TOSSED BY THE WAVES

By Erin Reilly

To request permissions, contact the publisher at
erinreillybooks@gmail.com

Paperback ISBN 9798842499557

Cover by Erin Reilly and Katy Teets
Printed by Amazon KDP
Published independently

erinwritesthings.com

for the ones still searching

Chapter One

Elliana

"Come on, Syd. We're going to be caught."

Sydney's loafers scuffed on the pavement as she halted beside me. She brushed her hair out of her face and greeted me with a look of utter exhaustion.

"We're cutting through the teacher's lot, not robbing a bank."

When I looked at her, my face as serious as hers, she let down her guard.

"Sorry. Lead the way, Captain."

Sydney was right, of course. There weren't any administrators hauling toward us with pink slips in hand, and there might as well have been a tumbleweed rolling across the soccer field that stretched between us and the gym. But none of that mattered to me, and we both knew it. We were breaking the rules, and there was a chance someone would see us. That was that.

Shockingly, we made it back into the school without a scratch and without sounding any alarms. Once inside the doors of the girls locker room, where we found ourselves at the exact same time every day, we were greeted with the bittersweet (but mostly bitter) smell of sweat and light perfume. To anyone else, it was unnerving. To us, it was home. During basketball season, that is.

The gym was much different. In the locker room, Sydney and I could joke around, relax until the exact moment we had to put our pinnies on and head out with the rest of the team. But as soon as we stepped into the gym, even on a practice day like this one, there was a job to do. There was a team we couldn't let down and a person whose expectations we had to meet.

There were two coaches at St. Jane's that students were actually afraid to play for. First was Coach Allenson, head of the boys lacrosse team who turned red as a beet every time his players let in a goal, and who I'd seen breathe fire at least once. Second, and I imagine not surprisingly, was Coach Pieter. The sole reason that Pieter was scary, so to speak, was because of his conditioning practices. All through tryouts, and in any down time he could find during the season, we were running. Hard. A week rarely went by without the puke count making it into double digits, and that was saying something, since he never let a girl join the team who wasn't in impeccable shape.

And yes, this was just a high school team.

Other than the conditioning and his expectations, Coach Pieter was incredible. He was kind, mostly, and he wanted to influence us as people as well as just players. The general consensus was that he was much scarier before you made the team, and turned into a sort of father figure once you became a regular. I'd always had a hard time connecting to people, so maybe the father figure part would've been a stretch for me. But I looked up to him. In fact, I admired him. He liked perfection. He lived for it, actually.

"Alright, let's see," Coach Pieter said, studying his playbook like he'd never seen it before. "Eldridge, Rose, let's have you go purple. Watson, Frag, black."

Sydney and I both scrambled, flipping our pinnies inside-out as Piper Frag did the same. It was always a toss-up, whether you'd wear your pinnie on the right side at the beginning of practice or not. Sydney and I sometimes made bets on it. I usually won.

"Actually, Frag, purple. Sorry," Pieter said. "Sienna and Bella, go black."

"Aye aye," Piper said, ever the class, or team, clown.

Once the sorting was through, Coach relayed the last of his instructions.

"Alright, purple will run the offense first. Sienna, I want you on Elliana. Bella on Syd. We're going man-to-man. Full court press. Pluto first then we'll go from there."

"Starting on the sideline?" Piper asked.

"Mmm," Pieter mumbled. "Baseline. I want to see the press."

Basketball, I'd learned, involves knowing a completely different language. Since I didn't start playing until seventh grade, Sydney had to teach me everything she knew. I grew up with athleticism in my blood, so basketball itself came pretty easily to me, but just one two-hour practice the summer before I made the team left me feeling like I'd been surrounded by aliens for an entire afternoon.

Now, I was well-aware that there was more to the word "pivot" than that one episode of *Friends*, and traveling was not just something you needed an airplane to do. Although, I guess I didn't know much about that either.

For forty minutes, like high-sprung clockwork, we ran plays, hustling up and down the court as if our very lives depended on it. When it was finally time for a water break— they were always about five minutes overdue—Coach Pieter headed to his office for the blocking pads while the rest of us slunk down onto the floor, our legs pulsating and lungs begging for air that we certainly weren't going to get.

But despite the exhaustion, there was always room for chatter. For Sydney and me, we usually found ourselves sitting with Piper Frag and Amari Watson, a sophomore and junior respectively, who found our friendship to one another both fascinating and heartwarming. I usually brushed off the glares of perplexity that Sydney and I were given whenever we hung out, and Piper and Amari were no exception. Besides, I was lucky they even wanted to talk to me. In a few years, they'd probably all be Division I athletes, scoring baskets on scholarships and working their way to playing professionally. Sydney included.

"So who do you think he'll start Saturday?" Piper asked, always curious, in a hushed voice. Talking about playing time was basically grounds for exile.

Amari shook her head, her fingers wrapped around her shoelaces as she pulled them tight. "No idea."

Sydney curled her lip. "Probably the same as last week, yeah?"

"I don't know," Piper shrugged. Then, she turned to me. "Hey, maybe you'll start on the wing. He did have you in purple just now."

I tried not to laugh, but a breath of one slipped out. "I've never started."

Amari sat up straighter, joining in on Piper's stance as Sydney just looked on. "But you work hard. And Sienna is really starting to piss Coach off. It's like she's never heard of a three-two zone before."

"But I don't start," I said. My face was getting red with the thought of it. "Really."

For most of my basketball career, if you could call it that, I was what one would refer to as the sixth man. I never started the game on the court, but I was usually the first to sub in. Really, it was what I preferred.

While everyone else whined and whispered about their lack of playing time in the locker room or on the bus when Coach Pieter wasn't around, I hoped for more time on the bench. I'd much rather have been able to watch on as each game began, figuring out the style of the other team while our five starting players went against them. Starting on the court would've been far too much pressure. Subbing in was quieter, like I was just taking over what someone had already started.

The idea of being one of the first on the court, all eyes on me and the pace of the game in my hands, made me nauseous. Thankfully, Sydney could tell.

"Don't sweat it," she said to me quietly as Piper and Amari were pulled into a conversation about backyards with the rest of the team. "If he plans on starting you, he'll give you a heads up. And I'll be out there with you."

"Yeah. Okay."

"And maybe it would be a good thing."

I just looked at her, watching as her hands went up in surrender.

"I said *maybe*."

4

"I bet Elliana's will be perfect," Piper said then. Sydney and I turned, my straightened ponytail hitting my shoulder gingerly while Sydney's curly flyaways fell into her face.

I shook my head. "Elliana's what?"

"Backyard," Piper sighed, almost whimsically, draping her hand over her forehead. "You'll have the perfectly cut grass and the patio with the furniture that's matchy but not *too* matchy."

Another teammate joined. "And an infinity pool that looks over the ocean."

Then another. "A husband who takes the kids water skiing on the weekends."

"And the dog who wins the puppy pageant at the end of the Thanksgiving parade every year."

After another gulp of the water from her Gatorade bottle, Sydney joined in. "All this from a conversation about shrubs?"

Piper sat up on her elbows, her space buns sticking out in two very different directions and her chin turned up like she was addressing royalty. "Do you object, Ms. Elliana Rose?"

All eyes were on me now, and truthfully, I couldn't disagree. Or I didn't want to, at least.

Sure, they were poking fun at my want—no, my need—for order and perfection. But I liked the thought of it, too. I loved the idea of my life turning out perfectly, with all of its pressures floating away with the clouds and successes falling together like dominoes. Just the idea of my life turning out, no matter who I needed to be to get there, was enough.

Sydney knew it too, mostly because she was there when it wasn't perfect. When there was no order and when everything went dark. Sure, Syd and I were complicated. An odd pairing, to say the least. She was tall, where I was short. She had crazy, beautiful, curly hair that was sometimes wound into just as crazy braids, while I never left the house without straightening every strand of mine. Sydney was loud, bold, popular, funny. I was just Elliana. But that was always enough for Syd, and she never pushed me to be anything more than that. I needed her.

"Not at all," I replied, satisfying the craving of all who awaited my obvious answer.

Everyone was bubbling at the surface, going crazy over hedges and in-ground pools, though we all lived right next to the ocean, and getting in the last of their conversations while Coach Pieter's inevitable return grew closer. I sat by, listening, chiming in when I was supposed to, putting on whatever face I needed to be a part of the team.

Then we stood, straightened our baggy shorts, and switched into our respective pinnie colors before resuming our game faces. Practice was hard, as it usually was, and only halted a few drills later when Sienna and Bella ran into one another head-on, a direct result of Sienna having no idea where she was meant to be. The collision caused a loud thud, one that made everyone hold their breath, and left one with a sore shoulder and another with a bruised jawline. We hesitated, held one another accountable for five minutes, then jumped right into another drill. And so it went.

But that crash, the thud that accompanied it, stuck with me. It was just further proof why I preferred the sidelines. There, you couldn't get hurt.

Chapter Two

Nell

"That does it. I'm obsessed with you."

Adrienne was circling me like a helicopter, tugging and pulling with *oohs* and *ahhs* flying from her lips like no one's business. I watched her in the mirror and studied the way the dress fell over my hips and landed at my feet, the way its shade of gray complimented my tanned skin.

"I love it," I told her. "Really, Adrienne."

She stood up, facing the mirror with me, our eyes meeting through it. "It's perfect on you."

I felt my cheeks redden. "Who would've thought?"

Adrienne lowered her eyebrows. "Well, me. And Luke. Your mom, too. And-"

"Okay," I said. "Point taken."

Adrienne smirked, reaching down to pull at the hem of the dress again. I couldn't blame her for how excited she was. Truthfully, we all were. We'd been looking forward to the wedding since the first time we heard Adrienne's name in our house nine years before.

My older brother, Lucas, was in the seventh grade when they met. It had been one of the hardest years we'd ever gone through as a family. There was a certain lull, a hush, that fell over our house. We didn't know what to do with it.

Luke, specifically, had been struggling with what it meant to be sad. As a thirteen-year-old, he was pretty lucky that the feeling of sorrow was foreign to him. I was looking to him, as was my little brother, Braeden, to be that happy kid through our rough time, too, and we were starting to think maybe he wouldn't be. Then came the 29th of August.

I was sitting at the kitchen table with both of my parents and Braeden, who was only eight at the time, eating an after-school snack and watching as the waves rolled and crashed onto the shore in front of our house. When the front door opened, we knew it would be Luke who walked through it. What surprised us, however, was the look on his face. A smile, and his freckles and rosy cheeks beaming so bright I was sure he'd been laying in the sun all day.

He slung his backpack onto the floor, something that likely made my mom squirm, and plopped down into the chair next to me. We all held our breath as we awaited what came next.

"I met the girl I'm going to marry."

I traded a glance with my dad, both of us laughing for the first time in months, and found Braeden doing the same. It was funny, and a ridiculous thing to assume Luke was serious. But then there was my mother, who held onto his gaze and read his smile like something she needed to decode. She believed him. Right there and then.

We knew very little how much that day would mean to all of us. Luke was right, of course, and my mom's belief in him was unbelievably warranted. Personally, I never would've thought Adrienne would mean so much to me, either. She became a sister, a friend when I needed one the most, and never wavered once as I grew from who I was at thirteen to who I was becoming at twenty.

Now, just one month before she and Luke would tie the knot, I was standing in front of her in the same house, my mom's same gaze awaiting us in the hallway. Only this time, I wasn't just her unassuming, soon-to-be sister-in-law. I was her Maid of Honor.

"Nell, if you don't get out here, Mom's going to explode all over the hallway."

It was Luke, who I didn't know was awaiting my impromptu dress-showing along with my mom. Now, I was dreading walking out there.

And then there was Braeden. "And you have to clean it up."

"I'm coming," I said. Then, to Adrienne. "*God.*"

Adrienne giggled, then swung my bedroom door open, revealing to me a full crowd in our spacey upstairs hallway.

There were Luke and Braeden (so far unamused), Adrienne's mom Ms. Brenda (adoring), my dad (brain gears working in overdrive for a Dad Joke), and my mom (tears behind gates, ready to rumble).

I caught Luke's smirk first. "Don't say it," I warned.

"You look great, Nell."

I turned to Adrienne. "He said it."

My mom stood from her cushioned stool, her hands out in front of her like I was a piece of art that she couldn't help but touch. "Oh, this is *stunning*."

"I was right, wasn't I?" Adrienne beamed.

"Man, what happened to your bowl cut and suspenders?" my dad asked. "This is not our Nell."

"Okay," I sighed, allowing my shoulders to finally slump as my mom and Ms. Brenda both took another look. "Can I go now?"

Dad huffed. "Ah. There she is."

"That color really makes your eyes shine, darling," Ms. Brenda said. "Glowing, you are."

"And I like it much better than the bowl cut. Even though you were cute back then," my dad added.

My mom's eyes were still wide. "You look like a *woman*."

"Gross." Braeden cringed.

This time, my sigh was audible. I let my mom take one more look, because of course I did, then turned to Adrienne. She met me with a smile and was ready to surrender, even if the rest of my family wasn't.

"Thank you all," I said slowly. "But I'm late for a run. I said I'd put on the dress and I did."

My mom's laugh came from her chest. "How are you late if you're running by yourself?"

I shrugged. "Just am. Can I go?"

I looked at Luke for approval, since it was only his and Adrienne's that I needed in that moment. He gave me his Thank You For Entertaining Mom smile and a nod, so I was off.

In my closet, I hung the dress carefully—it really was beautiful, and its sentimental value outweighed any rush I might've been in—then threw on the first pair of shorts I could find.

I changed out of my regular bra and pulled on a sports one, only sort of making sure I wasn't standing in front of my window, then began to tie my hair up into a loose ponytail. When I turned toward my mirror, I saw only myself this time, with freckles dotting my cheeks and color flooding my face. I was getting used to this version of myself, the way she could gaze so casually back at me like she was who I was supposed to see all along.

My eyes fell next to the part of my body that was beginning to become my favorite. Just below the line of my sports bra, in fine, dainty cursive lettering, was a tattoo. I ran my fingers along the words *find her*, that sat so innocently upon my ribcage, admiring their courage.

As I read the tattoo again and again and again, just like I did every time I saw myself, I couldn't help but smile, because I knew I was on my way.

The next morning, I took my run early so as to not face any interruptions from my family. I ran three miles, making a point to pass all of the places that used to mean so much to me when I lived here all year long instead of just in the summers. When I was about a block away from my house, I decided to slow my jog to a walk.

All around me, people were rising from their beds and their houses, ready to start their perfectly coastal summer days. The air was chock full of the scent I so loved, one of the ocean and pure bliss. I was crossing the street, crushing stray sand on the road with every step, when I sensed a bit of movement in the corner of my eye.

There was a pang in my chest as I stopped, my eyes stumbling toward the green house on the corner and finding it to be still, void of any people or movements. I took a deep breath, shaking the feeling of anyone being there, then jumped as the sprinkler in the next yard turned on. Before I knew it, the pang was gone, and I was walking again.

I tried to hide how heavily I was breathing as I approached my house. My forehead was in my tank top, wiping the sweat from it, when I heard a car door shut in front of me.

When it came to my house, for as long as I'd known, it was always a toss-up, a true mystery to find who would be walking up the driveway when I arrived back home at night. Lucas and Braeden were both popular at school, and my mom insisted on hosting everything, no matter how large the gathering. She loved a full house.

When I looked up, not at all convinced that wiping the sweat from my forehead made me look presentable, I found perhaps the most regular of visitors. Today, he wore a blue t-shirt, a pair of shorts, and of course, his goofy but charming-as-ever grin. I'd run past three miles of places with sentimental value, all of which brought me some sort of childhood nostalgia, but nothing compared to the way Ronan's smile felt like home.

He was just emerging from his car, his t-shirt catching on his seatbelt as he rose. Once he was released from its grasp, he looked right at me, like he saw me coming all along.

"Didn't anyone ever tell you you're supposed to become a N.A.R.P. after high school? You know, go downhill like the rest of us?"

Leave it to Ronan to make me laugh without even a hello.

The two of us embraced one another in a hug. We didn't have to say so, and it wasn't stiff, because it was just what we did. When we broke apart, I looked Ronan in his dark eyes.

"Sorry, a N.A.R.P.?"

"A Non-Athletic, Regular Person," he told me, his grin still plastered to his face as we began up the driveway together. "Someone who doesn't get up at the crack of dawn to run. On summer vacation, no less."

I turned to him. "Are you judging me?"

And just like that, Ronan's guard was down. His shoulders were softened and finally, we were back. With most friendships, a few months apart called for an hour or two of Awkward before you could jump right back into things. I was lucky that this wasn't the case with Ronan, even though he was really more Lucas' friend than he was mine. Maybe it was different when you grew up together.

"I'd never judge you," Ronan said.

"I know."

"So I saw that you learned how to ski," he said, effectively changing the subject, "and now you're all tan. And a traveler. And the Maid of Honor. What ever did Vermont do with our little—"

"Don't say it," I warned.

Unlike Luke, Ronan listened.

"Seriously. You look great, Nell. And happy."

I smiled, pleased that someone from home could recognize who I was becoming. It was different at school. My friends, my roommates, they had nothing to compare me to. No one to miss.

"I am happy," I told him.

"A good semester then?"

"Great semester. The best one yet," I said, choking down the fact that the last three months even had to end at all. "And skiing was easier than I thought it would be. But, I mean, I'm not a N.A.R.P., so."

Ronan nodded, his grin widening as he opened the screen door to my house, allowing me in first. "I'm not going to share my knowledge with you if you're going to use it against me."

"I'll take my chances."

I made a conscious effort to put distance between Ronan and me as we crossed over the threshold into my house. It took deliberate attention to detail to avoid the You And Ronan Are Next looks that we got from, well, everyone whenever we were next to one another. On wine nights with my mom and Ms. Brenda, those looks turned into words.

It started the summer before, when I was home from my first year in Vermont and Ronan and I saw one another for the first time. Every time he looked at me, there was something new behind his eyes, like he somehow saw me as more than just the little sister I'd been to him my whole life. I wasn't sure how I felt about it then, and an entire year later, I was even less certain. Ronan was one of my favorite people ever, and I was always able to be myself when I was beside him. But he was my brother's best friend, and the two of us being anything more would have just been messy. Plus, I didn't feel that way about him. I was sure of it.

Inside, I was welcomed with the smell of gourmet breakfast. With just a sniff, I could identify pancakes, hash browns, bacon, sausage, the lot. It was a sure sign that Luke was home, and a blessing considering he and Adrienne had their own house now. They must've gotten an early start with my mom.

"Ronan Little," Adrienne said, her voice shrieky and sweet all at once. "In the flesh."

"Embry," Ronan said, stepping into our naturally lit kitchen and pulling Adrienne into a hug not unlike the one we shared a moment ago. "But I can't call you that for much longer, huh?"

Adrienne's smile remained as they separated. "You can call me Embry forever."

Lucas glanced over his shoulder, flashing a playful look at Adrienne and Ronan, who towered over her. "What's wrong with my last name?"

Ronan shrugged. "It's connected to you."

Luke, Adrienne, and Ronan were as close as could be, best friends since the day the universe made it possible. So their conversation was able to jump right over the usual pleasantries and catching-up that most high-school-turned-college friends had to endure. Instead, they started talking about Best Man Duties, those of which Ronan would have to perform in just a month, and the rest of the goings on that would take place before then.

I headed to the fridge for my water bottle, attempting to keep my distance from the breakfast so my sweat didn't infiltrate its wonderful scent. Though I was happy in Vermont, and was finding something new there every day to fall in love with, nothing compared to the way the light from outside poured through the windows of our house. Our living room, kitchen, and entryway were open-concept, so it often felt like the ocean could come right inside if it wanted to. The waves always had a seat at our table.

As I stood in the kitchen, my water bottle sweating all over my hand, I watched as the waves rolled in, some softer than others, and crashed so graciously on the damp sand. The sky was an electric shade of blue, contrasting perfectly from the deep navy that the water held. I found myself captivated by it, oblivious to everything else around me, as was often the case when I was in front of the ocean. Like Luke's cooking, Adrienne's excitement, Ronan's smile, my mom's sentimental glare, it brought me home. It always did.

"Nell?" When I turned around, Luke was looking at me, his expression quizzical as he stood over a sizzling pan of bacon. "You okay?"

I smiled. "Fine."

"We were just talking about how excited we are to see you and Ronan walk down the aisle together."

I blinked hard as I tried to recall the part of the conversation where I agreed to marry Ronan. Before I could embarrass myself, however, I realized that they were talking about Luke and Adrienne's wedding day, not the one between Ronan and me that would never happen. Then, I pictured it too: the two of us walking down the aisle, arm-in-arm, supporting the happy couple the way we always had, the way everyone expected us to. It would be perfect, just as Adrienne had hoped. Even if there were a few things missing.

I let out a laugh, shooting Ronan a look. "That is if I don't trip him."

Ronan shoots a playful one back. "I am the definition of grace, Nell. There is no tripping me."

"Well, I'll give it my best shot."

14

"Just don't hurt his pride," Luke said. "It's wearing thin these days."

Ronan's jaw dropped. "Ouch, Lucas. Ouch."

Adrienne shot up suddenly from her spot at the table, joining me at the kitchen counter. I was beginning to wonder if she'd ever stop smiling. I didn't want her to, of course. I was just impressed.

"We're doing a beach day while your mom and I talk tablecloths and napkins. Join us, please?"

I let out a sigh. My arm had been twisted, and there was no going back.

"I just have to shower first. Don't want to stink up the whole coast of North Carolina."

Adrienne's smile grew, somehow, with my satisfactory answer. "Fabulous. It's been too long."

To this, Lucas pondered, "When are you leaving, Nell?"

I tilted my head, needing more.

"For Vermont," he added.

"Oh," I said, almost too immediately. "Saturday. I'll be back Monday."

Now, Ronan was confused. "Vermont? Didn't you just get back from there?"

I nodded, slowly so as to keep my cool. "It's my roommate's birthday, and my friend who studied abroad all semester just came back home. So just a weekend to celebrate. Then I'll be back for good," I said. "For the summer, I mean."

I was given three nods of approval, one more pensive from Ronan than I would've imagined, then made a quick exit up the stairs. It seemed as though I needed to tighten up my interrogation skills, as just the simplest of questions threw me right off my feet.

As it turns out, the story I told my brother and my parents and everyone else was just that: a story. A tale. A fib, if you will. I wasn't going to Vermont to visit the friends I'd just left a few days before. I was going to Pennsylvania, and I was going to find Finn.

Chapter Three

Elliana

The scoreboard horn rang out, sending a momentary jolt through my veins and lifting every teammate around me from their chairs, the ones on the court starting the group hug that would only grow bigger within the next few seconds. I sprung from the bench, trying my hardest to feel it, whatever it was that was in the air, and was pulled into the mid-court celebration by a sweaty and smiley Sydney. We'd just won our first playoff game, and she was largely to thank.

She'd scored twenty-six points, a feat unheard of for a sophomore at St. Jane's. Every time she touched the ball, the crowd was on its feet, anticipating a SportsCenter moment from the girl I was lucky to call my best friend. The whole night was exciting, and exactly what a playoff game was supposed to feel like. At least, I hoped.

We gathered in the locker room, all of us sweaty and panting, and punctuated Coach Pieter's entrance with another round of cheers. We'd all worked hard, and Coach certainly wasn't the exception.

"*That* is what I'm talking about!" he exclaimed as he slapped his clipboard with his hand, Assistant Coach Jenna trailing behind him. "That kind of second half is exactly what I was talking about at practice. They saw you fight in the first, expected you to fight in the second, but thought you'd play tired. I didn't see one tired person on that floor today."

All around me, everyone was tuned in, aching for the reassurance and validation that was spewing from Coach Pieter's mouth. I could feel Sydney's leg bouncing beside me, forever restless, and could see Bella Crow's doing the same on the other side of the room. We sat on the floor, on benches, on our shoes, gravity only pulling us down because we'd been running for what felt like hours. Besides that, we were on a high, the smell of sweat and triumph filling the air.

"Amari, that was an incredible game," Coach said then, giving credit where it was certainly due. "Never stop shooting from the arc. I don't care if it goes in or not."

Amari's slightly discouraged look—likely stemming from the few times the ball did not, in fact, make it in the basket—turned appreciative. She should've been proud. I never would've dared shooting the ball from that far away. And if I did, it certainly wouldn't have gone in.

"Sydney," Coach said, turning on his heel and stopping when he met Syd's smiling face. Before he could continue, another round of cheers rang out, and I placed my hand on her shoulder before giving it a hard shake. "Twenty-six points. Eight rebounds. Six assists."

It was rare for Coach Pieter to offer statistics so willingly and immediately after the game. He always wanted us to think more about our passion rather than the numbers. This, obviously, was a special occasion.

"I knew you had it in you," he said to Syd. "Did you?"

Sydney shrugged. Behind us, a couple of our teammates laughed. If Sydney didn't know she could play like that, she was sorely alone in that thinking.

"I don't know."

"Good. Well, whatever mindset you went in with, bottle it. Please. For us."

Another round of laughter, then Coach turned to me.

"Elliana," he said, causing me to gulp. There was no way I was next. "Great work on defense. That's what I mean when I say I want the man-to-man to be tight. That guard looked like she wanted to slap you for the entire second half."

Next to me, Piper snorted.

"I'm glad she didn't," I said quietly.

Coach nodded, his smile growing. For some reason, he always liked it when I spoke, no matter what it was that happened to come out.

"But you made her want to," he said. "That's all you've got to do."

Coach went on, for the next few minutes, about Piper's assists, Bella's box-outs, Sienna's quick-thinking (which, for the rest of us, wasn't that quick), before talking about what we needed to work on for our next playoff game, opponent still To Be Determined. Once we changed from our uniforms into our matching sweat outfits, courtesy of the St. Jane's Varsity Booster Club, we were on the bus, headed home.

As I sat in my seat, my feet planted on the floor and backpack in my lap while Sydney talked to Coach Jenna, I thought about the game. Coach Pieter's words were kind, and I was happy to hear that he was pleased with how I played. But the truth was, I could've been better. I ran through every instance where quicker thinking or faster running on my part would have resulted in a higher score or a better game. By the time Sydney plopped down next to me, making me bounce on the bus seat cushion, I'd counted twelve.

Before I could offer any sort of greeting, which I didn't need to, Sydney's head was on my shoulder, her arm splayed across my leg. I could feel her warmth making its way onto me. Finally, without knowing I needed to be, I was relaxed.

"Number eighteen was a bitch," she said like it was what she'd been holding in for the past three hours. "She kept pulling my jersey. Not even just when I had the ball."

"Really?"

Sydney nodded. "And she had dead eyes. Like a snake or something."

I tilted my head. "I think snakes' eyes are actually pretty cool."

"Okay. An owl, then."

I tilted my head again.

"Just believe me. They were dead." Then Sydney sat up, the glow of her phone lighting up her face. She typed something onto it, smiling just enough that I knew who she was talking to, then turned to me. "You down for Archie's? Henry's already there."

And there it was. Our post-game, sometimes post-nothing, tradition of greasy sandwiches and greasier fries while we sat across the table from Sydney's sweet-as-ever boyfriend. It could've easily been one of my favorite things, maybe even something I'd look forward to, if only I could guarantee it would be just the three of us. Unfortunately, that was never the case. Ever.

"Of course," I said. "How'd the swim team do?"

"Lost," Syd replied. "Wasn't even close."

This, of course, wasn't a surprise. Unlike our basketball and lacrosse teams, the swim team was at the lowest point of the Varsity Sport Totem Pole at St. Jane's. This year, the team was made up almost exclusively of sophomores, with the exception of Abel Ailish—he was a senior, only for the third time, and rarely was allowed in the water out of the fear of him drowning. They'd miraculously made it into whatever postseason swim looked like, but not one person on the team or at St. Jane's in general thought they'd make it past the first round. As it turns out, they didn't prove anyone wrong.

When we pulled up to the school, the only lights to greet us being the ones from parking lot posts and waiting parents' cars, Sydney and I grabbed our things, exchanged some words with our teammates, and headed for Archie's.

The sidewalk that stretched in front of us was quiet, occupied only by the two of us and a college-aged boy walking his dog a block ahead. Though we were covered in dried sweat and our lungs were still recovering from the game, the air that we walked through was soft, as if the world had set its thermostat to room temperature.

"You played great today," Sydney started, breaking the silence between us that, while unusual, was comfortable.

I looked at her, a laugh I'd probably get scolded for escaping my chest. "Well, you played *twenty-six points* great."

Sydney rolled her eyes. "I hate it when you do that."

Though I knew what she meant, I had to ask, anyway. It was better to play oblivious. "When I do what?"

"Ignore compliments. Make yourself small," she said. "I get it, Elliana, I do. But you're not really helping yourself when you don't let the good things in."

This part of our conversation was unusual. There were great things that came with Sydney knowing exactly who and how I was. But then there were the days where I felt her getting sick of it. The days where, though I knew she loved me, I could feel her trying to change things. We both knew it was a losing battle, but Sydney was nothing if not driven.

"You had, like, six steals and four assists. And you're a great teammate. Loud on the bench, encouraging," she continued. "I see the look in your eyes when you come off of the court. You don't even look a little bit proud of yourself."

I tucked the stray pieces of hair falling in front of my face behind my ears, remaining silent because I could feel that she wasn't done. Then, she hit me where we both knew it would stick.

"Did you even feel it? Any of it?"

We were almost to Archie's. I could just make out the neon red *OPEN* sign that tilted every time someone opened the door it hung on, and I was sure I could see Henry's car in the parking lot. We were close, but Sydney needed an answer, and the silence wasn't comfortable anymore.

"I want to," I admitted, my voice low and my gaze on my feet. Lower, if it could be.

The truth was, I didn't feel anything. At least not to the extent that everyone else seemed to. Every time I saw Sydney with a smile on her face that she just couldn't contain, after a good game or better day, or when I saw my brother so sad that the curl of his lip made my mom break down and cry, I was jealous. Not because I wanted to have a good game, and not because I wanted to face whatever doctor's appointment or bad test grade my brother was handed that day, but because I wanted to feel something the way they did.

The only feeling that cut deep, and was so painfully familiar that I could see it coming before it hit, was one I couldn't even identify. It was a sort of worry, I guess, that came when I was out of place, doing something or existing somewhere that I wasn't supposed to be. So I held onto the feeling of comfort, with certain people or places, on the

20

sidelines, in line with the rules. There was no worry in perfection, in order, so I lived for it.

Sydney knew all of this, perhaps better than anyone. It was part of our day-to-day, something that probably kept Syd herself from getting some of the things she wanted out of life. But sometimes she just needed to check in, to make sure nothing inside me had come alive overnight. I always hated to disappoint her.

"Maybe next game," Sydney said, now sporting a sympathetic smile. "Could be your SportsCenter moment. You never know."

I smiled, too, thankful for the mood-lift. "You never do."

Inside Archie's, the two of us were greeted by the strong scent of, well, everything. From chicken tenders to loaded fries to sandwiches with cheese so melty it might've been soup, Archie's had a distinct personality. There was a constant flow of high school students, not unlike Sydney and me, crowding at every table, and conversations so loud you couldn't even hear yourself think. The walls were lined with photos of our town's sports teams, all of which came from St. Jane's or Arbor High, the public school a few miles in from the coast.

It wasn't crazy, then, that when we finally found Henry, he was seated at a table below a photo that Sydney and I were in. It was of our Junior Varsity basketball team, which we'd both made in our eighth grade year, standing mid-court after the last win of our undefeated season. Sydney and I stood in the front row, crouched over so the camera could find those behind us, with our arms around each other. I was focused on it, the way our smiles matched, when I was yanked from my trance by none other than Foster Baxton. Bax, as most liked to call him.

"Hi there, Elliana."

Sydney and Henry were only engaged in a quick hug, but Bax knew his chances were highest when Sydney was preoccupied. What exactly did he need chances for? I had no idea.

If there were a list of people I felt most comfortable around, Bax would've been dead last. Actually, he wouldn't have been on the list at all. Ever since the day I met him (fourth grade: phonics class), I always felt like there was something off between the two of us. Every other acquaintance I'd made in my life had been balanced. An instant click, or not. A little bumpy, or not. Awkward, or not. For me and Bax, it was always a whole lot of something on his end, and nothing on mine. That was all I knew.

"Hi, Bax," I said politely, avoiding his eye contact and finally meeting Henry face-to-face.

All of our lives, I'd been watching as boys looked at Sydney. In the hallways, on the beach, during basketball games. She never noticed, but she was certainly a head-turner. It was only last year that some of the boys at school, juniors included, started to vocalize their infatuation with her. Over just one weekend in the summer, she'd shot down three boys, all on the beach. She was persistent in convincing both me and herself that she'd let down her walls when the right time came. After the thirtieth boy that had asked her out, I wasn't sure anyone would ever meet her standards.

And then came Henry.

Henry had always been around, actually. He'd been in our class since fifth grade. Unbeknownst to Sydney, he spent every one of those years hopelessly in love with her. She claimed he was just friendly—which, absolutely, he was—but I always knew his feelings lived much further within him than his manners. Everyone else did, too.

So he asked her out on a real date, just the two of them, one Thursday afternoon while me and Bax watched from across the school parking lot. Needless to say, she went. And then it was Henry and Sydney, forever and ever. It was adorable, the way she was just an inch taller than him and the way his bright eyes and blonde hair contrasted with every one of her dark features. Everything about them was complimentary to the other. It was beautiful.

Now, when Henry's eyes met mine, I was always welcomed with kindness and a little bit of something else. Maybe it was gratitude for sharing my best friend with him. Little did he know that I wanted them together as much as he did. Henry brought out the best in Sydney. I wanted nothing more than that for her when she was always doing it for me.

"Congrats on the win," Henry offered.

I nodded, pressing my lips into a smile. "Sorry I can't say the same to you."

Henry waved his hand. "It's a good thing. If we won, we might've started thinking we had a chance," he said as we all sat at our characteristically red and white checkered table. "So what are you guys going to get? Sandwiches?"

"I'm thinking fries," Syd offered before looking at me. "Are you going to get your sandwich? The tomato pesto?"

I was about to answer when Bax sat forward, making his presence known once again. I wasn't sure if his hair was still wet from the swim meet or if he just had that much gel in it, but the light from above us was making it sparkle.

"Hey, Elliana, I don't think I've ever seen your hair not straightened."

I looked down and found that Bax was right. My sweat from the game must've caused some of my hair to curl, something it always wanted to do naturally. Now, more than half of it was still straight, but I didn't like the lack of symmetry, and I was beginning to zone out on it.

"Oh. Um, yeah," I said slowly.

Bax's expression reeked with interest. "It looks good like that. I like it."

You're fine, I told myself. I could feel Sydney looking at me, so I looked back at her, pulling my eyes away from my hair without a second thought. She lowered her chin, sensing that something was off. If I'd known what it was, I would've told her.

Her eyes were soft as she asked me again. "Are you going to get your sandwich? We could split fries."

I nodded, but felt light-headed as I thought about agreeing. I'd dealt with Bax's random, pointless comments for years and never batted an eye. But for some reason, this one was getting to me. Maybe I was taken by the noise from Archie's, or the smell of the food, or the exhaustion I was feeling from the game. Whatever it was, I didn't feel right, and I had to go.

"I think I might get it to-go," I said, itching for a way out.

Now, Sydney was concerned.

"What's wrong?"

I shook my head. "Nothing. I'm just– I'm tired, that's all. I think I'm going to go now, actually."

When I stood from my chair, Sydney did, too. She wasn't going to make it easy, but that was what she was there for. I couldn't stand the feel of Bax's eyes on me. I had no idea what Henry was thinking. Whatever had happened was quite literally nothing. I couldn't figure out for the life of me why it was such a big deal.

"Are you sure?" Syd asked. Then, quietly, "Is it what I said earlier? I didn't mean to–"

"No, Syd," I said, flashing her a smile quickly as the room began to close in on me. "I promise I'm fine. Just need air." I turned to the table, finding Henry with a concerned expression and Bax with a slightly offended one. "I'll see you guys at school tomorrow."

Sydney put her hand on my shoulder gently. "Elliana."

This time, my look told Sydney what she needed to hear in order to let me go. It was one of those feelings, of worry or discomfort or anxiety, that came from something being out of place. I'd be fine by tomorrow. We both knew it. So Sydney just nodded, releasing my shoulder from her hand and watching as I walked away.

It took me a few moments outside to get used to the fresh air again. As I breathed it in, I felt my hands rise to my throat, for some reason aching to make sure it was still there. I felt the straps of my backpack holding tight to my shoulders, the legs of my sweatpants swishing against my shins, the hug of my socks against my ankles. Houses and cars and trees were sitting idly in their places as I walked past, all of them looking so differently at night than they ever did in the morning. My brain was spinning, replaying everything from the warmups before the game to every second that passed as I walked. Of all of the feelings I was numb to, I wanted so badly for whatever this was to be one of them.

A few moments had passed by the time I realized I was actually walking home alone in the dark. I wasn't afraid, and was sure that I needed the fresh air and solitude as soon as I stepped out of Archie's. But *alone* and *dark* were two things that, when put together, made my mother panic relentlessly. She never really had a reason to be that way; it was just one of the parental urges that stuck with her and made its way into my everyday life.

I was hoping I'd get lucky and that my mom would have been asleep (impossible) or in the garden (slightly less) or on the back deck (a toss-up) when I got home, and that she wouldn't see me take on the driveway alone, when I heard the muffled sound of a car's exhaust creeping up behind me.

There were two options. First, my mom's worst nightmare could've been coming true, in which case I would have proof to give Sydney that rules were to be followed for a reason, should I survive to tell her so. The second option, and the much more preferable one, was what I found to be true as I turned my head. Beside me now, stopped on the side of the nearly empty street, was not a car but a truck that I knew all too well.

I walked up to the truck, peering through its open passengers' window, pretending to be surprised that the only person inside was the driver.

"Hm," I mumbled, lifting my chin up and pointedly sniffing the air. "Is that a new freshener?"

"Ocean Breeze," he said, his charming and perfect smile stretching gingerly across his face. When his eyes met mine, he narrowed them. "Why are you walking alone in the dark?"

"Don't tell my mom," I joked, but not really. "It doesn't really smell like the ocean."

"Too fruity. Should be called The Ocean According to People Who Live In Skyscrapers," he said. Then, he slid sideways, reaching for the handle to the passenger door from inside. I knew, from experience, that this was the only way it opened. He pushed it out toward me, then met my eyes again. "Come on. I was headed to your house, anyway."

To anyone else, this exchange might've seemed strange. A guy his age—tall, athletic, handsome—slowing to a stop, picking up a girl that looked like me. But for us, this was normal. Finn was family.

So I got in, and we headed together toward home, leaving my night and his behind us. I sank down into my seat, listening to Finn talk about the last musical he'd seen, adding my input where I could. It didn't take long to feel comfortable again. He was safe.

On Thursday, enough time had passed since the game that Sydney was no longer on high alert, jumping every time I made a move to be sure I wasn't having another panic-like-attack. I was thankful, because normalcy was what I liked. With Sydney back to normal, I could be too.

So after practice, Sydney and I headed to the beach. This was another tradition of ours, but unlike Archie's, we rarely had to speak it into our schedules; it just happened. We'd come home from practice together, to my house since it was closest, drop our bags on the floor, kick off our shoes, and head for the shoreline. Before we knew it, we were sitting in the sand, alone together, staring out at the ocean.

I never knew what it was that Sydney saw while we sat together, or if it was anything more than just the waves and sky before us. Maybe she was just taking in the peacefulness of it all, appreciating the beauty that we had at our fingertips. Or maybe she was thinking about Henry or basketball or her summer camp friends who were much more exciting than I could ever hope to be. I, on the other hand, was always thinking about the same thing. Rather, I was always searching for the same thing.

The ocean itself was vast, deep, mysterious. I could only ever see what was on its surface—the waves, the glimmer of the sun, the occasional animal. But I knew there was more hiding within it, so much beauty and wonder that I'd never see for myself. For some reason, when I sat there, I felt as though the ocean and me had that in common. Beside it, I felt closer to the version of myself that didn't have such a hard shell. The version of myself that wasn't the way I was. The version that wasn't afraid.

I looked for her everywhere. In the clouds, which today were dancing across the sky, teasing the sunset with carefully painted strokes of pink and orange. It resembled a work of art, so bold and so brave that I wanted to grab ahold of it, try it on for myself. I looked for her in the waves, in their sloppiness, their freedom. Sometimes, when they were soft enough that I could stand above them and see my reflection, I looked for her there. I was never surprised, but always disappointed, to see the same person staring back at me that greeted me in the mirror every morning.

I was studying the water as it rolled over my feet, covering them like a blanket before sliding back down the sand only to come back up again, when I heard a pair of footsteps drawing toward Sydney and me. At first, I didn't look. Our beach was busy and tourists and residents alike passed us all the time, sometimes in groups of ten, while we kept our peace. It was valuable, after all.

These footsteps, however, stopped just as they neared the left side of Sydney, who was on the left side of me. We shared a look, then turned around, a bit skeptical.

I wasn't expecting to recognize the girl standing beside Sydney when I turned, but I immediately found myself wishing I did. I couldn't figure out what it was that was so unique about her. But within the split second I took to study her, I just knew there was something.

What I could point out was that she was beautiful. She was glowing, with bright red hair and freckles all over that popped so much they looked fake, though I could tell for certain that they weren't. In one hand, she held her shoes, a tote bag hanging loosely from the other one, and she wore a pair of ripped jeans and a faded Bon Iver t-shirt. Her clothes didn't hug her the same way everyone else's did, her manicure was chipped and the colors she wore didn't seem deliberately matched. But somehow, she looked like she belonged there. Right in front of us.

We still hadn't said anything, had we?

"Hi, sorry–" she said, her smile emphasizing the beauty she already held. "Are you Elliana?"

"Me?" I asked. I wasn't sure why I sounded so surprised, as Elliana was my name. I just couldn't believe she knew it. "I– yeah, I am."

Her smile grew a little wider, dimples appearing on either cheek, like I was the one she'd set out on her beach journey to find. Frankly, I was a little scared.

"Cool. Do you know if your brother is home? I was supposed to work on this project with him. I'm a little early." Sydney and I were listening intently to every word she was saying. Noticing this, the girl laughed, mostly at herself. "Yeah, this is– this is weird. I guess I could just go knock on the front door–"

"He's not home yet, actually," I told her, surprising myself. "Lacrosse practice."

"Ah. Right."

I couldn't tell if she was embarrassed or if she felt awkward because she didn't have a clear out, but neither really seemed to be true. She tucked a piece of her curly hair behind her ear while I thought of what to say next.

"You can wait here with us if you want," Sydney said joyously, easily expressing the same sentiment I was wracking my brain for.

To my surprise, there was barely any hesitation in her step as she lowered herself to the sand, taking the spot right next to me. Then, she held out her hand, beginning a gesture I didn't think any teenagers did anymore, and offered to shake mine.

"I'm Mo."

I shook her hand, mine flimsy compared to hers. "Elliana."

Mo smiled before reaching out to shake an amused Sydney's hand. I wondered what she was thinking of all of this.

"Sydney," she said, her voice much more confident than mine.

Mo's soft expression remained as she sat back, sticking her hands into the sand without a care of what they might encounter. "You two go to St. Jane's, too?"

I nodded. I had no idea what expression was on my face. "We're sophomores," I said.

"Are you a senior?" Sydney asked. "How have we never seen you before?"

Mo let out a one-beat laugh through her nose. "A senior, yeah. I just transferred."

I tilted my head. "For one semester?"

"Dad's job," Mo said.

I didn't know the slightest thing about her, nor if I would ever see her again in my life, but I was beginning to envy her. She was so lax, so chill, about everything. Even her voice knew it.

"That blows," Sydney said, glancing over at me to make sure I was still engaged in the conversation. "St. Jane's isn't so bad, though. And at least you've got this at your disposal."

Mo tilted her head to the side, looking out at the ocean after Sydney motioned toward it. "Yeah. Lots to see here. It's quiet, too," she said. Just as I was beginning to get comfortable, as I was a master of the small talk, Mo turned to us again. "So do you two have nicknames? Or are you always Sydney and Elliana?"

It was a simple, albeit strange, question. Beside me, Sydney considered it, intrigued by how the conversation had turned to Get To Know You so quickly. "Some people call me Syd. My little sister used to call me Dippy because she couldn't figure out how to say my name. I'm not sure if you'd count that."

Mo laughed, a contagious one at that. "Dippy. I like it."

A second later, I felt Mo glance at me, awaiting my answer. I just looked at her, already finding myself to be mentally apologizing for how boring I was. "Uh– just Elliana."

Mo's smile matched the one she offered Sydney, which made me feel good rather than embarrassed, though I wasn't sure why. Then, she surprised me again.

"We'll work on that."

I was taken a little bit. I was sure she didn't have a problem with what my actual name was, as she didn't seem to be the kind of person who would insult my parents' choices so flatly. But I could tell she was serious. Part of me wanted to know why.

"So is Mo short for anything?" Syd asked then. "Or is your mom just much cooler than mine?"

This time, Mo's laugh had something behind it. With the slight shake of her head, and a glance at her feet, she said, "It's short for Morrigan."

And just when I thought she couldn't get any cooler.

"That's beautiful," I said.

I seemed to have surprised Sydney, as well as Mo, who looked at me graciously. "Thanks. So is Elliana."

I looked at Mo then, too. Her eyes were a rare shade— kelly green, almost—and held courage, even in the smallest of moments like this one.

Behind us, I heard the back door to my house open, which was only possible because of how soft the waves in front of us were. I turned around to find my brother, lacrosse hoodie on and hair an absolute mess, waving to us.

"Mo!" he shouted. "Sorry I'm late! We're in here!"

I could see his friends milling about behind him, Finn the tallest among them, and just couldn't imagine what Mo was about to walk into. I watched as she waved back, saying nothing. She turned to Sydney and me, her hair falling all over the place without a care.

"Catch you guys later. It was nice meeting you, Syd," she said. Then, to me, "And Elliana."

"You too," Sydney said as I just nodded.

The two of us watched then as Mo made her way across the sand and up the steps to my house. I felt Sydney turn back, at least toward me if not the water, but I kept my eyes on the house.

"So, Bax was asking about you in Homeroom today."

My eyes readjusted, finding the reflection of the beach in the windows of my house rather than what was going on inside. Then, I heard what Sydney had said.

"What?" I turned around to face her, unable to read her expression. A smile was growing upon her lips and I could just feel that a laugh was coming. I shook my head. "What?"

Then, Syd shook her own head, raising her eyebrows as she finally turned back toward the water. "Nothing."

I shrugged it off, whatever was happening, and turned back toward the water, too. The sun was just about to meet the horizon, planning to duck under it within the next hour or so. As I watched, I thought about the look in Mo's eyes. She was so bright, so carefree. Her hair and her jeans and her voice painted the picture of someone living life exactly the way they wanted. Maybe I was being presumptuous.

I looked toward Sydney again in an attempt to read her opinion on the matter. "So," I started slowly, "she was cool, right? Like, different?"

Sydney nodded immediately, a genuine smile on her face, agreeing without even looking at me.

"She was cool."

Chapter Four

Nell

"I just love that suit," Adrienne said, side-eyeing me and arranging her sunscreen and water bottle neatly on the sand beside her. She was laying out on her towel, the sun beating down on us already, and had a pair of green sunglasses sitting just right on the bridge of her nose. "Where'd you get it?"

I looked down at myself. I was wearing a strapless black bikini that hugged me just right and covered enough of my ribcage that my tattoo could still remain hidden. The suit was cute, I had to admit, and was something High School Me wouldn't have been caught dead in. Thankfully, though, she was dead, and here I was to bask in that glory.

"I don't know," I told her. "The top might be one of Genevieve's."

"Might be?"

I shrugged. When it came to me and Genevieve, my college roommate of two years now, there was no telling what kinds of clothes I'd come home with at the end of the semester. Once we moved in together, our wardrobe became one. For me, it was a blessing. Genevieve arrived freshman year with a style I could only dream of having—spunky, colorful, a bit careless. Now, I was getting there. The bathing suit top was proof of it. Although, I wasn't entirely certain I hadn't bought it myself.

"I remember when you got yours," I pointed out, nodding at the royal blue bikini Adrienne was wearing.

Adrienne lowered her eyebrows. "You do?"

"Ocean City. My junior year of high school." As I began to recount the story, the memories started to flood back into Adrienne's mind, too. I could see it on her face. "You were wearing a white bathing suit, and if I remember correctly, the ice cream you were holding was blue—"

"And then the seagull!" Adrienne exclaimed.

"It was Ronan's fault," I remembered. "He was teasing it with the french fry."

"What was Ronan's fault?"

I turned around, totally unafraid of Ronan's wrath which, as we all knew, didn't really exist. He was approaching with a towel in one hand and a football in the other. Beside him, a sunglasses-wearing Luke was carrying snacks.

"Ocean City," I explained. "When the seagull went after your french fry and knocked Adrienne's ice cream all over her suit."

"Wasn't it Italian Ice?" Luke asked.

Ignoring this, Ronan tilted his head. "How was that my fault?"

"You were teasing it," I said

Ronan turned to Luke. "Weren't they your french fries?"

Luke shrugged. "Yeah, but you were teasing it."

Ronan should've known better than to go up against Luke and me. Adrienne was sure to always hold the middle ground—Switzerland, as Ronan liked to call it—but, believe it or not, Luke and I never disagreed. For a brother and sister with two years between us, Braeden trailing me by three, we were impressively close. Not only did Luke allow me so willingly into his friend group at such a young age, and never once wavered, but he always took my side. We were raised to have each other's backs, and Luke took that more seriously than anyone.

Ronan, as years of practice allowed him, knew when to surrender. "Fine," he said. "But for the record, Adrienne, that bathing suit color you have now is electric. And electric is cool. So you should really be thankful."

"Thank you, Ronan," Adrienne obliged. "I'll forever be indebted to you."

Luke, shaking his head, took a seat next to me. Neither he nor Ronan ever felt inclined to put towels down before they sat. I always noticed, but never said anything. There was no point.

"Do you know what Mom has planned for the seventh?" Luke asked.

Almost immediately, I shrugged. The seventh of July was two days before Luke and Adrienne's wedding, which meant it was right in the middle of my mom's painstakingly intricate plans for their week of festivities. Most of them were small—a brunch with the girls in the wedding party, an evening to separate napkins and decorations—and took little to no thought on my part. Unless Adrienne asked for my help specifically, I tuned out the rest. I was planning to go with the flow, something I knew Luke would've loved to be doing, too.

"I think it's just drinks and dinner. Nothing big," I told him, pulling from what little knowledge I had about the party she was planning at our house.

Adrienne sighed. "We've told her a million times she doesn't have to host anything. She's doing so much already."

"You know she just wants everyone to see the garden," I said.

"I just don't want her to do too much," Luke said, his finger drawing a circle in the sand between his feet. "Everyone's seen the garden."

"Then she wants them to see it again. It means a lot to her," I said. I turned to Ronan, finding him utterly distracted by a misplaced lace on his football. "She'll be okay. Ronan and I will keep an eye on her. Isn't that right?"

Ronan shot up with the sound of his name. "Right. We've got everything under control."

Though this was meant to sound convincing, it wasn't. Not even a little bit. To emphasize this, Adrienne let out a laugh.

"What, are you stepping up your organizational game for the wedding?"

Ronan's hand lifted to his heart, oh-so-hurt at Adrienne's dig. He looked at me, his jaw dropped. "Can you believe they don't believe in us?"

"Oh, we know Nell is very capable of handling things," Luke said.

Ronan clicked his tongue. "Hey," he said, with absolutely nothing else to back himself up.

Luke leaned back on his hands now, relaxing as this was hardly an argument he needed energy to win. "Ronan, I had to submit your college applications for you because your laptop broke and you waited until the night before."

Ronan nodded, as this was a fair point. "Fine. But that was in high school."

Now, it was Adrienne's turn. "Remember when you were supposed to go on a date with Jess last summer?"

Ronan rolled his eyes, looking more defeated by the second. There was no further explanation, so I bit.

"What happened with Jess?"

Jess was one of Adrienne's bridesmaids. They'd been friends all throughout high school, and apparently Jess was a good one at that, but she was a bit of a tough egg to crack—not very talkative, rock-hard opinions, Resting Bitch Face, the lot. I'd never taken issue with her, but I knew for a fact that Ronan wasn't a huge fan. Not many people were.

"They had a date planned and Ronan left her waiting on the pier for an hour," Adrienne told me.

Beside me, Luke laughed.

Ronan let out a sigh. "I fell asleep!"

Adrienne knew this, but evidently wasn't happy about it. "I had to tell her your dog died."

"I don't have a dog."

"Well, not anymore. He died."

I turned to Ronan, noticing that, for the past five minutes, he'd only been attacked. Though all of this was warranted, sometimes he needed a hand to grab onto. The one person who'd always extended theirs, however, wasn't on the beach with us. So it was my job.

"Aw," I joked. "What was his name?"

Ronan smiled nostalgically. "Sparky."

Luke shook his head. "That's the worst name you can give a dog."

"What's wrong with Sparky?" Ronan asked.

"It sounds like he got stuck in an electrical socket."

Adrienne curled her lip now, her eyes growing softer. "I always wanted a dog named Tucker."

"What about Blake?" Ronan asked.

Luke was intrigued. "For a dog?"

Ronan nodded.

"I like it," Luke decided.

While Ronan took his triumphant name suggestion to heart, I stood from my towel, a movement I had two reasons for. First, looking back and forth between Luke and Ronan was dizzying. Second, the conversation, like the many I'd encountered between the four of us over the past few years, was starting to feel empty. There was a chance that my next few days would change that, for better or for worse. But for now, I just needed one thing.

"I'm going in the water."

By the time I set foot in the Pittsburgh International Airport, I'd concluded one thing: I was in way over my head.

From a distance, setting off on a secret trip to find Finn in Pennsylvania seemed so compelling. I was excited by the thought of it, and had not an ounce of fear. But then I was in the air, flying away from home and toward a place I had never been, in search of a person who might not even be there at all. A person who certainly wasn't expecting me.

I'd gotten out of bed early enough—and skipped a run, I might add—to do some much-needed research on the man in question. What I found, I wasn't at all surprised by.

Finn had gone to Carnegie Mellon (which I knew), stayed there all four years (which I figured—Finn wasn't a quitter), and earned several accolades for his academic and stage performances while he studied Drama and Music Theater. He'd been most intrigued by the Directing program, as his name appeared in several articles that included it, dating all the way back to his sophomore year. All of these things—the longevity, the success, the horizon-broadening—made perfect sense to me. They were just added and sensible pieces to the

36

puzzle that was Finn Cooper. The puzzle that, at one point in my life, I wasn't sure I could live without.

The thing with Finn was that I never thought I'd have to learn any of this through an internet search. I always figured that he'd reach out if he needed me, or that we'd catch up every time he came home. But then he never needed me, and he never came home. So here I was.

After all this time, it was taking mental and physical preparation to see Finn again. I wasn't nervous, necessarily, but it had been awhile, and he didn't know me anymore. I knew when Luke and Adrienne got engaged that it was finally time to find him and figure out what happened, but part of me couldn't shake how long it had been since the last time I'd seen him. What if I'd changed too much?

For all I knew, Finn could've packed up the second his stay at Carnegie Mellon was over, fled the city, and headed for Mars. But if every moment we'd spent together—late nights at the beach, hushed conversations while noise swirled around us, crying over moments that seemed so small from this far away— told me anything, it was that I knew Finn. Even after all these years, I had a hunch that he'd fallen in love with the city, or something within it, and made a home more welcoming than the one he used to know. Maybe it was just hope.

So I had a feeling Finn was in Pittsburgh. But as I walked through the airport, headed for an Uber driver named Teresa, I was realizing that the city was huge. And daunting. And nothing like home. And, to top it off, I didn't even know where to start.

As his academic achievements on the internet stood to show, Finn loved musicals. When I remembered this on my way to the airport, a light bulb ignited above my head. Finn was always a theater guy. He was the only one who would ever watch *Mamma Mia* or *Hairspray* with me when we were kids, the other boys claiming it was much too girly. So, I did some further research and looked into the Broadway productions that Pittsburgh had to offer, and I hit the jackpot. There was an ongoing production of *Hamilton*—a musical about history,

Finn's other obsession—right in the city. And there was a show tonight.

It was a long shot; I knew it. I was walking outside, wearing ripped jeans and a t-shirt with just two extra outfits and a goal so wildly unattainable it was laughable, planning to look for one person at a Broadway musical in a city of hundreds of thousands. The more I thought about it, the more I wanted to puke.

So, I decided I'd start with lunch.

"Nell?"

I smiled, sliding my backpack off of my shoulders. Finally.

"That's me."

"Just headed Downtown, dolly?" asked Teresa, who nearly blinded me with her hot pink blazer when I slid into her passengers' seat. Her car smelled strongly of an apple-scented air freshener, even though it was July, and she had a thick southern accent.

"Yes please," I said. Once I was settled in the seat, I turned, finding Teresa already focused on the task at hand.

Normally, I'd have gone out of my way, making sure that Teresa didn't feel like I was just using her to get from point A to point B, and start a conversation. But I was already tired, from both the plane ride and the conversation with Luke on the way to the airport that preceded it. He'd asked questions about my roommates, our weekend plans, my flight schedules. All, in this case, would be normal things to be curious about. But Luke trusted me, and him asking specifics made me nervous. Like he was onto me. If anyone's knowledge of my trip to Pittsburgh would have spoiled my entire plan indefinitely, it would've been his.

So when Teresa turned up her rap music, seemingly content and bobbing her head along to it as we headed toward a load of traffic, I leaned my head against the window. I watched as we passed by characteristically Pittsburgh things that I'd seen in pictures and in exposition shots on *Dance Moms*—Genevieve watched it for hours every Sunday night like she was attending a midnight church service with Abby Lee Miller as the priest—only lifting my head when we stopped in a line of traffic. I looked ahead of us at the growing population of bumpers and brake lights, then over at Teresa.

"I can just get out here," I said, a polite smile on my face as I eyed a row of crowded restaurants on the next block.

Teresa raised her eyebrows. "You sure? I don't mind the wait."

"I'm sure. I could use the walk," I answered, scooping my backpack from the floor and waiting for Teresa to unlock the car before reaching for the handle.

"Suit yourself!"

When I looked back at Teresa, her smile was so genuine and her eyes were so kind that I felt a pang of guilt for ending our journey together a few minutes early. But then I blinked, hard, and remembered that this was just the kind of thing I used to care about, but hadn't for a long time. Now, I was doing what I needed to. It didn't make a difference to Teresa and I knew it. So I decided to take advantage of the fact that we'd never see each other again.

"Speaking of suit," I said, grabbing her attention as I stepped out of the car. "That is a spectacular blazer."

Teresa's eyes lit up even more, warming my heart in a way I didn't know they would, and she lifted her hand to her heart. "Well, aren't you just the sweetest thing? Thank you!"

I nodded my head, then thanked her before shutting the door and finding my way to the sidewalk. The air around me was fresh, a combination of the bustling city and the nearby water and the newness of the summer sun beating down onto me and everyone else. I felt it then, the freedom that I was seeking when I booked the trip to Pennsylvania and came up with the (admittedly loose) plan to find Finn. I was by myself now, doing something just because I wanted to. High School Me was quaking, and I loved it.

With that, I made a mental note to text my mom and Luke in an hour when I was supposed to land in Vermont. Fingers crossed I made it there safely.

I'd always been fascinated by the way cities could hold so many things in such small places, so I felt a boost of adrenaline as I walked down the sidewalk, backpack holding loosely onto my shoulders, toward a crowd of restaurants and shops and street lights. It wasn't long before I was standing in front of a pizza place called Jay's, appetite bursting. It was a petite brick building sandwiched between a flower shop and a boutique dress store, complete with black bistro tables and chairs. I was a sucker for outdoor stand-up menus, which Jay's conveniently had just to the right of their entrance, so my decision to eat there barely took much brain power at all.

The menu itself sold me even more. The first option of pizza, by the slice or the pie, was titled "An Apple A Day." It had a cheese-stuffed crust and was topped with basil, apples, pine nuts, asiago cheese, onions (yuck), and balsamic vinaigrette. In my head, I could hear what Luke would be saying about the combination as if he was standing right there next to me. *The basil and the balsamic compliment one another*, he'd say. *The pine nuts are just for a crunch factor,* and *If you want it without onions, just ask.*

There was a part of me that was beginning to wish I'd told Luke and Ronan and Adrienne and everyone else about what I was doing. Maybe it would've gone over well. Maybe the past four years had been a mistake, and maybe everyone was finally willing to admit it. Luke and Ronan might've even come with me, and maybe I could've heard Luke's take on the pizza in real life rather than just in my imagination.

I was thinking all of this, ready to begin dwelling on it while I surveyed the other pizza options, when I felt a tug on my pant leg.

I looked down, expecting to see a nosey dog or something like it, when I instead found the most adorable of all little girls staring right back up at me. She blinked her bright blue eyes which ignited against her light brown skin, and tipped her head up a little further, her curly black pigtails bouncing as she did.

"You're pretty," she said, her voice sweet and soft. With just two words, she'd already made my trip. Pack it up, Pittsburgh. I'd gotten what I needed.

"You're pretty, too." I crouched down so I could be eye-to-eye with my new small friend. She looked right back at me, wildly unwavering for such a young kid, and flashed me a smile. I was beginning to wonder why she wasn't being scooped up by a parent or a sibling or an incredibly irresponsible babysitter. "What's your name?"

Beside us, a roar of laughter erupted from an outdoor table at Jay's, but I kept my eyes on my friend.

"Freya," she said.

"Freya," I repeated, refraining from a handshake for several reasons. "I'm Nell."

"Hi Mel," she said, quick on her feet even if she was a little off. Then, she lowered her eyebrows at the same time I lowered mine, confused by my confusion. I couldn't help but laugh, though I was beginning to think that Freya might've been able to outsmart me if she wanted to.

"Are you here all alone, Freya?"

Freya shook her head, pigtails swaying. "I'm here with my daddy. He's tall."

"Right," I said, thankful to Freya for narrowing down the tell-tale characteristics of her dad. A tall man. Great.

After a quick glance around us, where I saw many tall men but none who looked like Freya or who were walking our way, I looked into her sweet eyes again. "Do you know where he is?"

Freya began to nod, but then a voice—as soft as Freya's but with a bit of an edge to it—answered my question for me.

"Freya!" the voice said. "Jesus," he muttered under his breath.

I was halfway turned around, fully ready to console this father of Freya's and let him know that she'd only been in front of me for a few seconds, when he said a name I hadn't heard in a very long time. One I wasn't sure I'd ever hear again.

"Elliana?"

Chapter Five

Elliana

"Rose," Coach Pieter said pointedly, snapping me out of the trance I was in. "In for Taylor."

We were nearing the end of the fourth quarter and the score had been so close the entire game that I was sure I'd find gray hair on my head by the time I got home. I was standing on the side of the huddle, glancing up at the scoreboard when Coach Pieter called my name, subsequently forcing the anxiety back into my chest that began to fade when he put Sienna in for me five minutes before.

When I sat down on the bench next to Sydney, watching as Coach Pieter drew Xs and Os and arrows on the small whiteboard he held in his hands, I tried to put myself back in the headspace it took to be on the court. I liked sitting on the bench, cheering Sydney on, watching the other team—the North Coast High Dolphins, who apparently wanted to make it to the championship, too—try to keep up with us as we did with them. I'd been sitting there for exactly four minutes and thirty-two seconds of playing time. Now, the pressure was on.

When Coach Pieter looked at me, I gave him my full attention, trying my best to ignore the feeling of my ponytail sticking to the back of my neck.

"Stay on five," he told me. "She won't drive to the basket because she's afraid of Sydney, so if she pump-fakes, she's not going far." He turned his attention just a few inches to my right. "Piper."

I took a deep breath, or twelve, while Coach spewed out directions and comments to Piper and Amari and Sienna. I could feel Sydney's leg bouncing beside me while a pit sank deeper and deeper into my stomach. She'd already scored eighteen points, and was carrying the team in stats and energy. I prayed to God that my entering the game wouldn't mess any of that up. When the buzzer sounded, I stood up, straightened my shorts, and headed for the court.

Seconds after Sydney patted me on the back, ensuring me that I would be okay, I found Number Five. Her jet-black hair was pulled and twisted into tight french braids that fell around the middle of her back, partially covering her last name, Jovey, which was printed on her jersey. I situated myself next to her at the top of the arc, waiting for the referee to hand her teammate and Syd's mark, Number Fifteen, the ball. As I stood, surveying the court and everyone on it, I saw Jovey smile at me. I offered one back, then felt a sudden wave of confidence as the ball was inbounded.

The gym was on fire. Every fan and friend and teammate and coach was on their feet as the game went on, back and forth like a tennis match or a Presidential Debate, for the next two minutes. I could barely feel my feet as I ran—offense then defense then offense again—and was so zoned-in that I couldn't have been distracted even if a group of dinosaurs decided to take up a portion of the bleachers and catch the last few seconds of the game. In a similar sense, I had no idea where my family was sitting. But I knew they were watching.

I'd been doing okay. Nothing detrimental had happened, at least not to me. But I could feel overtime weighing down on my chest like an anchor. I knew our team was tired, and I really wasn't too confident we'd win if we had to play for eight more minutes.

So, when the whistle was blown with just four seconds left, us down by one point, and Coach Pieter called a time-out, I was hoping I'd be called out of the game. This was certainly the worst-case scenario, and the possibility that the ball could end up in my hands might as well have been strangling me.

"How are we? Good?" Coach Pieter said, not breathing for long enough for anyone to answer. Not that we would, anyways. "Get some water."

To my dismay, I sat next to Sydney on the bench, concluding immediately that Coach had no intentions of pulling me out of the game. At least there was still a chance that

I wouldn't have to touch the ball. There were five of us, and only four seconds left. I'd say the odds were pretty good.

"It's going to be an inbound on the side of the court," Coach said as he drew an X in pink marker on the side of his basketball-court-shaped board. "I want Elliana to start with the ball."

Maybe I should've just stopped hoping for things altogether.

"Sydney, you've been doing a good job of making yourself open all game, so they're going to think we're looking for you, but we're not."

Coach went on, for the twelve seconds left in the short time-out, and detailed the way Sydney would fake a run to the opposite side of the court, while Amari and Piper would free themselves of their defenders after Sienna would effectively get in their way by setting picks. In layman's terms, if Sienna and Amari and Piper did their jobs exactly as Coach said, I'd have two options. Once the ball was out of my hands, the fate of the game was no longer up to me. I just had to hand it off. Easy.

But when the referee blew his whistle a moment later, whatever Coach Pieter drew out on the whiteboard was not what was unfolding in front of me. I had the ball in my hands, only seconds to get rid of it, and no teammates to be found. I could hear shouting coming at me from every direction, unable to make out any exact words, and had Jovey's hands flailing in my face to distract me from an open pass to Amari or Piper. Lucky for Jovey, her teammates were doing a good job of making sure they were covered.

What Coach Pieter surely wasn't expecting, and what was the only way I saw to relieve myself of the world of anticipation surrounding me and the game, was Sydney. She was on the complete opposite end of the court, jumping up and down so that I could see her, hands in the air and all. I didn't look for Amari or Piper or anyone else before making my decision. I didn't have a choice, really.

I took the ball in one hand, wound up, and hurled the basketball through the air—baseball-style, like a centerfielder.

44

Then I held my breath along with everyone else in the gym, and watched in slow motion as the ball traveled over Amari, Piper, a jaw-dropped Sienna, and every Dolphin, before landing in between Sydney's hands. There were two seconds left on the clock when Sydney readjusted herself just inside the 3-point-line. There was only one when she shot the ball, holding her follow-through as time stood still and the nearby Dolphins scrambled tooth and nail toward her.

There were some gasps (hundreds), a buzzer (frightening), and then a swish (so, so sweet).

Game over. Sydney wins.

The crowd went nuts while our team and hefty student section flooded the court. Before I blinked, I was surrounded, and I didn't even know by who. Somehow I found my way to Sydney, and our team engaged in the most excited, happiest, jumpiest group hug we'd ever had. All I could see were the smiles on my teammates' faces, though I could hear the chatter and excitement of the crowd that surrounded us, too. I wondered what it looked like from the outside.

Three days later, I was heading up my driveway after another post-practice trip to Archie's with Sydney and our counterparts. Sydney had continued down the sidewalk, her basketball pounding against it as she walked, after observing the collective amount of cars in front of my house and lights on inside of it. She wasn't antisocial by any means, just tired. We both knew that upon entering my house at an hour like this, you'd need a serious second wind. I didn't have one, but I lived there, so.

The state of my house at night was a strange phenomenon. On one hand, I always knew what kind of atmosphere I'd be walking into. My older brother Luke and his friends would be occupying the living room or the kitchen, my younger brother Braeden would be sitting somewhere close but not too much so, listening and observing the chaos, and my parents would either be sleeping and pretending not to hear what was going on downstairs, or partaking in the nonsense themselves.

On the other hand, I never had any idea what to expect. I'd come home to several laughing fits, game nights, dance parties. One time after basketball practice, I was slung right into an argument over who would make the best salad. That debate in particular wouldn't have stood out to me, but I did find it interesting that the contenders were not my brother and his friends themselves, but Ryan Reynolds and Tom Holland. Needless to say, the debate went on for hours. I'm not entirely sure it ever ended.

The one constant of my arrival home was that I was never invisible there, not to them. I'd be thrown into the mix, landing right on my butt in the middle of their perfect circle. I was always welcomed like just another piece of their puzzle, even though we all knew I wasn't like them. We all knew I never would be.

This time, when I made my way from our entryway and into the living room, where the daylight that usually ignited its walls and furniture was long gone, everyone was on the floor. *Footloose* was playing softly on the television, a bowl of guacamole and an accompanying one of chips sat on the coffee table, and I could smell brownies baking in the oven.

The first person I spotted, likely because he was the closest to me and the loudest, was Ronan.

"I'm just saying," he was saying, "I don't think it would be that cute."

"Is that a dig at me or you?" asked Finn, who was sitting right beside Ronan with his back against the couch.

"Neither," Ronan said. "Sometimes when two really hot people have a baby together, the baby isn't cute. It's like their genes work against them, or something."

"So you're saying you and Finn are both hot," Adrienne, Luke's girlfriend and by far the saint of the bunch, said, her eyebrows raised.

Finn let out a laugh and shook his head, while Luke, sitting opposite Ronan and Finn with his arm around sweet Adrienne, actually pondered the idea.

"Give an example," Luke said.

Ronan shrugged, a goofy smile on his face. "Well, your parents are hot."

My duffle bag slipped off of my shoulder and landed on the floor with a thud. At the same time, Adrienne turned around and met my eyes.

"Elliana!"

At the sound of my name, everyone turned toward me. Ronan kept his goofy grin, but I could see in his dark eyes that he'd be returning to his argument soon. Adrienne and Luke met me with their usual smiles, which always made me feel loved, while Finn's expression said that the night had only gotten better when I walked in. When I looked at him, sometimes I could believe it.

But now, I had questions. For Ronan, specifically.

"Are you saying I wasn't a cute baby?"

Ronan smirked again, then leaned back on his hands so as to seem relaxed and not at all intimidated. "You were adorable. So was Braeden."

Ronan's comment got a laugh from everyone, even though we all knew it was coming. Mostly, he was right. My mother was beautiful. She was a nurse, a great one at that, but had always been told that she could've been a model or an actress in a heartbeat if she wanted. She was tall and blonde with big green eyes and, as Sydney liked to point out, was "curvy in all the right places."

My dad, a mousy dental student when they met, was now a full-time practicing dentist with curly brown hair and a freckled face. They pleasantly complemented one another, and when they had Luke, he was a perfect combination of the two. Now, he stood a few inches taller than me while Braeden was surely headed in that direction. They had blonde-ish and brown curly hair respectively, and faces that had all the girls at St. Jane's doing double-takes. With a family so beautiful and bright, it was a mystery how I turned out so boring.

"You guys ready for the championship tomorrow?" Luke asked me, reaching forward for a chip to fill with guacamole and ignoring Ronan's comment all together. "Sienna Brandon said Coach Pieter had you guys running in circles at practice yesterday."

I tried not to think too much about practice the day before, where Sienna's sentiment was valid as could be. The team we would face in the championship was tough, and Coach Pieter wanted to make sure we were ready.

"Something like that," I said. "Today was easier."

"Well, I can't wait to see you guys play again. That game was so intense," Adrienne said, her eyes wide. "I almost lost my voice."

"It's too bad no one was filming that last play," Finn added. "It would've been on SportsCenter if they were."

I let out a laugh as I made my way to the end of the couch in the living room. When I sat on it, I felt my bones and muscles settle for the first time in days.

"Only Sydney can pull off something like that," I said.

Like clockwork, there was a general downshift in the mood of the room. It wasn't only Sydney who didn't like when I discredited myself. I usually tried not to say anything, good or bad, about myself around Luke and his friends for that very reason. This time, I hadn't even noticed.

"Not the shot, Elliana, the pass. Sydney made that shot ten times already before then. No one thought she'd miss," Luke said.

Adrienne shook her head and placed a hand on Luke's leg. "That's not to say it wasn't good."

"No, it was great," Luke says. "But no one else in that gym would've made that pass."

"I almost passed out when I saw you look at Sydney," Ronan added, forcing a laugh out of me.

"He's not kidding," Finn said. "He turned purple."

"Good school spirit," Adrienne said, making Ronan giggle.

"Well thanks," I said quickly, readjusting myself on the couch and hoping to cut the conversation short. Thankfully, a text message chime on Adrienne's phone did that for me.

"Shoot," she mumbled. As she began to stand up, she planted a quick and unexpected kiss on Luke's lips. Beside me, I watched Ronan squirm, Finn laugh, then Ronan elbow him in the side all in one perfect motion. Their predictability was second to none.

"Late?" Luke asked, smiling like an idiot. He couldn't help it when he was with Adrienne.

"Told my mom I'd be home ten minutes ago." She sprung up on her feet and retrieved her bag, a purple St Jane's Musical Players tote, from our front hall closet, then turned to the rest of us as she drew open the door. "See you all tomorrow! Good luck, Elliana! Love you!"

Right when the door shut, Adrienne seemingly gone with the ocean breeze outside, it opened again. She peeked her head inside, her eyes meeting Luke's like they were magnetized to them. "Don't forget about the brownies in the oven."

Luke nodded his head, his smiling not having faded in the slightest. "You got it, Chef."

Now, Adrienne's business-like expression turned soft. "Love you."

"I love you, too."

The door was barely closed tight before Ronan let out a sigh. He leaned his head back on the couch cushion beside me. "Observing young love is exhausting."

"Aw," I said. I patted his head with my hand, his curly hair bouncing as I did. "Your day will come."

A few minutes later, the oven timer went off at the same time that there was a knock on the door. I took a quick survey of the room, then was overcome with confusion. Luke and his friends were popular, but not many others found themselves in our living room past 10 o'clock.

Ronan headed for the oven—my fingers were crossed that he remembered to use a mit – while Luke wearily went to the door. On his way, he turned back to Finn and me who both shrugged.

Luke's hesitation, however, stopped the second he opened the door. He drew it open with excitement when he saw who was standing on the front step, and I could tell he was smiling even from behind him.

"Oh, hey Mo," he said. He drew the door open wider and stepped aside, letting the cool breeze inside and revealing a sweatshirt and messy bun-sporting Mo. It was nearly eleven o'clock now, and she looked as if she'd just had her morning coffee. Her cheeks were rosy and her eyes were bright enough to light up the room.

"Hey," Mo said, stepping into the house carefully. "I think I left my phone here earlier. I would've called, but, you know."

"Ah," Finn said suddenly. He reached his hand underneath the coffee table, retrieving a green-cased phone. "I was wondering what this was."

"That's it," Mo said with a laugh, meeting Finn's eyes before finding mine. When she did, she paused. Maybe it was only enough for me to notice, and maybe it wasn't a pause at all. But I was sure it was. "Oh, hey–"

"Oh, sorry," Luke said, shaking his head and following Mo into the living room. "Mo, this is my sister, Elliana."

"We met actually," Mo said. She turned to Luke. "I took the beach route the other day. Ran into Elliana and her friend…"

"Dippy," I said, surprising myself and apparently everyone else in the room, except for Mo, that is, who clicked her tongue and pointed a triumphant finger in my direction.

"Dippy. Yes."

I felt myself smile, then sat up a little bit straighter. The energy in the room seemed to change then. It felt warmer, more energetic. Maybe it was just Mo.

"You know," said Ronan, who I would've almost entirely forgotten about if not for the smell of sweet chocolate now wafting my way, "Elliana and Syd are playing in one of the biggest games of the year tomorrow. You should come."

At the sound of Ronan's offer, I felt something fall on my chest. Mo being at the game would've meant two more eyes watching my every move. Two bright, green, captivating ones that for some reason I felt the need to impress.

"Ah. Basketball, right?" Mo asked.

Finn nodded. "The championship game."

"Right. My gym coach was going on about it all week." Now, Mo looked right at me. Whatever feeling it was that was sitting on my chest began to burn. Though it was my typical calming mechanism when attention was on me, I couldn't find it in myself to look away. "And I heard you had quite the game."

"She did," Luke said as he stepped a bit further into the house, putting himself between Mo and the kitchen. "Don't let her tell you otherwise."

At this, Mo let out a laugh like she knew why Luke would say such a thing. Like she knew me.

"I won't."

"Well, if you don't make the game, at least come for dinner after," Ronan offered. "Luke here is quite the cook."

"Yeah?" Mo turned to Luke once more, her side profile just as perfect as the rest of her.

"I dabble."

The same laugh that erupted from my chest then came from Ronan and Finn, too. If "dabble" meant that Luke was a better cook than any of us were at anything, then sure. He dabbled.

Really, Luke had been cooking since he was fourteen. It started with him watching my dad cook or bake and helping out here and there, but then he moved onto YouTube videos and our grandpa's old recipes. Now, he'd gone through just about every cookbook in the house and had even started a recipe book of his own that he kept in a spiral notebook above the microwave. He was phenomenal. Braeden liked to refer to him as Gordon Ramsay, but my mom would always say he was too sweet for that nickname.

Mo was about to ask about the cooking, as we could all see in her expression, but Luke wasn't much of a bragger, either.

"Want some brownies?" Luke said instead. He nodded toward the kitchen where Ronan was now pulling a spatula out of one of the drawers under the countertop. "They've got marshmallows and peanut butter."

"Don't worry," Ronan said as he turned, waving the spatula in his hand. "I had nothing to do with them."

Though Mo was new to the group—an addition that slipped right under my nose without me really knowing it—she seemed so comfortable. I envied the way she carried herself like she belonged right there with us, messy red hair, ripped jeans, and all. I wanted to know how she did it.

Once Mo expressed that Luke's offer was one she couldn't pass up on, she joined Luke and Ronan in the kitchen. Seconds later, Ronan was making them laugh while he served brownies onto one of my dad's favorite plates. I was just watching them when I felt Finn beside me doing the same.

I studied him for a moment, too. It was like observing Finn in his natural habitat—perfectly content watching as his friends made fools of themselves. As long as he was in their company, he was always okay. I was happy Luke and Ronan were safe for him, and that I sometimes was, too. It was no secret he didn't feel that way at home.

"Are you staying tonight?" I asked, my voice low enough that the kitchen-goers wouldn't hear me.

When Finn smiled, I knew it was because he was grateful he always had a place with us. But I could also see the pain behind his eyes. I always wanted to find a way to get rid of it, though I couldn't control the way his parents treated one another. The way they treated him.

"Probably."

I offered a smile back, then let my eyes flicker to the television. "Do you want to finish the movie?"

Finn glanced toward the screen, where one of his favorite scenes was unfolding.

"You've got a big day tomorrow," he told me.

I shrugged, knowing for certain that I'd be kicking myself in the morning for staying up so late. But this was Finn.

"It's almost over, anyways."

"Are you sure?"

I flashed Finn another smile, one I didn't have to force, then patted the couch cushion beside me. A few minutes later, we were joined by Luke, Ronan, Mo, and a plate full of brownies.

There was still that feeling in my chest, and an extra one that came with the dwindling time between where I was and where I would be at the game the next day. But even if it was just for a moment, I was happy to be sitting there. To be taking it all in, whatever it was.

Chapter Six

Nell

As it turned out, the person I'd come in search of was the last person I was expecting to see. But I knew there was only one soul in Pennsylvania, and maybe in the whole world, who would've called me by that name. When I heard it, I felt out of place, like I'd done something wrong and everyone in earshot had just gotten word of it. The truth was, that name didn't belong to me anymore. I was someone else now.

For these reasons and so many more, I felt like I was moving in slow motion when I pulled my attention from Freya and turned around. The second my eyes met Finn's, I felt every ounce of myself deflate.

"Finn-"

I caught one glimpse of his face before he pulled me in. I was embracing the hug as much as I could, and I felt the confusion bubbling up inside Finn just as the last four years were rising as a lump in my throat. He held me tight, pressing one hand up against the back of my head and the other on my backpack.

When I stepped back from him, I realized I was crying. The lump in my throat came out as a sort of sob-sigh, and an almost identical one came from Finn. I thought I knew what seeing him again would feel like, if I were to ever get the chance, but nothing I dreamt of could've possibly compared to the way I felt.

For a second, Finn took me in. All of me. My appearance, my emotions, the way I was carrying myself. So I did the same. Appearance-wise, he hadn't changed much, but he did look a bit more mature. He still had Harry-Styles-like, curly brown hair that was just a touch longer than it was the last time I saw him. His eyes were still kind, albeit a bit more tired, and he still slouched a little bit when he stood. It wasn't enough to notice, really, unless you were me. And I was, so I did.

What I was relieved about, and what I hadn't really identified as a worry of mine to begin with, was that I could tell his heart was the same. I could feel it already, and he'd only said one word.

"What are you—" He shook his head, his words escaping him. "You— you look so—" His eyes widened, and his chest was rising and falling with every breath he managed to take. "I can't—"

"Finish a sentence?" I cracked, lifting my hand to wipe a stray tear from my eye. Then, I watched a smile grow on Finn's face, and suddenly every ounce of stress I'd endured to be standing where I was—in Pennsylvania and in life—was worth it. I wrapped my arms around him and held him tight again before he could respond.

"You're so different," I heard him say while my ear was against his chest. "What are you doing here?"

"Good different?" I asked as I looked up at him, stepping back to put space between us again.

"I don't— I don't know," he said. "Yes, good different. Not that there was anything wrong before, I just—"

"I know," I said, saving him from the stammering that I was used to hearing from my family over the past few years.

"What are you doing here?" he repeated.

I watched Freya inch a bit closer to Finn, finding comfort next to his leg as she reached up for his arm. He kept his eyes on me, but wrapped his hand right around hers like it was nothing. Like it was instinct.

Next to us, Jay's was still spilling over with customers, all of whom seemed satisfied as could be. Part of me felt like I wasn't even there, like this was some dream that I had tried so hard to manifest for myself and that I'd soon wake up from. I just couldn't believe I'd found him. I would've asked someone to pinch me, but I had a feeling Freya might've taken my request a bit too seriously.

"Getting pizza," I said instead. When Finn didn't move an inch, not with his feet or his eyes or his expression, I shrugged. "I was looking for you, actually."

"You were looking for me," he repeated.

"Not actively," I countered, awaiting the first of several funny looks I was sure to get for how extensive my plan was. Instead, Finn was just looking at me like he couldn't believe I was in front of him, but also as if he'd never seen me before. I imagined my stare was identical to his, so I took another quick look at Jay's. Then I turned back toward Finn and the little girl who called him her dad—if every question I had sitting in my throat were to have been ranked, that was number one—and flashed a smile.

"We've got a lot to catch up on, huh?" I asked.

At this, Finn nodded, glancing down at Freya after realizing that I did, then looked back at me with eyes filled with so many stories I thought I might burst. Then he squeezed Freya's hand a little tighter. "How about lunch?"

"Thanks," Finn said to our waitress, a girl with firetruck-red hair and a nose piercing so shiny that Freya even expressed her admiration of it.

I decided on a slice of plain cheese pizza. Luke once insisted that I must broaden my horizons and try something with more flavor, more variety. So out of my natural-born sibling-spite, I always ordered cheese. I also found it easier to compare pizza from different places if I ordered the same kind, so at least I had a reason to back myself up should Luke ever question my choices. If he didn't, Ronan surely would've.

In front of me, Finn spotted a pink crayon underneath his placemat. He reached for it and then flashed it in front of Freya, who was already crafting a masterpiece on the sheet in front of her with the three colors she had. When she spotted the pick crayon, her blue eyes ignited with fire. "Don't forget this one," Finn said.

"Legendary," Freya replied with perfect diction.

I let out a laugh (how could I not?) and turned to Finn with so much confusion and adoration in my eyes that he laughed, too.

56

"It's her new favorite word," he told me while she tuned us out, focusing now on the ear of the elephant in front of her. "Sutton used it once last week and we haven't heard the end of it."

"Sutton," I said aloud. The name felt so special once spoken, though I was sure I didn't know the extent of it.

Finn nodded, a smile forming again on his lips. "Freya's mom," he said. "We met freshman year."

"At Carnegie Mellon," I said, tying together the loose ends as best I could. I wasn't sure how sensitive the topic was, or anything about the topic, really. So I was treading carefully. We both were. When Finn nodded, I kept going. "So a little over three years ago."

Finn nodded. "Right."

"And how old is Freya?"

Finn bit his lower lip. "Four."

"Four and one third," Freya corrected him. She raised her eyebrows and pulled a laugh out of him.

Finn looked at Freya, then back at me, like I didn't even know the half of it. I didn't even know a third. "Right. Four and one third," he said then.

I nodded, albeit slowly. Though things were clearer, I only had more questions now. Finn looked and acted like a father figure to Freya for every second I'd been watching him, so the fact that his title wasn't biological didn't change much in the way I saw the situation. The most overwhelming feeling I had was one of loss for the four years that I could've been there for him. That I could've known.

During my pause, I noticed that Finn was still looking at me the way that he did after we hugged. Like I was a new person, someone so intriguing and worth studying. To him, I was. And he didn't even know my name.

"So Sutton—"

"Is amazing," Finn said to me, the smile on his face now bursting. Freya was coloring the elephant's trunk green, while the ears were blue and the rest of it was pink. To my surprise, everything was perfectly between the lines. Luke, Braeden, and

I could never. Not at that age. "You can meet her if you want. I mean, if you're staying long enough. Which brings us to—"

"I'm not done asking questions."

Finn laughed, then leaned forward on his elbows. Evidently, I had more explaining to do than him. Which, to be fair, wasn't fair.

"I can't just be in Pittsburgh to hang out with one of my best friends?"

"Elliana, it's been—"

"It's Mel." Freya didn't even look up from her coloring sheet. But dammit she was quick.

Finn looked between us and shook his head. "Mel?"

"Nell," I said slowly. "I go by Nell now, actually."

"Nell," Finn said. Like Sutton's name from my mouth, it had a nice ring to it. I didn't realize how badly I was aching to hear him say it.

"You ordered soda with your lunch, you're in Pittsburgh all by yourself, wearing ripped jeans, and your name is Nell."

I couldn't help but laugh, so I did. To my left, a table of friends erupted in cackles too, one of their voices coming out in a shriek.

"Not quite how you imagined our reunion, huh?" I asked, feeling the sun as it beat down on my forehead and the black bistro table between us.

Finn's smile was still there, but faded a bit at my question. He glanced at Freya before giving me an answer, one I wasn't expecting.

"I stopped imagining a reunion a while ago, actually."

Finn's words hit me like a slap in the face. Not one that came from Finn himself, but the situation, I guess.

I had no idea why Ronan and Luke stuck so closely together while Finn exiled himself to another part of the country. I'd witnessed their bond my whole life and deemed it unbreakable, so I was sure the reason for the permanent separation was bad. But never once did I imagine a future of mine without Finn in it. I always knew there'd be a time to find him. I guess I figured he'd felt the same way. Now, I was wondering when he'd lost hope.

So I decided to answer his question.

"Luke and Adrienne are getting married."

Just like that, Finn's shoulders dropped, and the color fled his cheeks. I knew the wedding news would have hurt him, solely because of how involved in it he would've been if whatever happened just hadn't happened. But there was so much history I didn't know about, and it seemed that my words came out like a slap, too.

"Oh," Finn said finally, forcing his shoulders and his mood back up. "They must be so happy."

"They are." I bit my lip and folded the paper napkin in front of me. "I want you to come to the wedding."

Silence. Everywhere.

"I wasn't invited," Finn said after a beat.

"Yes, you were," I told him. "Just now."

"Nell–"

"Will you at least think about it?" I was suddenly desperate, as if I didn't know Finn's presence at the wedding would take convincing. Loads of it.

Finn sighed. I could almost hear his heart beating.

"You came all the way to Pittsburgh to ask me that?"

I frowned. "That's not an answer."

"And how were you expecting to find me, anyways?"

"If I tell you, will you think about it?"

Finn grinned now, as if my negotiating was just another characteristic of mine that he wasn't expecting. He would've been right not to.

"That's hardly a fair exchange."

As sort of an intermission, perhaps for the both of us, our waitress returned, balancing steaming slices of pizza on a silver tray. I leaned back, simmering myself the same way the pizza was. Next to Finn, Freya set aside her elephant and crayons, readying herself for the food like no other four-and-one-third-year-old had ever done before.

"Those are big," she noted, making eye contact with the waitress before nodding at the pizzas.

"They sure are!" the waitress said, endeared. "We have to fill you up before you have a fun day with your mommy and daddy."

"Oh, she's not my mommy," Freya said matter-of-factly. "My mommy is tall."

Instead of being offended, I laughed at the fact that our height difference was the distinction Freya chose to highlight between Sutton and me. Then I looked at the waitress, who seemed to be only slightly mortified.

"Oh, I'm very sorry. I was mistaken."

"No worries," Finn said as she set down the last piece of pizza in front of him. It looked floppy, like Ronan's hair. "Thanks."

The waitress returned to the rest of her duties, and Freya reached forward for her pizza, her hand stopping to hover over it as the steam floated upwards from its cheese. "Too hot," she noted.

"Just give it a couple of minutes," Finn told her. "The cheese is better that way, anyways."

Funny, I thought, it was Luke who taught Finn and Ronan the perfect timing of pizza slice consumption. I decided not to say it, though, because maybe I was getting somewhere.

When Finn looked up at me, I was looking right back. It was obvious I'd come with an agenda, and I would've been damned if he wasn't even going to consider it.

"So were you just planning on walking down the street and tapping on every shoulder you could find? You know Luke has my number," Finn said.

"I didn't want Luke to know I was coming."

Uh oh. Backtracking. It was time to expose myself. For better or worse.

"I remembered how much you loved theater, so I was going to see if I could find you at a show." I paused, swallowed a gulp of air that tasted like pizza. "Tonight."

Finn's laugh was breathless, and it forced one out of me, too.

"*Elliana*," he said in disbelief.

Freya looked up. "Mel!"

"Mel." Finn shook his head. "God. *Nell*."

My story was already so ridiculous, so I decided to keep it going. "I bought a resale ticket last night for a Broadway show. It might not even be real," I said.

"And you were going to, what? Search the hallways for me?"

"I had nothing else," I explained, laughing and grateful that Finn was already making fun of me, a true staple of the friend group of our past lives.

"What show were you going to see?"

"*Hamilton.* Since, you know, you liked history–"

"Daddy went to *Hamilton* last night," Freya said suddenly, a bite of still-too-hot pizza lingering in her mouth. She shut her eyes tight to swallow it, then took a breath and studied the crust as she went on. "With Mommy too. I stayed with a babysitter even though I'm not a baby. She didn't like popsicles and her name was Crazy."

I was surprised, but mostly stuck on that last part.

"So I wasn't that far off." I turned to Freya. "Crazy?"

"Her name is Maisie," Finn explained, "and you still came to Pittsburgh, where there are hundreds of thousands of people, expecting to run into me at a show. Do you hear how crazy that is?"

"Says the one sitting across from me at lunch. In Pittsburgh. Where there are hundreds of thousands of people."

"Okay, fine. But–"

"So you'll think about it," I pressed. Freya raised her eyebrows, seemingly impressed by my persistence.

At this, Finn sighed again. Yeah, I was being hard on him. But I had to be. I hadn't even asked any of my other questions yet.

Finn took his time thinking up a response. He took a sip of his water, the condensation dripping from the glass and onto the table, then set it down with a gentle clink.

"How long are you staying?"

"Finn—"

He widened his eyes a little, as if giving me a sign to stop and think. So I did.

"Until Monday."

"So two days to catch up then," he said.

I felt almost defeated, like maybe there wasn't a chance I was going to get him to consider. But, like he said, maybe we had time.

I sat back in my chair. I wasn't surrendering, but I was letting down my wall. I had lots of practice doing that recently.

"Two days."

"Are you staying with us?"

"I was going to get a hotel-"

"Stay with us," Finn insisted, a smile on his face as he glanced at Freya again. I was noticing that he did this every minute or so, just to be sure that she was okay. That she was happy. With him, I couldn't imagine a reason she wouldn't be. "God knows I owe you one."

"You don't owe anyone anything," I told him. Then, the thought of a possible late-night conversation with Finn, like the ones I used to hold so closely to my heart, popped into my mind. One look at him told me that he was remembering them, too. So I surrendered. "Thanks."

At my confirmation, Freya's eyes shot up again, her pizza slice slamming down onto her plate with a thud.

"I'll show you my seashells!"

Chapter Seven

Elliana

"Not a chance in hell."

We were sitting on the bench, an overtime period sticking its nose right in our faces, and out of courtesy, Piper had just asked Sydney if she wanted to sit out for a few minutes. Though it was very much against the coach-to-player etiquette that Coach Pieter had instilled in us long ago, a request by Sydney for a break would've been warranted. In fact, it probably should've been required.

There were thirty-two minutes of game time behind us, and Sydney had been on the court for every single one of them. She hadn't made a single mistake, and I didn't only think that because she was my best friend. Every time the ball was in her hands, the chance of us scoring got astronomically higher. She was so much fun to watch, and the energy she brought when we stepped in the gym was contagious. It might've actually been the best game all of us had played the whole season. The only problem was that the Palm Hill Cougars were keeping up.

So now we were tied, and the championship was hanging over our heads like something we could touch but not quite grab ahold of yet. If it was possible, there was even more excitement in the air than the week before at the semi-final game. This time, we were so close to something that we could taste it. Apparently the crowd could, too.

Coach Pieter substituted Sienna for me at the same time he pulled out his white board and began to draw his usual shapes and lines across it. I was relieved that I could stand then and watch, even though my playing time was also nearing the thirties, and found myself zoning out on the section of bleachers behind our bench.

Normally, I would've been paying keen attention to every word Coach Pieter was saying. But I was nervous, and I thought that maybe if I just caught a quick look at my family, I would be able to calm down and zone in. But then I actually found my family, and the opposite happened.

First, I saw my parents, both sporting purple St. Jane's t-shirts. Even from a distance, I could tell that my dad was telling my mom a story that at least he thought was funny. His face was a certain shade of red, a result of withholding laughter, and my mom's smile was bouncing like she just couldn't contain it but was trying very hard to. In front of them, Braeden was leaning into Luke, showing him something on the phone he'd just gotten. From so far away, the two of them looked even more alike. I wondered how identical they'd be once Braeden grew into himself.

Next in the row were Adrienne, Finn, and Ronan, in that exact order. They were facing away from Luke and Braeden, but they were all wearing similar St. Jane's shirts and goofy expressions, so anyone could tell they were together. What drew my attention the most, and simultaneously sped up my heartbeat, was who their attention was focused on.

When I first met Mo, I had the feeling that she was the most relaxed person I'd ever encounter. With that, I made the assumption that she didn't care. About anything, I guess, because that's how I saw people like her. But every day that she came around, I was finding that to be less and less true.

That morning, just hours before Sydney and I were due in the gym with the rest of the team, I was standing beside my locker. I had a presentation during ninth period, so I was straightening my shirt and brushing through my hair with my fingers, glimpsing periodically into the tiny mirror that hung in my locker door, when a group of seniors turned the corner into our hallway.

I didn't recognize any of them, so I kept my attention on my shirt, tucking and untucking it because I needed something to do and because my brain was telling me I had to. As the group's volume grew louder and closer, I felt a pause in their momentum, and then I felt someone stop beside me. When I turned, I saw Mo.

64

She flashed a smile across her freckled face and caught my immediate attention. In a split second, I noticed that her oxford shirt was more untucked than mine, and her tie was looser than everyone's. I was typically bothered when any St. Jane's student didn't care enough about their uniform to wear it appropriately, but with Mo, I didn't think that was it. I had a feeling that maybe her shirt was untucked for the same reason mine was pulled so perfectly tight. Because it had to be.

"You look like you're in rough shape," Mo said. "You get in a fight?"

"What?" I said, glancing down at my shirt again as if I hadn't been staring at it for the past three minutes. "I do?"

"No," Mo laughed. "You look great. I was joking."

"Oh."

Mo was still smiling when I looked up at her again, like she was actually happy to be standing beside me in the hallway. With anyone else, this would've been the time where an Awkward Silence would invite itself into the conversation and not leave until I was red in the face. Instead, Mo's eyes widened a bit as she focused on the miniature poster hanging in my locker, so I followed her gaze.

On the first day of school, Adrienne claimed that having only a mirror hanging in my locker might make me look like a narcissist. She said she was joking roughly twenty-five times, and I of course believed her, but I still couldn't stop thinking that maybe she was right. So, after lunch that day, Finn took it upon himself to hang the poster he'd had in his own locker since eighth grade just under the mirror in mine. Now, every time I opened it, I thought of him and Adrienne, and it made me smile. So maybe the reason for it didn't matter so much.

The poster itself was a painting of Shakespeare's *Romeo and Juliet* next to Broadway's *West Side Story*. Finn was obsessed with the comparison between the two and found the poster at a craft fair that Ronan's parents took the boys to in seventh grade. The fact that it held so much meaning to Finn made his hanging of it in my locker that much more special. Thank God I hadn't ripped it.

"Do you like Shakespeare?" Mo asked, eyeing the top half of the poster.

"Not really."

"Oh," she said. "Okay. So musicals, then?"

I looked at Mo, then back at the poster. I knew I enjoyed watching musicals, but I was never sure whether it was the act of viewing or the actual content that I was a fan of. Part of me thought that it might've just been the company.

"I don't know," I told her.

"You don't know?"

I shook my head, then shrugged. "I don't mind them."

"Hey, Mo?" said a boy in the still-loud group behind us. "How do you say 'fuck off' in French?"

There was an outburst of laughter from some of the students in the group, a collective eye-roll among the others. Mo offered me a polite smile, a silent apology for the interrupting, though I didn't mind it. Then she turned to the boy whose blonde hair was covering one of his eyes, and said, "Je suis occupée avec mon amie."

The boy's smile reached his ears. "Thanks!"

I watched as a tall girl thumped the boy in the back of the head and Mo turned her attention back to me. It was such a short interaction, but somehow I felt like she'd won.

"Is that really how you say that?" I asked.

She shook her head, then took a breath and looked as if she was going to say something, maybe even change the subject, when someone else from the group behind us spoke up.

"Mo!" It was another boy, this time with short black hair. "You have calc next period?"

As if this was her cue, she turned back to me before offering any sort of response.

"Good luck today," she said, then rejoined the group before I could get a word in.

I watched as she walked along with the other students, the way they rambunctiously chatted with her and one another, and noticed that she didn't look entirely interested in anything they were saying. It was a kind of look that most people tried to hide, but that she was wearing proudly.

I straightened my shirt one more time, closed my locker, and then concluded that those two minutes were probably the last I'd spend with Mo. It was just how it went. One conversation with me was usually enough for anyone to decide that I was too boring for their liking. I had no business thinking someone as exciting as Mo was any different.

And then, here she was.

As the buzzer sounded and I made my way to the front end of the bench with Sienna, I tried to block the image of Mo—the images of the rest of my family, too, though I was much more used to them—out of my mind. One more set of eyes on me meant more pressure, and I wasn't exactly prepared to carry it. Besides, maybe she was just there for the company, too.

When the referee handed Sydney the ball, and she inbounded it after the tweet of his whistle, the gym came alive again. Coach Pieter had given us benchwarmers specific instructions: be loud.

This, in basketball terms, means that even if you're sitting on the bench, your teammates that are in the game should be able to hear what you're seeing. If there's someone setting a pick on one of your defenders, tell her. If a Palm Hill Cougar sneaks down to the baseline without anyone seeing, shout about it. If there's nothing to yell about, yell anyways. So that was what we did.

For what felt like hours, the scoring went almost rhythmically back and forth. Our team ran a zone defense, imitating a synchronized dance team every time the ball swung from one side of the court to the other. I kept yelling to Sydney, acting as the eyes in the back of her head whenever the Cougars tried to be sneaky. I was sure she could hear everyone else in the gym yelling the same exact things as I was, but she always had a way of singling out my voice. It was just one of those things.

When the ball bounced off of a Cougar's shin with two minutes left in the overtime period, the score was tied 70-70. So Coach Pieter called a time-out, and my heart sank to my feet.

"Elliana, in for Bella. Sienna, in for Taylor," Coach said, just as I suspected he would. Bella and Taylor both looked tired, and he just couldn't have that. Fresh legs meant a better chance at winning. I just wished I didn't have so much energy, or that it wasn't obvious, at least.

"We're going man-to-man," Coach said, ditching the white board and looking at all of us directly. "Sydney, take number forty. Elliana, I want you tight on twenty-four."

The three point shooter, I thought. *Crazy ball-handling skills and hasn't missed a shot all game. Great.*

It wasn't odd, per se, that Coach only assigned Sydney and me specific players. He knew our skills better than we did, and he'd been watching the game with more attention than anyone. Plus, in terms of stats, Sydney was the best defender on the team. I was up there, I guess. Offense certainly wasn't my specialty.

"Sydney, hands off on defense," Coach said, his parting words. "Two minutes. Give me everything you've got."

The buzzer sounded again, this time with seemingly more gumption than before, and I walked out onto the court beside Sydney, doing my best to block out everything else around me—the cheers, the murmurs, the excitement, the scoreboard. All I needed to focus on were the nine other people on the court. That was it.

Before the referee blew his whistle and restarted the chaos that was overtime, Sydney and I exchanged a look. Mine was full of angst and fake confidence, while Sydney's game face reeked of reassurance and trust. I envied her, but I was also worried. Sydney had four fouls. We were only allowed five per game, so one more would have her sitting on the bench next to Assistant Coach Jenna, and I'd lose my right hand man. I was no use on the court if Sydney wasn't there, too.

Our first offensive run down the court resulted in a three-pointer by Amari, which put us ahead but didn't give anyone in the gym relief. If it did, it didn't find its way to me.

As the ball made its way back down to our side of the court, I positioned myself in front of Number Twenty-Four. She wore a tight headband and her long red hair was thrown up into a ponytail that had nearly fallen out several times throughout the game. Now, it was sitting on top of her head, but I had a feeling it wouldn't be for long.

Thirty seconds of game time left us up by four points, and the gym was the loudest I'd ever heard it. Right as the scoreboard clock indicated that there was one minute left, there was a roar from, well, everywhere, and only after the fact did I realize it was because I'd stolen the ball.

We had possession now—the ball was quite literally on our side of the court—and since we were up, we slowed down the pace.

"Pluto!" Coach Pieter yelled from the sideline. Coach Jenna shouted the same thing, directing Piper and Sienna to switch sides of the court.

When they did, and when Amari handed the ball off to Piper like the play called for, she started dribbling around her defender like a WNBA player. It was mesmerizing, the way she moved. I wanted nothing more than to be able to just watch.

Pluto, our typically seamless, time-consuming play, was soiled when Sydney wasn't open under the basket. She kicked the ball back out to me and, though I was open, I passed it back up top to Piper who took a three-point shot and missed. The Cougars retrieved the rebound and moved up the court quickly, scoring a jump shot of their own before we could even blink. Now, we were only ahead by two.

It was dizzying, watching the game unfold before me while also trying to participate in it. Every time the ball made its way to my hands, I found myself trying to get rid of it as quickly as possible. There was too much on the line, not just for our team but anyone experiencing the game at all, for its fate to be left up to me. Unfortunately, Coach Pieter disagreed.

After another missed shot by Piper that she took after a handoff from me, I heard a sigh come from our bench. "Elliana," Coach said, not quietly but only loud enough for those on the court to hear it. I hoped. "Shoot the damn ball."

Not a chance in hell, I thought, eyeing Sydney as he said this. Instead, I just nodded, positioning myself in front of number twenty-four again as the clock wound down below the thirty-second mark.

"Flex!" yelled the Palm Hill coach, his face as red as Ronan's was green—just one look up into the bleachers and it was obvious—and his clipboard shaking beneath his grasp. "*Flex*! Ashley, get to the wing!"

Ashley, a tall, very stompy, forward, also known as Number Forty, did just that. The ball landed in her hands after a few passes and a missed shot, and since she had Sydney defending her, I took a breath, letting my guard down because I knew I could. But then, in one swift yet bumpy motion, she charged right into Sydney while putting up a shot.

I watched as Syd tried to hold her ground but stumbled backwards, just as anyone would've. It was a hard hit, and I felt the whole gym gasp when I did. She had taken a beating all game, and the referees hadn't been much in our favor, so I was relieved when the nearest one blew his whistle.

This was actually a good thing, with great timing. We were up by two points, with fifteen seconds left, and it was our possession. I felt myself begin to smile, the tightness in my chest loosening the slightest of bits, but then I saw the number the referee held up to the scoring table. The foul wasn't on Stompy. It was on Syd.

Even worse? The shot went in.

"Are you *kidding* me?" Coach Pieter shouted.

My feet took me to Sydney before my mind could even process what had just happened.

"Are you okay?" I asked her.

"Fine," she huffed. She made her way to the bench, heated, while the gym grew louder and louder within just a few seconds of time.

I was in shock, and trying to remind myself that this was just a basketball game, and that it'd soon be over, no matter what happened, when I heard more chirping from the crowd.

"You're blowing it!" said a woman from the stands.

"What, are you blind?"

"Just call the game already if you have a favorite!"

"That wasn't even *close*!" I was pretty sure that one was my father.

The referee seemingly had a skill that I wildly lacked: he blocked out everyone, finding himself on the sideline, holding the ball out to a Cougar, with the same blank expression he'd kept the whole time.

As for me, Sydney was on the bench, I was on the court, and with Stompy's foul shot that swished through the basket graciously, we were down by one point.

Yes, this was the worst case scenario.

It was our turn to take the ball down the court, and Amari was taking her job as point guard very seriously. She wove in and out of Cougar after Cougar and made it to half court with ten seconds left in the game. The other team was holding every breath, crossing every finger. The crowd was *wild*—shouting and chanting and clapping—and the buzz that they created from the floor to the ceiling was fueling us. This was it. I knew it.

The ball swung from Amari to me to Piper to Bella, who subbed in for Sydney and looked as if she was going to hurl. There were three seconds left when she passed it off to Piper, and two when she passed it to me.

I looked for Amari (covered) then Sienna (lost) then Piper (too close), and finally, Bella (too far away). I was left with one choice: the worst one.

"*Shoot!*" said Coach Pieter's voice as it layered on top of everyone else's. I could hear every one. The fans I knew and the ones I didn't, my teammates, Sydney, maybe even the voice in my head.

So I took the shot, and I felt oddly confident as it soared through the air, its spinning coinciding with the buzz of the scoreboard and thus the end of the game, no matter what happened. I watched as it inched closer to the rim, and then circled it.

Right as I expected the ball to go in, and maybe even anticipated feeling something because of it, it fell out. I couldn't hear anything but the sound of its rubber pounding against the gym floor. And just like that, it was over.

It took all of the willpower I had not to crumble onto the floor as the Cougars' bench and fans stormed the court, engaging in a well-deserved celebration on their half of the gym. I felt all of the numbness like bee stings on my skin, my eyes glossing over just as Sydney made her way to me. I could barely even see her, and for once I didn't want to.

"Elliana," she said, her voice hardened and quick. "That was not your fault. You played great. Don't think about it."

"You did what you were supposed to," Coach Pieter assured me. I hadn't even realized I'd made it back to the bench. Coach lowered his face, forcing me to look right into his eyes. He shook his head as the rest of my teammates lined up to shake the hands of the Cougars.

"Elliana, you played an outstanding game. You had an outstanding season" he said. I tried to look away from his eyes, but Sydney nudged me right back. "Don't let them see you upset."

I nodded, my cheeks feeling red and warm and pale and flushed all at once. I wanted to hide, but I found myself in line, shaking clammy hands with the other team. I wasn't crying, at least not on the outside. I hadn't done that in years. But something was happening inside of me, and it wasn't good. I had a feeling nothing would be for a while.

I coasted through the post-game antics, treating every word of encouragement and pity as if it was just white noise that flurried around me. I didn't hear a word Coach said in the locker room, but assumed that it was the usual: he was proud of us, we played well, and he had fun this season. If anything was truly important enough to require action on my part, I knew I'd hear it from Sydney later.

Our walk to the parking lot, however, was silent. Until I mentioned that I was going to take a rain check on Archie's.

"You sure?"

I nodded. "Luke's making dinner. Circus will probably be there if you want to join."

"Henry's already at Archie's," Sydney said, though I could tell she was smiling. "But I'll see you tomorrow, yeah?"

I nodded again, my shoes scuffing on the pavement as I reached the passenger's door to my dad's car. I watched through the window as he turned the radio down.

"Just don't beat yourself up, okay?" Syd said, her parting words.

I drew the door open, forcing a smile as Sydney's basketball began to pound against the pavement. "Good game, Syd."

The car ride home was mostly silent, just as I suspected it would be. My mom and dad never forced Luke, Braeden, or me to talk about anything we didn't want to, solely because they wanted us to be comfortable enough to say how we felt. They didn't want us to run away or avoid the hard things, though. Just take the first steps. And sure, we'd had plenty of heavy talks as a family over the years that might've been quicker or easier if my parents were the first to bite. But it was an unspoken rule. The tough conversations started on our terms.

So it wasn't until the car was in park, our house stretching above us while my dad and I unbuckled our seatbelts, that I began this one.

"Was it a bad shot?"

I watched as he gently let go of his seat buckle and it slid back up on the belt. He knew what I was really asking. "It was a great shot, and nobody else was taking it. You had no other choice."

I nodded then, taking a deep breath as I pushed the door open and stepped out into the warm, ocean-scented air. In contrast to the sweaty gym, it was sweet and fresh.

As I stepped into the foyer beside my dad, I was hit, of course, by many things. First, there was the noise. I could tell Ronan and Finn were there, and assumed Luke and Adrienne weren't far. In the living room, Braeden was sprawled out on the couch, likely avoiding my mom's subtle nudges for him to help with the dinner preparation. Which, delightfully, brings me to the second thing that I was smacked in the face with upon entering the house: the smell.

It was a rare blessing, I knew, that my house often doubled as my favorite restaurant, but I had to guess that it was the same feeling. Every time I walked inside and Luke was home, I smelled one of my favorite dishes. Because of him, I had hundreds of those.

My dad gave me a quick shoulder-squeeze when I set my duffle bag down on the floor next to the hall closet.

"Everyone's really proud of you," he told me.

I nodded, tucking his compliment and the pity I felt because of it away as I ran up the stairs to my bedroom. When I returned downstairs twenty minutes later, I sported the scent of lavender soap and clean laundry, while the kitchen smelled devourable. Thankfully, I was in the mood to eat.

I took a visual attendance upon entering the kitchen, and found that I was only caught off-guard by one thing. That in itself might've been a record.

Like a film that I watched over and over again, there were a few usual things happening in front of my eyes. Luke was finishing up the creation of dinner, handling several dishes all at once because he'd never accept help even if it was offered to him, while my dad did exactly that, standing by just in case. Beside them, Adrienne was tossing a colorful salad, one of her special ones, while my mom poured white wine into stemless glasses and carried on a conversation with her.

At the kitchen table, Ronan dealt a deck of cards between himself and Braeden, sitting beside one another in their usual spots. Finn sat opposite them, watching along because he wanted to and not because he wasn't invited to partake. What was odd, and what caused my breath to catch in my throat while I made my way over to them, was that Finn wasn't just watching the card game and awaiting my arrival. He was also talking to Mo.

The invitation that Ronan offered seemed so fleeting to me in the moment that I'd forgotten about it entirely. Clearly, that was just another difference between Mo and me. Now, I felt a bit like a foreigner at my own dining room table. Not that I really minded.

"There she is," Ronan announced, perfect timing as he dealt the last card in his hand to Braeden. They both picked up their half-sized decks, laying the best of their cards on the table and hiding what was in their hand from one another.

I eased my chair out from under the table and sat on it, consequently melting into its light brown fabric.

"That was quite a game," Finn said, nudging me with his elbow. "You played great."

"Seriously," Ronan said. "We sat by the guys' team and they want to have you at their practices next year to teach defense. You're like a cheetah out there. And that's a direct quote."

"From who?" Adrienne asked, looking over her shoulder and flashing me a smile and a wink.

"Me," Ronan replied.

I didn't feel like I'd done anything to deserve their praise, but I knew I'd get shot down if I expressed it. Plus, for some reason, I could feel the weight of Mo's presence beside me, and I didn't want to sound more pathetic than recent events were making me out to be. So instead, I just smiled.

"The only reason you lost is because of that stupid ref," Braeden muttered. "He sucked."

"Braeden, be kind," my mother said, suddenly appearing behind me. She gave me a shoulder-squeeze akin to my dad's, then set a glass of wine down at her spot at the table.

Like me, my mother craved perfection. She was always happier when I did my homework straight after school, or when I was ready for basketball practice with enough time to spare that we could get stuck in traffic and still be punctual. Perfect was the way our family worked, the way our house was arranged, the way the light poured in through the windows in the morning. She deserved for things to be that way. So I knew, deep down, that she was probably disappointed in the missed shot, too.

"Need any help, Stella?" Finn asked. Every friend of ours was on an obligatory first-name-basis the second they set foot in our house. No exceptions.

My mother shook her head and flashed Finn a smile of contentment. "It's almost ready."

"Stella?" said my dad from the kitchen, at the same time Luke said, "Hey, Mom?"

He nodded in the direction of the lemon chicken dish in front of him. He wanted her to taste-test, which she knew, so she was off again.

Beside me, Finn's eyes were back on the card game in which Braeden had just laid down the ace of hearts.

"Ronan, you just cheated."

Ronan lowered his eyebrows, his head jerking backwards as he studied his cards. "I did?"

Finn nodded. "You passed when you were supposed to pick up."

"I was?"

Braeden's palm went right to his face. This kind of thing happened often with Ronan. He never meant to cheat, but he didn't really pay enough attention not to.

Next to me, Mo let out a quiet laugh. I was too close to look right at her, so I didnt. Instead, I stared through the windows behind Ronan and Braeden, straining my eyes to find the horizon. The sunset was long gone, and all of its colors with it. There was no use.

"So that was my first basketball game," said Mo, knocking me out of my self-inflicted trance.

"Really," I said, finally turning to look at her. It seemed she was captivating in any lighting, or at least in every one I'd met her so far.

She nodded. "It was great. Didn't know what I was missing."

A laugh escaped my nose. Beside me, Finn was still explaining the rules of the card game.

"Great until the last ten seconds," I said in a low voice.

"What was wrong with the last ten seconds?"

Now, I looked into her eyes, and found them to be surprisingly genuine. She wasn't joking.

"I blew the game. Missed the last shot. Did you watch that part?"

"Well, did you have another choice?"

I shrugged my shoulders. "No, but–"

"That's not true, actually," she said. Now, her expression was playful but serious all at once. I wasn't sure how she did it. "You could've not taken the shot. And then you would've definitely lost, and you wouldn't have even tried."

I considered this, trying to think of a quick defense. This wasn't as easy with words as it was with basketball. "I guess–"

"So, instead, you took a risk with the game on the line and everyone in the gym watching you. And you're mad at yourself for that?" Mo asked. She was looking into my eyes now, searching for something. I had a feeling she wasn't going to find it. "I'd be proud. I mean, if I were you."

Okay, so she'd just completely stumped me, and she didn't even know me. I was terrified, to say the least, that she'd found her way into my brain with such ease. I wasn't exactly sure if that said more about her or me. Then again, I didn't have any time to think about it.

"El-li-a-na," sang Adrienne, skipping my way and wrapping her arms around my shoulders, save for her hands which she kept in the air. "Sorry. Salad hands."

"I see that," I laughed.

"Wait 'til you try Adrienne's salad," Ronan said to Mo, apparently understanding the card game enough to look away from it. "It's ten times better than the meal."

"I can hear you," Luke said, joining us at the table with a steaming bowl of roasted potatoes. To put it frankly, they smelled like heaven.

"I know," Ronan replied in the same tone.

Finn leaned forward, looking over Adrienne and me and offering Mo a smile. "You sick of this yet?"

Immediately, Mo shook her head. "No," she said. Then she leaned forward, directing her attention, and thus all of ours, at Ronan. "But I think you cheated again."

Ronan looked down at his hands, revealing to himself and anyone who knew the game they were playing that he had, in fact, cheated. While his head tipped back in defeat, everyone else's did in laughter. Braeden set his cards down on the table, declaring that he'd already won anyways, and began gathering the rest to put back in the box.

As always, the punchline was perfectly timed. Dinner was ready, and thus the end to a horrible day could finally begin.

If the ocean were watching, it would've seen a night like any other. Rosy cheeks, conversations erupting with laughter, the clinking of silverware on plates of all different shades of blue. But as I sat, feeling my chair beneath me and the people all around me, I felt light, like a weight I hadn't accounted for was being lifted off of my shoulders. I traded a look with my mother when I realized this, curious if she, like Mo, could see right through me.

But instead of being interested in my look, she just smiled, nodding toward the chicken on my plate. I gave her a thumbs-up, indicating that it was good while Luke and Ronan fell deeper into a debate about the versatility of sporks.

I shelved my opinion on the topic because I didn't really have one, but listened as Finn inputted his usual middle-ground stance. Right on time.

"Maybe it depends on what you need the utensil for. Sometimes a spork can be more useful, sometimes a spoon. And so on."

"Nonsense," Ronan said.

Chapter Eight

Nell

"...usually walk most places, and Sutton works from home with pretty flexible hours so we don't have trouble getting Freya to and from school, either. It's a great location."

"It's beautiful," I said, taking in my surroundings as we approached the door to Finn's apartment. His building was cleaner than I expected it to be, probably because I'd spent the majority of the past two years in a packed dorm building.

When he drew open the door to Apartment 18F, I was immediately, though adorably, pushed aside. Freya decided to burst between Finn and me, gliding into the apartment and kicking her shoes off before continuing any further.

The apartment, like the house I grew up in, was bright, which was only the first thing I noticed about it. Light poured in from all angles, splashing itself amongst the walls and the furniture in artful patterns. The room I stood in led into the kitchen which led into the living room. There, I saw a sectional couch that looked like it'd swallow me whole (in a good way) if I were to sit on it, and complementary warm-toned blankets and decorations on the coffee table and the walls.

My eyes quickly found their way to a round kitchen table that sported a vase of yellow tulips and an open laptop. There, I found Sutton. She immediately struck me as poised and beautiful, and not just on the outside. She had curly brown hair, big round glasses that sat perfectly on the bridge on her nose, a cardigan wrapped around her shoulders, and papers scattered all around her. Now, there was also Freya on her lap.

"Mommy, this is Mel," she said, smiling in my direction and cozying herself on Sutton's dark green sweatpants.

Though Sutton offered me a smile, she was visibly confused. Finn, noticing this, set his keys down on the kitchen counter and then positioned himself next to me again. "Elliana, this is Sutton. Sutton, Elliana," he told her. "From home."

The word *home* caused a tickle to start in my throat. Ever since Jay's, I wasn't sure how Finn felt about my spontaneous and uncalled-for visit, seeing as he gave up hope on all of us a long time ago. But it was nice, and somehow a little heartbreaking, to hear that he still thought of me as someone from home. At least that hadn't changed.

"Elliana…" Sutton said, her buttery voice still sounding curious as she reached her free hand out to shake mine.

"Rose," I said.

"Oh, my God," she said then, her eyebrows raising as her eyes widened. When she stood, she was a few inches taller than me, though still shorter than Finn. Her beauty reminded me of someone I used to know. "Wow, I– I didn't ever think I'd get the chance to meet you."

She looked at Finn then, who still sported a smile, but now held something else in his eyes, too. Lucky for me, I could still tell what it was: *We'll talk later.*

"Likewise," I said.

Sutton adjusted her cardigan. "What brings you here?"

Now, Freya looked up at me with her big blue eyes, awaiting the answer she'd already heard. It was funny: if I didn't know the whole story, I wouldn't have been able to tell that Freya wasn't actually Finn's daughter; she looked just like a combination of the two of them. His freckles and smile, her curly hair and light brown skin. Bright blue eyes, just like the both of them.

"I, uh–" Now, I looked at Finn, completely in the dark about how much I was allowed to share. After four years of knowing nothing, it was strange to see Finn's blank expression, no fear behind his eyes. I should've guessed he'd never keep anything from her. "My brother is getting married in a couple of weeks. I came to extend an invitation."

I watched, and bit my lip, as Sutton processed the information, her eyes going blank, too, with the thought. When she took a deep breath, I was expecting the worst. Of course, she didn't give me that.

"That's a very personal invitation," she said, breaking my eye contact only to see what Finn was thinking—to check in. "Paper ones are overrated, in my opinion."

I let out a laugh, one mostly of relief. If this was Sutton's immediate reaction, I wondered if she might be inclined to help with my convincing of Finn.

"Your brother is Luke, right?" she asked, crossing her arms over stomach.

I nodded, both enthusiastically and reluctantly. "He's marrying Adrienne."

"Right," Sutton said, trading a look with Finn again. "Well, that's very exciting news. And has Finn accepted the invitation?"

Now, we all turned to Finn. Even Freya, who had fully taken over Sutton's chair.

"He's thinking about it," I told her, hoping for the best that it was the truth.

At this, Sutton let out a laugh, and I had a feeling it was because she knew the extent of it. It warmed my soul to see that someone else knew Finn just as well as I did. As well as I used to.

"I think we can get him to budge," she said, leaning a little closer to me. After shooting Finn an eyebrow-raise which he returned, Sutton's attention was back on me. "Are you staying for dinner?"

"She's staying until Monday," Finn said, finally inputting himself into the conversation now that the hard part was over. I couldn't say I blamed him.

"Great," Sutton proclaimed, hands now on her hips. "We have time to get to know one another then."

I couldn't help but smile. "I look forward to it."

"Me too," Finn said, stealing Sutton's words from her mouth while he slowly and finally made his way to her side. When he did, he reached his arms out for Freya. "Now let's let Mommy get back to work." He turned to me. "Deadline tomorrow," he said quietly. "Rockstar things."

"But *I* want to work!" said, well, no one ever. But this time, it was Freya.

"How about some *Little Mermaid*? We haven't hung out with Ariel in a while," Finn suggested.

At this, Freya surrendered, standing upon Sutton's chair, arms outstretched. Once Finn was holding her, he headed toward the sectional couch. Freya turned her attention to me then, so I followed behind.

"I love Ariel," she told me. "I love Molly, too, from *Bubble Guppies*? I was her for Halloween."

"That's awesome," I said. "I bet you looked great."

She nodded. "I had pink hair."

I stood correct.

When I was Freya's age, I was a turtle for Halloween. The year after that, a dolphin. My entire array of childhood Halloween costumes solely consisted of aquatic animals. Though Molly, the half-fish, half-human, maybe-mermaid looking character, as Freya explained, wasn't exactly a real aquatic creature, it seemed Freya and I had quite a bit in common.

After a few minutes, Finn was able to get Freya settled in front of the movie. She was wrapped in a cream-colored blanket with brown sea turtles stitched delicately onto it, which she told me was given to her by her grandmother. I assumed it was Sutton's mother that she was talking about, but then the question of Finn's parents' involvement crept into my mind right beside the hundreds I already had. So, I was more than happy to hear what he said to Freya next.

"Nell and I are going to go out on the balcony to catch up. If you need something, come get me, okay? Mommy can hang out once dinner's done."

Freya waved us off, completely engrossed in the first song of the movie and the colorful images that accompanied it.

On our way to the balcony, which I was excited as ever to see, I caught Finn catching Sutton's eye, and watched as she mouthed, "Thank you." Next thing I knew, we were outside.

The city air was much different from that of the ocean. With just one gust of wind brushing up against my face, I could feel the distinction. The breeze was warm, but instead of sunny it felt busy, and instead of quiet it felt loud. When Finn closed the sliding glass door behind us, and we took seats opposite one another at a yellow table with yellow chairs, I took a deep breath. I wasn't very accustomed to city air, but I had a feeling I'd be needing it.

"It's nice out here when it's not windy," Finn said, reading my mind. And it was nice. But for some reason, sitting across from Finn, I wanted to cry again. I'd missed him so much that even the moments together were hard to swallow.

At some point during my seconds-long zone-out on the city, I realized that Finn was looking at me. He wasn't awaiting my start to the conversation we knew we had to have, but just studying me. Like I was a new version of the person he used to know all those years ago. Exactly like that.

"You're different, too," I said, acknowledging what I knew he was thinking.

He was smart not to deny it. "How so?"

I shrugged. "Well, you're older."

This got a laugh out of Finn, which, in turn, drew one out of me.

"I'm serious," I said. "You're raising a child, with an incredible girlfriend. You live in this gigantic city. You have facial hair."

Finn frowned. "I had facial hair in high school."

I nearly snorted.

"Thanks," he said, instead referring to what came before the facial hair. "It wasn't all easy."

"But it's beautiful," I pointed out. "Your life, I mean."

Finn nodded, taking his turn to look out at the city. I gave him a moment. Part of me was hoping he needed it.

When he looked back to me, his face just as familiar as it had ever been, I could see the bottoms of his eyelids watering. I wasn't ready for a sob-session, though I could've easily partaken in one. So I got to talking.

"Have you heard from your parents?" I asked, starting with the first question that came to mind.

When we were in high school, I had a feeling that Finn would separate himself from his parents as soon as he was given the chance, but I wasn't sure exactly what that would look like. I expected more of a subtle tie-cut: maybe a Christmas or two at home and then nothing. But I didn't expect him to be this far away all the time, both in distance and in heart.

"My mom called once last year."

"Did you answer?"

He nodded. "She wanted to tell me she left my dad."

For what I imagined wouldn't be the last time, I didn't know what to say.

"Your dad," I said. "Is he—"

"I don't know," Finn said in a curt manner. That was that. "She asked how I was doing. I thought after twenty-something years, it might actually feel good to hear her say that."

"It didn't?"

"At first, maybe," he told me. "But then I told her all about Sutton and Freya. I don't know why."

"Was she happy for you?" I asked, hoping with every vein of my being that the answer was yes. It was the least she could've done. Honestly.

But, of course, he shook his head. "She said I was being careless. That I was throwing my life away for some girl and wasting my money."

I couldn't help but let out a laugh, though this wasn't funny and we both knew it. I just couldn't believe what kind of audacity a person like that could have to say something so ridiculous. To Finn, especially.

"So I told her that Freya's happier than I ever was at home," he said, his demeanor softening at the end of his sentence, like he'd gotten it all out. He took a deep breath, glancing into the apartment through the glass door that stood beside us. "Sutton's a great mom."

Now, I watched the way Finn sat, the way he stared in through the window, the past repeating itself over and over again in my eyes and maybe even his. "They're so lucky to have you, Finn," I said, my voice almost breaking at the end. "I'm happy for you. You finally have a family."

Finn looked quickly back at me, like what I'd just said was the most urgent I'd ever spoken.

"I've always had a family."

I nodded, my heart forcing me to look down at my hands rather than up at him. It was like I couldn't bear it anymore, the fact that we'd once been so close and were now so far apart, which felt strange, because maybe now I still had a chance to fix it.

"Finn—"

"Yeah," he said. He knew what I was going to ask.

"Why didn't you ever come back?"

This was what seemed to get him, even though he was expecting it and neither of us had much left to begin with. Now he looked down at his hands, his long eyelashes batting a couple of times while he sat there.

"They didn't tell you," he said, not as a question but a realization.

I shook my head. "Who? Ronan and Luke?"

This time, Finn didn't nod, and he didn't look up at me. But, after all this time, only then did I realize that whatever had happened was *bad*. Probably worse than I'd imagined. And now I wasn't sure I even wanted to know.

The weeks that ended my sophomore year might've been among the most confusing days of my life. For several reasons, actually. My mind had been elsewhere, dealing with things it didn't know how to tackle, and probably dealing with them the wrong way. But then, slowly, I started to notice that something had happened between the boys, too.

They were as close as they'd probably ever been, their lacrosse season winding down and graduation just around the corner. And then, it was like a bomb hit. A quiet, sneaky little bomb.

86

Finn stopped coming over, which was alarming enough in itself, but particularly odd because there were only a few days before he left for Pennsylvania. Luke and Ronan were acting like nothing was out of the ordinary, dodging every question asked and all topics of conversation that included Finn. Neither of them went to his graduation party—a celebration that his grandparents threw because his mom and dad couldn't be bothered—and then Finn left. Then Ronan left. Then Luke and Adrienne left. And that was it.

At the time, I didn't think it was going to be as big of a deal as it was. I thought maybe it was just a little fight, or something, and that it was better if I didn't get involved. But then, well, here we were.

"Finn," I said now, my voice filling with anger for something I didn't even know about. "What happened?"

"Nothing."

I just looked at him, my eyes narrow. He knew I didn't believe him.

He sighed. "I sold 'em out."

"What?"

"I sold them out. Luke and Ronan."

I shook my head. I didn't understand. "Sold them out to who?"

Now, he finally looked up at me. Before he could say anything, though, I could tell it was going to be a lie.

"Do you remember senior night? For lacrosse?"

I felt a catch in my throat. I'd trained my mind and my heart not to think about that night, and I was sure I'd finally exiled it far enough away that it couldn't hurt me anymore. But now he'd only said seven words and I wanted to combust. Instead, I just nodded.

"Remember how I was the only senior to start the game?"

The lacrosse-related details of that night were in a deep part of my memory that I wasn't sure I'd ever opened. But now, when I actually thought about it, I did remember.

"Sure," I answered.

"Luke and Ronan didn't start because I sold them out to Coach Allenson. On accident."

I shook my head. "I'm— I'm lost here. Sold them out for what? Being idiots?"

"For drinking before the game."

"Like, alcohol?"

Now, Finn laughed. Or, sort of. He still had that look on his face, the one of guilt and regret that I just didn't like.

I, on the other hand, was shocked again. I wasn't disappointed that they'd been drinking. They were seniors in high school, and I would've been dumb to think that they'd never done it. But I just didn't think that was them, and I thought I knew them all so well back then. I thought I knew them better than I knew myself.

On top of all of that, I was surprised that Luke was able to hide such a thing from my mother, and that Coach Allenson only made them sit for five minutes. Drinking on school property, or at all, for that matter, was a serious offense at St. Jane's. Sister Bridgette would've had their heads if she'd found out.

"Okay," I said. Something still wasn't adding up. "So they sat for the first five minutes of the game?"

Finn nodded.

"Uh-huh. And you haven't talked in four years because of five minutes?"

Now, it was Finn's turn to lose his words. When we made eye contact, I had a feeling he knew how I felt, but I said it anyway.

"I don't believe you."

"Well, that's what happened."

"Finn, you're not missing Luke and Adrienne's wedding because of a stupid game four years ago. That's absurd."

"Elliana—"

"It's Nell," I said, sounding much harsher than I intended to. But, to be fair, I was angry. It wasn't just the three of them that lost time together. I'd been affected too. No one ever thought to tell me that it was over something so miniscule.

"I'm sorry," Finn said, settling himself and the conversation. Now we just looked at eachother, knowing full well that neither of us wanted to fight. That wasn't who we were, or who we'd ever been. "I'll think about it, okay?"

Though I'd announced this to Sutton inside, it was the first time Finn had budged, so I took it as a win. I'd learned the hard way that even the smallest of moments can change everything, and maybe this was one of them.

I sat back in my chair, taking what I could get and keeping in the back of my mind the fact that there was certainly more to the story. Finn, apparently sensing that my walls were down, leaned onto the table with his elbows.

"So," he started, his tone having done a one-eighty. Oh God. "Have you talked to Mo?"

In the ever-replaying film reel of my life, this was the question that ended every scene and started every new one. It was always there, lurking, reminding me of my answer to it. I'd gotten so good at hiding from it that I'd forgotten how much it hurt to hear the words spoken aloud.

"No."

Now, Finn was the one in the dark, and I was who couldn't be understood. Back to high school we went.

"What ever happened between you two?" he started. "I mean, I guess I sort of know what happened. But before she left—"

"Nothing," I told him.

Before I could be angry at myself for fibbing, Finn let out a laugh. No, a giggle. Like he and Ronan had just pulled a prank on fifteen-year-old Luke.

"You're funny, you know that?" he said then.

Of course there wasn't a doubt in his mind that I was lying. What was I? See-through?

"You know if I really want the story, I'll get it out of you."

I crossed my arms over my chest. "I don't think you know how to do that anymore."

At this, Finn's expression said one thing: *Challenge accepted.*

Before he could give the challenge a go, however, the sliding glass door opened. And what a sweet, sweet sound that was.

When I looked over my shoulder, I found a smiling and blanket-free Freya staring right back up at me, her eyes brighter in the natural daylight than they were inside. *The Little Mermaid* certainly wasn't over, but maybe she'd seen enough.

"Wanna see my seashells?" Freya asked, her eyes on me.

God, I wanted to take her home with me.

"I would love to see your seashells," I said. I pushed up from the table and stood from my chair, Freya and I both turning to Finn.

Freya's smile grew bigger when their eyes met. "Coming?"

"Right behind you."

Chapter Nine

Elliana

"Elliana, can you give me a hand?"

With the sound of my mom's voice, I stood from my spot on the couch, where I was reading a romance novel set during a school musical. Henry had suggested the book to me, and so far it was pretty good, though sometimes I found high school love stories hard to believe. It was just something about the way the characters were so sure of what they wanted, and then knew exactly how to get it. Things like that always felt foreign to me.

On the far side of the living room, the one opposite the ocean, my mom was holding a painting against the wall, her hands on each of its lower corners. It was a large canvas with an abstract-like painting of waves rolling into a sandy shore. We'd had it for as long as I could remember, but until now it had been leaning up against the wall in the room Finn often slept in.

"Can you just make sure this is straight?"

I obliged, retrieving the level from one of our coffee tables and holding it up against the edge of the painting, our limbs playing Twister with one another.

"It's straight," I told her.

She released the painting with a sigh of relief, then stepped back to take it in. Once she was beside me, I looked between her eyes and the art work, settling on its intentional brush strokes and bold colors.

"I should've hung it up years ago," she told me, keeping focus on the painting.

"Why didn't you?"

She shrugged. "Wasn't up to it."

It was moments like these, when the words were thrown right out into the open air, that I remembered the kind of life my mother lived, and the things she carried. Sometimes, when she was burning so bright, making everything so perfect, it was easy to forget that she had more bad days than good ones, or that she had to overcome pain and dread just to hang up a painting. When I remembered, I always felt bad, like maybe I didn't know enough about it. But then, I knew I couldn't ask.

"It really ties the room together," I told her, studying the painting.

"You think?"

I nodded, earning a smile and a gentle hand on my shoulder.

"Me too," she said.

Within another moment, it was just me in the living room, as she'd noticed the sun peeking through the kitchen windows and gone off to the garden. My solitude restored, I made my way back to the couch, leaving the paperback unopened on my lap as my attention went immediately and unapologetically to the horizon.

Sometimes, in the moments of quiet, it was as if I had a secret line of communication with the sunset. It felt like, if it were just the two of us, I could understand what its colors and patterns meant. Sitting next to Sydney, I was always looking for the version of myself who was one with the ocean, who called adversity her good friend. When I was by myself, it was almost like she was looking for me.

I was thinking this, watching the clouds dance slowly across the sky, when my eyes flickered toward the back porch and caught onto something else. More specifically: Thing One, Thing Two, and Mo.

Ronan opened the door, allowing Finn and Mo to pile into the house in front of him. They were dressed in beachwear, as the season proudly called for, and obviously carrying on a conversation that had started before their trek inside.

"You don't think it would be Braeden?" Finn was asking.

Ronan, shaking his head, said, "No way. If Luke made him give a speech in front of the whole family, he'd kill him."

"Right," Finn said. "Then I don't know."

"Maybe Elliana does," Mo said then, the first to notice me on the couch, though certainly not the last. She smiled in my direction. "Hey."

"Hey," I replied, keeping my cool. "Maybe I know what?"

Finn kept quiet, leaving the talking to Ronan.

"We're talking about Adrienne and Luke's wedding."

I raised my eyebrows. "They're getting married?"

"Well, eventually," Ronan said. "Finn thinks Luke will wait to propose until their junior year of college, get married the summer after senior year. I think it'll be sooner than that."

"And Mo agrees with Finn," Mo said, making me laugh.

"The point is," Ronan said, he and Mo trading a competitive yet friendly look. "We were talking about who Luke's Best Man would be."

Truthfully, this was a toss-up. The kind of relationship that the three of them had together was what most teenagers and even adults longed for. They were so comfortable with one another, it was almost like they'd all shared a womb, and there were rumors at school that they actually did. The three of them had spent their whole lives together, but individually, their friendships with Luke were special all on their own.

Since the day Ronan and Luke met, which was in kindergarten, they loved each other. Yeah, when you're little you have a certain kind of love for your friends, and it's wholesome and adorable all at once. But with Ronan and Luke, it was different. It was like they knew they'd get each other for the rest of their lives, and they were prepared to stick together no matter what that would look like.

As they grew up, and Ronan just got goofier and goofier, Luke was always there to straighten him out. Conversely, there wasn't a moment that Ronan wasn't spending trying to make Luke laugh. I was pretty sure that this was what saved Luke at one point in our lives.

Then, of course, there was Finn. Besides the fact that he was one of the kindest humans to ever exist, and therefore impossible to resist some sort of connection with, Finn and Luke's friendship came really easily, too. One of Luke's greatest accomplishments in the first grade was inviting Finn over to our house and getting him to talk. He was so quiet at school, so observant, but even back then Luke knew what kind of person he was going to be, the kind of force he'd be in his life.

Over the years, Finn had always been a cushion, someone Luke could fall back on and someone who could, and often did, comfort him with just a look. The second he found out that Finn preferred spending time at our house over his own, he knew he'd never let him go.

Then there were Finn and Ronan together, who, like Sydney and me, the rest of the school couldn't quite figure out. Finn was so cool and collected, Ronan exactly the opposite. It only took seeing them in an environment like this one—home—to know that they were made to be friends. They took opposites attracting to a different level, because deep down they both had the same kind of soul: a good one.

These three different friendships strung together, and this was what you got. Three boys who could insult each other with the bat of an eyelash, with no offense ever taken, but who would go to the ends of the earth defending one another. As proof of this, there was a scar on Ronan's finger—I again took notice of it as he debated the Best Man Phenomenon—from a lacrosse game two years before where a player from the other team gave Finn, who'd been having the game of his life, a concussion. The next play down the field, which Finn wasn't even watching, Ronan checked the same player so hard that he broke his own finger. Luke acted as padding for the player, since he saw it coming and didn't want Ronan to get in trouble. And this was how it went.

So, no. I didn't know the answer. I doubted Luke ever would, either.

"Maybe both of you," I suggested.

"You think?" Ronan asked. "Can you even do that?"

"You can do anything you want," Mo said, "if it's your wedding. Who cares?"

"I like the way you think," Finn pointed out, heading to the fridge.

This was the general consensus, actually. We all liked the way Mo thought. Which was why, in the two months that had passed since the dreadful championship game, she'd been a pretty consistent member of our household population. I was learning that she wasn't only cool, but very honest, quite blunt, and astoundingly opinionated. It wasn't something she offered unless asked, however, which somehow made her that much more intriguing.

Once water bottles and snacks were acquired by the beach gang, a conversation comparing the sideburns of Ronan's Uncle Art to those of Mo's history teacher, with photo evidence of both, ensued. Just as I thought I was clear to return to my book, however, I was pulled back in.

"Hey Elliana, where's Syd?" Ronan asked, cracking open a water bottle.

"With Henry," I said, which had pretty much been my solid answer to that same question over the past two months.

Since basketball and swim ended, Henry and Sydney had more freedom to spend time together. I was almost always invited, unless it was a pre-planned Date Night which, in my opinion, didn't happen often enough. Between hanging out with me and Bax at Archie's weekly and their alone time, it seemed like they were getting pretty serious, and I certainly didn't want to get in the way of that. So I was spending more time with Luke and his friends than I normally would during the springtime. I hated to admit it, but I might've even preferred it this way. Maybe it was the Bax of it all.

"You should join us on the beach," Mo suggested, nodding toward me.

"Oh, I don't know," I started mechanically. "I have homework."

"It's Friday," Mo countered, her head tilted slightly.

At this, Ronan grinned, taking the spot next to me at the table. He looked between me and Mo. "Ah, this is one thing you must not know about Elliana. All work and no play."

"Hey," I started, but that was it.

"Come on," Finn countered, his hand on the back of my chair. "You only get us for two more months. You can't just wait until dinner every night to hang out with us."

I glanced out at the beach, where Luke and Adrienne were sitting, surrounded by empty towels and inflated footballs, waiting for the rest of the bunch to join. It was only 70 degrees outside, but it was the warmest it had been since the fall, so it felt like the heat of the summer was upon us. My hair was straight and I was comfortable inside, but it sure was enticing. Plus, the company wasn't half bad, and I did want to slow down time.

"Fine," I surrendered, meeting only Finn's and Ronan's eyes. "But I have to change, so I'll meet you guys out there." I was hoping this would give me extra time, either to delay my arrival or decide against it entirely, but that was the opposite of what happened.

"I'll wait for you," Mo said.

And she did. When I returned five minutes later, a pair of shorts and a t-shirt thrown over my bathing suit, she was standing in the kitchen, looking out at the ocean through my favorite window in the world.

"Ready?" Mo asked, to which I nodded.

We made our way outside, the sun warming my skin like an old friend, and headed straight for the shoreline. We were just about off the back porch when I thought the Awkward Silence was going to find its way to us. I probably should've known better, just based on who I was next to.

"I'm surprised you're able to stay in your uniform for that long," Mo pointed out without looking at me. "Mine comes off the second I get home or I go all Tasmanian Devil."

I shrugged. The truth was, I liked wearing my uniform. It was the one constant between me and my peers. The one thing that didn't set me apart.

"Sometimes I forget I even have it on," I admitted, likely digging myself a deeper, lamer, hole. "So how are you liking St. Jane's? I mean, besides the uniforms."

Now, she looked right at me, as if trying to decipher what kind of answer I was looking for. Mo was the kind of person, I'd learned, that liked to skip the small talk and jump right into the stuff you really had to think about. I couldn't blame her if she had a hard time talking to me.

"It's alright," she said, her focus back on the beach. "It's much different than the school I went to back home."

"Where is home again?" I asked.

"New York."

"The city? Or the part of the state that people get mad at you for referring to as the city?"

At this, Mo actually laughed, and I couldn't believe it. Just the summer before, I'd met Sydney's cousin Laurel, who strongly disliked when anyone assumed she was from the city. She was from a village way upstate in New York, quite the opposite from the city, and was proud of it. Now, I was too, but not for the same reason.

"The city," she told me. "But you're absolutely right about the other part."

I smiled, my eyes focused on the way my feet sunk into the sand with every step. Now the conversation didn't seem so scary, but I wasn't sure what had changed.

"So what's so different about St. Jane's?"

"It's smaller," she started. "And quieter. But the people here are cool."

In front of us, Ronan fumbled a football pass that Finn had thrown to him, spilling soda all over his feet in the process.

"Are you sure about that?" I asked.

Mo's laugh surprised me again. She shook her head. "That kid is going to be the death of himself."

I watched as Mo studied Ronan, an overwhelming sense of amusement in her eyes. The sound of Adrienne's laugh trickled into my ears, and at the same time, I thought I might've seen something else in Mo's smile. Something I'd seen in Adrienne's many times before.

"You know," I said. "Ronan's a really great guy. And he's single."

I felt Mo's eyes on me again, so this time I turned, only to find a bigger smile on her face. And, under the freckles, a bit of confusion. Uh oh.

"What?" I asked.

She kept her smile, but now hid her teeth, as she shook her head. "Nothing. But I think I'll pass."

Thankfully (I think), we'd made it to the rest of the group. From her striped towel, Adrienne tipped her head back to look at me.

"I didn't think you were joining us!"

"I was guilted," I said, looking at Finn, whose expression held nothing but pride. For this, Adrienne offered him a fist bump, which he triumphantly accepted.

"Good," Luke said, receiving a wild pass from Ronan and catching the football over his shoulder. "You two can put an end to Ronan's debate."

Great, I thought. Now we were deliberating about Best Men in front of Luke? I knew this friend group was basically an open book, but this seemed like it was maybe crossing a line. Which one, I had no idea.

"What debate?" Mo asked.

Luke raised his eyebrows in the direction of Ronan, who now had a pair of red sunglasses—Tony Stark-inspired—over his eyes.

"Alright," Ronan started. "So, you know what individual pieces of spaghetti are called?"

I looked at Mo, for some reason, and found that she was just as relieved that the debate had switched from wedding to pasta in the time it took us to get outside. She widened her eyes at me, as if giving me the honor of answering this ridiculous question.

I nodded slowly. "Yes."

"Okay," Ronan said. "What is it?"

"A spaghetti?"

"Yes, but what's the more general term for it?"

Everyone was looking at me now, but it was Ronan's eyes that I could feel burning into mine, even behind the shades. "A noodle," I told him.

Luke threw the football back to Ronan, his expression mostly blank.

Ronan nodded. "Okay. So, if you order a dish at a restaurant that consists mostly of those individual things, what would you call it? And you can't say spaghetti."

I looked at Luke, in slight disbelief that this was actually a debate. "Really?"

He shrugged, withholding his laughter.

"I don't know," I said.

Next to me, I heard Finn laugh, and caught a glimpse of Adrienne's grin.

Ronan, however, was as serious as a heart attack. "Yes. You do," he said. "What would you call it?"

I took a deep breath and didn't allow myself to actually think about the question. It was that ridiculous. "Pasta, I guess."

Luke, free of the football, pumped his fist in the air. "Yes!"

Ronan's shoulders sank and a sigh came from his chest. "You wouldn't call it noodles?"

I shrugged again, suddenly feeling as though I'd been questioned under oath and lied. Just as I'd run out of defenses, though, Mo came to mine.

"I think it would depend on the dish," she said, likely stealing the answer that Finn was whipping up, or repeating what he'd already said before we arrived.

Now, all eyes were on Mo.

"How so?" Luke asked.

She curled her lip, leaning back on her elbows as they rested on her green towel that sat next to Adrienne's.

"I think if it were, like, lo mein or some sort of egg noodles, I'd call it noodles. But if it were spaghetti or alfredo, I'd call it pasta."

Ronan and Luke both visibly considered this.

Adrienne, shades resting on top of her head, nodded. "So maybe it depends on the sauce. Or the lack thereof," she offered.

Finn nodded. "Right. Because you don't call it chicken pasta soup. It's chicken noodle soup. No sauce."

Mo turned to Finn, intrigued by his input, and also slightly amused. "Sure."

"Okay." Ronan looked at Mo, his gears turning so rapidly there might've been smoke coming from his ears if I looked close enough. "But wouldn't you call an individual piece of linguini a noodle?"

"Yes," Mo answered immediately.

"So what would you call a dish of linguini then? Even without sauce?"

"Pasta."

Ronan's head tipped back. "That doesn't make any sense!"

Adrienne, joining in Luke and Finn's collective laughter, sat up, her genuine and soft eyes finding Ronan's. "Maybe there's no rhyme or reason to what you call a dish with noodles," she said. "It's just baseless."

"There has to be," Ronan whined.

"Is this really what you spend your time on?" Mo asked, finally.

It seemed that the four of us already knew the answer to this groundbreaking question, but were all interested in hearing Ronan's answer regardless.

"It's a cultural debate," he told her, his goofy grin beginning to show behind his disappointment.

To this, Mo shook her head. Then, she stood from her towel, flattening it back out once she stepped off of it. "I'm going in the water."

"Me too!" Adrienne exclaimed, placing her sunglasses on the cooler beside her and offering her hand to Finn. It seemed all five of them were on the same page, with Ronan and Luke already wrestling near the water as the waves splashed against their shins.

Somehow, though she was the one who proposed the move, Mo was the last to make it to the water. To my surprise, she turned around just as she crossed the blurry line from dry to wet sand.

"You coming?" she asked.

I was proud of myself for making it this far. Since I wasn't planning on going against all of my gut feelings in just one day, I tucked my straight hair behind my ears.

"Maybe in a minute," I said.

Mo nodded, smiled ever-so-politely, then made her way to everyone else.

It was then that the strangest thing happened. I had the urge, like a pang in my chest, to join them. It had never happened before. I'd always been perfectly content sitting by and watching, cheering on from the sidelines. But now, as my toes dug into the sand, there was this responsibility growing inside me to start feeling something like Sydney so desperately hoped I would. Like maybe, after all this time, it was actually in my control.

Then, I watched as a gigantic wave towered over Adrienne, encapsulating her from head to toe while Luke stood beside and kept her from falling. Suddenly, the dry beach felt comfortable all over again. Just like it always had.

Chapter Ten

Nell

Sunday morning, I had only one regret: running.

I'd woken up early—not earlier than Freya, who apparently cherished her alone time before 7am—and taken a run without any knowledge of the day's plans. Now, after dinner, which was preceded by hours of walking around Pittsburgh so I could get the full experience, I was exhausted. Scratch that, I might've been dead.

"Have you ever had mac and cheese before?" Freya asked as my head was about to hit the wall. Literally.

I sat up straighter in my chair, deciding that not only was it a bit wimpy of me to be so sleepy at the table, but also impolite.

"I have," I said. "I've actually had your dad's mac and cheese before."

Freya's eyebrows lowered astronomically. She was kneeling on the chair directly across from me and leaning on the table because she wanted to be closer. She'd taken such a liking to me that Sutton had to pry her off of my lap to be buckled into her car seat earlier in the day.

"Before today?"

A laugh sounded from across the kitchen, where Finn was now scrubbing clean the dish used to bake the macaroni and cheese. I turned to Freya and nodded.

"You know who taught him how to make it?" I asked.

She tilted her head. "You?"

"My brother," I told her.

"You have a brother?"

"She has two," Finn said. He'd finished the last of the dishes, with which he'd denied any help whatsoever. Apparently even uninvited guests weren't allowed to lift a finger.

Freya whipped her head toward Finn, obviously awaiting an elaboration, the extent of which he already knew. "Their names are Braeden and Luke."

She smiled mischievously. "Luke sounds a lot like Puke."

This earned another laugh from Finn, and from me, too. Over the years, Luke had been called that nickname hundreds of times. I wondered if he would've liked it better if he heard the way Freya said it.

"It does, doesn't it?" Finn said.

"Do you have a sister?"

I met Freya's eyes, finding only a youthful curiosity radiating from them. It was an innocent question, one I should've been expecting. Still, I felt Finn shift beside me and noticed that I hesitated.

"No," I told her. "Just brothers. But that's not so bad."

Freya considered this, reaching forward to play with a piece of paint that had been chipped off of the kitchen table. "I want a brother."

"Okay," said Sutton, suddenly emerging from down the hall. "Crisis averted. Sorry about that."

I turned in my chair, offering Sutton a smile as she fastened her curly hair into a bun on top of her head. She'd taken an early leave from dinner to submit a script she thought she'd turned in already. I could hardly blame her. Not many recent college graduates had to balance freelance work, a graduate program, and motherhood all at once. It was no wonder Finn called her a superhero.

"You hear that?" Finn said, throwing an arm around Sutton's shoulders once she'd released her grasp on her hair. "Freya wants a brother."

Sutton snorted immediately, nearly causing me to do the same. Lucky for the two of them, it didn't seem Freya was dwelling on it.

"Mommy, did you know Mel's brother taught daddy how to make mac and cheese?"

Sutton nodded, reaching down to play with Freya's hair. "Nell's brother taught your daddy lots of things."

What a strange feeling it was to hear one sentence sum up an entire relationship, nevertheless one I'd spent my whole life admiring. Sutton was right. Luke taught Finn lots of things, just as Finn did for him and me and Ronan and Adrienne and everyone else. From so far away, this was a sweet sentiment. But once you really thought about it, it was friendship that we taught each other about most. Now, it seemed we'd lost all sight of that.

And all over just five minutes of a stupid game? There was just no way.

Freya's bedtime, though she'd been an angel all day, came with a bit of resistance. She remembered that it was my last night in Pittsburgh, and she wanted to eat up every second that came with it. This meant I had the honor of reading seven books while sitting at the edge of her mermaid-themed bed. Every single one was about the ocean, which she told me was her dream home—not beside it or near it, but in it. She even told me that I was pretty. Like Ursula.

This last accolade was accompanied by an apology from Sutton, who encouraged Freya not to equate her friends to villains, even if the villains were her favorite characters. I actually loved the compliment. Rare was the person who could find beauty in the girl who didn't look just like Ariel. I was just happy to hear that Freya could. The evil witch part, we could work on.

It was a few hours later, when even the city outside seemed to be calming down, that I was snuggled up on one end of the couch, a knit blanket around my shoulders, while Sutton and Finn sat comfortably on the other end. It felt like we were kids all over again, staying up talking after everyone else had gone to bed. This time, instead of crashing waves or my quiet living room, we were surrounded by cozy blankets and photos of memories Finn had created all on his own.

For me, these moments came with a bit of weight. I couldn't get over how surreal it felt to be this close to him again. To be a part of his life, even if it were just for a couple of days. The apartment we'd spent so many hours in, where I'd heard stories and learned about who he was now, was so new to me, and such a hard reality pill to swallow. But at the same time, oddly, it was exactly the kind of place I'd always pictured Finn. Wide open, not too many walls, plenty of room for ideas and songs and thoughts to swirl around the rooms. Most of all, it felt safe. That was how I knew he was in the right place.

"Alright, enough about me," I said, and justifiably so, seeing as the past twenty minutes had been filled with my voice. I didn't realize how much I was able to talk about something as simple as changing my major. I guess, when it came to Finn, it had always been that way; he could pull the words right out of me. "How did you two meet?"

Finn nudged Sutton gently with his shoulder. "You tell it better," he said.

Obviously in agreement, Sutton sat up a little straighter, lifting her head from his shoulder only to reposition. When she did, Finn's arm moved, too, but was still resting on her once she was settled, like it was meant to be there. For most of my life, I watched Luke and Adrienne behave this way, and saw love show itself even in the smallest of movements. I was overwhelmingly happy that Finn finally had something so special.

"It was fall semester of freshman year," Sutton started, taking a deep breath. I could tell by the look on her face that it was going to be a good story. "We'd been running in the same circles since orientation in August, but we'd never met. My roommate, Hana, however, was very fond of Finn. She'd been telling me for weeks that I just had to meet him, but everything kept falling through."

Sutton looked up at Finn, the two of them wearing matching, nostalgia-filled smiles that made me want to see their memories play out in front of me.

"So one night, Hana had an acting workshop on campus, and she came to me crying and saying she couldn't go because she was so sick. This was one of those things where you had to find someone to fill your place if you couldn't go. I felt so bad for her that I immediately volunteered myself, because what else am I going to do, you know?"

"Very brave," I noted, earning a laugh from Finn who knew that even this version of me would never do such a thing.

"Well, I came to find out that Hana was meant to play Finn's opposite in a number of scenes, all of which were being judged and graded by the top professors in the department."

I lifted my hand to cover my mouth. "Oh my God."

"Yeah," Sutton agreed. "So of course, I was terrible. I'm a writer. I don't do the stage work. Ever."

"You were fine," Finn said, nudging her again.

Sutton flashed Finn a look with wide eyes, then turned to me again. "I completely froze. I was so monotone, no one else on stage could understand me. I was about to burst into tears," she told me. "But then, Finn started saying all of my lines for me. Which he could do of course because he'd memorized them all ahead of time. And he nailed it. Put on such a performance that even the professors applauded afterward. They didn't care at all that I'd blown it."

I looked at Finn, whose expression said that this was all true. Of course, I'd believed it in a heartbeat. I hadn't heard a more Finn-like story in years.

"After that, I was loosened up, I guess, because I was able to do the scenes that came next. Not as well as Finn, obviously. But much better than that first one."

"So was it love at first sight?" I asked, hoping for the obvious answer.

"If you ask Hana, who was perfectly fine when I got home, by the way, then yes."

"And what if I ask you?"

Now, Sutton's smile of amusement faded just a little bit, and the shoulder under Finn's arm shrugged. "I had a nine-month-old baby at home. I wasn't really thinking about love."

106

Of course. I suddenly felt bad for asking such a question, but then I saw Finn's smile.

"It was for me," he said.

Sutton, turning back, looked him in the eyes like this was the first time she'd heard it, though I was sure it wasn't.

"Well, when I did start thinking that way, and we got closer, I was terrified to tell him about Freya," Sutton said then. "I was sure he was going to drop his jaw and run in the other direction."

"But he didn't," I observed.

Sutton shook her head, a smile on her face. "I invited him over to my parents' house. Sobbed my eyes out and told him everything." She turned to Finn now, her eyes finding his. "Do you remember the first thing you said?"

Finn nodded, his grin small yet genuine. "I asked what her name was."

Sutton turned back to me. "I knew it right then," she told me. "That was it."

What an astoundingly human moment to be convinced, with only a few words, that you're standing right beside your perfect match. Involuntarily, my own mind flashed toward all the phrases I'd heard, the ones that had that kind of potential or sparkled in a different light than the others. But even though they shone like gems, that side of my brain was dark, and I didn't have it in me to keep searching for them. Besides, this wasn't about me, and it didn't matter.

"Sounds like you," I said to Finn as our eyes met. His expression filled with gratitude, for this moment or that one or maybe both.

"Sounds like Freya, too," Sutton added. "Now it's the first question she asks anyone. It's like a weird, genetic hyperfixation that can't actually be genetic because—"

Then, as I was about to laugh, and maybe still did, Sutton's phone started to ring. The tone that emitted from it was an instrumental version of Taylor Swift's "betty." She and Adrienne, if they ever had the chance, would've been great friends.

"Shit," Sutton muttered, sitting up straight and away from Finn's arm.

"Clara?" he asked knowingly.

She looked at him, a sigh causing her chest to fall. "I don't want to."

"But you will."

She didn't disagree, but looked at me instead, an apologetic look on her face. "Don't go to bed until I come back out, okay?"

I nodded my head, and with it, Sutton was off. She'd made it down the hallway so quietly I didn't even hear a door shut, but I assumed one had. I looked at Finn. "Clara?"

"Her cousin. She's going through a break up and thought she was 'totally over it,'" he said, using air quotes for emphasis on the last part.

"But isn't," I guessed.

"Four calls this week."

"Ouch."

Finn's expression said that I didn't know the half of it, and the way he rearranged himself within his blanket said that he knew Sutton would be awhile. My sleep could, and would, wait.

Now that it was just Finn and me, it really felt like old times. I wouldn't have been surprised if we peeled back the living room curtains and the ocean suddenly appeared before us.

"So, she's perfect," I said, my voice hushed.

Finn shook his head, not in disagreement but disbelief. "Sometimes I feel like I'm dreaming when I'm sitting next to her."

I was so happy to hear this that I knew my face was showing it. Of course, me being me, I couldn't help but want to know the whole story.

"What's the deal with the father?"

Maybe it was insensitive for a Next Question. But then again, this was Finn and me.

"Sutton's boyfriend senior year of high school. He wasn't a good guy, I guess. All of her friends hated him, her parents included. Then she got pregnant, and he ran."

I shook my head. "How long were they together?"

"A few months," he told me. "And apparently he wasn't the first of his kind she'd been with."

"His kind?" I said. "Meaning what? Assholes?"

Finn laughed and tilted his head, his voice still hushed. "When I met her parents for the first time, her mom teared up when I shook her hand. Apparently I was the only boy Sutton or her sister Izzy had dated that did. Can you believe that? Not one guy in five years even shook her hand."

"God," I muttered. "Well, I'm glad it never worked out with any of them. You're lucky to have each other."

"I'm glad too," he said, leaning back. "I can't imagine my life without her. Or Freya. Even though I get my nails painted with sparkles every few months."

"She does seem to love glitter," I noted with a smile.

Finn took a breath, his eyebrows raising. "Alright." He sat up straight, leaned forward, cupped his hands in his lap, and stared right at me. Actually, right into my soul. "I need to know about yours now."

"My what?"

"Your love life."

"I don't have one."

"Yes you do. And you haven't come all this way to not talk to me about it in the middle of the night," he suggested. "Come on. Anyone in college? Anyone I know?"

This last word, the one I knew he'd been wanting to say all along, hung in the air above the others. It was emphasized without any change in the tone of his voice. Like he was a magician, or something. And I knew exactly why he did it. Lucky for me, I'd mastered the art of omission.

"I started dating a boy named Ethan freshman year."

"Mhm," he muttered. "And why didn't that work out?"

I frowned. "Why are you so sure it didn't work out?"

"Because you're not gushing," he said. "And I can't hear it in your voice when you say his name."

I leaned back onto the couch, dumbfounded at how, after all this time, he still knew exactly who and how I was. Even though he hadn't met this version of me until this weekend.

"You're right," I said. "It only lasted a few months. He chewed with his mouth full and could never seal a Ziplock bag all the way. It drove me crazy."

Now, Finn's smile was beaming. "There's my Elliana."

There was a momentary silence between us, albeit a comfortable one. As much as I'd long buried that version of myself, sometimes it was nice to see parts of her come to the surface. The good parts, at least.

"So, there was Ethan. Anybody since then?"

I shrugged. "Nothing serious," I lied.

The corners of Finn's lips curled even further. With just two words, he'd probably heard the whole story.

"I know who I am, okay?" I said, his smile not faltering. "I'm finding my people and I'm finding myself. It just takes a little experimenting, that's all."

"I'm happy for you, Nell. Seriously," he said, and I knew he meant it. "And I'm guessing you don't want me to ask about Mo anymore, so I won't."

Finn, 1. Art of Omission, 0.

I crossed my arms. "Thanks."

"My pleasure," he said. When he looked down, likely considering a subject change, there was a shift in his demeanor, like something heavy was about to come from his chest. "So, how are they?"

He didn't have to specify for me to know who *they* were. Like me with Ethan, it was just in his voice.

"They're good," I told him. "I think they really miss you, Finn."

Obviously, I had no way of knowing if this was true since Luke and Ronan hadn't spoken a word about Finn. But this wedding was the first of the Biggest Moments of Their Lives, and one of the ones they'd spent every teen year talking about.

I had no doubt that Finn was in the back of both of their minds as it drew closer. Maybe, and perhaps more likely, he was at the front.

"If they missed me that much, they probably would've called."

I blinked a few times, hearing him. "Do you miss them?"

Finn nodded.

"And have you reached out?"

Silence.

"See?"

"It's complicated."

I nodded once. "Which means 'no.'"

Since this was Finn, I felt bad for pushing. Then again, I had a motive behind my trip to Pennsylvania, and I still wasn't giving up on it.

"You know, I have a pretty good idea of when you can reconnect," I started. "It's in a few weeks, actually, and–"

"I'll consider it, alright?" he said, his voice still soft but his eyes finally having lifted from his hands.

"You say that, but–"

"No, really," he told me. "I want to go. It'll just– it'll be complicated. But I'll consider it. I mean it."

This time, I knew he would. Maybe I could've done more, said harsher things that would've made him feel like the wedding was something he just couldn't miss. But there was also that part of me who wanted to leave a bit of room for Finn to take that step himself. In the end, that's what would matter. The space in between, being covered all on his own.

Monday morning, I found myself resting my head against the car window, watching as the airport outside drew nearer. I had an overwhelming feeling of resistance—to go home, to keep what I'd done a secret, to leave Finn. There were now two-and-a-half weeks until the wedding, and I wasn't dreading it by any means. But I had just invited a guest whose presence might've been detrimental to the wedding experience itself, all while reuniting with a friend I never should've lost touch with in the first place.

Basically, I'd put my heart into a blender and turned it on high.

Still, there I was, sending a text to my mom that my flight from Vermont was taking off. Really, I still had a while to find my way through the airport and board my plane. Before that, the goodbyes.

Sutton was the first, and she hugged the way most girls were afraid to. Like squeezing too hard would make them seem overly emotional. Really, we'd just bonded, and she was showing it.

"It was so nice to finally meet you," she told me once we were face to face, her glasses slightly fogged.

I took a deep breath. I couldn't put into words how grateful I was to be standing beside her. I hoped she knew it.

"Hopefully it's not too long before the next time," I said.

At this, Sutton moved a little closer, her words finding only my ears. "I'll make sure of it."

I was elated by Sutton's concrete stance, which was on my side. But when I turned to Freya and found another pair of sad, bright blue eyes staring back up at me, my heart was once again a smoothie.

I crouched down, sitting in a catcher's stance so we could be eye-to-eye like the day we met.

"I'm very happy I got to meet you," I told her, trying my best to keep my goodbye with the four (and one-third) year-old simple.

She reached up and threw her hands around my neck. I hugged her back, sort of like a girl, since I didn't want to break her.

"Will you come visit us again?"

"Absolutely," I told her.

When she released me, her eyebrows indicated that this next question was Life or Death.

"And will you bring seashells next time?"

I laughed, as did Sutton and Finn who both stood behind me. "Of course," I said. "And, you know, maybe one day you can come visit me and pick them out for yourself. There's always room at my house.

"I will!"

I felt Finn shift behind me then, and even though I'd been dreading saying goodbye since the second we reunited, the fact that it was finally here made me want to melt into a puddle on the sidewalk. When I stood up and turned around to face him, melting truly felt like the only option.

After studying Finn's face for only a few seconds, I found my feelings to be reciprocated.

"Come here," he said, pulling me in.

I'd never been very emotional, and I was still getting used to the idea that it was okay to be. With my head against Finn's chest, his arms pulling me close, I could feel my tears soaking his shirt. Normally, this was when I would've backed down, shut out anything that was allowing me to feel so sad. But this time, I knew, I had to welcome the tears.

"Promise we'll see each other soon," I said into his chest.

"I promise," I heard him say.

I felt him let go at the same time I did, like we were in sync, and found his eyes looking down at me.

"I mean it," I told him. "Even if you don't come to the wedding. I don't know why it's been so long, but it can't happen again."

"It won't," he assured me. Right then, I had the feeling he was going to apologize, like I'd mentioned the time jump to make him feel guilty about it.

"I love you, you know that?"

The guilt washed away from Finn's eyes upon hearing this, and the smile on his face finally forced one onto me. "I love you, too."

I pulled him into one last hug, even tighter than before. It said everything that I knew we both wanted to hear but didn't have the time for.

"You'd better go," he told me.

I sniffled, glanced anywhere but at Finn and his family, then took a deep breath.

"See you soon," Freya said.

God, I hoped she was right.

Chapter Eleven

Elliana

"So, when's Senior Night?"

This, in the grand scheme of things, wasn't a terrible question. But when it came out of Bax, I didn't feel the need to answer it. There were Sydney and Henry, though, who were both looking at me for confirmation. I had a feeling they knew the answer, but the silence was loud.

"About a month or so," I said.

The four of us were sitting on the bleachers, the scoreboard across the field indicating just a few minutes left in warm-up time before the game would start. If it were basketball, this would've been right around the time that the nausea would kick in, that I'd feel the urge to run out of the gym and never return. But this wasn't basketball. For that, I was thankful. For everything else, including my proximity to Bax, not so much.

We'd pregamed the lacrosse game—where the boys were competing against a team they were slated to crush—with fries and mozzarella sticks at Archie's. I was enjoying my time with Sydney and Henry, who were starting to look more like Love Birds than Sweet Hearts, but my social meter was running dangerously low. It was a good thing the air was warm.

"Are your parents coming to the game?" Bax asked.

"Senior Night?"

He shook his head. "This one."

I nodded, forcing Bax's attention behind my shoulder as I looked over it. Just up a few rows on the bleachers, my parents were sitting with coffees in their hands and listening to Braeden as he told them some sort of story. If Bax hadn't been staring at me for ten minutes, he might've seen them.

"Oh," he said, nodding as if he'd forgotten why he asked in the first place.

There was one Awkward Silence in the entire world that I didn't actually mind, and it was the one between me and Bax.

Maybe it was because it was less Awkward than it was Preferred.

Sometimes I thought that maybe I was too hard on him, even in my subconscious, because the one thing that scared me the most was what I held onto when it came to him. But then again, I couldn't really help it.

"I haven't seen your mom in a while," Henry noted.

"She's been working a lot," I told him, brushing a piece of hair behind my ear. "She can make the next couple of games though, and she has Senior Night off."

"She still on Labor and Delivery?"

I nodded. Before, my mom worked on the same floor at the hospital as Henry's mom, Jan. But then, when we were in eighth grade, my mom moved up a few floors. It was mostly to be around more babies, but also because the doctors up there were begging her to join them; they liked her that much.

According to Jan, the Psych Unit was never the same.

"Good," Sydney said, nudging me with her leg. "Those babies deserve her."

I was ready to dwell on it, and maybe even thank Sydney on my mother's behalf, when another conversation started. Almost.

It was Bax, again, and his eyes hadn't left mine since he'd spotted my parents.

"So, Elliana, do you—"

I didn't actually get to hear the end of this question because of a beautifully loud interruption that came in the form of Adrienne and Mo. And by that, I mean that Mo's shin connected with a bleacher just a few feet in front of me. She was graceful, of course, so she didn't fall. But it sounded like it hurt.

"F—"

"—abulous!" Adrienne exclaimed, saving Mo's swear word from entering the atmosphere.

I glanced at the scoreboard, biting down a laugh. There were only three minutes before game time, so this arrival was uncharacteristic. At least for Adrienne.

"Did you just get here?" I asked.

Adrienne, raising her eyebrows, glanced sideways at Mo, who was now rubbing her shin through her jeans. "We would've been here earlier, but we were cleaning out Mo's car."

"Was it messy?" Syd asked, intrigued as I was.

This, Adrienne just answered with a look.

Mo clicked her tongue. Immediately, I'd believed Adrienne, because a messy car definitely matched everything else about Mo. But now I was ready to hear what she had to say.

"We spent thirty minutes sitting in the back seat so I could teach you French," she said, looking at Adrienne who was now smiling. "If we're late, it's because you wanted to impress Luke. We could've cleaned the car in twenty."

Henry turned to Mo. "You know French?"

"Oui," she said without hesitation, earning laughs from our entire group.

"She actually knows four languages," Adrienne added. As if Mo could've gotten any better.

"Where did you come from again?" Sydney asked. "Mars?"

When Mo laughed, I felt it in my heart. Maybe she really was an alien, or some sort of otherworldly being.

"New York," she answered.

Henry raised his eyebrows. "Four languages? That's impressive."

Mo shrugged, seemingly not in love with the attention she was getting for it, but playing it off nonetheless. "Life's short. I want to get everything I can out of it."

Mo flashed me a smile with a hint of something else in it. I wondered if it was because I lived my life in the complete opposite fashion and she knew it. If it was, then maybe I should've felt bad about how obvious that might've been. But sitting there, her eyes still on me as the conversation went on for a moment, I didn't feel an ounce of bad, and it wasn't even the numbness. I felt good, whatever that meant.

Henry was so intrigued by Mo's multi-cultural knowledge that he was nearly exploding with questions about it. Naturally, I was beginning to zone out, watching as Ronan, Finn, and Luke made faces at each other while the team gathered at the bench. Ronan, who was standing beside the ever-rigid Coach Allenson, was crossing his eyes at Luke, who was hiding behind Finn so Coach couldn't see him laughing. Finn, though Allenson might not have known him well enough to tell, was about to burst.

When the first whistle of the game was blown a moment later, I heard Mo reveal to an excited Henry that, on top of English, she knew French, Mandarin Chinese, and Spanish. His jaw was on the floor when Sydney turned her attention to me, her voice low.

"I didn't think she could get any cooler."

I glanced sideways at Mo, who was listening to Henry talk about his dreams of studying abroad. "Me neither."

I watched as Luke moved the ball up the field, sure that Adrienne was probably tuned out of the adjacent conversation by now, too.

"You know," Sydney started then, her tone even lower than before. "Bax is still looking for a date to the sophomore dance."

I whipped my head around so I could look her in the eyes. I was fairly certain—no, positive—that Sydney knew how I felt about Bax. She was always putting herself between the two of us, ensuring that I was as far away from him as I wanted to be. This turn of events was fishy.

"I know," I said rather defensively.

The corner of her lips raised slightly. A smile?

"He also mentioned the other day how he wanted to ask you out."

"Sydney—"

"Would you go on a date with him?"

I slowly shook my head, and watched as the anticipation in Sydney only grew. Not only was Bax only a few feet away from us, but now I was wondering if this was actually what Sydney wanted. She was always wishing the best for me. Did she really think this was it?

118

"I don't– I don't know. Maybe."

"Maybe?"

"Why are we talking about this?" I whispered.

She shrugged. "I was just wondering."

"Well, wonder less."

On the field, the referee blew the whistle, and Ronan bent down to tie his shoe, his floppy hair falling over his eyes. Sydney watched it happen, then kept her eyes on the game as she whispered again.

"It could be fun to just try and put yourself out there more," she said to me. "You never know how you feel about someone until you really get to know them."

I pulled my eyes from the game and focused again on Sydney's face which, once again, I couldn't read.

"Are we still talking about Bax?"

Three days later, I was half of a mile from my house, the warm morning breeze from the ocean finding its way to my skin. This should have been relaxing, considering I'd been jogging for thirty minutes and was on the final and easiest leg of my run. But then there was Bax's question from Tuesday night, playing over and over and over again in my brain.

The game was over, and I was walking toward the parking lot beside Bax. Sydney and Henry were right in front of us, but apparently not close enough to hear when he cleared his throat. Three times.

"What are you doing Sunday night?" he asked me, completely out of the blue.

I'd been trying to zone out, focus on every bit of my surroundings except for Bax himself. But with this question, my eyes fell on his hair. The white stadium lights were still holding onto it, illuminating just how much gel he'd used to make those spikes so spiky.

For the life of me, I couldn't think of an obligation I had other than discussing Marvel movies with Ronan or musicals with Finn. Frankly, that should've been enough.

"I don't think I'm doing anything," I said with instant regret.

Bax's face lit up. "Would you want to go to the boardwalk?"

The boardwalk was exactly what it sounded like: a long, boarded walkway lined with shops and cafes. In the case of our town, it ran for miles along our beach, and was punctuated by a pier with games and a Ferris wheel and more food. It was a perfect place for tourists—our beach hosted many of them, especially this time of year—and teenagers with nothing to do. I'd loved the boardwalk ever since I was a kid. The idea of being there alone with Bax, however, was not so appealing.

"Oh. Okay. Sure," I said, panic still coursing through my veins. "Like, with Sydney and Henry?"

Bax's triumphant smile that he began sporting the instant I said I was free was overcome with a look of fear. Since even the mention of their names didn't make Sydney or Henry turn around, I was really alone, and now I felt guilty. Bax had been wanting to ask this question for months. I was able to avoid it during school hours or at Archie's, but not now. Maybe there was a reason for it.

"Oh. Uh– no. It's just me. Is that– is that okay?" he said, stammering. "You don't have to come if you don't want to."

I took a deep breath, forcing a smile. It was just one night.

"No, that's fine," I told him. "I want to. Don't worry."

And there we were. A night alone on the boardwalk scheduled for three nights out. I wanted to grab Sydney by the shoulders, spin her around, and show her what I'd accidentally done. But she was too busy being in love with Henry.

Now, about a block away from my house, my watch started beeping, indicating that I'd hit the three-mile mark of my run. I slowed my pace to a walk and lifted the neckline of my oversized tee up to my forehead to wipe the sweat off. When I did, I heard a door swing open, presumably belonging to the house I was walking past.

Without thinking, I turned in its direction, expecting to see someone who I didn't know but who my parents probably did. Instead, I saw Mo.

Her skin was glowing characteristically and her hair was perfectly wild, a loose-fitting blue t-shirt and a pair of shorts completing her look. She'd just stepped onto her driveway when our eyes met, and I was suddenly very aware of how sweaty I was.

"You know what I love about the sun?" she asked, immediately clearing me of my morning fog.

I just looked at her, attempting to catch my breath before it was imperative that I say any words.

She smiled, recognizing my energy level as she got closer. "When we go to bed at night, everything is dark. The same color, even. So mundane, sad. But then the sun comes up, every morning, and everything is bursting in color. The ocean is all different shades of blue, the grass is green, our eyes light up. Everything in the world is brighter. And it's all because of the sun."

I, not surprisingly, was speechless. I wanted to look around, at the sky and the grass and the ocean, so I could find the world as she described it. Instead, I couldn't take my eyes off of her. When she turned to me, she laughed. I wondered what she thought her words sounded like. To me, they were profound.

"Wow," I said.

Nice, Elliana.

"Are you running from something?" she asked, her laugh subsiding as we fell into step together on the sidewalk.

I just looked at her, utterly surprised that she knew what was going on in my head. There was a chance that she didn't, and that her remark was her way of greeting me, post-heartfelt-observation, but I would've bet against it.

"I guess," I admitted.

Mo smirked. "What, uniform too wrinkled? Hair too wavy?"

I let out a laugh. "No."

"Then what?"

"I'm going on a date tonight," I told her, though I wasn't exactly sure why.

Here and there, my conversations with Mo were picking up. They were getting deeper than surface-level, bigger than small talk. I was learning more about her and she was trying to learn about me, and I really didn't mind it. In fact, I was having fun. But this blurting out of my own problems that I didn't even know I had—this wasn't me.

Mo turned to me quickly, her expression mostly entertained, slightly urgent.

"Are you?"

I nodded. "Unfortunately."

She was still looking at me. "You don't want to?"

I shrugged, keeping my eyes on the road that stretched in front of us. "Not really."

Mo nodded. It seemed like she understood, and I wondered if she really did.

"What's his name?"

"Bax," I told her. "Foster Baxton, technically."

"The kid from the lacrosse game? Spiky hair?"

I nodded, my breathing finally slowing to a human pace.

"Mm," she muttered. "You don't like him?"

"I don't mind him," I said, likely lying. As if I really knew the difference when it came to Bax. "He's just… I don't know. Not my type, I guess."

"So you're going on a date with someone who you sort of don't mind but who you're sure isn't for you," Mo said then. Just like with the championship game, it only took her repeating exactly what I'd done for me to understand it. "Why?"

"I don't—" I started, at a loss for any words. "I don't know. I guess I didn't want to hurt his feelings."

At this, I was expecting some sort of speech, like the one about how shooting that ball should've made me proud rather than ashamed. But this time, she looked down at the road with me, and I suddenly found myself at her level. Imagine that.

"I get that," she said.

"You do?"

We were almost to my house now. The smell of the ocean, combined with the conversation, was making me want to run into the water and never come back out.

Mo half-smiled. "I went on three dates last year with someone because I felt bad saying no. But when I finally did, I was a lot happier. I knew it was better for both of us because my heart definitely wasn't in it. You know?"

It was so strange, but I actually did know. It's not that I'd ever experienced that situation before, but I knew in my own heart that it's exactly how I'd have felt if I'd said no to Bax. On top of the guilt, that is.

"What did he say when you said no? Was he mad?" I asked, hoping for some wisdom should I have found the courage to shoot Bax down the next time.

Mo shrugged. "She got over it."

Though Mo didn't seem at all bothered by my wording, I suddenly was. Now we were on my driveway, and I finally allowed my eyes to meet hers.

"I'm sorry I assumed," I said.

Mo shook her head, her eyebrows furrowed, as if my apology was worse than my assumption. Right.

"Don't be," she said. "I gave up on boys in, like, seventh grade."

Her honesty forced a laugh out of me. As per usual, I was amazed by Mo. She was only seventeen and new exactly who she was. Just like the kids in those romance novels.

Not only was I proud, but also a bit honored. I'd always heard that coming out was one of the hardest things in the world to do, but Mo made it sound so easy. Maybe we were better friends than I thought.

"You're not missing much."

Mo laughed, too, and it warmed my heart. She gave me a suggestive look, but I was sure she knew what I meant.

"You'll have to let me know how tonight goes," she told me.

Then, she was opening the screen door to my house, the smell of pancakes and sausage hitting our noses at the same time. And that, apparently, was that.

But now, the conversation replaying in my mind was the one that led us to the door. I didn't know what it was about Mo, maybe the way she worded things or the way she smiled in the quiet moments, but talking to her was easy. Even if the topic wasn't.

About thirty minutes later, however, another conversation took over. This one, I wanted to end as soon as it began, and it was Braeden that took the first bite.

"Elliana's got a date tonight."

We were about to sit down for breakfast—the whole crew minus Finn, whose whereabouts were almost at the front of my mind. Luke had prepared a feast of pancakes, sausage, hash browns, fruits of all colors and sizes. I'd been basking in the glory of its scent before Braeden dropped a figurative bomb on me.

"Where's Finn?" I asked, turning to Ronan who was more intrigued by what Braeden had said than I wanted him to be.

"Said his parents needed him for something," Luke said, trading a look with me as he placed a plate of pineapple slices and strawberries between Braeden and me. "He'll be here soon."

I wanted to give more attention to this answer, as Ronan, Adrienne, and Luke likely did, too. Finn's parents never needed him. They never even acted like they wanted him.

"You have a date?"

This question was asked by my dad, whose eyeline I couldn't meet without feeling the burning stare of my mother's. What happened to the tough conversations starting on our terms?

"It's not a date," I said, fiddling with the corners of my napkin. I was thankful that Mo, who sat to my right, was keeping quiet, since I explicitly told her earlier that my evening with Bax was, in fact, a date.

Any mention of a boy in my house, ever since Luke met Adrienne, was like news of a new pope. Braeden was still too young to be teased about potential Perfect Matches, but my love life was fair game for any and all speculation. Especially at the breakfast table.

"Who's her date with?" my dad asked now, thinking himself funny, and turning toward Braeden.

"Foster Baxton," he told him, or, everyone.

"It's not a date," I repeated. "We're just going to the boardwalk."

"That's where Adrienne and I had our first date," Luke noted. I knew he wasn't really prying, just stating a fact. But it didn't help.

Now, my mom leaned forward in her chair, her stare bursting with interest. "When did Foster ask you out?"

Finn's empty seat next to me was starting to feel like a vortex I was being sucked into, and at the same time, a wall that was about to collapse onto me. If his presence were there instead, I wouldn't have felt so trapped.

I took a deep breath and tipped my head back. "Thursday," I said curtly, feeling an ounce of guilt for using a harsh tone with my mother. "But it's really not a big deal. Can we not make it a big deal?"

I was pleading, really, and maybe I was overreacting. But my entire body felt hot, like I was melting, and the air in the room was getting thick.

"Isn't Foster Baxton's father the principal at the elementary school?" my dad said, ignoring me and turning to my mom.

Adrienne lowered her eyebrows. "That's his dad?"

"Oh, he's a nice guy." My mom was excited now, the idea of our families merging forming into one big fantasy in her eyes. "The kids love him."

Adrienne turned to Luke. "His brother's in our grade. RJ."

My mom let out a sigh of approval. "Well, I just think this is great."

Next to me, Mo shifted, like she was going to say something. I braced myself, wondering whether it was going to help or hurt, when Ronan beat her to it.

"Luke, you might have some competition for cutest couple in the family."

"I'm going outside for a second." I abruptly stood from my chair, pushing it out but not back in as I made my way to the front door.

There was something pulling me back to the table, perhaps the part of my mind that wanted me to stay between the lines and be the daughter and sister and friend who didn't cause any problems. But I couldn't breathe, and as much as opening the door felt like a blatant disregard for the rules I'd set for myself, the fresh air was what I needed.

I sat down on the steps, feeling the cool cement through my shorts, and closed my eyes. Seconds later, I heard a car door. I should have guessed; alone time didn't exist at the Rose House.

"You okay?"

Of course this was the first thing Finn asked, even though he was the one who was late to breakfast and looked like he'd just seen a ghost.

"You first," I said.

Finn's smile didn't reach his eyes. By the time he made it to me, he'd let out a sigh and run a hand through his hair.

"My dad's sick," he told me.

Though I thought my heart was already in my stomach, I felt it drop.

"What? Sick how?"

He shook his head, another deep breath causing his chest to rise and fall. "Something with his lungs."

"Is he going to be okay?" I asked, to which Finn only shrugged. "Are you okay?"

This, I knew, was complicated. A parent being sick was one thing, but when the parent wasn't actually a parent, I imagined that was an entirely different one.

He offered a very Finn-like smile, then nodded in my direction. "Your turn."

"Just needed some air," I told him.

Finn unsurprisingly took my hint, then placed a hand on my shoulder as he drew open the door and stepped inside. I hoped being beside Luke and Ronan was the medicine he needed, and was thinking about it when I heard the door open again.

"Do you want to be alone?"

When I turned around, I found a look of empathy on Mo's face. Usually, she looked fierce, unbothered.

I shook my head. "You can sit."

When she did, her posture was much more nonchalant than mine. She folded her hands in her lap.

"I don't do well with pressure," I admitted. Though this was probably obvious, she didn't say it.

"That's okay."

These were only two words, and basic ones at that, but I'd never heard them before. At least, not when it came to the way I was. I knew that everyone had to deal with how panic-ridden I was, how everything that seemed so small to them was earth-shattering to me. I also knew that everyone, likely including Mo, wished I was different. So to hear that it was okay, well, that was something.

"If you don't have a good time with Bax tonight, you can just leave. You have no obligation to him," Mo said then, offering an option I needed. "You're in control of your own life. I'd hate for you to coast because you're afraid of a little mess."

Mo looked at me then, so I looked back. The May sun had already darkened her freckles and lightened her hair. Pretty or beautiful or stunning didn't quite sum her up. There had to have been a better word.

I shook my head. "I don't know how to not coast." I was surprised, not only by the fact that I was speaking this out loud, but that I'd thought of it at all. Words never came easy, but those ones did. "It's who I am."

"It's who you think you are," she countered, taking a breath. "I don't mean to always be giving you unsolicited advice—"

"It's okay. I need it," I interrupted. This made her smile, so naturally I did, too.

"I just think you'll be a lot happier if the choices you make are your own. Choosing yourself first doesn't have to be selfish," she said. "And you're capable of more than you think. You just have to believe it."

What she was saying was hard to hear, but the way she was looking at me when she said it softened the blow. It also made my hands tingle.

"What makes you think that?"

Mo shrugged, for the first time without an immediate and visible answer.

Finally, she found it. "Intuition."

I didn't respond to this, because I couldn't and I didn't need to. Instead, I watched as Mo's eyes lingered toward the side of my house, where a family of yellow flowers were peeking around the corner.

"Is that a garden?"

I nodded, though she wasn't looking at me anymore. "My mom's."

"You'll have to show me sometime. I love flowers." She turned back to me, the fierce and unbothered glimmer right back in her eyes where it belonged. "But now, Ronan is about to demolish all the pancakes, and that is not acceptable."

Mo stood, not bothering to dust herself off, and offered her hand. I could've gotten up by myself, and maybe even should've, but I was making a choice of my own. Besides, I liked the feel of my hand in hers, even if it was only for a second.

Chapter Twelve

Nell

"Did you get your Ben and Jerry's fix?"

I was so focused on fixing the broken clasp of a bracelet Adrienne had given me that I didn't hear my dad walk into the kitchen. With the sound of his voice, I dropped the piece I was holding onto my lap. Four tries apparently wasn't enough.

"Huh?"

"Ben and Jerry's," my dad repeated in the same tone. "In Burlington."

"Oh. Right." Now I left the bracelet on the table, joining my dad in the kitchen so my slip-up wasn't obvious. "Yeah. We made all of our rounds."

It had been three days since I returned from my trip to Pittsburgh, and I hadn't been questioned about it once. I even showed Braeden pictures of Genevieve and me on Church Street—we took them before I left at the end of the semester, when I started planning my fake trip—and he barely studied them. I knew I'd hidden my whereabouts pretty well, but I didn't think it was seamless.

"Did you know they have a Jimmy Fallon flavor?"

This was the most Adam Rose a question could get. My father had three loves: my mother, the Avengers (which he and Ronan frequently bonded over), and Jimmy Fallon. This probably said a lot about us kids—his fourth love, I guess.

I nodded. "'The Tonight Dough.' It's Genevieve's favorite."

"I knew I liked her," my dad said with a smile.

Then, like we'd been directed by some outside entity, both of our gazes fell upon the window above the kitchen counter. It led to the side of our house, and through it, I could see delicate fairy lights and the tops of trees that were amidst their summer bloom. I could also see the tops of two familiar heads.

"Just about two weeks now. Can you believe it?" my dad asked.

I took a deep breath. He had no idea.

"No," I admitted. "I can't."

"Do you remember when he first told us he was going to marry her? How old was he then?"

"Thirteen," I told him. "I was eleven."

My dad sighed, shook his head. "I thought he was crazy."

"Mom didn't," I said.

I watched his eyes soften as his head shook slightly. "I think she saw Adrienne as a saving grace. Nothing was too crazy for her then."

I thought back to that time in our lives, my mind flickering toward the parts of it I usually blocked out. I shook them away, focusing my attention back on the trees and the lights that glimmered in the sun.

This wedding, and everything that accompanied it, was the italicized word in that paragraph of our lives. It certainly wasn't the end, but it stood out. Our eyes would be drawn to it forever.

"I'm going to the beach," I told my dad, who was now completely zoned-out. Maybe I should've asked what he was thinking about, but I didn't want to know.

When I made it to the shoreline, I slipped off my cover-up, allowing my skin to soak up the warmth I'd been depriving it of while I stood in the air-conditioned house. Then, as if no one was watching, which I wasn't sure was true, I completely immersed myself in the water. As the waves washed over me, the weekend in Pittsburgh was on replay in my mind. I desperately wanted to feel good about it, to smile at the thought of seeing Finn again after so much time had passed. At the thought of meeting his family.

But then there was what was coming. I wanted so badly to know that things were going to work out, to know that I'd done the right thing. But there was no way to be sure. It was a good thing I had plenty of distractions.

I was back on the beach, nearly dry and laying flat on my towel, when a breeze washed over my right leg only. There wasn't a cloud in the sky, so when I opened my eyes, sitting up slightly to lean on my elbows, I wasn't surprised to see a shadow towering over me.

"Alright, who said you could get this hot?"

Lo and behold. Sydney Eldridge, in the flesh.

Of course, when I looked up at her, squinting once I removed my sunglasses, we were wearing the same bathing suit. A black bikini with a blue trim. I'd gotten mine on a visit to the Adirondacks with Genevieve, so the matching was purely coincidence, but not at all shocking.

I stood up, pulling Syd into a hug before offering any sort of response. After freshman year, Sydney worked a summer-long basketball camp in Georgia where she attended college. So, really, we hadn't been around each other for more than a few days at a time since our high school graduation and subsequent moves to different states. Sometimes, if I thought about how much I missed her, I couldn't handle it.

"Seriously," she said.

I spun around like a model, my wet hair sticking to my back while the dry strands twirled around me.

"And you're confident?" She raised her eyebrows. "What did Vermont do with my best friend?"

I rolled my eyes, let a laugh out of my nose and nudged her on the shoulder. "What did *Georgia* do with mine?" I asked, my eyes falling on her arm muscles that had grown twice in size since the last time I saw her. "You'd better leave your shirt on. Don't wanna destroy all this self-love I have."

"Oh, shut up." She joined me on the sand, spreading her towel out right beside mine.

We were acting as though we hadn't spoken in months, but it had really only been a few days since our last phone call—before Pittsburgh, to be specific—so there wasn't much catching up to do.

"How was the trip?" Syd asked. A few hundred feet to our right, a group of teenagers was having their picture taken by a sun-hat wearing mom.

This was the part of summer on the beach that was as annoying as it was entertaining. We were cursed with crowds, being a tourist town, but we also were able to watch people experience fleeting vacations right in our backyard. Bothersome, maybe. But it made me realize what a privilege I had when the place so many chose to spend their precious free time was the same place I called home.

I shrugged, waving my hand at a fly who had landed on my knee. "I'll answer that after the wedding."

She lowered her eyebrows. "Is he coming?"

"I don't know." Though I was sure my entire family was in the house, I was still keeping my voice low. "He said he'd think about it."

Syd looked out at the ocean, the waves crashing rhythmically in front of us. "This is you and Finn," she said. "I'm not worried."

This meant a lot coming from Sydney. For so long, I didn't realize how close I'd gotten with Finn or Ronan or Adrienne because of how set I was on Sydney being my one and only best friend, my other half. It was only recently that I realized there isn't a limit to how many people can love you. So my problem, as I might've said, wasn't really a problem at all.

"Have you seen the dress?" Syd asked next. On to the important stuff.

"Sydney, it's the most beautiful thing I've ever seen," I told her, practically drooling. "You're going to pass out."

She raised a finger to her temple. "God, I cannot handle that."

"Maybe it's just that Adrienne's wearing it."

"She is practically a real-life princess," Syd agreed. "And what about yours, *Maid of Honor?*"

I frowned. "I sent you a picture of it."

"I know," she said, "But how does it feel to wear it?"

Honestly, though I was itching to take it off the day my family gathered to see me in it, I felt special in that dress. Maybe it was just that Adrienne had christened it years before, or that putting it on made everything feel so real.

"Great," I said. "Special."

There was a silence that washed over us then. I thought it was because we'd reverted to old habits, our collective attention lingering on the horizon in search of something bigger than the two of us. But after a moment, I felt Sydney's eyes, and they were on me.

"What?" I turned to her, and she was still studying me.

"I just like seeing you like this," she said with a shrug.

"And how's that?"

She grinned. "Happy."

Sunday morning, Luke and my parents were busy planning the food layout of the pre-wedding party at our house, so I had the honor of accompanying Adrienne to the venue.

Both the wedding and the reception were to be held at The Royal, a breathtaking resort that sat on the waterfront downtown. Every girl that grew up in our town and the adjacent ones dreamt of being married there. For being on the brink of a lifelong Dream Come True, Adrienne sure looked green.

We'd just finished walking through the Banquet Hall where the reception would be—the ceremony was set to take place in the Coastal Room, which was as beautiful as it sounded —with the wedding planner named Natalia. It was the last time Adrienne would see the place before it was all set up on the day-of, so Natalia was all business—blazer, high bun, dangly earrings, the lot.

"...and you'll have absolutely nothing to worry about. Leave the stressing to me."

This was Natalia's catch phrase, as I'd heard it four times within just an hour of walking the grounds. I wanted to ask if her stress-handling applied to Maids of Honor who went behind the backs of the married couple and invited an exiled childhood friend to the wedding. I had a feeling I knew the answer.

"Thanks so much, Natalia," Adrienne said in her buttery voice. Natalia smiled, satisfied. "We'll see you in a couple of weeks."

With that, Natalia was on her way, and we were on ours. In the parking lot, Adrienne finally let out the breath she'd been holding in. I felt it move my hair.

"So?" she said, like she was in a hurry. "What'd you think?"

"I can't believe you're getting married there," I said, giving her my biggest smile. "It's so— it's so beautiful. Like the castle in *Beauty and the Beast* but not as scary."

She whipped her head toward me. "You were scared of *Beauty and the Beast?*"

"The palace is literally alive." I shook my head. "Not the point."

She laughed, though it faded a little too quickly, and I noticed. Once we were in the car, Adrienne fastening her seatbelt, I noticed something else. She was biting her lip.

"What are you nervous about?"

Cover: blown. At least it wasn't mine.

She released her lip to protest. "I'm not nervous."

"You were biting your lip."

"No, I wasn't."

"It's still red," I pointed out.

This, she didn't question. She tipped her head back onto her seat's headrest and let out a breath not unlike the one that slapped me in the face a few moments earlier. I could see in her eyes that she was about to say something to rock the boat. Or, car.

God, I could not handle cold feet.

"I feel like Luke's not telling me something," she said.

"What do you mean?"

As much as I was Luke's sister, I was also Adrienne's friend. And, in this case, Maid of Honor. Luke was fair game for worrying. I was glad Adrienne knew it.

"I don't know." She stared at the ceiling, possibly looking for an answer on it. "He keeps getting quiet. Like he's nervous or— or second-guessing. And if he has doubts, that's fine. I just wish he would tell me. But I don't want to ask because then—"

"Adrienne. Luke has never been more sure about anything in his life. He has no doubts."

She turned to me then. "How can you be sure?"

I shook my head. "Because he loves you."

This answer was simple, and apparently satisfactory. Adrienne backed down, simultaneously shaking and nodding her head. Of course he loved her, and of course that was enough.

I was happy to see that the worry had washed away from her face, and that her poor bottom lip could rest. But then, a few days later, it was my turn to panic. And, quite frankly, it hit me like a truck.

The heat outside had been nearing absurdity. So the party, so to speak, was inside. In our living room, more specifically.

I was sitting on one of the sofa chairs, and had just finished watching a video on Braeden's laptop when Sydney flashed her phone in front of my face.

"What about that one?"

"I'm reaching my screen limit," I joked. It was only the thirtieth hairstyle she'd shown me, so maybe I was overreacting. I studied the photo anyways, trying my best to refrain from cringing. "You want me to look like Effie Trinket?"

Sydney frowned, her phone retreating to her eyes only.

"It's not that bad," she sighed. But then I watched as she looked at the photo again and cringed herself.

"Is it good?" Braeden asked, referring to the video he'd shown me.

I nodded. "Perfect."

"Okay," Syd said next. "This one."

This next hairstyle was better, but still not good. There was too much volume, and I didn't like poofs.

"Adrienne said I can just do something simple," I told her instead of outright shooting it down like I had the previous million.

"What did Adrienne say about simple?"

It was Luke, finally. He and Adrienne had been due at the house for hours. We were all going to go over the plan for the wedding day—hair, makeup, picture-taking—and I was dying to see if I was going to find the same quietness in Luke's demeanor that Adrienne was so worried about. Of course, when they entered the house side-by-side, they were both sporting their typical in-love glow. I wasn't surprised.

Adrienne, flashing me a content look, made her way to the couch where Luke would soon join her. Before that, he made a pit stop in the kitchen, sticking his fingers into the bowl of leftover dough from the cookies I'd just put into the oven.

"You're going to get sick," I told him.

He frowned, sticking the dough into his mouth anyways. "What are you, mom?"

Sydney let out a breath. "I think Elliana is back. And she ate Nell."

I rolled my eyes. "Fine. Get salmonella for all I care." I turned to Syd. "If you find something I *like*, I won't shoot it down. I'm just particular."

This, Sydney accepted. I knew what she was saying was out of love, so I wasn't bothered in the slightest. At least now we could poke fun at who I used to be.

"Alright, Nell, ready?" Adrienne asked, drawing open her super-neat and color-coded notebook that had every detail about the wedding day and the few prior. I'd flipped through most of it before, but figured it was best to entertain Adrienne and listen to it a few more times.

As was evident by the increasingly buzzy air in our house, the stress and excitement of the wedding was starting to seep through the windows and doors. I'd assured Luke and Adrienne over and over that I, along with Ronan, whose current location I couldn't put a finger on, had everything under control. But, truthfully, I had a bad feeling, and I wasn't quite sure where it was coming from.

Adrienne was almost through with her plan about the out-of-towners and how they'd be accommodated when Luke joined her on the couch. He sat down quietly, so as not to disturb her as she spoke, and put his arm around her shoulders. Then he just listened.

I only saw the look in his eyes change when Adrienne started talking about our side of the family—it was ten times bigger than hers, and us kids only knew about ten percent of it, give or take. I knew that detail was the biggest stress for Luke, and honestly, it was one of mine, too. The last time any of my dad's brothers or mom's cousins had seen any of us, we were those little, do-no-wrong kids who were being shaped into the best versions of themselves at private school. Now, we were all grown up. Or at least trying to be.

"Then, after the first dance, we'll do the toasts," Adrienne said, now quickly moving through the bulleted itinerary of the reception. "Ronan will go first, and then you. How does that sound? If you want to do it the other way, that's okay too. I'll just have to tell Natalia."

I felt Braeden let out a sigh of relief next to my leg. Lucky for him, getting out of toast obligations.

"Ronan first is fine," I said, shelving any preference I had. There was no need to make a fuss over something that small, anyways.

"Great." Adrienne smiled. "Then we'll just have cake and the mother-son dance. Then, party."

At this, Luke let out the breath he'd been holding in. Okay, maybe he was nervous. Just based on his smile, though, I could tell it was more reception-based than it was Adrienne. I wondered if I was allowed to ask him about it.

"No father-daughter dance?" Sydney asked then, stopping at another hair photo and flashing it in front of me. This one was better. By far. I actually might've been obsessed.

"I love it," I told her quietly, awaiting Adrienne's answer to the question.

"Oh, I–" Adrienne shook her head, her smile remaining. I could see the gears grinding, searching for the politest way to answer. "My dad's not coming."

Sydney's smile that resulted from my approval was quickly overcome by a look of guilt. "I'm such an idiot. I knew that. I'm sorry."

Ever since Adrienne came into our lives, and even before, Ms. Brenda was the only one around. I'd asked Luke about it one time, and he told me that Adrienne's dad, a surgeon a few towns away, stopped trying to be involved in Adrienne's life when she was five. Since then, it was just something we all knew. Including Sydney, who must've been too preoccupied in high school to take permanent notice. I blamed Henry.

Thankfully for Syd, Adrienne—a warrior and sunflower wrapped up into one little person—was never bothered by the assumptions that she had both parents in the picture. She took it like a champion, just like everything else.

"No worries. Really."

We moved on to the details of the Thursday night party at our house, a conversation which mostly included sighs from Braeden and the biting of nails by Adrienne. I'd just swung my leg over Braeden's shoulder when the front door to the house whipped open with a *bang*. Adrienne's sentence was cut in half, and every ounce of attention in the room was immediately turned to Ronan, who burst into the foyer, seemingly with a purpose.

"Woah," he remarked, grabbing ahold of the door and gently pushing it closed behind him. "Man, it's hot out there."

"Why are you so stompy?" I asked.

Ronan frowned. "I am not stompy."

"You almost took down the front door."

He clicked his tongue. "Must be I don't know my own strengths, then. Like the Hulk."

Braeden looked at me, anticipating a response.

"Maybe, but you cannot pull off Bruce Banner."

"That's the biggest lie you've ever told, Elliana."

Touché.

"Jesus Christ," Sydney groaned, leaning her head back on the couch. "I need a chainsaw."

Braeden laughed. "Why?"

She looked at me, then Ronan. "To cut the sexual tension between you two."

My eyes widened. "*Sydney*."

Ronan didn't protest, which made my position even harder to hold. He just smiled, like he almost agreed. God.

Like the saving grace my mom believed her to be, Adrienne leaned forward, just out of Luke's arm, and focused her gaze on Ronan. He'd just gotten settled on the floor and was straightening his shirt.

"Alright, please tell us why you stormed in here with such vigor so poor Nell doesn't dissolve into that seat."

He cocked his head. "Vigor?"

"Enthusiasm," Sydney noted.

Ronan nodded. "I waited two hours in line at the DMV to renew my registration, just for them to tell me it wasn't up until September."

"It says the date on the sticker," I told him.

Ronan threw his hands up in the air. "Woah. Are you flirting with me?"

After Sydney snorted beside me, I leaned my head back onto my chair. What ever happened to the Ronan that I could love without being accused of being *in* love with? The more I thought about it, the more I dreaded walking down the aisle with him.

But when I picked up my head, taking a deep breath, Ronan offered me one of his real smiles, goofiness included. All was forgiven then, and he decided to change the subject, likely on my behalf. This small moment of quiet, however, was the last one I knew before every vein in my body was overcome with panic. Sheer, debilitating panic.

"Oh yeah," Ronan started innocently. "Guess who I ran into at the store."

No guesses, only slightly raised eyebrows.

"Mo."

This one word, name, sound, was enough to take my soul right out of my body. The next part of the conversation, I experienced from the outside. I wasn't in control of my heart or my mind. I didn't know what my face looked like.

"O'Brien?" It was a stupid question, sure, but my brain wasn't processing.

"No, the other Mo," Ronan joked.

I could feel my heart beating in my ears. "She's in town?" I asked with more of a jolt than I intended. "Why?"

There was a pause before Luke's slow and skeptical answer. "The wedding?"

Adrienne was visibly curious as to why my voice had raised and my heart had dropped. If only she knew. The problem was, none of them did. For so long, I thought that this was a good thing. The best thing. But now I just looked crazy.

"She's helping her dad pack up the house. He's moving back up to New York after the wedding to be closer to her," Adrienne told me, a fact everyone else seemed to have known.

I turned to her much too quickly. "I didn't know she was coming to the wedding."

"Have you even looked at the guest list?" Ronan asked.

"The last time I checked, I didn't–" I shook my head, pressed my eyelids together so tightly I was seeing stars. "I didn't see her name."

"You two haven't talked?" Luke asked.

Next to me, Sydney was silent. She was the only one who knew the whole story. I intended to keep it that way, but I'd always been an open book when it came to my friends. Whether I wanted to be or not.

The mere thought of seeing Mo again terrified me to my core. I wanted to kick myself for not thinking she'd be at the wedding. Of course she would. She and Luke and Adrienne had probably remained close throughout the past four years. Unlike their relationship with Finn, I'd just never asked.

As I was thinking this, and everyone was staring intently at me, the oven timer started beeping. With it, the smell of cookies flooded back into my nose, and I could see clearly again. I stood up, filled my chest with air, and went toward it.

"I'll get that."

In the kitchen, after I safely removed the cookie sheet from the oven and placed it on the stovetop, my eyes wandered through the window and to the shore. I could almost feel the heat radiating from the sun as it set over the water. My eyes fell naturally to the waves crashing along the sand underneath the hazy sky, and then I closed them. When I did, my imagination got the best of me, flashing to a golden sun lighting up the face of a freckled girl with curly red hair. I shook the picture away, took a breath, and went back to my friends.

I wasn't Elliana anymore. Things were different.

Chapter Thirteen

Elliana

It had been three hours since Foster Baxton showed up on my doorstep wearing a sport coat—I was almost too warm in a tank top, so I couldn't imagine what his shirt underneath looked like.

We'd just eaten dinner, the cuisine of which wasn't at all different from a typical night at Archie's, and were now walking toward the pier. The Not Date was actually much different than I was expecting. Bax wasn't the same when he was by himself; he was tolerable, for one. Maybe he was just nervous.

By suggestion of Mo, I decided to dress casually. And by that, I mean that I was wearing ripped jeans for the first time in my life. My hair was straight as a pin, but I let Adrienne throw a braid into it ten minutes before I left. On top of that, I was wearing blue Converse with green socks. I was practically unrecognizable.

"So have you started looking at colleges yet?" Bax asked. His hair was lacking its usual gel-like glimmer. It was brushed out, and looked remarkably soft. I almost felt guilty that he'd put so much effort into the night.

"Not really," I started, leaving out the fact that I tended to avoid the college conversation at all costs. Even though it was two years away, the idea of leaving home scared me more than I wanted to admit. I had no intentions of going very far, but it would still be a big change. "A couple of local schools, but nothing too extensive yet. You?"

"My mom wants me to look at schools in Michigan." Next to him, a little boy ran past with a cloud of blue cotton candy on a paper cone. He barely noticed.

"Why Michigan?"

"She lives there," he told me.

I turned to him, taking note of his lack of googly eyes. "I didn't know that."

"She moved there with her husband when I was eleven. My brother and I stayed here because we didn't want to switch schools."

Huh. No one had a good time that year, it seemed.

"That sounds complicated."

Bax shrugged. "Not really."

Since this was bordering on big-talk, I was starting to grow uncomfortable. Unfortunately for me, I didn't really know a way out of it.

"Do you ever see her?"

"At Christmas. And every other summer. But that'll probably change once I move out."

I wasn't naive enough to think that everyone had the kind of family that I did. But I was always caught off guard by how complex some of my peers' home situations were. I couldn't imagine only seeing my mom for that amount of time each year, and I was lucky that I didn't have to.

"I'm sorry," I said, and I really meant it.

"Nah," he said. "It's just about how long I can stand her husband for, anyways."

"Not a nice guy?"

He pursed his lips, stuck his hands in his coat pockets as we made a left turn onto the pier. Now, we were walking over the ocean. I breathed it in.

"He's nice. He just tries too hard to be a father figure," he claimed. "Me and RJ already have one of those. We don't need another one."

This was precisely where I lost any words of advice I'd been wracking my brain for. I had no expertise here, so I went out on a whim.

"One of my brother's friends has two dads," I told him. "Maybe we weren't all meant to have just one."

Once this was out in the open, I realized just how much I believed it. Not only would it be painstakingly boring if every family looked the same, but the world would be deprived of so much love.

To my slight dismay, Bax didn't seem as convinced. He shrugged his shoulders, his lips forming a diagonal line. "I guess when you put it that way. Sure."

We were still walking, albeit slowly, toward the end of the pier. Around us, there were couples and friends and families all enjoying romantic nights of their own. I wished I could've said the same.

With an impending change of subject, Bax's face lit up again. "Oh, speaking of that, do you know Piper Frag?"

I nodded. "She's on the basketball team."

"She is?" His eyebrows furrowed. "Well, anyways, I heard that she's, like, bisexual now or something."

There was a whole lot to unpack there, but I found myself stuck on one word in particular.

"Now?"

"I guess she had a girlfriend in South Carolina or something last year. But before that she'd only dated guys. And I guess she's still into them, too."

I wanted to ask, well, so many things. But Bax just kept going.

"Sonny Rosenthal was going to ask her to the sophomore dance, but now he's not."

Involuntarily, though perhaps not surprisingly, my mind flashed to Mo. She was so confident in who she was, so open in talking about it, that I was sure she was willing to defend any conversation regarding the subject that had gone awry. I wondered what she would've thought of this one.

Not only that, but I was pretty sure Piper Frag's sexuality wasn't up for debate by anyone but Piper herself.

I slowed my pace slightly, making a conscious effort to be deliberate with what words I used next.

"Why is Sonny not asking her to the dance?"

Bax looked me in the eyes. Back and forth, like I was the one missing something. "I guess he feels weird."

"Because she likes girls?"

"Well, yeah," Bax offered almost innocently.

144

I wasn't sure if anything wrong had even happened, but I didn't feel right. My skin was itching and my blood was beginning to boil. I wasn't one to get angry, and I rarely judged people for their beliefs, but being a part of this conversation felt dirty. If someone felt weird around Mo because of who she chose to love, I would've been mad. I had no reason to believe this was any different.

"Wait," I said, stopping in my tracks. This, Bax couldn't miss, so he stopped, too. "I'm not saying that I do, because I don't, but would you still have asked me out if I liked girls?"

He wasn't expecting that; it was written all over his face. He shook his head. "Like, exclusively?"

"No. If I was bisexual like you presume Piper to be."

"Yes." He hesitated before he repeated himself. "Yes. Of course I would've."

I nodded, royally unconvinced. "And if the whole school knew that I also liked girls, would that have changed the fact that you were going to ask me to the dance when we got to the end of this pier?"

I'd promised both Henry and Sydney I wouldn't reveal to Bax that I knew of his plan, but it looked like I wasn't sticking to any of my rules tonight.

Bax's gaze turned desperate, looking at me for his answer instead of at himself. "I don't– I don't think so."

I took a step back, doubling the distance that was between us. I was visibly upset, and now people around us were noticing, silencing their conversations and adjusting their views to listen in. I didn't care, and that alone was liberating.

"You don't think so."

"I mean, no. No, it wouldn't change anything. I asked you here tonight because I like you, Elliana. That's it."

He was panicking now, and I started to feel guilty about it. I never meant to make him squirm, and maybe it wasn't my place to be so upset. But just when I was going to back down, or was thinking about it, he spoke again.

"Wait. Do you, though?"

"Do I what?"

His eye twitched. Literally. "Like girls."

"I just told you—"

I stopped myself, taking a second to glance out at the water. The sun had already set, so there was no sign of light. But the waves were still moving all around me. I could hear them, if I listened close enough.

Like Mo said, if I wasn't having a good time, I could just leave. It was my life, and I wasn't coasting. Not tonight.

"Have a good night, Bax," I told him, offering a smile and turning away.

"Elliana—"

I waved over my shoulder. "See you at school."

I found my way back down the pier, weaving in and out of the crowds. From moms holding toddlers on their hips to teenagers carrying arcade tickets and sugary drinks, the place felt alive. As yet another turn of events, I did, too.

Once I made it to the boardwalk, I slipped off my sneakers and socks, holding them tightly in my hand as I opted for the beach. My toes dug into the sand with every step, and the breeze that touched my skin kept the fire in me burning. Now I knew why Mo preferred this route.

When I arrived home, the house was mostly dark, save for the light coming from the den down the hall from the kitchen, where my mom was probably reading. She liked to wait up for us kids, especially on nights like this one where Luke was with his lacrosse friends and I was on a date. The last part, of course, was a rarity. But it still counted.

I still had some time before I was due home, so I didn't stay in the house very long. I wasn't ready to sit in my quiet room or detail the night to my parents. Though I knew my mom would have my head if she saw me walking home via the beach, I needed to be next to the waves. So I left my shoes on the deck and headed back to the sand.

When I sat, I made sure that my jeans remained dry— they were actually Adrienne's and not mine—but was close enough to the water that my toes caught the ends of the bigger waves. I wasn't sure I wanted to think about the date, or about why my cheeks and ears were so hot. I didn't try to ask the sky what had happened, or look to the moon for advice. I knew that whatever I was feeling had something to do with me, and maybe I should've tried to figure it out. But what I couldn't stop focusing on, and what was the loudest voice in my head as I sat there, was that I was *feeling* something. It wasn't astronomical and it wasn't worth screaming off of a mountain top, but there was something making the blood in my veins move faster and bringing color to my face. That meant something, I knew it.

Of course, this not-thinking could only last so long. After a few moments, each wave that crashed before me started to sound less like a beautiful note in the ocean's song and more like a question about what had happened at the pier. And then a question about Piper Frag. And then about Mo. And then—

"Aren't you supposed to be at the boardwalk?"

I turned around half-way to find Luke, his hands in the pockets of his shorts and his dirty blonde hair peeking out from underneath the purple hood of his sweatshirt. He took one look at my face and likely realized the magnitude of my sitting on the beach. Within the next few seconds, he was sitting beside me.

"I thought you were at a lacrosse party," I noted, avoiding the elephant on the beach.

"Braeden needed a ride home from his friend's house so I left early," he told me.

I nodded. "Where are Finn and Ronan?"

"Musical rehearsal, parents' anniversary dinner."

"And Adrienne's at rehearsal too?"

Out of the corner of my eye, I saw him nod. "Looks like you're stuck with just me."

Now I turned fully, and found him to be staring out at the waves just as I was. "That's not a bad thing."

Luke smiled, and I knew I didn't owe him any sort of explanation for my questioning. It was just strange to see him alone, but not at all weird that we were. It was actually kind of nice.

"So are you going to tell me why you're sitting alone in the dark?"

I shrugged my shoulders. "I wasn't really planning on it."

This was an uncharacteristic response, and it forced a laugh out of Luke. After he saw the smile on my face, he tried again.

"Are you alright?"

I dug my toes further into the sand. Maybe I did want to talk about it.

"I don't like Bax."

Luke sat with this for a second, and I wondered what exactly was going through his mind. He took a deep breath, the next look he gave me being a protective one.

"Did he do something?"

I shook my head, saving Bax from a midnight visit from Luke and his posse. "He just said something I didn't like," I told him. "Not about me, but about someone I know. It didn't feel right."

"What was it about?"

This question was one I didn't know I was afraid of. If I told Luke everything, what would he think? I wasn't sure how much he knew about Piper. Or, more importantly, Mo. It wasn't my place to tell him what she'd told me, but now I was worried that my defensiveness could be taken a different way. Silence, I figured, would probably be worse.

"It was something that felt sort of homophobic," I said, meeting his eyes then looking away quickly. "I don't know if it was, and it might not even be my place to be mad–"

"Elliana," Luke interrupted, his voice sincere, "you can be upset about something even if it's not directed toward you. Having compassion is a good thing, not an intrusion."

Of course Luke was right. There was just something so urgent about what Bax had said, something that felt like a punch in the gut. I hadn't been this upset about anything in years. But I certainly didn't want to show it.

"Well, there's definitely not going to be a second date," I told him. "There shouldn't have even been a first one."

At this, his smile grew wider. I could see the white of his teeth even through the darkness. "So it *was* a date."

Luke might've been exactly what I needed when I needed it, but rest assured, he was still my brother. With this collective, silent agreement, Luke threw his arm around both of my shoulders.

"Don't worry about Bax," he told me. "No guy will ever be good enough for you anyways."

After school a few days later, I accompanied Adrienne and Mo to Magnes' Makings, a shop on the boardwalk that sold upcycled clothing. When we arrived back home, Adrienne headed to the den with my mom to go through some of her old nursing school equipment. The less Adrienne had to buy within the next few years, the better.

I was sure, however, that within a few minutes there'd be laughter coming from down the hall, a sign that productivity wasn't a priority. I smiled just thinking about it. Adrienne wasn't just a saving grace for Luke.

As for me, I was headed to the shoreline with Mo. She insisted that it was too perfect a day to be sitting inside, and after the past few days at school with Bax's words running rampant in my mind, I wanted the fresh air, too. Alone time with Mo was just a plus.

"So you want to study fashion?" I asked once we were together on the sand.

On the way home from the boardwalk, after I painfully recounted my date with Bax (save for some details), Mo and Adrienne talked about college—their orientation dates, the people they knew going to their schools, what they'd heard about the experience. I wanted to tune out the conversation, because the thought of everyone leaving was certainly not a good one, but I was invested.

"I do," Mo said, her hair blowing in even the smallest of winds. "I think it'd be cool to have an influence on the way people express themselves, and clothing plays a really big part in that."

I nodded, though it wasn't something I really knew. The furthest my fashion sense went was a plaid skirt and matching tie, and I could hardly claim it as my own.

"I want to minor in Latin, too," she continued.

I raised my eyebrows. This was new. At least to me. "Does anyone even speak Latin anymore?"

Mo let out a laugh. It was obviously a valid question.

"Not really. But most of the languages we do speak are derived from Latin," she told me. "The language is actually considered dead."

"Why are you going to spend all of your time and money on learning it, then?"

There was a pause. "Because I want to."

Right.

In front of us, the sun was beginning its descent. Though its colors were vibrant and bold, the picture that the sky was painting was soft and inviting. Golden Hour was taking on its newest meaning with every second that passed.

"So which language is your favorite?" I asked then. "Out of all the ones you know."

We'd made it to the water now. Like it was my job, I sat down on the sand, allowing my legs to feel its coolness. Mo stayed in front of me, walking the imaginary line that the waves were making like a tightrope.

"Probably French."

"Why?"

"It's romantic." She looked at me with a smile on her face and a rosiness filling her cheeks. "Sometimes I imagine myself living the rest of my life out in Paris. Staying in a small apartment with the person I love, doing things tourists would never. If I wouldn't be limiting myself so much, I might even start now."

Now, I let out a laugh. For someone so go-with-the-flow, this sure sounded like she had a plan.

"I never would've thought you were the romantic type."

Hearing this, a new kind of look flooded Mo's face, one I hadn't yet seen. She was surprised, and maybe even a little offended. The latter faded very quickly, however. I barely had time to worry that I'd hurt her feelings.

"I guess I see what you mean," she told me. She'd gone back to her tightrope, some of her curly hair falling in front of her eyes as she walked. She didn't push it away. "When I was little, there were rumors at school that a meteor was headed straight for Earth, and that the world was going to end. Do you remember that?"

I nodded. I was in the fourth grade when that happened. I cried for a week.

"Well, the way my dad tells it, it was the most hysterical he'd ever seen me."

I was laughing just at the thought of it. "Really?"

"And not because I was afraid of the meteor. I didn't even care that some of the boys in my class were saying that it was headed right for New York."

"What were you upset about, then?"

"That the world was going to end, and I was never going to get the chance to fall in love."

I lifted my hand, involuntarily as ever, to cover my mouth. "You said that?"

Her grin grew wider, the look I was so worried about now a world away. "Word-for-word."

"How old were you? Twelve?"

"Ten," she corrected, but only because I'd asked. "Almost eleven."

Right, I thought. Two grades ahead of me in high school, but less than a year older. This was something Mo shared in passing one day, and I hated that it had slipped my mind.

"Wow," I said. "Well, now the whole Paris thing makes perfect sense."

Mo's smile remained, but this time she brushed the hair away from her face. Now, I could see her eyes.

"Have you ever been?" she asked.

"To Paris?"

"In love."

Mo had stopped walking, and for a second, the sound of the waves was the only thing coming to my mind. I shouldn't have had to dig for an answer. Mine was simple.

"No," I told her. "Which is kind of embarrassing, I guess."

Mo's laugh was soft and sweet. "I'd hardly say that." She was walking again now, on the tips of her toes, with a bit more of a bounce in her steps. "I haven't either. In case you were wondering."

"I was."

She smiled again, and I realized that she had been for most of the conversation. She was never really smiling when I saw her in the halls at school, but always was when she was around us—Luke, Adrienne, Finn, Ronan, and me. It made me wonder what kind of people she knew back in New York, what kind of life she had. I wondered if she was happier here.

"Well, I'm sure Rose will have the chance to fall in love."

For once, I thought I knew my place in a conversation. But now I was lost.

"Who's Rose?"

Mo grinned. "Your alter ego."

"Oh good," I laughed. "You're back on the nickname thing."

"Come on," she said, finally taking a seat next to me. I took a deep breath. "You have to want a nickname."

"I like Elliana. My parents would probably agree."

"I like Elliana too," Mo said, a hesitant pause at the end of the sentence, as if she'd said something wrong. She shook it away, and so did I. "But it should be reserved for people that don't know you. Like teachers."

"Well, some teachers do call me Rose. They all had Luke, so."

Mo shook her head, as this was apparently a valid excuse. "Okay. Ellie."

"There are three Ellies in my class," I countered.

"Elle?"

I shook my head at the same time as Mo. It was a pretty name, but it just didn't fit. I was glad she agreed without my having to put up a fight.

"Fine," she said. "I guess it'll just come to us."

There was such a simplicity in the way Mo joined the two of us together into one. We were such opposites, but somehow the harmony of *us* sounded so good together. Maybe it was just me.

"It will," I said, though I still wasn't fully convinced about the nicknaming of it all. I just liked talking to her, so I was willing to entertain the idea. "I have one more question about the French thing," I said, turning to face Mo completely.

"Shoot," she told me.

"What's the best phrase?"

"The best phrase?"

I nodded. "Like, your favorite thing to say," I clarified. "Maybe that doesn't make sense. I never took a language, so—"

"No, it does." Mo paused, her toes now digging into the sand in front of us as she thought about it. I was honored that she was putting so much effort into such a silly question. "Ce n'est pas la mer à boire."

For a moment, I believed I was going to be able to figure it out, like I had some language-barrier-defying superpower. But I was stumped. This, Mo took immediate notice of. She flashed me a smile as she turned back toward the water.

"It's not as if you have to drink the sea."

Chapter Fourteen

Nell

"I think we need a code word."

"For what?"

Ronan took a deep breath. "For if the other groomsmen hate me and I need an out."

This, I knew, was just not going to happen. Of course, I had no other choice but to entertain the idea.

We were standing on the beach awaiting the arrival of the bridal party. The rest of it, that is. So far, it was the happy couple, Ronan and me, Adrienne's two good friends from nursing school—Logan and Renna, cousins who grew up in Colorado together—and Braeden. We were waiting on both of Luke's other groomsmen—Brett and Jackson, both business majors and one attending culinary school with Luke in the fall—and Jess, Adrienne's friend from high school who had a severe case of Resting Bitch Face. I hadn't seen her since I was sixteen, but apparently she and Adrienne had remained close. I wondered if she'd gotten softer.

The beach day was planned with remarkable luck. It was just a few days before the wedding festivities began, the whole party was arriving the same morning, and the weather turned out to be beautiful. There were few clouds in the sky, a light wind to keep the heat at bay, and a sparkling ocean at our fingertips. Of course, it was Adrienne who had done the planning, so perfection was what I should've expected.

Weather and timing aside, I was crumbling. Both physically and emotionally. I'd taken a six-mile run in the morning in an attempt to clear my mind from the thought of oh-so-many things, but all I'd done was exhausted every muscle in my body. Add to that the fact that I hadn't slept in three nights—the thought of seeing Mo again at the wedding was not only keeping me awake, but giving me unshakable nightmares—and this was what you had: noodle bones, noodle brain, and the inability to have a normal conversation with Ronan. Then again, that last part wasn't abnormal.

"Okay," I said, watching as Adrienne tightened the back of Logan's lime green bikini top. "What's the word?"

Ronan thought on it, obviously not for long enough. "Hulk."

I felt my face drop. "Hulk?"

He nodded.

"Isn't a code word supposed to be something you can actually work into a conversation?"

He frowned. "I can work Hulk into any conversation."

I let out a sigh. I had no fight left in me, which was definitely not a good thing so early in the week.

"Fine," I surrendered. "What if I need one? Should mine be different?"

"Why would you need one?" Ronan asked, searching my expression for an answer.

I shook my head. "For the same reason. If they hate me and I need an out."

At this, Ronan let out a laugh. For the life of me, I could not figure out what was funny.

"What?"

He was still laughing. He raised his hand up to pat my bare shoulder and shook his head. "No one could ever hate you."

I wished that this part of our conversation wasn't punctuated by the entrance of Brett and Jackson. I felt bad that I'd given in so easily to Ronan's assumption that he could be hated when the idea of someone feeling that way about me was so comical to him. Lucky for him, in just a few days he'd have the opportunity to see someone hate me firsthand. At this point, I wasn't even sure who would take the cake in that sense. The options were only growing.

A few minutes later, the party finally began with the arrival of Jess, whose involvement in the wedding Ronan had entirely forgotten about. To say we were the most chaotic and underprepared of all Best Men and Maids of Honor everywhere would have been a vast understatement. Hopefully we still had time to turn it around.

By the time Braeden switched to the second playlist of the day—a privilege that came with aux cord control—I concluded that Jess had not only gotten softer, but now she was *nice*. I also found that Jackson, Luke's roommate who was joining him at culinary school, was incredibly funny and charming. If Sydney hadn't already been taken, I would've given her a call.

Brett, the last of the groomsmen to make my acquaintance, was just as charming. It might've been because he looked almost exactly like Corbin Bleu—he'd been told he was his doppelgänger on several occasions—but also because he was so gung-ho on learning about Braeden and me. I found it hard to turn away from anyone who made that genuine of an effort. Looking like one of my favorite Disney Channel stars was just icing on top.

Then there were Logan and Renna who, if they'd gone to St. Jane's, would've fit perfectly into the group of friends that used to sit around the fire pit on the beach at night. Our group of friends, I mean.

They were both kind, talkative, interesting. Renna, for example, spent her spare time teaching contemporary dance to women in their thirties and forties who always dreamed of being on stage but never got the chance. Logan had a black belt in jiu jitsu, but looked like she wouldn't hurt a fly. Talk to one, maybe, but not hurt it.

Most of all, they were weird and they knew it. That was what told me they were meant to be on the beach with us now.

After a few hours, I was so tuckered out that I wanted to float on top of the waves and drift off into the setting sun. But just as I'd finished a riveting conversation with Ronan, the comfort of whom I was really grateful for, I spotted Adrienne walking back into the water where the party had just relocated. She was holding her water bottle, walking her normal walk, and biting her lip.

"I think everything's going pretty well, don't you?"

I'd made it to her side in record time, while also keeping my cool so as to not draw any attention to the situation that was obviously dire. In response to my question, Adrienne released her lip and offered me a smile.

"I'm glad everyone's getting along," she told me. "Not that I was worried."

I nodded. In front of us, Ronan and Jess were joined by Jackson. I saw an immediate release of tension in Ronan's shoulders, but I couldn't laugh. Not now.

"How's Luke been?"

I was poking around. Testing the waters, so to speak. We all knew I was never discrete, at least not anymore. Adrienne could probably see right through me. By the way she looked at me, I wasn't entirely convinced otherwise.

She let out a breath, and I watched as the smile on her face grew a little bit faker.

"I think I know what's bothering him," she told me.

I studied her face, then realized that the smile she was wearing was so no one else suspected our conversation was going this way. Adrienne was a sweetheart, but also quite clever.

"Is he still being quiet?"

She nodded, laughed at the way Braeden was hanging onto Luke's shoulders just in case one of them looked on. I hoped the waves were drowning us out enough, and I was sure my face wasn't as convincing as Adrienne's.

"He's gotten quieter. But it's mostly at night. I can tell he's thinking," she said.

"Why?"

She blinked a few times, prepared herself to break whatever news she needed to. I held my breath.

"Because. Someone's missing."

Someone was missing. Okay. Was the wedding turning into a search party? I watched her expression, waiting for the rest of the explanation.

She turned to me, her fake smile faltering. I could see the desperation in her eyes, but not all of it.

"From all of this." She motioned toward the water, where her groom and wedding party were all existing in perfect harmony.

My mind immediately rewound to the way I'd reacted to the news of Mo's attendance at the wedding. If Luke and Adrienne had known somehow, and if they'd kept her out of the wedding party on my behalf, I would have been devastated. I looked right into Adrienne's eyes, hoping to find some confirmation of this so I didn't have to say it aloud.

"What do you—"

"Finn."

Suddenly, the waves hitting my knees couldn't possibly have been refreshing enough, while the sand beneath my feet wanted to pull me under. I blinked, likely several times, and attempted to gather my bearings before Adrienne noticed that she'd just ripped my heart out through my ears. To my dismay, I wasn't quick enough.

"Nell," she demanded. "What is your face right now?"

I shook my head, and my voice came out quieter than I anticipated. "How do you know that's what's bothering Luke?"

Her answer came out before I even breathed.

"Because it's the same thing that's bothering me."

This made perfect sense. And, at the same time, it was the most confusing thing I'd ever heard. If Adrienne and Luke were so upset that Finn wasn't coming to the wedding, why had I gone all the way to Pittsburgh to invite him?

"Why don't they talk?" I asked, neglecting any attempt I'd been making to hide the depth of our conversation from the others.

Adrienne was on the same page. "I've been trying to figure that out for four years."

"You've never just asked?"

This was a face I'd never seen on Adrienne before. It said *I can't believe you actually just asked me that question*, and it made me laugh.

"Sorry."

"Luke used to just say, 'It's bad,' and Ronan would say, 'You don't want to know.'" She used air quotes for both instances, then settled herself before we caused a scene. I didn't care so much about that anymore. This was invigorating, and the closest I'd gotten to the truth in the last four years. She and I were both in the dark, but at least we were together. But then, maybe we were getting somewhere. "I think it has something to do with their last lacrosse game."

I lowered my eyebrows. "Do you remember if they were drinking before?"

Now, I knew what this looked like, but I hadn't really thought this far ahead. Obviously.

"Drinking? Like, alcohol?"

What an odd thing to say. I nodded.

"I don't–" She blinked, hard. "Why is that your next question?"

"Do you remember?"

"Is that a tattoo?"

In the grand scheme of things, this is probably as thrown off as I could've possibly been. I nearly fell over.

I'd gotten the tattoo just after Spring Break, so the fact that I'd hidden it for this long was pretty impressive, I had to admit. If I hadn't been wearing the wrong bikini top, I might've even lasted the whole summer.

I followed Adrienne's gaze to my ribcage and—would you look at that—there it was. I traced my finger along it, which was an invitation for Adrienne to do the same, then shrugged.

"I guess so."

"*Find her,*" Adrienne said sweetly, admirably. "I love it. What does it mean?"

"I don't really know," I said, which I knew she'd never believe. But we had business to take care of. "Were they drinking?"

"When did you get it?"

I sighed. "This year, at school. Don't tell my mom."

At this, Adrienne smiled. She probably figured she'd get the story when I wanted to tell it, which certainly wasn't now. Back to business we went.

"I don't remember if they were drinking," she told me. "Why does that matter?"

Just ahead, Brett and Renna pulled Jackson out of his conversation with Ronan and Jess. I watched as Ronan's eyes politely searched for Luke, then for an end to the conversation, as Jess kept talking. Now, time was ticking.

"I didn't go to Vermont."

Understandably, this was confusing.

"What?"

"I didn't go to Vermont." Here came the word vomit. "I flew to Pittsburgh and found Finn and I invited him to the wedding. And I told my whole family and you and Ronan that I was going to Vermont because I thought if any of you found out what I was really doing, you'd stop me."

Adrienne breathlessly looked away from me, her eyes falling to the water in front of us. If anyone else looked over, they would've thought I'd just told her she had three months to live.

"I'm sorry," I said quickly, quietly. "I shouldn't have gone behind your backs, and I know how disrespectful it was to intrude on the wedding like that. You have every right to—"

I stopped because Adrienne held up her hand. She was probably thinking about how best to yell at me without causing a tidal wave.

"Is he coming?"

I shook my head and shrugged at the same time. "I don't know."

Her chest rose and fell quickly as she took a sharp breath, then another one.

"Are you having a panic attack?" I asked.

"No," she told me. Underneath her words, I heard a laugh. When I looked at her again, after checking our surroundings to make sure we were still in the clear, her lips were curling into a smile. It was a small one, carrying so much

160

weight that I knew just what it meant, but it was still there. For that, I could finally breathe. "Nell, you did a good thing."

"I did?"

She nodded, still deep in thought. In the silence, I remembered just how the conversation started. Since Adrienne already had so much to think about, as did I, what was one more detail going to do?

"He told me that they haven't spoken because he sold them out to Coach Allenson for drinking before the game."

All the thoughts fell right out of Adrienne's ears and into the ocean. She looked back up at me, puzzled as ever. "*What?*" she huffed. "That's ridiculous. There's no way all of this is over something so small."

I shook my head. "I know."

She was silent again, attention back on the waves. After a moment, her eyes grew softer, and she almost looked sad.

"Is he still with that girl? The one he met freshman year?"

Now, this question meant plenty of things, many of which I couldn't put my finger on. Maybe I wasn't the only one with a big secret, after all.

"Sutton?"

Now she was smiling again. "Yeah."

I nodded, albeit slowly. "He lives with her and her daughter in the city."

Adrienne lifted her hand to her heart, her face showing nothing but love and relief.

"Um—"

"Oh," she said, shaking her head. "Finn and I talked a couple of times, but it kind of fell off after that year. He got super unresponsive, like he didn't want to hear from me."

"Really?"

She nodded, her eyes going blank with the thought. "It tore me apart."

My miniscule heartbreak was interrupted by the pull of Ronan's eyes. He was still in front of us, now standing with Jess and Renna, and looked desperately like he needed an out. Even if his eyes weren't screaming it, his body language was.

"Nell's actually a Marvel fanatic, believe it or not," he announced.

I knew what was coming, so I turned to Adrienne. She was catching on, but I could still see the past replaying in her eyes.

"What do we do?" I asked, not about Ronan but about the Big Picture.

"Hey, Nell, didn't you say your favorite movie was *The Incredible Hulk?*"

Adrienne turned to me quickly, the fake smile having returned. She was good.

"You get Finn to come to the wedding."

I nodded, then immediately stopped. "What about Luke and Ronan?"

There was a beat, then a breath. "Don't worry about them. It's been long enough."

"Nell? The Hulk?"

Adrienne and I were on our way now. To the rescue, if you would. I was nearly shaking from the inside out. I felt excited and nervous and hopeful and maybe even a little bit angry still, that so much time had been taken from us and that the memories we used to share together stopped so prematurely. Only now, I finally had hope that we might see those days again. I knew, in the end, it would be worth it. Whatever it took.

"I do love Marvel," I said, joining Ronan's side and nudging him with my elbow to let him know I was there. "I'm actually more of a Black Widow fan, though."

Chapter Fifteen

Elliana

I kicked off my shoes right as the air conditioning made it to my skin, and before I made it further than the doormat. I was trailing behind Ronan and Luke, who did no such thing, and beside Mo, who followed my lead.

"So. No to pressure, but yes to rules."

I glanced over as she said this, then shrugged. She was right, I guess. I just didn't love hearing it out loud, and I wasn't sure why.

"I'm just trying to figure you out," she said.

This phrase could have been used in a condescending way, but Mo said it with a smile, and somehow I knew exactly what she meant.

"Me too," I told her.

The boys bustled down the hallway, Ronan making Luke squirm by telling him all of the bones in his body were "wet right this second." They were supposed to be recycling the pizza boxes from the beach, but I had a feeling that task was going to take longer than it needed to.

Though it was getting late, our night still had some promising momentum. We'd eaten dinner at the house, courtesy of Chefs Luke and Adam Rose, and everyone came. The regulars, of course, plus Sydney and Henry, Adrienne's mom Ms. Brenda, and Ronan's parents. It was the biggest crowd we'd had in a while, and we'd been carrying the fun on at the beach, where a fire had been roaring, for a few hours.

Normally, I stayed at a fire like this one late, unless I had school or basketball in the morning. This time, I had both—Coach Pieter was starting our summer workouts early this year, and that meant a Team Lift before the first bell.

But now, even though most of the crew had gone home, I was having much too good a time to stay in for the night. Maybe I'd regret it in the morning, and maybe I had a pit in my stomach for going against my usual ways. There was just something about the night, about the memories I knew we were making, that I wanted to hold onto for a little bit longer.

"I don't know why I feel the need to follow the rules," I told her. "They've always just worked for me."

I'd never been a liar. Not once, actually, at least in recent memory. But there was something in my voice that suggested this reasoning wasn't exactly true. I did know why I had a need to follow the rules, and it wasn't always that they'd worked for me. I could've pointed to the day that necessity made its way to my bones in the form of fear. But I wasn't going to.

"Well, everyone has their shtick," she told me. "And if it's a part of who you are then it's not a bad thing."

Mo had picked up her shoes and was heading to the front door with them in her hands. I wondered if she would've kept them on had I not been accompanying her.

"How do you figure that?"

Mo turned to me, her face serious. Her cheeks were rosy beneath her freckles. "There aren't any bad parts of you."

I nodded, though it took all of me not to list every thing I could think of about myself that would fall under the Bad or Undesirable categories. I had a feeling that I'd only start blushing if I did. Mo, like the rest of Luke's friends, had learned to quickly shut down my self deprecation. With her, though, it felt like she came into my life with that instinct.

"You're not taking the beach route?" I asked instead.

Mo drew open the front door, twisting her hair into a knot on top of her head as the fresh air stormed inside.

"I told my dad I'd grab us some pizza from the gas station." She let out a mix of a breath and a laugh. "He swears it's the closest you can get to New York down here."

"You're getting pizza at eleven at night?"

She grinned. "It's our shtick."

Right. There were rules, and then there were midnight trips to places most people preferred to visit only in the daylight.

We couldn't have been more opposite from one another; the universe reminded me of it every day. But then, here we were.

After I said goodbye to Mo, and she to me, I retrieved a blanket from the living room, then headed for the beach. It was only Adrienne and Finn left, and as I approached them from behind, I could hear a conversation unfolding. I didn't want to interrupt, so I slowed my pace.

"...and my family was never like that. Even before my dad left, it was always just my mom and me," Adrienne was saying, her silhouette outlined by the dancing fire.

I watched Finn nod, his blank stare aiming at the flames. "Yeah, if me and my parents all sat at the dinner table together, I'd think the world was ending. If it's not screaming, it's silent."

Adrienne looked at Finn, her eyes studying the sadness in his. "I hate the quiet." She looked down at her feet that sat crossed in front of her. "I think that's why I've always been so drawn to big families."

"And friends that are family," Finn agreed, meeting her eyes. They shared a smile, one I never could have taken part in. They related on a level that I was lucky not to, and I hadn't ever realized it.

I was close enough now that they could've heard my footsteps, but they didn't.

"Luke doesn't always get it," Adrienne said then.

I stopped in my tracks. Talking about their complicated families was one thing, but I didn't want to be involved in a conversation about Luke had they kept going when I arrived. It wasn't my place.

"When I try to explain it to him, I mean," she continued. "He's had this family his whole life, you know? And when everything happened with Stella, I think it just made them all so much closer without them realizing it. It sounds awful, but even then I was jealous of what they had and I didn't."

"There's nothing wrong with that," Finn said, like he'd felt it too. "I'd have no idea how to handle something like that with my family. I'd just turn to you guys."

I felt a pang in my chest and continued to hold my breath, thinking about the way Finn's face looked when he told me his father was sick. He seemed so confused, his feelings so complicated. Maybe I should've done more.

Adrienne nodded, though her mind was elsewhere now. "I don't know what we're all going to do in the fall."

Finn reached over naturally, placing his hand on her shoulder. "We'll be back before you know it."

Since they'd finally moved past feelings and memories too dark for me to handle, I decided that now was a good time to reenter the conversation. So I took the few steps I needed to be beside Finn, where I could feel the heat from the fire, and handed him the water bottle he'd politely asked for.

Finn flashed me a smile. "You're the best."

"You ready?" Luke asked suddenly.

I turned to find him stepping carefully over the pile of firewood next to Adrienne. He handed her a sweatshirt and then his own hand, pulling her gracefully to her feet.

"Thank you," she said, cozying herself next to him. She turned to Finn and me. "We're going to walk to the pier and back."

I nodded. After all of the chaos that ensued over the last few hours, they deserved some alone time. Now, though, I was wondering how long Luke had been behind me, and if he'd heard the same things I did. If I had to guess, he was probably moving too fast to notice.

"Make good choices," I told them. Finn laughed.

The two of us were alone then, a common occurrence in the ever-spinning record of our lives on this beach. The waves crashing in the distance and the fire crackling right before us were creating a peaceful soundtrack. I was so comfortable, in the presence of both Finn and the ocean, that I could've fallen asleep. But then, it wouldn't have been one of our Late Night Talks if there was no talking.

"So how did Syd and Henry take the news of the bum date?"

This was typical of Finn, to start the tough conversation in a light way. Begin with Sydney, sure, but I knew where it would end. At least I thought I did.

I pulled my knees to my chest, rearranging the blanket as it draped over my legs. "They expected the bum part," I told him, which he didn't deny because everyone expected it. "Not so happy with the Bax of it all."

Finn snorted. "The Bax of it all," he repeated under his breath.

There was a pause. In it, I knew I had two choices: to let Finn ask what he wanted to ask, or to bring it up myself. I wasn't sure if it was the looming morning hours or the damnation of my lifelong shtick, but my choice surprised me.

"Did Luke tell you what he said?"

After dinner one night, Luke had noticed my mind was elsewhere. To be fair, it had taken me twenty-five minutes to do the dishes, which was practically my specialty when it came to chores. So he asked and I answered. Then, I went up to my bedroom and stared at the ceiling, replaying that night on the boardwalk over and over and over, desperate to figure out why Bax's words made me feel the way they did. I kept coming back to one answer. Now, it was hidden somewhere upstairs, never to be found again.

Finn looked over at me, reading my face like a novel. "He said he'd let you. But you don't have to tell me if you don't want to."

I knew Finn meant what he said, just as much as I believed what Luke had told him. Though I typically felt nothing, I was realizing that the boys always made me feel respected. That was for sure.

"He was telling me about how Sonny Rosenthal doesn't want to ask Piper Frag to the dance anymore."

Finn blinked. Obviously, he was expecting much worse.

"And this is bad because Piper really likes to dance," he joked.

I shook my head, a smile fighting with what was coming next on my lips. "This is bad because he was going to ask her until he found out that she is also into girls."

These words were caught in the wind, but Finn heard them, and I knew he had questions. I, however, had to march on, or I knew I never would.

"And he was saying it like Sonny was justified," I told him. "So I asked him if he would've gone on a date with me if he knew I liked girls. I don't even remember what he said, but I can't get the way he said it out of my head. It was as if the whole concept was... wrong."

"The concept of liking girls?"

I nodded. "I felt like it offended him." I took a breath. "Maybe I took it the wrong way."

"Nothing you feel is wrong." Finn was looking at me now, emphasizing his words with his eyes. "Ever. You were uncomfortable, and you did something about it. I'm so proud of you for that, Elliana."

This hit me right in the heart, and it made me realize just how rare that instance on the boardwalk was. It replayed before me once more, my fingers toying with a pulled thread on the blanket.

"I've just never been one to stomp away."

Finn nodded, curled his lip. "Maybe it felt personal."

Half of my heart sank into the sand, while the other half found itself clogged in my throat. I knew what this meant, but I didn't want to.

"What do you mean?"

I waited what felt like hours for his answer, though he didn't really have to think about it at all.

"I mean, you and Mo are really close, right?" I gulped, while he unknowingly kept going. "Maybe you were just hurt because you know what he said would've hurt her." He elbowed me, a smile on his face. He had no idea the weight of the breath I'd just released. "You have empathy."

Right. It was empathy that was keeping me awake at night. Empathy who was setting fire to the idyllic life my basketball team crafted for me the week before playoffs. The perfect backyard, the husband who would take the kids water skiing on the weekends, the puppy-pageant winning dog. What did all of that look like if my choices were offensive? Who was I if I wasn't exactly the person everyone thought I was?

"Yeah," I said, a sort of cry escaping me in the form of a laugh. In front of me, the waves had calmed, the flames swaying along with their rhythm. "Empathy."

The sophomore dance: the one night that every sixteen-year-old at St. Jane's started looking forward to when they were ten. It was the first dance, officially, that any of us were allowed to attend. I was having a wonderful time avoiding it.

Instead, I was sitting on my living room floor, listening as the rain outside pounded against the many windows that surrounded me, and gluing.

Sydney was at the dance, Adrienne was baking with her mom, and the boys were at lacrosse practice, likely getting so soaked that my mother would have a cow upon their return home. So it was just Mo and me, using the entirety of our living room rug to put together posters for the boys' Senior Night, which was coming up all too quickly. I didn't have a creative bone in my body, so this was all obviously Mo's idea. But if I had to judge our work, I'd say we made a pretty good team.

"Okay. Little, seven. Rose, six," Mo was saying as she sketched a bubble-like number six on a piece of white construction paper. "What number is Finn?"

"Eight," I told her.

She sat back, her marker pausing above the paper. "Did they do that on purpose?"

"What?"

She pointed to Luke's poster, then Ronan's, then Finn's. "Six, seven, eight."

Now I sat back. For as long as I could remember, they'd worn those exact numbers on their jerseys. This was the first time I was putting together that their choices might've been intentional. Or, that Mo was putting it together.

"Probably," I said, hoping to play off my ignorance. Oops.

Mo giggled, then leaned forward again, her marker meeting the paper with grace.

We'd come right home from school with supplies to make the posters, so we were still sporting our uniformed looks. The minute we'd gotten into Mo's car, which smelled lightly of lemons and was still spotless from the day Adrienne helped her clean it, Mo untucked her uniform. She loosened her tie, threw her hair up into a bun, and let out the biggest sigh I'd ever heard from her. It took me thirty minutes to untuck mine and to loosen my tie, but when I did, I understood just how relieving it was. Now, as we sat on the carpet together, I felt looser. Imagine that.

I was thinking about just how comfortable I was when I heard Mo's voice again.

"I'm proud of you for not going to the dance tonight."

"It's very much like me to not go to the dance," I pointed out. "It's not some big accomplishment."

Mo kept drawing. Her lines were perfectly curvy. "I disagree."

Of course she did. Part of me wanted her to. A big part. "How?"

"I think it would've been more like you to go to the dance just because your friends wanted you to," she explained. "It's easy to give in, and it's enticing. But you didn't."

I wanted to tell her that I was proud too, of the way she held herself and the way she was able to get inside my head like no one else. If it weren't for her, I would've been at the dance. I would've let Bax's words sit inside of me until they went away, and I wouldn't have *felt* anything. It was the brightness of her eyes and the confidence in her voice and the truth in her words that were making my choices more my own, and I wanted to thank her for all of that. But then Mo looked up, just as the sun was beginning to peek through the clouds in front of us.

The new light coming through the window captured Mo in a way it wouldn't hold many others. She was always radiant, always glowing. In that moment, she was golden.

I couldn't comment on it, nor could I thank her. Before I could even blink, she was off.

She sprung up, first stopping with her hand on the sliding glass door that led to the back deck. She slipped off her socks, placing them neatly just in front of the door.

"What are you doing?" I asked.

I watched as she slid open the door, the muffled sound of the rain immediately becoming louder and clearer, then paused before turning to me. "Come on."

I just sat there, staring back at her, reestablishing myself as the one who sat still while everyone else went on and did their crazy things. Mo shrugged her shoulders, then stepped out onto the deck. Within seconds, her white uniform shirt was spotted with giant raindrops. I watched a few roll down her face.

"What are you doing?" I asked again, louder.

She took off her tie, tossing it on the deck as she shouted back over the rain. "It's a sunshower."

I shook my head. I must've missed the lesson in school where they taught us to run out into the pouring rain as soon as there was a crack in the clouds.

Mo watched my face, enticing me with her own as I stayed still. She nodded once over her shoulder before closing the door behind her, saving the inside of the house from the rain.

After a moment, I stood, unable to take my eyes off of Mo as she made her way down the first set of steps and onto the landing. The picture that surrounded her then was one that most cinematographers dreamed of capturing. The sun was creating a series of hazy lines that shone over the dark gray clouds surrounding them. The ocean was the audience, while the sky was putting on a show. In the middle of all of it, there was a girl, living every moment the way she wanted.

I could feel myself breathing. I studied the clouds and the rays of sun that streaked them, then watched as Mo took a deep breath, tipping her head back so the rain would fall in her face. She closed her eyes at the same time I opened the door.

For a moment, we stood beside each other without a word. She'd only turned with a smile when I joined her, then retreated to taking it in. I wanted to feel it too, whatever it was, so I shut my eyes. The rain was falling in sheets around us, the drops kissing every part of my bare skin. In the silence, I felt light, like something loud and daunting had made an exit from my mind.

When I finally opened my eyes, Mo was watching the clouds.

"They're my mom's favorite," I said, breaking the silence that wasn't really all that quiet. "Sunshowers, I mean. Especially over the ocean"

Mo grinned. "My mom's, too."

This was the first I'd heard of Mo's mother, which I'd only imagined was intentional. I didn't know what to make of the sudden mention, so I stayed quiet.

"She left when I was thirteen." Mo turned her head slightly, keeping focus on the sky but making the conversation more intimate nonetheless. "I sat her and my dad down one night and told them I was pretty sure I had a crush on a girl at my school."

I gulped, hoping to God this story didn't go the way I was thinking it might.

"They both responded well, I thought. My dad told me he loved me and my mom just smiled," she told me. "A week later, on a Thursday, I came home from school in the pouring rain and she was just gone. Didn't even wait until I was there to say goodbye. My dad was a wreck."

There was a desire within me to become one with the rain, wash away on the beach and float out into the void of the ocean. But then there was that other part, the one that wanted to cling to Mo and never let her go.

"Mo–"

"And then," she said, flashing another smile at me to assure me that it, and she, were okay. "And then the sun started to creep through the clouds. It was like the sky opened up just for the two of us. We watched it through the window. It just kept getting lighter and lighter. We couldn't ignore it."

"So you went outside."

Mo nodded proudly. "We had to claim sunshowers as our own, you know? So I grabbed his hand and we went out onto the sidewalk. We started dancing," she told me. Finally, she turned my way. I looked right into her eyes, trying to decipher whether I saw tears forming in them or if it was just the rain. And then she went on. "So now I dance in every one. Doesn't matter where I am."

I nodded. Really, it was one of the most beautiful things I'd ever heard. There was a ray of light in the darkness and Mo held a tight grasp on it. I was so touched, but not surprised. But then-

"Wait," I said, shaking my head slightly. "You're not dancing."

Mo turned to me, grabbing my hand, and I realized it was not just the rain in her eyes. "Not yet."

If we were soaking wet on the deck, I didn't know what to call us when we made it to the ocean. I didn't think twice about running through the crashing waves with Mo, or about who might've been watching the spectacle through their windows. I didn't care that my skirt was acting as a sponge for the salt water as the tide splashed against me, or that the air touching my skin was growing colder as the sun started to retreat behind the clouds.

What I did care about, overwhelmingly so, was that I felt safe. I was so far from the shoreline, so far from neat and dry, that I thought I'd be afraid. But now I was in the ocean, dancing solely to the beat of the waves, and I felt like myself. Whoever that was.

"It looks good," Mo said.

The sun was completely hidden now, and the sky had turned dark. But I could still see Mo, even through the rain.

I settled myself, focusing only on her eyes. "What?"

She nodded toward me. "Your hair."

When I looked down, I saw my hair, which was now curling wildly, sitting on my shirt and my shoulders and sticking to my neck. Where one stray curl normally filled me with angst, I didn't entirely mind the way it looked now.

"Thanks."

"This is what you're so afraid of?" Mo was grinning as she reached out and spun a strand of my curly hair between her fingers. The proximity sent sparks throughout my entire body. When she looked into my eyes again, I thought I was going to burst into flames.

"I guess—"

"Nell."

She was still looking at me, filling my heart and confusing me at the same time. "What?"

"Nell," she repeated.

I couldn't help but laugh. Of course now was the time she'd speak another nickname into existence. But this one—it felt different. It wasn't Elle or Rose or anything else. Not even close.

"Did you just come up with that?" I was smiling so hard I probably should've been embarrassed. But there was no way I was letting that change how I felt.

Mo shook her head. "No, you did."

I didn't know what to say, really. I'd never liked any nickname. But the way Nell sounded, especially coming from Mo, was special. It held more meaning, somehow.

"So, what?" I said loudly, the rain picking back up all around and above us. "I'm not Elliana anymore? I just change everything about myself?"

Mo's demeanor changed. She took a step forward, her hands finding my wrists. I watched as her eyes darted back and forth between the two of mine, her expression serious and kind and maybe even loving all at once. I could barely breathe.

"You don't need to change anything about yourself."

"Then—"

"I just—" Mo looked up at the rain, probably, like me, wishing it would quiet down for just a moment. "I know I haven't known you for very long—"

"That's okay." There was a smile on my face that forced a smaller one onto hers. "You can say it."

She took a short breath. "I just think you're more you when you think less like Elliana. She's not who you think she is." This was spoken with urgency. She squeezed my wrists tighter, but not too much so. Her voice came out quieter this time. "I see it in you."

I nodded, took a second for myself to watch the rain falling. In a way, it was still beautiful. Even without the sun.

"I look for that version of myself sometimes," I admitted. "You make it sound so easy."

"It's not," she told me. After a pause, she looked into my eyes again. One final push to convince me of who I was. "But nothing matters."

I laughed, because, well, I had to. If Mo had to sum up the exact opposite of my life motto since I was eleven years old, that would've been it. She knew this, I was sure, but she said it again.

"Really. Nothing matters," she told me. "Your life deserves a you that doesn't apologize. That doesn't think twice about what you're doing because of the way it might affect someone else. It's your happiness that's at stake. Everything else is white noise. You just have to remember that."

Truthfully, I didn't think there was a possibility I could ever forget what she'd just said. It was so heavy, so much of everything all at once, that I wanted to bottle up the words and save them forever. The look in her eyes, the way I felt, the scene being painted around us as we spoke—they were all telling me that I wouldn't have to. She and I weren't going anywhere.

"Okay," I said, hoping that the look on my face would tell her how happy I was. "Nell it is. But only to you."

Mo grinned, the light in her eyes beaming. "We'll test it out."

Chapter Sixteen

Nell

We were lucky Adrienne had chosen the date for the Bridal Party Beach Day wisely. Just twenty-four hours after my confession under the burning sun, we were back inside. The cause? Torrential downpour.

The truth was, we needed the rain. Had the sun continued to shine the way it was, none of us would have wanted to stay in the house, and there was work that needed to be done. For me, that meant helping Braeden edit together a montage of videos he had collected over the years to play at the Thursday Night Party. For everyone else, it was napkins.

"It's a good thing you have to take video editing classes at school," Braeden said, looking over my shoulder as I sliced off the end of a video of Adrienne and Lucas at their eighth grade graduation. "This would suck without them."

"I don't *have* to take them. I want to," I told him, the compliment giving me cause to smile anyways. "And you were doing just fine before I got home."

I was playing this off with as much chill-ness as I possibly could, but inside I was bursting from Braeden's subtle recognition of my skill. For my whole life, I'd never really been good at anything I enjoyed. There was basketball, sure, but that brought me much more anxiety in my early years of playing it than it ever should've. There was also surfing, which I'd enthusiastically learned a few years ago, but that was just a hobby. With school, though, I was starting to find a passion. It wasn't full-blown just yet, but as soon as I switched from the Biology major—the most natural path for myself, or so I thought senior year of high school—to the Communications major, my creative eyes were effectively opened.

Now, I got to spend my time at school with images—still and moving—and was learning how to tell all sorts of stories, many of which I didn't even realize I had inside of me.

The major switch was just one of many choices that were as scary as they were needed, and so far it had been paying off. As proof of it, the video montage was turning out beautifully. I couldn't wait to watch the whole thing with everyone at the party.

"What if the music fades back in with the pictures at the end?" Braeden asked as I scrolled mindlessly to the part of the video he was referring to.

"A marvelous idea," I said, making him laugh. I turned slightly as I dragged a line up on the audio track. "What do you want to do when you get to college?"

"Me?" Braeden shrugged, a grin on his freckled face due to my lack of response. "I don't know. Maybe I'll be a dentist like dad. Or a cook like Luke."

I looked into his eyes, a twinge of discomfort in his. He was always the little brother, the last to be asked these kinds of questions. He didn't have answers at the ready like Luke and I did. But maybe that was a good thing.

"Just do what you like," I told him, turning back to the computer to save him from a full-blown advice session. "You don't have to be like anyone else. Just remember that."

I saw him nod. "Yeah. Okay."

"Uh oh."

This relatively urgent remark came from the kitchen where, for the past thirty minutes, I'd been trying not to look. Every surface—the counters, the table, the stovetop, even the chairs—were covered in supplies for the pre-wedding party that was now just days away. There were bowls and plates and tablecloths and the most beautifully subtle of decorations, among about a million other things. My mother, being my mother, wanted to make sure everything was accounted for so there was no last-minute rushing around. The napkins, allegedly, had other plans.

There was a bit of rustling, a momentary pause that fell over the rest of the room. Something was out of line, hence the *uh oh*, and this was Stella Rose. Order was her shtick.

"What is it?" Luke dared to ask.

More rustling, then a shake of her head. "The gray napkins. I've counted them fifteen times," she muttered, moving onto another box. "They have to be there somewhere."

It was almost laughable how still the air was in the room, when seconds ago it had been bustling. Ronan and Adrienne were frozen above a series of floral centerpieces they'd been putting together, Luke and my dad were like statues in the kitchen, and now, Braeden and I, in full pause while the video continued to play on low volume in front of us. I'd already had a heavy feeling in my chest—I had Finn to thank, since I'd called him six times in the past two days with no reply—so any added panic was not going to bode well with me.

"How many more do you need?" I asked.

My mom bit the nail of her thumb. "A couple of packages."

This was met with an eyebrow raise from my dad. "The manager of the store said they were almost through their last shipment when I was there yesterday."

My mom turned quickly in horror, because the faltering of their napkin pattern was certainly detrimental to the potential success of the party. Luckily, I understood the need for perfection more than anyone else in the room.

"I'll go right now," I said, setting aside Braeden's laptop.

"It's downpouring," my mom pointed out, her sentence emphasized by a gust of wind that blew a sheet of rain against the ocean-side windows.

I flashed her an Everything is Fine smile and headed for the door. "I love the rain."

"I'll go with her!" Braeden announced. He followed directly in my footsteps, earning another worried look from my mother, and from Adrienne.

"Are you sure?" Adrienne asked.

"We'll be right back," I assured them, hoping to God that the pause in the room would have vanished by the time we returned back home.

As I eased the door shut behind Braeden and me, I saw my mom give my dad a familiar look. It was the same one she'd given me when I'd played my last basketball game, when I moved to college, when I tried on my dress for the wedding. We were growing up, all of us, and even the little moments reminded her of it. I was pretty sure she hated it.

With so much luck I barely believed it, the party store in town had just the right amount of napkins left for us. The sigh of relief Braeden released at the checkout counter made me realize he'd been just as nervous as I was. So, the crisis averted, I decided we had grounds for celebration. Braeden immediately suggested french fries from Archie's, and there was absolutely no denying him that.

On the way to the diner, however, I took notice of the songs Braeden had chosen to play through the aux cord. Though it was raining, and the badgering was likely unnecessary, I *was* his older sister, so I had to.

"I can't believe you listen to Gracie Abrams," I started.

"This girl I–" He paused, long enough that I knew what it meant, but short enough that I couldn't get a word in. "This girl I'm friends with sends me songs sometimes."

"This girl you're *friends* with?"

We'd made it inside Archie's, which used to feel so much more like it belonged to me than it did now. While Braeden looked around, likely ensuring that his Friend Who Was A Girl wasn't in earshot, I did, too. The ambience—the noise, the sweet and greasy smell, the warm lighting—was all the same, but the people inside it were different. Most obviously, Sydney and Henry weren't beside me. That, in itself, was a strange feeling. And then there was the way Braeden's expression twisted, which made me want to laugh.

"I can't be friends with girls?"

"You've always been friends with girls," I noted as we claimed our spot at the back of the short line. "Not girls who get you to listen to Gracie Abrams and Lorde."

Braeden couldn't disagree with this logic; it was just that good. Instead, his cheeks rosied, and he tilted his head. "Okay," he muttered, his guard officially down. "I guess she's more than my friend."

I elbowed him, hard and out of true anger. "You have a Lucas-and-Adrienne-level girlfriend and you haven't told us about her?"

"We are *not* Lucas-and-Adrienne-level."

"What's her name?"

Braeden sighed. "Rowan. And she's really cool and nice and I think she likes me so please don't tell Mom or Dad or Luke because I don't want it to become a thing."

There was an abrupt wave of guilt that washed over me, and it had nothing to do with how close the girl's name sounded to Ronan's. All of a sudden, I'd realized what I was doing – pestering about a potential romance, not taking no for an answer, making it a Thing. Sure, it was my job as Big Sister and Middle Child to get what I wanted in a conversation like this with Braeden. But when I was on the other side of it all those years before, it was nearly catastrophic.

"It won't be a thing," I assured him. "But I do expect frequent updates."

"Thanks. I don't want mom to give me that look."

Braeden was grateful for my answer, as was I. But just after we ordered our fries and found a spot by an empty table to wait for them, the entire conversation and every feeling that accompanied it was ripped from inside me. I'd heard the familiar clang of the sandwich shop door, which wasn't out of the ordinary. But this time, with the clang, there was a shift in the atmosphere of the sizable room we stood in. The air felt lighter, the lights softer. When I realized why, I could barely breathe.

The line at the counter was nonexistent now, so she walked right up to it, not pausing to take attendance like Braeden and I did. She wore a light green raincoat, pulling the hood down to reveal that her hair was much shorter than the last time I'd seen her. The top half was pulled up into a messy bun, while the bottom half, curly as ever, fell just below her shoulders. I couldn't think hard enough to focus on her outfit, but I could tell it suited her. Just like the faded blue nail polish on her fingernails as she reached for her purse.

"Shit," I whispered, turning my body around fully to face Braeden. I knew he'd grown to be taller than me, but now that I was this close, I realized just how much. Too much.

As far as I knew, Braeden had no reason to believe that I had a reason to avoid Mo. But, given the circumstances—me facing directly towards him, my face flushed, my eyes wide—he picked up on the severity of the situation pretty quickly. It was a good thing he was smart.

"What's she doing?" I whispered.

Braeden's eyes flickered down at me, pondering just how ridiculous I was about to become. "She's just ordered."

"A sandwich?"

Now his gaze on me was stronger. "How am I supposed to know that?"

"What's she doing now?"

"Paying." There was a beat. Maybe that was my heart. "Is it weird that I'm watching her?"

"No," I told him. "Keep doing it."

Braeden's lips curled into a slight smile, though his eyes were still on Mo. "She sees us."

Shit.

"She's coming over here."

Shit.

Braeden's whispers were gone with the ambient chatter that surrounded us. It took almost everything I had to gather myself and force my body to turn in Mo's direction. When I did, I found her to be glowing, smiling, and the most beautiful person I'd ever seen and ever would see again for as long as I lived.

So, she hadn't changed.

"Hey, Mo," Braeden said nonchalantly. Impressive.

"Hey. I didn't see you guys over here," Mo said.

Hearing her voice again, the way I knew I remembered it, was sweet and sour all at once. I wanted to turn back time. But here I was, staring so intently my eyes were beginning to burn.

My voice came out softer than I wanted it to.

"Hi."

And now, I never wanted to say anything else for the rest of time.

"You getting fries?" Braeden asked. I wanted to be thankful for him, but his celebration suggestion was the reason we were at Archie's in the first place, so I was having a hard time finding gratitude.

Mo nodded. "For me and my dad. Late lunch. You guys?"

"Same," Braeden offered. "Had to escape a napkin fiasco at the house."

I heard Mo's laugh, and wanted to bask in it, but when I looked up at her fully, finally, I noticed something. She hadn't looked at me. If she had, I didn't notice. And I would have noticed.

"How's the wedding planning going?" she asked.

I watched her gaze as it intently remained on Braeden. Even in the sandwich shop lighting, her eyes were a glowing shade of green. I was so focused on them I didn't even hear how Braeden responded.

"Order number eighty-eight!" called a high school girl with an Archie's visor on from behind the counter. Music to my trembling ears.

"That's us," Braeden noted, putting a few inches of space between us.

"I'll see you guys soon." I watched Mo nod, smile politely at Braeden. Then, in slow motion, her eyes found mine. The chatter surrounding us disappeared, and for a moment, all I could hear was my breathing, and her voice, but not this one. The old one. The one from before. "It's nice to see you, Elliana."

Before I could process, well, anything, Braeden let out a laugh through his nose. I knew exactly what it meant. Mo, obviously, did not.

She was confused, but her smile hadn't completely vanished. "What?"

"Oh–" Braeden looked between me and Mo a few times, like we were the ones making things complicated. I guess he had a point. "It's just– I haven't heard anyone call her that in, like, years."

Mo's nod stopped halfway, her eyes slowly finding my face which was flushed once again.

"What do they call you now?"

My hesitation felt massive, and it likely was. But when I allowed my eyes to settle on Mo's, it felt like all of my worrying, and all of the tightness in my chest, was useless. It felt like nothing mattered.

"Nell."

Mo's eyebrows shot up, like I'd said that my new nickname was some long, medieval word, and not the one that she picked out herself. A part of me thought that she might've been upset, but then, as she studied me, a flicker of a smile returned to her face.

The last time she and I were face-to-face, I was someone else. It wasn't only that my hair and my posture and my clothes were straight, but the inside of me was darker, more closed-off, courtesy of my own outlook on life. Mo was the only one who'd ever seen it and who knew I could even be someone else. Or, she was at least the only one with enough gumption to say it.

"It suits you."

"Thanks," I said quickly, inhaling a deep breath and nudging Braeden with my elbow.

Again, he took the hint. "Well we'd better go to our... fries. See you, Mo."

"See you."

In the car, I finally took a breath. My face was all different shades of everything—red, purple, awkward. It was only when I was in my cushioned seat, hair and skin soaked from the rain we trudged through, that I could finally think. Braeden, however, had other plans.

"What *was* that?"

He shut his car door, the radio immediately blaring a Lorde song when I twisted the key in the ignition.

"Nell."

I placed my hands on the steering wheel, then rested my forehead on my knuckles. They were cold, and I realized the rest of me was, too.

"Why was that so weird?" Braeden pushed, reaching to turn the volume down.

I decided that acknowledging Braeden's question was the best way for me to figure out the answer myself, so I sat up and took a pointed breath, watching the raindrops pound down on the windshield. Then, my leg started to vibrate. When I reached for the source (my phone), I saw Finn's name.

Braeden saw it, too, and was apparently set on fulfilling his Little Brother Duties by asking about every movement I was, or wasn't, making.

"Finn? Why is Finn calling you?"

His name was bright and loud and beautiful as it sat on top of my screen. At first, there was no hesitation in my fingertips; I moved quickly to answer it. But then I froze. Finn's call this close to the wedding could mean two things: he was coming, or he wasn't. It was crunch time now, and so much else was piling up on my plate, so I knew the answer he was going to give me would be it. If my missed calls were any indication of what he was going to say, I didn't have high hopes.

Braeden's voice got lower. "Do you still talk to him?" Then, "Are you going to answer it?"

These were questions that my movement offered replies to. I slid my finger across the bottom of the screen then pressed the phone up to my ear.

"Finn?"

"Hey." His voice was distant at first, but clearer the second time. "I, uh– hey."

"Did you forget that you called me?" I asked, poking fun but also a little curious as to why he was so scattered. "You haven't been answering my calls. I was getting worried."

"I'm sorry," he said immediately. There was a rustling on the other end of the line, and I thought I might've heard Sutton's voice. Then, there was a deep breath from Finn and more silence.

"Are you drunk?"

He laughed, and it somehow calmed me. "I'm not drunk," he told me. "I just– I called to tell you two things and I was sure I wouldn't change my mind, but now I don't–"

"Finn. Tell me." My voice was low, desperate. If those three days in Pittsburgh meant as much to him as they did to me, this was going to be okay. There had never been a thing we couldn't say to one another. Things were going to be better again. This was the start.

"I'm coming to the wedding."

I dropped the call. Literally. The phone fell onto the floor, and I scrambled to pick it up from between my feet. As I put it back up to my ear, I could still hear Finn.

"You there?"

"Sorry," I panted. "You're coming? Really?"

I was afraid still, because of course I was, but there was so much excitement coursing through me now that it didn't matter. Finn was coming to the wedding. I'd done it.

I figured he was nodding, or pacing, or biting his lip. In the distance, there was an upbeat, child-like tune playing.

"But it's going to be complicated, and I need you to know why."

This, I imagined, was the second thing. I didn't bother to brace myself. Nothing could have been as big as the picture I had in my head now. Ronan, Luke, and Finn all under the same roof again. Our family back together. It was going to be perfect.

"I'm just going to say it once," Finn said then.

I could feel Braeden looking at me, questioning the smile on my face.

"I was in love with Adrienne."

The pounding in my heart had reached my eyelids, and now it was in my throat.

"You–" That was it. That was all I had.

There was no way.

I tried again. "*What?*"

"I said I'm only saying it once."

"But– you–" I closed my eyes hard, or maybe blinked a few times. I wasn't sure there was a difference. "But Adrienne and Luke–"

"I know," Finn said. "I know. We can talk about it later, okay? I'm hiding in the bedroom and Freya is getting suspicious."

I believed him. Every word, precisely. But I was having such a hard time coming to terms with it. I tried, hard, to replay every instance of our youth together, to find hints that could have revealed what he was telling me now. But there was no use, and there was no time. Like he said, we'd talk about it later.

"Okay," I surrendered, taking a breath and searching for parting words. "Wait. You don't– now–"

"No," he assured me. "No. I love Sutton more than anything. I promise I'll tell you everything later. We have time."

This, for some reason, was what got to me. Not only did my lungs fill with air, but a pool of tears flooded my eyes. I felt one, big and warm, roll down my cheek as I swallowed down a sob. I had so many more questions. Not just for him, but for Adrienne and Luke and Ronan and maybe even myself. But Finn couldn't have said anything truer. We had time, and his acceptance was proof of it.

"So you're coming home," I finally managed.

I couldn't see him, obviously, but I could feel the smile through the phone. "I'm coming home."

Chapter Seventeen

Elliana

"I'll be back in ten," Finn whispered through the almost-darkness.

He was off to his parents' house, where he was being summoned to bid farewell to an aunt that was visiting. It was the middle of the night, and any other time he wouldn't have gone. But graduation was around the corner, and I knew he was aching to see some kind of nostalgia pooling in his parents' eyes. Maybe the midnight trip was just another chance to see if he could find it.

Evidently, Finn wasn't going to be missing much in the few minutes of his absence. We'd been playing cards for hours—a game called Pitch that Mo had learned in New York and taught us a few weeks earlier—and everyone was exhausted. As proof, they were all asleep.

I was awake, if only because of the reminder my mother had slipped me that I had a basketball scrimmage in the morning. It was her first instinct after she took notice of my presence in the living room and matched it up with the time. I could hardly blame her. Months before, I would've been in full-blown panic mode at this hour. But now, I was too comfortable to move.

It was mostly Ronan's fault. He'd been sitting between me and Sydney for every card game, and his eyelids began to grow heavy only a few minutes into the first one. They'd been suffering through extra-tough lacrosse practices as the season was nearing its end. Luke and Finn were handling it just fine, but Ronan was struggling to stay awake in the in-between moments. Just being next to him was enough to make me tired, and once the games ended and everyone settled down, our living room turned into an impromptu slumber party.

Since Henry and Sydney had called it a night a little earlier, there were only the six of us left. Luke and Adrienne were occupying a couch, looking almost annoyingly cute with every glance, and Ronan had migrated to one of the loveseats where he was so sound asleep that even a hurricane wouldn't have woken him. I was still on the floor with my back resting against one of the empty chairs. I could've easily found somewhere softer to lay—my bed, even—but Mo was next to me, so I didn't feel at all inclined to.

We were shoulder-to-shoulder. My knees were tucked up to my chest, my arms hugging them, while Mo's legs were crossed in front of her. It had been exactly seven minutes since she'd fallen asleep, which I knew because it had been the same amount of time since she started resting her head on my shoulder.

Everyone else was already out, so it was just Finn, Mo, and me. I thought all three of us were chatting, but Mo was apparently tapped out, too. Throughout the conversation, which focused solely on the difference between watching musicals on stage versus on a television screen, my eyes were growing heavy, as was the rest of my body. I kept thinking about what might have happened if I'd just tilted my head and rested it on Mo's shoulder, but it was more intimate of an act than I thought I was capable of. I wasn't a hugger, really, and I had never been one to show affection toward my friends through any kind of touch. So I just didn't, even though my heart and my mind and my body were telling me it was okay.

But then, she did it.

Finn was in the middle of a sentence, and all of a sudden, the words he muttered vanished in thin air. All I could hear was my heart beating. Surely, as much thought as I'd put into it wasn't behind Mo's decision to lean. She was probably just so tired that it didn't matter who was next to her; she needed a pillow. But this small moment, which had quickly turned into eight, sent my heartbeat on a rollercoaster ride throughout my body. The rush was like a tidal wave, and it hadn't yet subsided.

"When was that photo taken?"

188

This voice came out strained, like it was fighting sleep. Only after surveying the room did I realize it had come from my shoulder.

"You're awake?" I whispered. Mo just shrugged, so I turned my attention slightly to the frame in question. It sat in front of us on the coffee table—a wooden frame with a professionally taken picture cozied into its center. In the photo, Luke, Braeden, and I were smiling youthfully with our arms around one another. The boys had on khaki shorts and blue shirts, while I wore a blue dress to match. My eyes were drawn most to my hair, which was being held back by a tan headband and was curly as ever.

"I was ten," I remembered. "My dad had professional photos taken as a birthday gift to my mom."

"You're the cutest kids I've ever seen," she observed, making me laugh, albeit silently.

Mo sat up, cracks sounding from her sleepy bones as she rose. With her head off of my shoulder, I felt like I could finally breathe without making too sudden a movement. But I also felt colder.

"It's my dad's favorite photo of us," I told her. "He keeps a copy of it in his car."

The picture had been fastened to the sun visor in front of his driver's seat for as long as I could remember. It had become a piece of the car's interior, and at some point I must've stopped acknowledging it. But I was sure my dad never did. It was his favorite picture because of how contagious our smiles were, how much we were bursting with happiness. For me, the picture was just a reminder of what we had and what we felt. We didn't know anything other than happy then. We were lucky.

"How very wholesome of him." Mo stood up, stretching her arms over her head and then out in front of her. Even in this state—wild hair, baggy sweatshirt, mismatched socks—she was breathtaking. "I have to go clean my room before my dad gets home in the morning. My promise is bordering on four days late."

"What does your dad do again?" I whispered, the term *again* being used loosely, as I wasn't sure I'd ever asked in the first place.

"He's a firefighter."

"Right." I yawned, standing to meet Mo as she slowly began her trek to the front door. "And you had to move across the country halfway through your senior year for his job? Aren't there fires to fight everywhere?"

The smile on Mo's face told me she'd wondered the same thing. But the shrug said she didn't really care. "Big promotion, I guess."

"Hm." I reached to unlock the door, because I knew she'd forget to if I didn't. "Well, I'm glad you're here."

Mo paused as she drew open the door, her radiant eyes settling comfortably on mine. "Me too. I'll see you tomorrow, Nell."

"See you."

When the door was finally closed, I rested the back of my head against it. I felt as if I was floating on a cloud, and every time she walked away I went higher and higher. Soon, I was going to lose track of the ground.

"Want a brownie?"

I jolted, hitting the side of my head on the door frame. "*Shit,*" I muttered, which was almost as surprising to me as it was to Adrienne, who was headed for the kitchen, her eyes now wide as could be.

I shook my head. "No, thanks."

A moment later, Adrienne sat next to me at the kitchen table, the smell of her warmed brownie waking up my nose. The rest of me, sleepy as ever, apparently thought it would be fun to toy with my own emotions. And maybe even Adrienne's.

"How did you know Luke was the one?"

Though this was asked at a very low volume, the two of us simultaneously glanced in the direction of the living room. Ronan and Luke were both still sound asleep on their respective couch and chair. It wasn't that my question to Adrienne was

190

some big secret, but this was obviously girl talk, so it was good that they were asleep.

"The first time?"

I nodded. I did have a reason for asking, so I just needed to come out and say it. "Like, how did you know it was love, and not just friendship or admiration?"

"I think love is a little bit of friendship and admiration," she told me, taking a bite as she thought about it. "Luke showed me new things about myself, and about the world. I knew my life was going to be better with him in it."

I had lots of people in my life who made it, and me, better. So my mind could have flashed to just about anyone. But it didn't. My thoughts were pointed, specific, painting an image of a sunshower and an outstretched hand.

Thank God Adrienne had more to say.

"I didn't know anything about love back then. But, God, the way he made me *feel*. I almost couldn't handle it." She shook her head. "Everything about him—the sound of his voice, the color of his eyes—made me feel more like myself. That's how I knew."

My eyes were beginning to pool with tears. Warm ones, that I had no plans of stopping. I wouldn't have stood a chance.

"And it hasn't stopped," she continued. "Every day with Luke is the best day of my life. We're young, sure. But I know my heart."

Yeah, I'd asked the questions. But it didn't necessarily mean I was ready to hear the answers. If she kept going, I was sure I was going to combust.

Adrienne's dessert plate was nearly empty, and the expression she offered me was one of utter concern.

"You okay?"

I wiped a stray tear and sat up straighter. "I'm just— I'm happy for you both."

Adrienne curled her lip and stood from her chair before pulling me into a hug. "I love you," she told me as I leaned into her. "You're going to find that one day, Elliana. I know you are."

I sniffled back another set of tears before they ended up on Adrienne's sleeve. "I hope you're right."

The next night was almost identical.

Luke and Ronan were asleep on the floor, Adrienne on the chair just above Luke's head, and I'd just said goodbye to Mo, who was on a late-night pizza run. This time, Finn's absence was thanks to his need for a clean set of clothes for school the next day. I was just slipping out onto the back deck, my mind in desperate need of clearing, when he returned.

"Elliana?" he said quietly across the room. "Where are you going?"

I nodded toward the back deck. "Want to come?"

The ocean was loud and the breeze was not quite warm as I sat on the top step of the deck. All I could think about, and all I'd been thinking about for a full twenty-four hours, was what Adrienne said. Luke showed her new things about herself and the world. Everything about him was a new part of who she was. He made her *feel.*

Though this was all so easy to comprehend, and maybe even obvious, I now had a roadblock in my heart. Who was Mo if not the exact person Adrienne described, but in my own life? And why didn't I want her to be?

I was thinking all of this, and maybe even planning on saying it, but had to do something else first.

"Did you talk to your parents?" I asked, keeping my gaze on the abyss in front of us so as to not seem too pushy.

"My parents talked," he told me. "Loudly. Behind a cracked-open door."

So, they were fighting. This wasn't new, but I still didn't like to hear it.

"How's your dad?"

Finn shrugged. "Haven't talked to him. Seems the same."

"I'm sorry," I told him. "I wish it were different for you."

It could've been the color of the sky, the emptiness swirling around us, or the mere context of the conversation, but saying this put a rock in my throat. No one deserved the home life Finn had, but it might've hurt even more to see how effortlessly he carried it.

As proof of this, Finn nudged my knee with his, a solemn smile on his face. "They're just showing me what not to do, right?"

There was a moment of stillness then, the two of us turning back to the sound of the waves. With it, I sensed that Finn wanted the conversation to end.

"Remember the night I went to the pier with Bax?"

This, obviously, came out of nowhere. I saw it on Finn's face, and he saw it on mine. He only nodded, but I could tell he knew where I was going, even though I didn't.

"And he said those things that I told you about," I explained.

Finn nodded again.

"What did you mean," I started slowly, "when you said it might've felt personal?"

His eyebrows fell a bit. He'd already explained himself, and was obviously prepared to do it again. But he was confused, understandably.

"I'm sorry if I was wrong, I just–" He paused. "I thought maybe you cared because of Mo. Like if her feelings might've been attached to what Bax said–"

At first, I wasn't aware of Finn's pause. It wasn't until I turned to him, my cheeks soaked with tears, that I realized what exactly was happening.

"Oh, Elliana," he muttered, wrapping his arms around me without pause.

My head was against his chest, my hair sticking to the tears on my face. I couldn't believe how fast my heart was beating. With every thump, I thought I was going to explode.

In an attempt to calm myself down and slow my breathing, I tried to convince myself that what I was about to say wasn't a big deal. This was Finn I was talking to. I had nothing to worry about. But as much as I believed that, my body was behaving otherwise.

"I think it felt personal because it was personal," I muttered before taking a breath that caught in my throat.

I felt Finn nod. He pressed his head against mine and stayed there.

"I'm sorry," I told him.

Now, Finn backed away, only to look directly at me. I saw tears pooling in his eyes. Even in the darkness, they were still so blue.

"You have nothing to be sorry about." His head was shaking slightly, his eyes desperate to convince me that he meant what he was saying. Then, they softened. "Do you want to talk about it?"

I shook my head immediately. This was what I did. I let things build up inside of me until they didn't exist anymore. The pressure, the rules, the past. Of course I didn't want to talk about it.

But now, there was that girl who I looked for in the clouds. She was on the brink of being exposed, but so different from who I thought she was that I desperately wanted to keep her away. She'd found me in the darkness, and now I had to confront her, whether I liked it or not.

I slowed my breathing, remaining in Finn's arms but letting my eyes linger back to the void.

"I don't know what I am," I told him, "and it's all– it's confusing and I don't want to be making a mistake–"

"Hey, hey." Finn looked at me again. "You don't need to be absolutely sure. Ever." Now, a smile grew like a flower on his lips. "I'm so proud of who you are, Elliana."

I laughed, though the noise didn't really make it all the way out. "You sound like a broken record."

"I'm okay with that." He squeezed my shoulder a little tighter. "Thank you for telling me."

I felt as though I'd just played an entire basketball tournament. My lungs were begging for air while, in the meantime, forcing out every last breath. I let out an audible sigh, finally pushing my hair away from my eyes, a family of tears accompanying it.

Finn leaned forward, his eyes avoiding me, likely for the same reason mine did at the beginning of our conversation. "Can I ask you something?"

My brain had quieted and I was sure I could handle anything now, so I nodded.

"Is it Mo?"

I didn't even blink. "Is it that obvious?"

Finn didn't either. "No. But it'd be fine if it was."

I sat up now, fully clearing my cheeks of tears and straightening myself out so I could breathe properly. Finn released me but stayed close.

"I'm not going to do anything about it."

His face twisted. I didn't know why he was surprised.

"Why not?"

"Because the thought of doing something is terrifying," I explained, as if it was obvious. To me, it was. "And I've only just come to this conclusion."

Finn sat with this for a moment. I could tell he had a lot to say, but was being careful with how he approached it. Maybe it was a good thing he did. I was fragile.

"I said it wasn't obvious," he started, treading carefully, "but I didn't mean it in a way that I can't tell how good you and Mo are together. I think she brings out something in you." There was a sadness in his voice, one I didn't expect. It sat behind a load of love. "Something that was missing. And, God, Elliana, I haven't see you cry since Paisley—"

Before I could even hear her name, he was apologizing.

"Oh my God. I'm so sorry." He turned to me, and I saw the blues in his eyes again as well as the whites. "I'm so sorry. I didn't mean to bring that up."

"Finn, stop." I could feel heat growing in my cheeks. I was okay. "It's fine."

His voice was quieter this time. "Okay. I'm sorry." He settled himself, as did I. The thumping wasn't so harsh anymore. "What I mean is," Finn continued, "I feel like you've been numb since then. Forgive me if I'm wrong-"

"You're not."

He nodded, turning to me again. "But then Mo comes around, and you're *living*. You don't sit back anymore. Your cheeks have been rosy for weeks," he laughed, slowing his pace. "Even if that means crying on the deck at midnight, I don't think you should ignore it."

The truth was, I didn't want to. Finn couldn't have said it better. The sidelines, the shore—they were always my safety. I fell back on them every time I was pushed further than I wanted. But with Mo, the more I was pushed toward her, the more comfortable I felt. I just wished it wasn't so scary.

"She's leaving in three weeks," I said flatly. "And maybe she doesn't feel the same way."

"She'll come back," he said in the same tone. "And do you want my honest opinion?"

I lowered my eyebrows. What a dumb question. "Of course I do."

"I think she does."

Eyebrows: raised. "You do?"

He nodded. "So does Adrienne."

"Adrienne thinks Mo—" I shook my head. "You've talked about it?"

He grinned. "You're not at *every* late-night fire."

Huh. Obviously, this Elliana Gossip was news to me. But in a way, it was kind of exciting.

I tried to hide my smile. "So why do you think that, then?"

He curled his lip. He was smiling, too, but there was no hiding it. "I don't know a lot about love, but she definitely doesn't look at Adrienne the way she looks at you."

I laughed, and it felt good. Warm, even. "Well, Adrienne is with Luke."

Finn's expression was comical, unexpected. "I know."

"It would be pretty bad if Mo had feelings for Adrienne."

196

"Right," he noted with a chuckle. "Well, okay. How about this: I was walking out of the house the other day when Mo was coming to hang out with you."

I shook my head. This was barely proof. "Okay—"

"And I saw her fix her hair."

It wasn't that big of a deal. But wasn't it? Mo was The Queen of Carefree. I didn't want her to think I cared what she looked like, because I didn't. But maybe Finn had a point. Maybe, just maybe, it mattered.

I narrowed my eyes. "Really."

He nodded, a triumphant smile gracing his lips. He'd convinced me. I wished it wasn't so easy.

With this, I let the ocean fill my lungs. I didn't know what I was going to do. As much as I wanted to be Nell, I was still Elliana, which meant I was notoriously unsure. But maybe this was okay. Maybe this was how it felt to figure yourself out.

I did know one thing, however, and it was that I wouldn't have been able to handle what was going on without Finn. He was Luke's friend, through and through. But maybe, like Adrienne, he was my saving grace. I didn't know what the last few moments would've turned into if I'd been sitting next to Sydney or Adrienne or Luke or Ronan. I could've guessed it would've been okay. But with Finn, I just knew.

This time, I was the one to slide my arms around his body. There was no hesitation from him to do the same.

"I love you," I said into his shoulder.

"I love you, too."

Chapter Eighteen

Nell

Four days.

There were only *four days* until the wedding. Two days until the party at our house. One day since I found out that Finn was coming home.

Everyone was on edge, and it wasn't just the buzzing air that was telling me so, but our faces and characteristic behaviors. Because they were anxious, Adrienne and Luke were spending quality time together, as doing so would surely calm them. My mom was in the garden, for the same reasons, while my dad was grilling dinner for everyone.

All of this was common, yet not. These were our usual habits when stress was running free around us. But, at the same time, this was the biggest thing since the Big Thing. So, the wedding wasn't only nerve wracking by nature, but a life event whose imprint on our lives we could actually control. It was a big deal, and it had to be perfect for Adrienne and Luke. Even if they didn't say so.

I hadn't stopped thinking about what Finn told me, and I hated how much it changed my feelings surrounding his homecoming. Since the phone call in the car, I'd stopped trying to wrack my brain for hints that would've led me to figuring out his feelings for Adrienne sooner. It'd been so long, and there was just no point. But what was complicated before was now practically life or death, and it was all my fault.

I didn't regret visiting Finn. I knew deep in my heart that he needed to come home. But now, I wasn't sure whether it was the right time to initiate the reunion. This was Adrienne and Luke's wedding. If I was the one to stir the pot and jeopardize the happiness that should've been flooding from that day, I wouldn't have been able to live with myself.

It had been done, though. And there was no way I was retracting Finn's verbal invitation at this point. So I had to stand by it. Plus, I knew it wasn't all over a stupid game, and that felt good. Whatever that was worth.

Since all of this and more was on my mind—the run-in at Archie's being the second-biggest, and so prominent I couldn't even think about it—I succumbed to my own characteristic behavior and decided to head for the beach. The sun was beginning to set, and it was calling my name.

"Nell? Is that you?"

Apparently, the sun wasn't the only one.

"It's me," I said to the flowers peeking around the side of the house. Or, my mom.

She revealed herself. Like the flowers, she was perfectly upkept. Her hair was tied back into a neat bun, her clothes perfectly ironed with their colors complementing her tanned skin. The only part of her appearance that was askew was the pair of gardening gloves she wore, the fingertips covered in dirt. Even then, they looked right.

"How are you doing, honey?" She asked as she set a pot of purple flowers on a bench to her right. I could hear my dad's burgers sizzling behind her.

I shrugged. "I'm fine. How are you?"

She let out a breath and offered me a smile, both of which answered my questions for me. Her oldest was getting married. I didn't even have to ask.

"Ready for the big family reunion?" I asked instead. My dad chuckled over the sound of the grill.

As much as Luke, B, and I felt like we had to be on our best behavior for the incoming family, it was worse for my parents. Both of their families lived on the other side of the country, and weren't exactly thrilled that they'd chosen to start theirs in North Carolina.

"You could say that," she joked, then shook it off. "Are you headed to the beach?"

I nodded, glancing down at my sweatshirt and shorts.

"I'll be in for dinner in a few minutes," I told her. "Just needed some air."

She smiled once more. "Me too."

A few moments later, I was laying on the sand. I'd pulled my gray hood over my head, allowing only my own thoughts to circulate my ears as I stared up at the sky. The wind didn't stand a chance against what was going on in my mind.

Above me, the clouds were miniscule, wispy. Surrounded by a pink glow, they were fading slowly as the sun sank down below the horizon. I took deep breaths as I watched, my eyes begging to see something other than what was playing out in front of me. It didn't feel like so long ago that I'd believed there was something more to the sun and the ocean, their mere proximity giving me hope. I used to think I'd find answers within them. Now, with everything that was going on, I didn't even want to bother.

Luckily, I didn't have to. I was studying the shape of the cloud right above me when my heart rose into my throat. Whiplash.

"Are you alive?"

I jolted into a sitting position. It was amazing how blind I was to the peacefulness of the moment right up until it was ripped away. In this case, I was met with a goofy smile and a pair of raised eyebrows. Of course, Ronan thought this was funny.

"No," I said breathlessly. "You scared me."

He chuckled, taking a seat next to me. "I see that."

When I sighed, I caught another glimpse of his face. He was so kind, so loving, so soft. I hated that I couldn't find it in myself to be angry.

"I just had lunch with the nearlyweds," Ronan started, shaking his head as his chest rose and fell with a sigh. "Adrienne's going crazy."

"Can you blame her?" I laughed. "She's getting married in four days."

He shook his head. "She was just so jittery. I've never seen her like that. Luke had to calm her down, like, three times," he said, all of which was so easy to understand—the smallest of pills to swallow. "And then she started asking about Finn."

Once again. Whiplash.

"She– what?"

This was surely a new record: the mention of Finn's name from Ronan and Adrienne both within a week. I was beginning to think that, leading up to the wedding, we'd all had the same feelings. I just couldn't believe I was the only one who'd done something about it.

He shrugged. "It was weird."

I sat still, unsure of what I could really do or say. But I'd kept the secret for so long (from most people, at least) and I could feel it bursting under my skin.

"What ever happened between you three?" I asked innocently.

Ronan's eyes found mine, likely in search of what answer I might believe. Lucky for me, there weren't any.

"Just grew apart, I guess."

I couldn't help it. All of a sudden, it was all right there on the tip of my tongue. I turned to face him fully, my hood falling down the back of my neck when I did.

"I happen to know that's not true."

His cheeks immediately reddened, and he looked as if I'd just told him I had an eleventh toe. He didn't ask me to explain, but the silence was ear-piercing.

"I went to visit him."

"You–" he shook his head, his eyes closed tight. "What? When?"

"A few weeks ago. Vermont was actually Pittsburgh."

I watched as this was computed, then piled it on a little bit more.

"I stayed for a few days. We caught up and he told me everything. He's doing really well, in case you were wondering."

I could tell just from his face that this hurt. I didn't feel good about it.

"Does Luke know?" he asked, his voice low.

"No. Adrienne does," I admitted. Then, "I invited him to the wedding."

This, evidently, was the biggest of bombs I could've dropped. Not only was the impact of it quickly impending, but it was also wildly uncharacteristic of me. He knew it, and so did I.

"You're joking."

I shook my head.

"You have to be."

"I'm not."

Ronan's hands went to his temples. He was frustrated because I hadn't told him sooner, and I understood because I felt the same way. But for me, it had been four years, not a couple of weeks. Finn was my friend, too. It was only now that I was angry about it.

"Nell, you don't understand. He told Luke and me that he was in love with Adrienne."

"I know."

His face twisted again. "You know?"

I nodded.

"And you're okay with that?"

This was Ronan's final reach. He was in search of something to grab onto—my hand, my heart, my mind. Of course, if I were still who I was in high school, I might've reached back, told him everything was okay and he was right and we'd figure it out together. But I wasn't still the person I was in high school. Frankly, no one was.

"Maybe I wouldn't have been four years ago," I said, almost defensively. Sitting beside Ronan, it was a strange feeling to not have laughter bubbling in my throat. "But things have changed. You don't know him anymore, Ronan. You and Luke made sure of that."

The shift in the air was evident, and the change in demeanor was plastered all over Ronan's face. Now, I wasn't the sweet Elliana he knew in high school or the Nell he might've been interested in. I was a stranger sitting behind him on a windy beach. There was discomfort between us and I didn't like it.

Ronan stared straight forward. I thought I saw tears pooling in his eyes.

"You're willing to jeopardize Luke and Adrienne's relationship for someone you haven't spoken to in four years."

My response came quickly, and I didn't hold it back. "You haven't spoken to your best friend in four years because he was honest with you about a feeling."

When Ronan turned to me then, I thought I was going to burst. It might've been the second-worst I'd ever felt. I'd long gotten over the fear of hurting others' feelings because of putting myself first, but this felt almost dirty. Ronan was family.

"Come on." I nudged him in an honest attempt to lighten the mood. "It's not like he killed your imaginary dog."

Not even a joke was getting through to him. Cue my final reach.

"Don't you miss him?"

Ronan's pause was thoughtful, and I appreciated it. Maybe we weren't in agreement, but much closer to understanding than when the conversation started. I knew that part of him was in there somewhere. I just needed time to find it.

"Of course I miss him." When his eyes found me, his demeanor shifted again. It was lighter. "Uh– Mo."

"What?" I shook my head. "No, Finn–"

"No," Ronan said pointedly, nodding over my shoulder, "Mo."

I craned my neck to look over my shoulder. Lo and behold, there she was. She walked casually along the beach, shoes in hand, just like the first time I saw her. It was mind-blowing. Four years had passed and she'd only gotten brighter.

I was impressed with myself, however, when the feeling that began coursing through me upon seeing her wasn't panic, but instead warmth. Maybe it was just the chill from my conversation with Ronan. A break from the tension would have been nice no matter who was the cause.

When Mo spotted us, I couldn't read her. I couldn't tell whether or not she actually wanted to make a pit stop, but now it looked like she was going to anyway.

I turned quickly to Ronan, trying to read his face, too, with no luck.

"Hey," he said softly to Mo. "Still got taste, huh?"

Mo looked down at her shirt, which Ronan's compliment was nodding towards. It was a deep shade of purple, and had faded art featuring the band Queen printed onto the front of it. Four years ago, her hair would've blocked some of the logo. Now, it was clear.

She grinned. "You thought I lost it?"

Ronan's grin both filled and broke my heart. He needed the smile, but only because I'd taken it away.

"Never." He flashed Mo another grin and then turned to me. "I'll catch you guys later. Told Luke I'd help with something."

This was another lie. He needed an out and I understood. But, God, I wanted to believe he wasn't going to run inside and spill our conversation to Luke. Or worse, my parents.

When he stood, I reached my hand up to his, immediately grabbing his attention and, apparently, Mo's.

"Ronan," I said, hoping my silent plea for confidentiality was evident.

"I'll talk to you later, okay?"

"Okay." I paused. "Don't—"

"I wouldn't."

With this, and the heap of air my lungs latched onto, Ronan was off. Then there were two.

I didn't hesitate to turn my gaze to Mo, who still stood just a few feet away from me. It wasn't until our eyes met that she decided to sit down. The silence that followed in the next few seconds was unsure of itself.

Then, I thought of Mo's face, the way it contorted when I grabbed Ronan's hand. It probably meant nothing, but a part of me wanted to assure her of it. Not that it would have mattered.

"I invited Finn to the wedding but now it might be even more problematic than I imagined because apparently he was in love with Adrienne when we were in high school and that's why he and Ronan and Luke haven't talked."

I'd certainly overshared. I blamed my lack of experience dealing with things like this, and also the way Mo still made me feel. I watched her out of the corner of my eye, fully expecting her to stand up and walk away, because I was obviously no longer the girl she used to know. But instead, she laughed.

Maybe, the more people I told of Finn's arrival before it happened, the less casualties.

"Sorry," I said through my own laugh.

"No." She shook her head. "That was just a lot."

I nodded. "It is," I agreed. There was another silence then, and in it I recognized she had no advice to give. Or, she didn't want to. So I went a different direction. "How's New York?"

"Good," she said simply. "Cold. How's Vermont?"

I shrugged. "Cold. Are you just back for the wedding?"

"And to help my dad. He's moving back up to the city," she explained.

I hated the small talk. I wanted to know if Mo still saw the world the way she used to, and to feel alive because she did. I wanted her to feel alive because of me.

I was thinking this for too long, however, because the air quickly grew uncomfortable. We both felt it.

"Well, I told Adrienne I'd help with her rehearsal dress," Mo said, standing up rather quickly.

It took all of me not to reach for her hand, too. But that would've meant so much more than Ronan's. So I just nodded, turning my attention back to the waves like I didn't care. Obviously, that couldn't have been further from the truth.

"I'll see you," I said.

Mo just flashed a smile before heading for the house. When I heard the door shut behind her in the distance, I promptly returned my back to the sand. Then, all of a sudden, I was back.

I looked to the clouds and the pink swirls that had gotten brighter over the last few chaotic moments, and I searched within them for the euphoria and radiance that crept into and filled my life a few short years ago. Although, this time, I knew I didn't have to look far. She'd just walked away.

Chapter Nineteen

Elliana

At this point, there were several factors contributing to my exhaustion.

First and certainly foremost, I had been crying. For most people, this was probably a minor inconvenience, a temporary energy block if anything. But I hadn't cried in five years. Not a single drop. Now, I'd been teary-eyed (at the least) for three days, mostly at night after everyone else left the house or went to bed in other rooms. I didn't know why, and I couldn't stop it.

Second, it was a Saturday in the almost-summer-springtime. So not only were tourists beginning to crowd our beach like ants at a sugary picnic, but I also had basketball. Sydney and I had been up since six o'clock in the morning, playing back-to-back tournament games against teams from different towns along the coast. We'd won both, and since Amari was out with a shoulder injury, I'd been given the responsibility of Point Guard. That, in itself, required no elaboration.

Finally, my mind was moving faster than it ever had been, and this was saying something. I couldn't stop thinking about Mo, what I'd told Finn, what Adrienne told me, what my parents might think, and Mo. But instead of dealing head-on with any of it (mostly because I didn't know how), I was taking a nap. On the kitchen table.

Technically, I was sitting on a chair. My arms were folded in front of me and resting on the table while my forehead rested on them. I would've been upstairs in bed, or sprawled out on the couch. But today was Senior Ball at St. Jane's. So it was quite a momentous occasion.

My mother was milling around the kitchen, straightening things and holding tightly onto her camera while the dance-goers all got ready—upstairs for the girls and downstairs for the boys. It was a fuller house than usual, since there were the regulars and also the dates. To add to it, Sydney had accompanied me home from the basketball games because Adrienne wanted help with her hair, and she was an expert among us amateurs. So, since Braeden was in a room down the hall fiddling with a video camera with my dad, I was alone, and not to mention in desperate need of a second wind. Hence the table nap.

I wasn't actually sure how long it had been since my head hit the table when I was jolted straight up into a sitting position. Considering the fact that my hair had dried significantly since my shower and I certainly had red prints on my face from my arms, I would've guessed it had been a while. Nevertheless, when my eyes shot open, I was incredibly disoriented.

"I'm so sorry," I heard Mo say quickly. "I didn't mean to move the table."

It took my eyes a second to adjust, but when they did, I was speechless. Literally.

Mo, on a daily basis, was captivating. She had a constant glow that followed her around like a friendly spirit. But when I looked at her today, I was blown away. Half of me was likely at the end of the pier by now.

Mo's dress was a dark shade of green, a shiny fabric with small and simple flowery details. She wore her hair straight and parted down the middle, like mine usually was but so much better. It was quite the contrast from her typical, carefree appearance, but she wore it just as well. And her beauty wasn't just on the outside, which made her glow even brighter. I envied her very existence.

"It's okay," I said quietly, studying her. I cleared my throat. "You look– you look incredible."

"Thanks." She smiled, haphazardly taking the seat in front of me. "You okay?"

I nodded, taking in a shaky breath. "Just tired." I rested my chin on my hand then. I needed all the support I could get. "Is everyone else ready?"

Across the room, I saw the stovetop clock switch to 5:45 p.m., which meant we were fifteen minutes past Adrienne's very hopeful picture-starting time. I wasn't surprised, and neither was Mo.

"Adrienne and Alaina are. Jess has asked Sydney to fix her hair about, oh, fifteen times."

None of this was really surprising, except for the fact that Sydney was taking so many orders from Jess—Ronan's date who I wasn't sure he actually wanted to go with. Adrienne was always very punctual, and Alaina—a fellow drama club student that Finn had asked to the dance—arrived at the house hours earlier with her hair and makeup already done. I certainly wasn't surprised that Adrienne and Alaina were waiting on Jess while Mo wasn't, but I was glad. It meant a few extra moments alone, and apparently, despite my exhaustion, I was going to take advantage of them.

"So you didn't want to go to the dance with anyone?" I asked.

Mo sat up a bit, intrigued. She mirrored me with a slouch and rested her chin on her hand, too. I held back a giggle.

"Remember how you felt about going to the dance with Bax?"

I nodded.

"Pretty much everyone at St. Jane's is Bax."

I tilted my head slightly. "You mean, like, homophobic?"

She thought about this for a second, and wasn't too quick to disagree. "I mean, some are. But every school has those kinds of people," she told me. "I just meant that there isn't anyone there that I'd really want to spend a whole night with. No one that isn't here, at least."

"Yeah," I laughed. "Judging by the look on Ronan's face this morning, I have a feeling he'd rather go with you. Finn too, probably."

Mo flashed a grateful smile, one that lingered longer than I expected. "They aren't the only ones I was talking about."

Cue the second wind.

I knew exactly what she meant, and I wanted to throw up. In a good way, if that was possible. But, of course, I couldn't show how much her words had energized me. I didn't know how strong her feelings were. I didn't even know *what* my feelings were. So, my expertise: a subject change. Sort of.

"What about your friends from back home?"

When I studied Mo's face, I realized this was one of the first times she didn't immediately understand what I was saying. It was almost funny.

I elaborated. "Was there anyone back there that you could stand to spend a whole night with?"

Now, Mo's face softened. "I guess so. I wasn't really close with anyone in New York. I spent a lot of time alone."

I couldn't stop the frown that made its way to my lips. "Really? But you're friends with everyone here."

She shrugged and pushed her hair behind her ear. "It's not as complicated here."

Now, I sat up. I didn't need my hand to hold my head up anymore. Mo's lack of elaboration was doing it for me. "What do you mean?"

"I came out in seventh grade," she explained. "The people I knew didn't really understand."

"So you lost all of your friends?" It broke my heart just to ask, and even more that I saw the answer on her face before she spoke.

"In a way, yeah," she said with a sad smile. "It was definitely a change of scenery when I came here and met all of you."

"I can't believe they all just abandoned you."

"It's not that big of a deal," she told me. "They stuck around, but it was different. They weren't willing to try and understand. I didn't want to waste my energy on making them."

210

There was the Mo I knew. She didn't ever apologize for who she was, and not even when her mother and friends turned their backs on her at such a young age. I wanted to commend her for it, and ask her how she learned to be so brave. But then there was my mom.

"Oh, Mo!" she exclaimed, crossing the floor from the sliding glass door to the table. "You look incredible. That dress is fabulous on you."

Mo stood to greet my mom, her usual slouch having erased itself flawlessly. My heart was full at the sight of the two of them standing side by side, but I still felt an urge to correct my mom. *Incredible* and *fabulous* didn't even begin to describe Mo. She, at that and every moment, was everything.

"Thank you, Mrs. Rose."

My mom huffed, placing her hand on Mo's shoulder and pulling her close. "My family calls me Stella."

I felt these words in my chest. My mother was unbelievably loving toward any friends that walked into our house. Oftentimes, she was more of a mother to them than their own, Finn being the shining example. But her evident love for Mo and recognition of her beauty made me smile in a way no interaction ever had before. It meant something so much more to me than what I could see.

Like all beautiful moments, however, it was fleeting. The boys had arrived.

My mom spun on her heel, nearly taking Mo out with her shoulder-length hair. "Braeden, honey, are you recording?"

All of a sudden, Braeden appeared from the back hallway like he was on a mission. He held his new video camera like dropping it would initiate explosions, his eyes laser focused on the screen. My dad trailed behind him, giggling, and found himself in the kitchen with the rest of us while the boys made their way up the basement stairs.

Finn was first. Though he always looked very put-together, tonight he looked endearing. He wore a gray suit with a matching waistcoat, and a red tie that would likely match the color of Alaina's dress, though I hadn't yet seen it. Behind him

211

came Ronan, and he too looked very charming. His floppy hair was brushed through, though not enough that its character wasn't recognizable, and he sported a black suit with a matching bowtie. I'd have said that he never looked better, but his expression—nervous, bored, and dreadful—would have disagreed.

And then came Luke. The color of his suit matched Ronan's, but the look on his face couldn't have been more dissimilar. His blonde hair looked anything but dirty, and his nervous expression was obviously due to the fact that his date was way out of his league. It was funny how, all of a sudden, he looked just like the kid who walked in the door all those years ago and proclaimed his undeniable love for the new girl in his class. It was almost as if he was still the same person.

My mom's spotting of Luke coincided with a massive gasp from her, and an obligatory eye roll from Luke himself. But then he saw the smile on her face, and one grew on his as well. As much as the Stop Growing Up looks made us kids squirm, nothing compared to seeing her happy. We'd learned long ago not to take that for granted.

"My boys," she muttered as she wrapped her arms around each of them. Once she made her way to Ronan, the nerves were wiped right off of his face. I hoped Braeden had captured the interaction.

I heard a door upstairs open, and then felt the air in the room shift again. Then, more gasps, and not just from my mother, when we saw the girls.

As I suspected, Alaina's dress was a bold shade of red. She was warranted in how confidently she wore it, as was Jess, whose slim white dress hugged her perfectly. I couldn't help but notice that her hair was pulled simply back into a neat and low ponytail, a style I couldn't imagine took much effort. Sydney, who was leaning over the railing in the upstairs hallway watching everything unfold, wore a slightly annoyed expression that told me just as much.

Like Ronan's returned dreadful look and Luke's nerves, Sydney's expression faded quickly when Adrienne started down the stairs. She was wearing the dress everyone had seen before—all but Luke, who we hid every picture of it from—and just enough makeup that you could tell she was wearing it, but not so much that it changed anything about her. The rest of the look could best be summed up with one word: elegant.

The dress was holding onto Adrienne perfectly, its grayness complementing both her tanned skin and her deep blue eyes, which had a bit of gray within themselves. The neckline and torso of the dress were simple—a plain fabric falling from a straight line. The skirt, however, was host to various layers, but somehow it was still simple. I couldn't have even imagined looking the way she did in a dress like that.

For this being only a school dance, I felt a whole lot like I was watching a princess movie. The way Adrienne floated down the stairs, the glow coming from every dance-goer, the newfound confidence the girls were wearing. Then, Luke did the honor of pulling me right out of the princess film and into our living room.

"Holy shit," he muttered, reaching for Adrienne's hands as she stepped off of the stairs.

My mom gasped again. "*Lucas.*"

Out of the corner of my eye, I saw Mo's eyebrows raise.

"He's right," she said, making everyone (even Ronan) laugh.

Adrienne blushed then embraced Luke as he pulled her in. Other conversations began as they had their moment, but I watched the way he whispered something in her ear, and I saw the butterflies from her stomach flutter to her eyes. There was never a time that I wasn't completely sure that the two of them were made for one another, but it was moments like this one that made me realize how lucky I was to be a witness to it. When all else in my life was scrambled, I could always look to Adrienne and Luke for peace of mind. They were more solid than anything.

The next fifteen minutes consisted of pictures. A multitude of them. Every pair imaginable was photographed together, and although my eyelids were growing heavier by the second, I was thoroughly enjoying the show.

If there had been superlatives for the photo session, dubbed by me, Luke and Adrienne would've obviously been crowned Cutest, with Finn and Adrienne's photo op coming in at a close second. I couldn't help but smile when the two of them stood next to each other. Their comfort with one another was obvious even through a photo, which never really told the whole story.

Funniest Pairing, or the Class Clowns, would've been given without hesitation to Ronan and Mo, whose banter with one another was both charming and a spectacle. Sweetest Picture, on the other hand, was a tie between Adrienne and her mother, Ms. Brenda, and my mom and Luke. I was enjoying the wholesomeness of the two of them side by side, Luke towering over my mom with my dad pointing a camera at them, when I was summoned.

"Okay, the whole Rose family," Finn insisted, offering his hand to my dad who handed off the camera. "Get in there, Elliana."

I straightened my black shorts, then found myself under Luke's arm, sandwiched between him and my dad. I smiled for the camera, but even if its lens wasn't facing me, I might've been shamelessly grinning anyway. Not only was my family a good distraction from what was on replay in my head, but I also felt safe beside them.

I didn't know what was next, or whether figuring myself out might have put a wedge between any of us in the future. But the way Luke held onto me, and the expressions of everyone else standing around the room watching as we smiled, told me that maybe I didn't need to be so worried. Maybe I'd always fit right there between the people I loved.

After (more than) enough pictures were taken, my parents slipped out of the frame and left just Luke, Braeden, and me.

"Stop slouching, Puke," Braeden said, poking the side of Luke's tux. He and I both laughed, and I was sure the photo that was snapped then would become my Favorite Of All Time. But then something else happened. Something big.

I'd retreated to the couch, watching over the back of it as my mother gawked at the sight of Luke, Finn, Ronan, and Adrienne remaking a picture they snapped in the same place in the eighth grade. I was pretty sure my quota for picture taking had been reached for the entire year, so I was happy to be sitting that one out.

On the other side of the room, Sydney was taking a photo for Alaina and Jess, posing them and fixing their hair before she took a few steps back and reassessed. Mo had just left their sides when she spotted me watching everything unfold.

"Elliana," she said slowly, immediately grabbing my attention. She waved me over to where she was standing by the fireplace. "Will you take one with me?"

"A picture?"

She nodded.

Ronan and Finn had apparently been relieved of their duties and were now just feet away from me, but I could only see the look of anticipation on Mo's face. If she'd asked again, I wouldn't have heard it over my heart beating.

"Yeah," I said finally, my voice a whisper.

Ronan stood in front of Mo and me, snapping the photo with a wide and goofy smile plastered across his face. Finn watched contently from behind him.

Standing next to Mo, there was a wave of confidence that washed over me, likely because it was radiating from her. I could feel her beauty in the same way I could normally see it, and it made me afraid of what my hand felt like on her waist. I wanted everything that she had, but I didn't want any part of me to bleed into her. Still, I couldn't stop the smile on my face.

"Best picture I took all night," Ronan said, and I knew he meant it.

Mo let out a laugh as she took her phone back. "Thanks."

"Oh, wait!" My dad said, scuttering our way. "Get back together, you two. Your mom will want one, too."

"We can just send those ones to her," I told him.

Mo lowered her eyebrows but her grin hadn't faded. She nodded back in her direction. "Come on."

My mind immediately flashed back to the last time she'd used that short phrase, and how unbelievably well things turned out once I'd finally followed her. This time, I didn't hesitate. So I was back by her side, a place I was beginning to live for. Or at least long for.

"Oh, Dad," I said, my shoulders slouching as I nodded toward the camera, where his pointer finger sat unknowingly and proudly in the way. "Your finger."

Instead of moving off of the lens, his finger cozied itself closer to the middle.

"No," I laughed. "Other way. It's still covering the lens."

He turned the camera around to face himself, a puzzled look causing his eyebrows to sink. I watched for just a second as he studied it, amused, before I felt eyes on me. Bright, green, captivating eyes. I turned to Mo, and there they were, looking at me in a way no one ever had before.

"What?"

She shook her head. "Nothing."

I watched as she turned back to the camera, the lack of noise coming from my dad indicating that he was done fiddling. But I kept my eyes on her.

"What?" I repeated.

She flashed a smile toward my dad, obviously bent on keeping the secret her eyes wanted to expose seconds earlier. Then, she squeezed my waist, pulling me closer to her and sending sparks throughout my entire body. All of it.

"Smile."

Chapter Twenty

Nell

I had nothing left. No brain power, no energy, no air in my lungs for an all-healing deep breath. Even sitting on our deck, my shins burning in the sun as I faced the ocean, I couldn't find solace. I had too many things on my plate, and an absurd amount were self-inflicted. But this kind of waiting—this longing for a weekend to be over so I could accept my fate—had never happened before. It was exhausting.

But among all of the things, there was a new bullet on the top of my Worry List. I'd never really fought with anyone, save for maybe once, if you could consider it a fight. I wasn't the same Elliana Rose from four years ago, and there were a lot of things about myself that I took the time to fix or to improve on. But I still didn't like seeing people upset, especially if I was the cause. So it was safe to say that my most recent encounter on the beach was keeping me up at night, and not just because of the way Mo's face shifted so starkly when I reached for Ronan's hand.

Luckily, this was the Rose House, and there was a party tonight. So Ronan wasn't far. He'd actually just arrived at my side.

"If I had a white flag, I'd be waving it," he said, his voice calm and sweet and everything good. There was that breath I needed.

I watched as he sat beside me, the two of us sharing the top step, and let out a laugh. "So you didn't come out here to continue our fight."

He lowered his eyebrows, his smile unwavering. "That was a fight?"

I shrugged.

"I'm sorry for the way I reacted," he told me. Now, my ears perked up. "I should've listened to you."

"It's okay."

Now, he let out a laugh through his nose. "Nah," he sighed. "It's not. We're family. There was no reason for me to walk away."

This, unfortunately, I could relate to. But Ronan wouldn't have known why, so I left it alone. With my pause, however, I gave him time to think and to act, and the way his next question sounded just about broke my heart. I didn't really know why.

"Is he coming tonight?"

I found raw nerves in his eyes then, ones I hadn't seen in a long time, if ever. I shook my head. "No."

His chest rose and fell with his breath. "Can I let you in on a secret?"

"I don't know if I should be trusted with any more of those."

Ronan nudged my shoulder, and it made me smile. So I nodded, giving him the okay to let it all out. I didn't even prepare myself for it.

"It's all my fault," he told me. "Finn wanted to tell me everything before he told Luke. I didn't even blink before making a big deal out of it."

I looked down at my feet. I didn't want to think about the three of them doing anything but laughing when they were together. "You were upset."

"I was irrational," he corrected. "Maybe we all would've been different if I'd handled it better. I think Luke could've come around."

"How did you handle it?"

"Told Luke in the locker room before our lacrosse game," he said. "I think I knew it'd get a rise out of him if everyone else was there, and I wanted him to react the way I did. Coach walked in when we were all screaming at each other. Finn backed down."

I shook my head, picturing it. "I hate the thought of that."

Ronan nodded, paused for a beat. "Me too."

Now, this is probably where I could've left it. But the conversation Ronan and I were having wasn't just an obligatory Best Man-Maid of Honor truce before an important wedding. We cared about one another, and even though he was long gone, I still cared for the Ronan from high school. I wanted to figure him out just as much as he did.

"Why did it bother you so much?"

He shrugged, but it seemed as though his answer was simple. "I've spent my whole life surrounded by good examples, you know? Your parents, Luke and Adrienne," he explained. "My parents immigrated here together when they were fifteen and got married at twenty-three. They've never broken apart, never so much as raised their voices at one another."

I lifted my eyes to him now, finding tears in his bottom eyelids as he explained.

"I always thought love was something concrete. I have a hard time believing it ever fades away once you find it," he told me. "When Finn told me he loved Adrienne, I thought that was it for all of us. I thought it was always going to be that way. So I didn't listen."

Never in a million years would I have dreamt this up as Ronan's explanation. But hearing him now, it made perfect sense.

"So, if love never fades," I started slowly, "then what about that?"

Ronan followed my eyes down to his hands. When he found what I was referring to—the barely pink scar on his finger—his face dropped. Six years earlier, the thought of someone hurting Finn was such an intrusion in Ronan's mind that he put his own body on the line to defend him. If that wasn't love, then I didn't have a very good idea of what was.

He nodded, blinking away a few tears as a gust of wind made his floppy hair bounce.

"Yeah," he said, his voice a whisper. "I guess I'm learning."

The daylight creeping into his dark eyes made me smile. Quite frankly, I was proud. I leaned and rested my head on his shoulder, a punctuation mark to our truce. It had been a tense forty-eight hours, and I was happier than ever that I had Ronan on my side for the next few.

"We're all learning."

Ronan nodded, and with it I could feel the fear he held for the next few days. I hoped he knew he wasn't alone in that, either. But then he surprised me.

"So who's the girl?"

I didn't want to make a big deal, for obvious reasons, but now my heart was in my throat. How the conversation had turned to Mo, I had no idea. I was going to take my time finding out.

"What girl?"

"You sounded very certain that he's not in love with Adrienne anymore," Ronan recounted. "So who's he in love with?"

Oh, dear God. I couldn't take all of this back and forth. I just couldn't.

I hoped my sigh of relief wasn't noticeable. "Her name is Sutton."

And on I went. About Freya, about Pittsburgh, about the babysitter named Crazy. There was no detail left behind. Sure, I might've been stealing Finn's spotlight, taking away from their reunion by offering his stories to Ronan myself. But I only had a few days worth of Finn knowledge. He had four whole years to unpack.

Five hours later, I was wearing a black cocktail dress, courtesy of Genevieve's Closet for Nell, and had my feet shoved into a pair of Adrienne's high heels. I was more comfortable and confident in the outfit than High School Me would've ever dreamt of being, but my feet were throbbing, and the night was still so young.

The Thursday Night Party, for utter lack of a better term, was in full swing. I'd already had countless conversations with family members who claimed they remembered me being all different variations of "this big." I didn't remember meeting many of them in the first place.

Now, I'd just handed off a pair of drinks to my cousins Brenden and Ashley, both of whom thanked me and lightly conversed in very New York-heavy accents. Just seconds before, I thought they were from California.

As much as I thought we were party animals before, I'd never seen our house as packed as it was. There was a light trace of music playing in the background, unapologetically being drowned out by all of the voices bouncing off of the windows and walls. A pink haze, courtesy of the sunset, was creeping into the already well-lit rooms, too. It was truly an oceanside party, even though the majority of it had migrated inside. Thankfully, we had plenty of napkins.

Though everything was going exactly as planned, likely because my mother was the one who planned it, I felt like I was spinning. Adrienne's family—all six on her mom's side who were in town for the wedding—were happy, but overwhelmed, so I was going out of my way to talk with them and make the night, and the upcoming festivities, more pleasant. My dad's brothers, on the other hand, kept stealing my attention to talk about basketball, though I hadn't stepped on a court in two years and didn't ever plan to again. There were several others— cousins my age, aunts and uncles, old friends of my grandparents—who wanted to know about my track at school, my roommates, my future plans. For a night that was meant to be solely about Adrienne and Luke, I sure had to explain the shell of my life story to lots of people.

Just as I finally spotted Sydney, who was rocking a red, floor-length dress and talking to a couple of bridesmaids, I was beckoned again.

"Elliana!" said my Grandma Laura. "Darling, come here!"

I begrudgingly made my way to my grandmother but hid my hesitance from my face and my shoulders. Grandma Laura was someone I only ever saw on the holidays, and my expectations of her personality, which started high because of how great my dad turned out, only fell with every visit. She had her ways, and she was more than stuck in them. She was cemented.

"So your father tells me you're into journalism now," she started, pulling me closer than I would've liked. She was taller than me even while I was in heels and she was in flats, and she'd done her graying hair so perfectly I would've thought she had someone do it for her. But I knew better than to assume she'd asked for any help.

"Well, my major is Communications," I explained. "But I'm more into the film and television side of things."

Even though I didn't exactly care what my grandmother's perception of me was, I still felt the need to be truthful. Maybe it was her grip on my shoulder, or the daggers her sister Marley and my Great Aunt Hellen had for eyes. I'd heard from my mother that none of the three were pleasant, so I shouldn't have been bothered about what they thought of me. But nevertheless, I wanted to soften their expressions.

So, to my dismay, my grandmother frowned. "You plan to make films in Vermont?"

I shrugged, albeit slowly. I couldn't be too quick to come back. "I don't know where I want to go after school."

"Well, you're not going to make much money waving a camera around in the mountains," she told me, the laugh that made its way out of her in the form of etiquette pointed at Marley and Hellen, not me.

I'd only taken a few classes in film so far, but I hadn't once thought about the money involved in it. Just the storytelling. It was a good thing Grandma Laura didn't have much of an influence on my subconscious. It could not handle any more what-ifs.

I flashed a smile and pretended to listen as she went on about practical jobs, like Adrienne's new placement as a nurse and Luke's path leading to culinary school and, later, countless opportunities as a professional chef. I already knew both of these things, and I was more proud than my grandma could've known, so I let my eyes wander. Of course, the first thing they found was curly, red hair sitting atop the shoulders of a short-sleeved black dress, the curls bouncing along as the girl sporting them laughed.

I could only see her side profile, and maybe it was just the lighting, but Mo looked different. I didn't study her so much on the beach, likely because I was busy rambling, and I was too nervous to really take her in during our run-in at Archie's. But now, as my grandma spoke, I could see the way her cheekbones had gotten more prominent, how her freckles were owning themselves. I never would've thought in high school that she had any sort of a baby face, but now she looked so grown up. It was funny, almost. Back then, I didn't think she could possibly be more mature. Add that to the list of things I was wrong about.

Just when I thought Mo was fully engrossed in her conversation with Renna and Logan, her eyes flickered toward me. I looked away quickly, so as not to seem like I was staring, which I was.

"... and he's got great friends," my grandmother was explaining, still on the topic of Luke and his apparent perfection. If he were next to me and not across the room, he would have snorted. "Like that Ronan."

That Ronan, I thought. Our Ronan. There was a difference.

"You know, I hear that you're very popular with the boys at school," she said to me then, drawing an involuntary and stunned look from me.

"Where did you hear that?" I asked, my voice light.

"Well, I guess I just figure. You're a very pretty girl, Elliana." She squeezed my shoulder again. "What about that Ronan? He's a good boy, isn't he? What's he doing now?"

I spotted Ronan across the room. Technically, *now*, he was spilling a hard seltzer on his pants without realizing it. But this answer was not what my grandmother was looking for.

"He's starting a graduate program for finance," I told her. "He just finished his undergrad in Ohio."

I kept my eyes on Ronan for a second longer, wishing to the ends of the Earth that we had some sort of telepathy.

Hulk, I thought. Nothing.

"You see," Grandma Laura continued, like what I'd shared was old information. "He's a smart boy, a great friend, I've heard. I'm sure he won't be scraping under the couch cushions for nickels and dimes." This last part came out a bit softer, as if she was almost aware of how shallow it sounded.

I didn't want to laugh, but I was coping. Plus, now Marley and Hellen were intrigued, or at least their eyebrows said so. "I guess we're just too good of friends to be anything else," I suggested.

My grandmother lowered her head, daring me to look her in the eyes. So I did.

"Those are the people you should be drawn to," she offered. "Your grandfather and I were platonic for ten years before I charmed him."

"More like wrangled him," Aunt Marley laughed.

Grandma waved her off, leaning into me again. "You have to think about your future, darling. It won't wait for you."

I watched Ronan across the room once more. He was conversing with Corbin Bleu, or Brett, with rosy cheeks and animated expressions. Just a number of days ago, Ronan was worried the other groomsmen wouldn't like him. What a silly thought that was.

There was a life I could have dreamt of with Ronan, and maybe it had the potential to be beautiful, with trimmed hedges and kids that played catch with footballs on the beach. He was a good person, and I knew that whoever he chose to spend his life with was going to be better because of it. But that person wasn't me, and now, with my grandmother's fingers digging into my shoulder, I was beginning to feel guilty for it.

"Yeah." I cleared my throat. "Well, you never know."

She smiled triumphantly. "You always know, dear." Her hair stayed perfectly still as she shook her head. She turned to Hellen, who was rubbing a speck of lipstick from her front tooth. "Now, it won't be long until we see those two walking down the aisle together, isn't that right?"

"Mhm," Hellen mumbled. Great additive.

I began to take in a deep breath as my grandma released me. I thought, perhaps, that I might've had an out then, but she kept on.

"I'm just surprised there's no one for you at that school," she joked.

All of a sudden, there was a hand on my shoulder, but my grandmother hadn't moved. When I turned to find who it belonged to, I finally found that deep breath.

"Sorry to interrupt," Mo said, to Grandma Laura and the group. Then, to me, "Nell, I think your mom needs you in the kitchen."

"Nell?" my grandma laughed. "What, Elliana is too boring a name now?"

I didn't even bother.

"I should go see what she needs," I said, placing a gentle hand on Grandma Laura's arm. "Excuse us."

The two of us turned away, standing as close to one another as friends would. Before I'd taken even one step, I could hear my grandmother's voice again, her tone unpleasant as she likely speculated about my attitude with Marley and the others. It was invigorating, the way I didn't care.

"What does she need me for?" I asked, holding my gaze hostage as it tried to wander toward Mo.

"She doesn't."

Now I turned, finding Mo's expression to be serious and, surprisingly, a touch nervous. "Oh."

"It just looked like you needed an out," she told me. So she was watching.

I took a pointed breath and shook my head, cursing the air for wanting to grow awkward as it sat between us. To discourage it, I offered a smile. "I did. Thanks."

For a second, I watched a smile grow on Mo's lips, along with the potential for some words, but then I was pulled back in.

"Hey, Elliana, you never finished telling us about school!"

This interruption was brought to us by my Uncle Drake, my dad's older brother who lived in Colorado and had two kids the same ages as Braeden and me. I'd been talking with him and Uncle Paul, Dad's younger brother with no kids, before I began to lose track of time. They were the basketball connoisseurs, and I didn't recall any of our conversation revolving around school. Then again, it had been an hour since I'd been on this side of the room.

I opened my mouth to apologize, or something, but I didn't get the chance.

"Who's this?" Uncle Paul asked. He had bright blue eyes and they were snaking happily between Mo and me.

I glanced at Mo, and she at me. The answer was easy, wasn't it?

"This is Mo," I told him. "My friend."

Uncle Paul reached out his hand. "I'm Paul. Adam's brother."

Mo took part in a firm handshake, then another as Drake extended his arm and introduced himself too.

"It's nice to meet you both," Mo uttered.

"You two go to college together?" Paul asked.

It was nice that they cared, or at least that they were trying to, but every word they spoke was making me squirm. Our past really wasn't that complicated, but standing next to Mo, so embarrassingly desperate to feel the way I did back then, it hurt my heart to talk about it. Even in this way, which was really nothing at all.

"High school," Mo answered when I didn't. "I went to college in New York. I'm the same year as Lucas."

"Huh. Would you look at that?" Paul said, elbowing Drake and nearly knocking his sweating beer from his hand. "Elliana gets along with Luke's friends."

This was more of a dig at Drake, I assumed, and maybe even at my dad. But for some reason, it felt like a dig at me. I'd spent years convincing myself that I belonged with Luke's friends just as much as he did. Now, just one comment was going to set me back.

"Um– Elliana," Mo started then. "Were you still going to show me the garden?"

My heart dropped. Like a rollercoaster cart after its peak, I felt it fall in my chest.

I turned to Mo, swallowing hard, then back to my uncles before I could get a read on what her face looked like. I had a feeling I knew, anyway.

"We're going to–" I swallowed again. After a breath, I was able to smile. "We'll catch you guys later." Then, I nodded toward the kitchen where I could see that red dress again. "I don't know if you remember Sydney, my friend from elementary school?"

Drake nodded immediately, while Paul tilted his head.

"Well, she's playing basketball in Georgia now. Division One," I told them. "I'm sure she'd love to talk about it."

This might've been a lie. Sydney probably wasn't going to love talking about basketball. But at least she had something to add to a conversation about it. I had nothing.

After a quick check-in with my mother, who had lost sight of sober hours ago and was enjoying a few moments of hysterical laughter on the back deck with Ms. Brenda and Ronan's mother, I was stepping into the garden with Mo. Thankfully, my heart had made its exit from my stomach. But now it was in my throat.

The sunset was through with its performance, and the night had brought with it a deep, navy blue sky. But even through the darkness, I could feel the spirit of the garden. It was undeniable, the charm it harbored.

I was surprised to find that Mo and I were alone as we stepped into the trees and flowers and under the fairy lights. More than that, I was nervous, and treading carefully. It was no secret, at least to the two of us, how significant this location was in our history. Though it was arguably the most beautiful part of the house, I'd always avoided the garden, and our past was just one more reason why. Now, I felt as if I was strolling through a time capsule.

And yet, here we were. I walked slowly, catching my breath as I took a seat on the concrete bench that sat just beside the stone path. I was doing my best to ignore the charm and the beauty of the place. Embracing the magic of its smell and its peace might have led me to feeling more than I wanted to.

"I can– I can go back inside," Mo said. When I lifted my head, I realized she'd stayed by the garden's entrance while I'd just continued on. "If you need a breather, or something."

I shook my head immediately, habitually. "You don't have to."

This was an invitation; we both knew it. But not just to enter the garden and take in the flowers and the lights. It was an invitation to talk. I was desperate for her to take it.

She nodded, taking her time and reaching for a low-hanging tree branch as her footsteps drew nearer to me.

Again, I had nothing left in me, and the next thing out of my mouth was probably very indicative of it.

"Do you remember the last time we were here?"

Mo's shock was visible, immediate. She laughed, but it wasn't funny.

"Are you joking?"

I bit my lip. It was a stupid question, but maybe it had broken the ice between us. I could only hope.

"I think about that night a lot," I admitted, my gaze on my feet again.

"Yeah?"

I nodded.

Mo paused. "Me too."

"You do?"

She'd made her way over to the bench without my noticing, and was taking a seat on the opposite end of it. There was enough room for two people between us. I had a feeling it was our past selves that occupied the space, daring us to push them away.

This time, her voice was a bit softer, less protected. Her walls were falling. Finally.

"I thought things were changing for you that night."

If it weren't for the dim lights coming from the trees and stone path, Mo would've been but a shadow in the garden. Still, she would've been just as radiant, and her words just as heartbreaking. I swallowed down a sob.

"They were," I told her, urging her to believe me.

She shook her head slightly, refusing to meet my eyes. "It sure didn't seem like it."

I was breathless. "Mo—"

She stood up, while simultaneously backing down. I'd never seen her regret anything, but the way she shut her eyes and shook her head made me believe she wished she could've stolen her words back out of the air.

"I'm sorry." she started. "I shouldn't have said that. I—"

Before my heart could completely shatter like fragile glass, the lights from the dark side of the deck flicked on, revealing both of our sunken faces and a very excited Braeden leaning his head into view.

"Nell!" he yelled, waving us over. "It's time for the video!"

Braeden disappeared quickly, and Mo turned back toward me.

"The video?"

I nodded, then led the two of us away from our joint landmark, my hand accidentally grazing hers as we crossed the threshold between the deck and the kitchen.

In the next beat, we were reimmersed in the party. Everyone who was outside or in different rooms had crowded into the living room—though it was big, it was not at all suited for this kind of population. I stood beside Adrienne and Luke and Mo and Braeden and had not a clue where Ronan was. I watched my parents snickering together from across the room, a gray napkin in my mother's hand, as Luke made an announcement on Braeden's behalf.

"Okay, hey everyone! Can I please have your, uh–attention?"

I knew a tipsy Luke when I heard one. I bit back a laugh. Adrienne, beside me, did the same.

"Braeden and Nell have prepared something special for us tonight," he announced. Then, his volume lowered. "Ready, B?"

I was still smiling when Braeden pressed a button on the remote and the video started rolling.

Everyone turned toward the television to find the most wholesome of compilations, starting with a video my mother took of Luke and Adrienne in eighth grade carving pumpkins together in the driveway. Then, there was a clip of the two of them walking hand-in-hand after a lacrosse game, and one of Luke watching in admiration from the wings of a stage that Adrienne was performing on—their tenth grade talent show, if I remembered correctly.

Those videos, and the ones that followed, were met by a series of laughter and sweet remarks from the entire room. I watched my mom wipe a tear from her eye during a video of them at their high school graduation, and I laughed out loud at a clip of Luke saving Adrienne's face from a football that was flying rapidly toward her. The one that followed was of the whole crew on the beach, and the star of the video, unsurprisingly, was Ronan, who was breaking out some never-before-seen dance moves with his sunglasses on upside-down. When the video cut, I finally spotted him across the room, his hair being tussled by a fellow former lacrosse player while his goofy grin shone brightly.

Then, the tv's frame was host to a video of Adrienne and Luke just before their Senior Prom, a day identifiable by Adrienne's beautiful gray dress and Luke's suit. I listened as a younger Braeden interviewed the happy couple about the goings-on of that day, but what caught my eye was what unfolded in the background.

First, I spotted Mo. She was standing with perfect posture in her emerald green dress, the one I remembered so vividly even without the video to jog my memory. Beside her, there was a girl in a bland outfit, with hair so long and taken care of it looked styled even though it was partially wet. She was talking to someone in front of her, completely oblivious to the way Mo was looking at her. To me, the girl next to Mo was such a stranger, so unfamiliar that I couldn't believe she was who I used to see when I looked in the mirror.

As a roar of laughter erupted around me, a result of Luke answering a question about Adrienne's appearance with ample stuttering and rosy cheeks, my eyes were pulled away. First, to my hands, one of which was anxiously toying at a hair tie around my wrist. Then, because I had to, I turned in Mo's direction. I looked into her eyes, which she was daring to keep on the screen, and found tears pooling in the bottoms of them. She'd seen what I saw, and she was hurt by it.

In an instant, I wanted to turn back time. I wanted to march toward the girl with the perfect hair and the dull outfit, shake her shoulders and tell her that what she was feeling was real. I wanted to tell her not to be afraid because letting go was going to be devastatingly worse than being brave.

I wanted Mo to turn to me now so I could convince her of it, too. So I could tell her it was real. When she did turn, finally, Adrienne nudged my shoulder.

"This one's my favorite," she whispered.

I watched the screen again as another video from Braeden's perspective unfolded on it. It began with Mo, whose face was lit up by the glow of a late-night fire and who smiled brightly at the grateful cameraman before he panned to Ronan who stuck out his tongue. The frame next found Finn, who just shook his head beside an unassuming Lucas—he didn't realize the video was being taken until it was too late. Finally, the tail-end of the video found Adrienne and me. When it was centered on the two of us, we simultaneously pulled the strings of our hoodies, so only our noses and mouths were left to identify us by. It was our laughter that took us to the next video.

I turned to a still smiling Adrienne and let a tear fall down my cheek. "Mine too."

Chapter Twenty-One

Elliana

"Can you toss me a marshmallow, B?"

Sydney held out her hands as Braeden hurled a white puff through the air. When it landed perfectly on target, a series of cheers rang out.

"Great precision," Ronan noted.

Henry nodded, his arm cozied around Sydney's shoulders. "You oughta be playing baseball with that arm."

"Don't give him any ideas," Luke said.

The nine of us, believe it or not, were sitting around a crackling fire beside the beach. The morning hours were getting closer and closer, just mere minutes away by now, and no one had cut out early. This was likely the result of two undeniable facts: we were having too much fun, and everything was about to change.

Earlier in the night, Ronan had announced that he'd done math for the first time in his life—the latter part an observation made by Finn—and had concluded that high school lasted for a total of seven hundred and twenty days. For the majority of the group, tomorrow was going to be the last one.

There was simply no reason to believe that this night would be the end of all nights like it. Only Finn and Mo were leaving for college in the next few weeks, while the others weren't off until August. Even then, we'd all be together again in no time. But it wouldn't ever be the same. While that was certainly cause for sorrow, it also meant we had to celebrate while we could. So, midnight had nothing on us.

Another thirty minutes had passed, and Sydney was well through with her s'more, when the entire course of the night was altered.

"You know what would be fun?"

It wasn't just my attention that was completely fixated on Mo every time she uttered even one word; the whole group seemed to be enthralled by her. So when she asked a question like this one, then nodded in the direction of the dark ocean, no one had to ask what she meant. By now, we just knew.

I listened to the waves as I considered her suggestion. It did seem enticing, a late-night swim on the eve of the last day of school. I had my reservations, of course. The beach was dark and empty, so if something were to have happened, there wasn't anyone around to help us. But maybe that was what made the idea so intriguing. The unknown, the risk.

"I'm in," Ronan said immediately, his confirmation seconded by both Luke and Finn as they traded enthusiastic smiles.

Adrienne leaned forward. "Me too."

"Me three," Sydney announced, grabbing ahold of Henry's hand. "And four."

Everyone who hadn't agreed verbally had now done so silently, with Braeden's face indicating he was all for the idea. So, naturally, all eyes were on the last one to join in.

"Yeah," I said quietly, clearing my throat. "Let's go."

I doubted that the lack of bathing suits or parental guidance was in anyone's mind but my own as we rushed toward the waves, but it didn't take away from the adrenaline running through my veins. I let my feet take me right in, and I didn't feel like there was something pulling me back. Only forward. And that something—the magnet that was drawing me into the water—was surely a person rather than a force. Maybe she was both.

We'd been standing, and effectively goofing off, in knee-high water for a few moments when I began to take in the conversations flourishing around me, and my cheeks rosied at their novelty. There were Luke and Adrienne, talking excitedly with Finn about their plans to visit him in Pittsburgh come fall. Ronan and Braeden were discussing the boys Senior Night for lacrosse, which was just hours away, and how quickly Braeden's own senior year would come. Then, there were Henry and Mo, the most unusual of pairings, drooling over their fascination with different languages. Their words and the stars that were painting a bold picture above our heads led me to believe that this was just where we were all meant to be. This was what it felt like to be in the water. To be a part of it.

"You know," said Sydney's voice, whose tone I had to trust in the few seconds that my eyes failed to make out her image in the darkness. When I found her, she was grinning. "I never thought I'd see you in the ocean in the middle of the night."

I laughed, because of course she didn't. No one did. "Me neither."

She was beside me then, the waves synchronously hitting our shins as she threw her arm around my shoulders. I felt her look in different directions, observing the same conversations I'd been. When she cleared her throat, no one else heard. Evidently, this was purposeful.

"So, do you like her?"

I shook my head instinctually, my skin immediately growing cold at the idea of admitting my feelings to another person. Then again, this was Sydney. It was surprising that it had taken this long, but I was still shocked.

"How did you—"

She clicked her tongue, but kept her voice low. "Elliana, I know what you feel before you even feel it."

I let out another laugh, but then stopped it short when I began to wonder how many other people in the water had been thinking the same thing, or if they'd noticed at all. Maybe it didn't matter.

"You have that look in your eyes," Sydney said then.

I swallowed down a breath, and not surprisingly, felt tears welling under my eyelids. "What look?"

"That's the thing," she said. "I've never seen it before."

I let this sink in for a moment. If anyone could convince me that a change I didn't see coming was a good one, it was Sydney. She'd been there for everything, even though I'd done this thing, so far, on my own.

"I'm sorry I didn't tell you, I just—"

"I know," she shook her head. "I've been spending too much time with Henry. I'm sorry, it's just that I sort of can't get enough of him. And I know it's still new but I feel so tingly when I'm around him, and—"

"Sydney," I laughed. "That's not what I was going to say."

"Oh."

"I thought you knew what I felt before I felt it," I joked.

"Apparently, that just expired."

We laughed for a moment together, and God, it felt good. I hadn't exactly recognized how much time Sydney had been spending with Henry, and I did miss her. But I was happy for her, for the new kind of smile on her face. If the way she felt about Henry was anything close to the way Mo made me feel, I wouldn't have blamed her if she never wanted to see anyone else ever again.

"I was going to say that I didn't see it coming," I told her then. I watched as, just a few feet away, Mo tipped her head back in laughter at something Henry said. In the distance, Luke and Adrienne's hands, interlocked, were swinging through crashing waves. "And it's hard to talk about," I went on, "because I don't really know what I am. If I'm— if I'm bi or what—"

"Elliana," Sydney started. I could feel her eyes on me, so I met her halfway. "What you *are—*" she paused, shaking her head. "It doesn't need to matter unless you want it to. Unless you figure it out and you want it to matter. You are beautiful, and kind, and a good person. The best person. That's what you are. That's what matters."

In the next second, I had my arms around Sydney, and she around me. I was also the luckiest person.

"I love you," I told her.

"I know," she said, her tone sarcastic and causing a synchronous laugh from both of us. "I love you, too."

I didn't know what time it was when we finally rounded up our belongings and started to head inside, all of us a symphony of shivers and laughter and breaths of relief that we'd once again made the best out of a night. I, for one, was on cloud nine. For the second time in just a few days, something that was so daunting to me became a relief that I never could've dreamed of. I was doing so much feeling lately, and most of it was overwhelming. But this—this was good.

So when I made my way up the steps, just one ahead of Mo and two behind the boys, I couldn't stop smiling. It was a good thing it was dark outside. The boys, who were engaged in their own love-fest and playing a game that seemed to revolve around movie characters, probably wouldn't have noticed anyways.

"Hm," Luke mumbled as they reached the landing. "Vision."

"Groot," Finn said.

Ronan's shoulders sank, and his head tipped back in defeat. "I was going to say Groot."

"Fine," Finn surrendered simply. "You say it."

I could see Ronan's smile even from behind him. "Groot."

"You lose," Finn countered. "I already said Groot."

I heard Adrienne laugh from a distance, and felt Luke perk up as he slowed his pace.

"Maybe we should let Ronan be Groot," he suggested.

Finn shook his head. "Why?"

"Because he only knows three words."

Instead of taking offense, Ronan joined in on the joke. It was an art he'd mastered, and I commended him for it. We all did.

"I am Ronan," he said in a deep voice, drawing giggles from both Luke and Finn. I giggled too, but then Mo's voice rang out quietly from beside me.

"Hey," she nodded toward the side of the house. "You still have to show me the garden. We can't forget."

Adrienne and Finn had reached the house now, the two of them slowly entering it with Ronan and Luke in tow. I glanced toward the side of the house where the garden was. I swallowed down whatever it was that wanted to erupt from inside me and found Mo's eyes.

"What about now?"

She grinned. "Isn't it a little dark to look at flowers?"

"You don't know my mom," I told her. "Come on."

I reached for Mo's hand then, and waved goodbye to Sydney and Henry as they followed the others into the house. The garden was only a few steps away, but I felt as though I was moving in slow motion. Everything was surreal—Mo's hand in mine, the pang in my chest, the floating feeling in my feet. Then I flicked on the lights.

If there was one thing to know about my mother, it was that nothing she did was small when she put her energy toward it. For the past five years, all of her heart and her mind—the parts that didn't belong to her job or my dad or us kids—went right to the garden. So it was beautiful. One of the most beautiful things I and anyone else had ever seen. One of.

First, there were the trees. All different kinds, which I couldn't even begin to identify, lined the stone paths of the garden. They were whimsical in the darkness, and they were host to all different sizes of lights and chimes and things. The fairy lights were my mom's favorite, and it was evident by how many of them sprinkled the branches of the trees and the leaves of the bushes. Because of the picture they painted, stepping into the garden often felt like a dream sequence. Tonight, I was beginning to think it was.

The next best part of the garden, and the part I caught Mo gasping at upon entering it, was the amount of flowers that littered it. There were dahlias, daylilies, irises, lavender, and plenty of others whose names I didn't know. Their colors were endless, and they existed in such harmony it was almost unbelievable. For a pride and joy, my mother certainly had something to brag about.

"This is—" Mo paused to catch her breath. I released her hand so that she could reach for a tree flower while I made my way over to the bench. "This is incredible. I can't believe I've never seen it before."

"It's my mom's hidden gem," I told her.

"I know, but—" She shook her head. "It's just— I can't believe you don't spend all of your time in here."

I shrugged.

"Oh, I love peonies," she said, eyeing a bunch of white flowers that surrounded the backside of the bench I now sat upon.

Normally, this was the amount of time that I could stand to be in the garden. Every time I'd been in it with my mother, I just walked beside her and the occasional guest, listening to her talk about the reason behind her flower placements. I liked to pretend I didn't exist when that happened. I could never wait to be anywhere else, just because of the feeling I couldn't shake whenever I was under the trees and the lights. Whenever the flowers and stones and colors were staring right back up at me. But with Mo, it was different. It had always been different.

"My mom does, too," I said quietly, referring back to the peonies. "They're her favorite."

"Out of all these, that's a beautiful choice," Mo said. She'd made her way to me now. I watched her eyes fall to the spot in the yard beside the bench—the cement plaque, I assumed. She read it, and I watched her shoulders drop. Then I watched her read it again. "Who's Paisley?"

This question hit my stomach before it hit my ears. I wasn't sure if I'd ever been asked the question directly, or if I ever had to answer it myself. I always had someone I would defer to. But coming in here tonight, I knew this would happen. And still, here I was.

"Nell," Mo said quietly, my pause uncomfortably long.

"She was my sister," I told her.

Mo shook her head, her eyes bouncing between me and the cement. I kept my eyes on her as she knelt down, gently wiping away the mulch on the bottom of the plaque to reveal the date carved into it. There were a few more seconds of quiet, ones she took to understand for herself, before she sat down next to me. Until that moment, I'd never seen her face so full of sorrow.

"Do you want to talk about it?" she asked, her voice hushed but not a whisper.

The answer to this question was usually so easy, such a formed response from deep inside of me. This time, it was just as easy. But it wasn't the same answer.

"My mom always wanted a big family. She actually told my dad on their first date that she wanted at least ten kids," I started, a faint smile on my face. I couldn't help but be reminded of Luke and Adrienne when my mother told stories like this. Even now, their similarity made me happy. "But, um, after Braeden, she started having trouble. Getting pregnant, I mean. I was still young, so I don't really know all of the details. But my dad says that she miscarried three times."

I saw Mo's face sink out of the corner of my eye but couldn't turn to read her expression fully. If I did, I wasn't sure I would've been able to keep talking. And this was big. For me, at least.

"Her third miscarriage was the worst, the latest in the term, and after it happened her doctors told her that she wasn't going to be able to get pregnant or carry a baby anymore. So, uh— so she was devastated."

I took a pause, and a big breath with it. This next part, I'd never spoken aloud before. Anyone outside of our family who knew the details hadn't ever heard them from me. "And then she got pregnant a year later. And it was like there was this ray of light all of a sudden, that we could all see. That we all felt."

Mo shifted beside me. She knew what was coming.

"She carried the baby full term, and both of them were healthy the whole time. The doctors called it a miracle. My parents named her Paisley," I said, trying to remember everything I'd blocked out for so long. "My brothers and I were at the hospital when she was born. We all got to hold her. She was the smallest little person I'd ever seen."

Mo let out a noise that was somewhere between a breath and a laugh, probably at the sentiment. She wiped a tear from her cheek.

I blinked hard. Then, I remembered the way Paisley's face looked, how perfect it was, how she looked like my mom and maybe even a little like me. I'd spent every day trying to forget what happened next, because I didn't want to believe that something so pure could've been taken away so quickly.

"They had to stay in the hospital for a couple of days because Paisley started to have some trouble. The doctors said that they were typical baby things, that she was still a miracle." I bit my lip. "Luke, Braeden, and I were at Ronan's house three days later when my dad called in the middle of the night to tell us she didn't make it."

Mo shook her head, and I heard her take in a hard breath. "How?"

"There was a lot of medical jargon thrown around that I never understood. In the end, her heart failed."

Now, Mo finally looked up at me, and I didn't hesitate to look back. We both had tears in our eyes, our cheeks rosy. I never wanted to see someone like her upset, but this felt different. This felt like something had changed, and it certainly had. The thought of telling anyone about Paisley had never once crossed my mind, not because I was ashamed but because speaking about it meant dealing with it. Sitting next to Mo, I felt like I could deal with anything.

"So that's why you don't come out here," she observed.

I nodded, but there was more to it than that.

"None of us talked for a week after she died. I didn't talk for longer."

"How much longer?"

I shrugged. "Long enough for my parents to be worried. For my brothers to think there was something wrong with me too," I recounted. "Do you remember when you were little, and you'd see someone fall on the playground?"

Mo nodded.

"Remember being afraid to do whatever they were doing, even if it was just for a second?"

And again.

"That's how I felt," I told her. "But I was afraid to live. Because she couldn't."

The years after Paisley died, all leading up to this one, had been dark. I was afraid of everything around me because of how harsh Paisley's short life had been to her. And, as much as I hated myself for it, I was afraid of my mom and her sadness. All I ever wanted was to escape.

"I'm so sorry," Mo whispered. Then, finding her voice, she turned to me again. "I'm sorry if I ever made you feel like you weren't getting the most out of your life."

My eyebrows lowered immediately. She couldn't have been more wrong about how she made me feel.

"You haven't."

"No, really. The Elliana and Nell thing— I'm so sorry if I pushed that on you, I didn't—" She shook her head, wiped away another stray tear. "I thought you were so apprehensive because of St. Jane's, or something. I had no idea."

"Mo, no." I took a breath, for once not lacking to find the words I wanted to say. "My life has always just been me making sure that everything was in line. Nothing could ever go wrong. For both my own sake and my mom's. I could never so much as breathe the wrong way."

She looked down at the peonies, waiting.

"I don't feel that way with you," I admitted.

When she looked into my eyes then, she stared so deep I felt it in my heart. I could tell she was looking for something concrete to hold onto, something that I could say that would make her believe I meant it. I didn't have that. Not yet.

There was a flash of a smile, but considering the weight of the conversation, it faded. "I'm glad."

Now, I was looking for something deep in Mo's eyes. Something that would tell me what to do next. Something that would tell me if what I was thinking—if what I wanted—was what was meant to happen. I looked away, if only to catch my breath.

"How— um—" I stumbled along these next words. "How long until you leave for New York?"

Her pause told me that she knew what I was thinking. Now, my heart felt like a jackhammer.

"A week and a half."

I nodded. I knew the answer, but hearing it again, my eyes and my hopes fell down to my feet. Now, I wasn't sure what I was thinking.

"I won't be there forever."

These words, and the way she said them, meant something. They mattered.

"Good," I said then, kicking my feet across the mulch beneath me and sporting a smile that I couldn't hide. The tears that had been welling in my cheeks and my eyes were now fluttering in my stomach in the form of butterflies. There was also something else—the magic of the garden, the way I'd opened up, the radiance flooding from Mo to me—that was making me feel especially confident. Before I knew it, I was acting upon it.

"Mo."

She turned her head toward me, her face glowing from the lights hanging above us, her eyes glowing all on their own. I felt light all over as my hand found its way to her forearm and slowly moved up it. We'd gotten so close so quickly, and I wasn't afraid. Not even when we were nose to nose. Not even when she stopped leaning in.

"Are you sure?" she asked, quiet as ever, her stare moving up from my lips to find my eyes.

I felt everything as I nodded. Everything good and new and terrifying all at once. I'd imagined my first kiss before. I'd envisioned myself on prom night or at a party or at school with someone I'd come to know and be infatuated enough with to hold close. I never pictured it being someone like Mo, and maybe part of me still felt wrong or off because it was different and it wasn't normal.

But I also never imagined myself smiling as our lips pulled apart and met again. I never pictured Mo's hand resting under my ear and on my neck and I never imagined I'd feel my heart swelling so big or my body somehow knowing exactly what to do. I couldn't have ever dreamt that merely existing would feel like this.

And yet, the colors around us, the warmth in the air, and the sound of the waves crashing into the distant shore were all playing parts in the moment that changed everything. It was like they all knew how to act, too, or like they'd been waiting all along to sit beside and watch. I was just happy they stuck around.

Chapter Twenty-Two

Nell

From what I'd heard, it was usually the morning after the wedding that came with the most nausea and dizziness, not the night before. Then again, not every wedding was like this one. I had a feeling none were.

We'd just gotten through with the rehearsal dinner in a small room at The Royal, which had gone by with surprisingly few hiccups. Ronan and I were tag-teaming conversations, ensuring that neither of us ran out of steam trying to make everyone happy and leaving virtually no worrying for Luke and Adrienne. According to the look on my mother's face when she and my dad pulled out of the parking lot just a few minutes ago, we'd done our jobs.

Now, all headed to one car, I could feel tension rising in my chest. Adrienne was biting her lip and Ronan was being eerily quiet, both signs that they were nervous about something, as much as I'd tried convincing them and their psyches to be cool. Braeden was clueless, droning on to Ronan about which young singer-songwriters were the future of the music industry, so I wasn't worried about him. But then there was Luke.

He'd been on a high all night, so smiley that I actually teared up at the sight of his happiness on three different occasions. Adrienne seemed happy too, and I really hoped that she was. But it was only a matter of time before Luke found out that we were all hiding something from him. And by a matter of time, I mean that there were mere hours left until Finn showed up at the wedding. I wasn't sure how anything was going to go down, or what the best way to go about it was. I was internally debating it when I felt an arm sling itself around my neck and shoulders. I didn't have to turn to know it was Luke.

"Nelliana," he joked, rustling my hair. "Maid of Honor."

"You're just now figuring that out?"

He grinned, a laugh escaping his nose. We were a few feet ahead of the other three and just about to the car, but Luke lowered his voice. "I'm really happy you're going to be standing up there with me tomorrow."

Shit. *Shit.*

I couldn't cry. I could *not* cry. Doing so would hint Luke into the fact that there was something bigger going on. But man, did that hit me hard. Luke had always been nice to me. This didn't have to be different. But, of course, it was.

"I'm standing with Adrienne, not you," I told him. But when I looked into his eyes, his kind, blue eyes and freckled face, the wall I built just seconds before tipped and shattered on the pavement right in front of us. The sound it made was ear-piercing.

"I'm serious." Behind us, Braeden accidentally kicked a rock that hit me in the ankle. I didn't flinch. "It means a lot to me, and I know I don't tell you a lot so I'm telling you now." He looked me in the eyes, and there were tears welling in his. God. "I'm lucky you're my sister. Not everyone gets to meet their best friend the day they're born."

Like Luke's, the tears were spilling over the edges of my eyelids now, so I wiped them away quickly. "It means a lot to me, too."

We'd made it to the car now. Braeden, Ronan and Adrienne were piling into their seats from the passenger side, so it was only Luke that could see me on the brink of waterworks. He gave me one last squeeze before reaching for his door handle.

"Best day ever, right?"

I forced a smile. "Best day ever."

Thirty minutes later, the universe made it evident that we needed to be clearer about which day we were referring to.

We were pulling into the driveway, the house a silhouette against the dark blue sky, its lights setting a warm scene. I'd just elbowed Adrienne for the fourth time, a signal that she was bouncing her leg and biting her lip simultaneously, when we spotted the same thing at the same time: a black SUV parked at the end of the driveway, right behind Ronan's car. Its lights clicked off just as Luke shifted the car into park.

Speaking for myself exclusively, I was frozen. But when I glanced over at Adrienne and poor Ronan, both of whom were sharing the backseat with me to allow Braeden shotgun, I felt a chill radiating from them, too. I could see Adrienne's whole face, which was nearly green, and only Ronan's dark eyes, which might as well have been stone. At least we were all on the same page.

"Who's that?" Braeden asked, reading only his own mind and not the room. "Didn't Grandma and Grandpa go to the hotel?"

Luke shrugged, sliding his key out of the ignition. "Probably one of mom's friends."

I watched Ronan slowly reach for his door handle before easing it open. I couldn't imagine how fast his heart was beating, how knotted his stomach was. I'd seen Finn only a few weeks ago and I was nearing combustion.

Adrienne filed out behind Ronan, while I found myself standing beside Luke. I was looking at my feet, to avoid looking anywhere else, when an expletive flew from Braeden's sweet mouth.

"Holy shit."

We'd naturally congregated by now, so I was standing, shaking, between Ronan and Luke when Finn came around the end of his rental car. There was a substantial amount of driveway between him and us, but even through the night I could see his face. He was clean shaven, his hair still as long as it was back in Pittsburgh, and his eyes were full of worry. Apparently, though, his lips didn't get the memo, because as he drew closer, I was sure I saw a smile.

Ronan said nothing, because he probably couldn't, while Luke's only reaction came from under his breath. I might've been the only one who heard it.

"No fucking way," he muttered.

There was a moment, drawing from Luke's words, that I decided I'd done the worst possible thing. Of course there

246

needed to be a reunion and of course Finn needed to be forgiven, but bringing him around on what was supposed to be the happiest day of Luke and Adrienne's lives when he was likely the only thing that had ever jeopardized that life—it probably wasn't the smartest thing.

But then Finn got closer, and Luke started walking, too. But toward him, not away. And with energy, not hesitance. Then I heard his words again and reevaluated their tone. Luke didn't want to banish him. He just couldn't believe he was real. I knew the feeling.

When Luke and Finn finally met, the rest of us still cemented like statues beside the car, they embraced one another and held on tight. I felt myself deflate as I watched it happen. It was as if a piece of life within me had been broken for years and was just stitched back together right in front of my eyes.

I couldn't breathe, and was watching Luke's shoulders shake when I realized that I was crying, too. It was a long moment before the two of them broke apart, looking each other in the eyes as Ronan, finally, approached with apprehension. I couldn't see his face, but I could see Finn's. That is, before he pulled him in, too.

There was always something so special about seeing the three of them together. Their connection had a spirit. It didn't matter what they were doing or who they were with or, evidently, how long it had been. You didn't have to be a part of it to feel it, and you didn't have to hear what they were saying to understand. You just did.

Ronan and Finn held onto one another for just as long, and it was the beat after they released each other that was crucial and time-stopping, at least for those in the loop. Adrienne had joined them, unfairly in the dark about just how much Finn's timing meant.

Finn held onto Adrienne like she was delicate, though we all knew she wasn't. I had a feeling I knew why. He needed to be forgiven first. But it was Luke, unsurprisingly, who put everyone at ease. While Adrienne had her turn with Finn, Luke put his hand on his back in support. I didn't see a flicker of confusion as he did so.

My heart was pounding on my ear drums, but somehow I was still able to make out the first words spoken once they were standing on their own again, all four wiping the rapid tears falling from their eyes.

"What are you doing here?"

It hurt to hear Luke's voice break. I hadn't seen him cry in years. But this, now, was good. This was important.

Finn's voice was filled with emotion, too.

"I was in the neighborhood." He grinned, and Luke did too. I couldn't tell what Adrienne and Ronan's faces were doing, but I had a feeling.

Luke's breathing was heavy. Behind me, a light turned on in the house. I felt Braeden shift to my left. I'd actually forgotten he was there; he was being so quiet.

Luke shook his head. I could tell he didn't know what to say. Not because there wasn't anything, but too much. "Do you— do you know? About the wedding?"

Finn nodded, his very slight smile unwavering as he noticed the ring on Luke's finger. His response, obviously, confused Luke. But it was then, in a slow-motion, of-course-this-is-happening, shit-your-pants moment, that Finn looked at me. Busted.

A wave of heat washed over me. There was a feeling of familiarity that battled with how otherworldly it felt to see those four faces staring my way, expecting something to come out of my mouth. Instead of an answer, because I didn't have one and because it was really only Luke who needed one, I stepped forward, parting the sea of friends and reaching out to Finn myself. When he held onto me, his hand on the back of my head, there was an unmatched feeling of comfort that grew in my heart. It felt just like that dark night nine years ago, and just like when I told him about Mo on the back deck in high school. Just like standing on that crowded street in Pittsburgh. Mostly, desperately, it felt like home.

That was when the door to the house opened, shining more light on us as my parents stepped through it. Within moments, it happened all over again—the crying, the questions, the confusion. The comfort. Then, the boys and Adrienne went to the back deck to talk—about everything, I assumed—while my mom asked to speak to me upstairs.

Time for my death sentence.

I sat down on my bed while my mother eased the door shut, my fingertips toying with the embroidered flower pattern on my bedspread. My mind, as much as I tried to convince it otherwise, began running through another conversation we'd had between these four walls.

It was a few months after we lost Paisley. The house had been mostly quiet, save for the abundance of flowers that had arrived at our house on a weekly basis. The kitchen counters were frequently stocked full of bouquets, baskets, even pots that held plants wearing every color of the rainbow and more. This was what people did. When something sad or tragic happened, they sent flowers. It was simply and beautifully human, and I didn't understand it.

My mom didn't know this much, of course, because I still hadn't spoken. But that day, something changed.

"Elliana, honey," she said, easing the door shut behind her. That time, I had my back against my pillows, and my eyes had been fixed onto the window until she came into the room. "Luke and his friends are on the beach. Don't you want to join them? Your dad is out there with Braeden."

I shook my head.

"What if I give Sydney's mom a call? I'm sure she would send her over."

And again.

I watched as she sighed, the weight of her body shifting the end of the bed as her breath sat in the air. I'd never forget how tired her eyes looked in that moment, or how hard I could tell she was trying. In the next beat, I noticed that there were freckles starting on her cheeks and shoulders. Summer was upon us, and she'd been outside enough that her skin was showing it. She'd been kissed by the sun, I thought.

"Why do they send flowers?" I asked.

She tried her hardest not to gasp, not to show that my voice was momentous in that second. "Who, honey?"

"When you lost the other babies," I started, sitting up, "they sent flowers then, too."

She nodded. I could see in her eyes that she was trying to concoct an answer that would satisfy me. Then I came up with one on my own.

"Is that how they come back to us?"

There was a hint of a smile on my mom's lips as she looked down, her fingertips finding the embroidery on my bed. She knew then, and I realized years later, that I was still looking to her words for something solid. If she said it was true, then it was true.

"I think so," she told me. "Those babies will always be a part of our family, so long as we have flowers. That's why everyone keeps sending them."

I nodded, glanced back through the window and watched as the setting sun began hitting the houses across the street. Its orange glow was beautiful, hazy. "Maybe we need to build a garden," I said.

It was an idea my mother obviously ran with, and held so close to her heart that she told everyone of our conversation each time she introduced them to the garden. Sitting on my bedspread, staring at the same flowers, I always remembered it. Even during the years I tried to forget.

Now, I had a feeling our conversation wasn't going to ring as sentimental. My mother sat next to me this time, her hands clasped on her lap. Uh oh.

"I'll give the sneakiness a seven out of ten, but the gesture itself an eleven. The logic, we may need to work on."

I was—well, I didn't know what I was. Stupefied was one word for it.

"You—" I shook my head. "You knew I invited Finn."

She nodded slowly, tilted her head and curled her lip. "Well, considering I had several conversations with Lucas regarding whether an invitation was appropriate or not, each of which ended with the same answer, I'm pretty inclined to believe it wasn't him," she said. Then she turned to me, a smile reaching the corners of her mouth. "Unless you prefer to blame it on Braeden."

I wanted to laugh, but I couldn't. I was sweating. "How did you know?"

"To start, you've been on edge since we visited you on St. Patrick's Day."

I let out a bit of a laugh, deciding then whether to defend myself or surrender, when she continued.

"You also share a Flying Miles account with your father. We knew about the trip the second you booked it." The giggle she let out then was involuntary, but warranted, and it forced one out of me, too.

Our laughter settled, and in the silence that followed, I thought about how much of a disaster everything could've turned out to be. Obviously, I wasn't as careful as I could've been. My mother had a lot on the line, too. She wasn't expressing any of this, so I had to ask.

"Are you upset with me?"

This was the question of all questions, and one I never asked growing up, simply because I was too afraid of the answer. Now, I felt as though I knew it.

She was quiet for a moment before she began to shake her head, and then she surprised me. "I admire you."

I looked up from the flowers again, meeting her eyes. They held bold shades of blue and green, a combination of Luke's and Braeden's and mine. "You do?"

She nodded. "It was risky and it could've been a mess, which wouldn't have been a big deal for most people, but I know it was for you. Or at least it used to be," she said. I took a breath. "Most importantly, you didn't just do it for your own sake. You took a big risk for your friends and for your brother. And so far, it seems to be going as planned, yeah?"

I found that familiar look on her face then, but wasn't at all inclined to turn the other way. This time, I reciprocated it. I wasn't the only one changing with time. Years ago, I had a feeling my mother wouldn't have reacted this way, at least not at first.

"With the exception of sharing a Flying Miles account with dad, then I think so," I told her, earning another laugh. "I wasn't sure it would."

She stood, straightening out the bit of comforter that she sat on. "Everyone's here that's meant to be now, and we have you to thank." She headed for the door, punctuating our conversation with an exit.

"Hey mom," I said quickly, my thoughts focused on all of the events that led to this moment. One event in particular. "Wait until you meet his girlfriend."

"Finn's?"

I nodded. "She's perfect for him. And that's a tough feat."

"It's a tough feat to be perfect for any of you kids," she told me, a new kind of smile on her face as she reached for the doorknob. "Would you like me to shut this?"

I shook my head. "You can leave it open."

With my mother gone, I laid back on my bed. A massive wave of relief hit me then. I felt lighter, but I also felt remarkably warm. Maybe it was the tension and subsequent chill that were finally able to escape me. Maybe I finally felt like I was home.

Everyone knew now. Not only that, but it was turning out to be *good*—the reunion, the secret-keeping, all of the pent-up panic that came with those things. Pending the conversation that was still happening on the back deck, the impossible might've just come to fruition. I was so exhausted, I was sure I could've slept for four days.

Which was why, when I opened my eyes the next time, I had no concept of time. My first thought was that I'd slept through the wedding. My second thought was that my first thought was the most ridiculous thing ever. And then I thought that I should probably get up, so I did.

I found Finn's and Ronan's cars both still parked in front of the house with just one glance through the window. The street was remarkably still, and every light in the houses of my neighbors had since flicked off. So, it was late. I could handle late.

The hallway, like the street, was dark. If I hadn't grown up wandering between my room and the bonfire in the middle of the night, there wouldn't have been a chance of me making it to the stairs now. So when I reached the bottom of them, my feet searching for the spots on each step that didn't creak, I was proud of myself. But then I hit a wall.

It took everything I had left—which, really, wasn't much—to withhold a scream, and even more to stay on my feet. But then the wall I'd run into reached out to me, steadying my shoulders. Then, it giggled.

"You scared me," I whisper-yelled. Though, really, the feeling of running into Finn at home in the middle of the night was unparalleled. I couldn't have been mad no matter how hard I tried.

"I'm so sorry," Finn whispered. "Everyone else is asleep. I was coming up to say goodbye."

My heart sank. There was no way.

"Goodbye?"

He saw the fear in my eyes and immediately shook his head. "Until tomorrow," he said quickly, his eyes darting between the two of mine. "The wedding. Remember?"

Of course that was what he meant. "I'm sorry, I just—" I shook my head, took in a deep breath. "So it went well."

He nodded, his hands retreating to the pocket of his sweatshirt while he looked over his shoulder. In the living room, where his gaze was pointing, everyone was asleep like he'd said. Luke was on the floor, his head leaning against the leg of Adrienne who was slouched into the loveseat. Ronan was on the couch, taking up only a small portion of it. His body was twisted slightly in a weird way, like he'd just been moved. Noticing it, I realized why. He'd been sitting with Finn.

"We've got a long way to go," Finn told me. The way he was beaming said just about everything else.

I nodded. "But…"

"But," Finn started, mirroring my tone. "It was good. Really good. Oh, and check this out."

I watched as he reached into his back pocket, easing something that crinkled out of it and flashing it in front of me. I couldn't make out every word through the dark, but I knew the outline of its shapes and the hues of its colors anywhere.

"An invitation to the wedding."

"And a plus two," he chuckled. "Adrienne said she appreciated the verbal one, but thought we should make it official."

I watched the smile on his face, and felt the way his bones were so settled into the house. It was like he'd never left. That, alone, was grounds for tears. Finn watched me wipe one away, then wrapped his arms around me in response. I rested my head against his chest and let him hold me together.

He turned his head and rested on me too. "Thank you," he whispered.

Five minutes later, I walked Finn to his car while he showed me a video of Freya running through the airport just after they landed in North Carolina. She was so excited, pointing and shrieking at every image of or reference to the ocean while her pigtails bounced freely up and down. I was looking down at my phone, waiting for the video to arrive on it and heading back up the driveway, when the front door opened.

I made immediate eye contact with Luke. He pulled his hood down before easing the door shut behind him. When he sat down on the doorstep, I had a feeling I was supposed to join him. So I slid my phone into my pocket and sat down, awaiting my sentencing for the second time in one night. Of course, I was more confident in Luke's inclination to pardon me.

He took in a breath, a sign that a long sentence was coming, if not a run-on one. But it was no use. We both saw her coming up the driveway, a small paper bag dangling from one hand. Luke called out to her first.

"Hey, Mo!"

She lifted a hand to wave, her face illuminated by the porch light coming from behind me as she approached.

"Am I interrupting a sibling meeting?" she asked.

She'd finally reached us, and though she remained standing, she situated herself to Luke's side, not mine.

"Nah," Luke laughed. "Couldn't have one of those without B."

I was trying to sense his tone, to get a precursor to what I was going to deal with when Mo inevitably walked away. But Luke was just Luke—kind, genuine, happy. I was hopeful it would last.

"Right."

"Oh, I meant to ask you this yesterday, but what was the name of the girl whose mom designed Adrienne's dress? She's your friend, right?"

As Maid of Honor, I should have known at least one of the two answers to Luke's questions, but I didn't. I also should've figured that Luke and Adrienne kept in touch with Mo since high school, especially considering she was attending the wedding and still felt comfortable walking up to our doorstep. But I guess that's what happens when you bar yourself from thinking about someone all together. You forget to remember the details.

"Lilly," Mo told him.

"*Lilly.*" Luke clicked his tongue. "I kept thinking it was Laina. Did she do fashion with you?"

I turned my attention back to Mo, which wasn't ever hard to do. Sitting here now, watching her converse with Luke, I felt like I was watching a tennis match.

"Actually, yeah. But we met in a Latin class we were both taking," Mo recounted.

It wasn't until my cheeks flushed that I realized her sentence hit me harder than the ones before it. Of course she was going to meet people at school and of course I had no place

255

thinking about what they would've meant. But what if one of them did? What if she'd *met* someone? Then what?

Luke grinned. "How'd that go?"

"Latin?"

He nodded.

"I'm not as good at it as I am with the others," she said.

"Can you say something in it?" Luke asked. "I've never heard anyone speak Latin before."

Because it's a dead language, I thought.

Mo pondered the request, her pause lasting only a beat. She lifted her eyes from the ground before she spoke. I was, in an unsurprising turn of events, entranced.

"Fluctuat nec mergitur," Mo said.

I traded a look with Luke, both of us stumped. Mo recognized our need for a translation.

"She is tossed by the waves, but she does not sink." At the tail end of the sentence, Mo looked right at me, her expression bold and unwavering. "Or something like that."

If we were going to play metaphorical word games before either of us talked about what happened four years before, Mo was going to win every time. I knew what she meant by what she said, and I wasn't sure whether or not I deserved it. Four years ago, maybe. But now I was different, and she didn't know how much. Maybe I needed to show her.

"Cool," Luke said, breaking the tension that I was sure he noticed while I kept my eyes on Mo. "Sounds nothing like it."

"Yeah," Mo sighed, breaking our eye contact. She leaned and set the bag she'd been carrying on the cement beside Luke. "Well, I just came to drop off some hair things for Adrienne. I'd better let you guys get some rest. Big day tomorrow."

Luke nodded. "We'll see you there."

She offered both of us a smile, but I didn't want to meet her eyes anymore. I didn't know what to do with them.

Luke waited until Mo was out of sight, but certainly not out of mind, to take that breath he started with again. I did, too, but only because the air in my lungs was dwindling.

"We're going to have to unpack that," he said.

I was so tired, physically and emotionally, that I couldn't hold anything in. Luke's words made me laugh, and I let them. Then I put my head in my hands and shook it.

"Later," I suggested.

"Okay." He nodded, laughing too. "And Vermont? Really?"

I kept my head in my hands, my voice coming out muffled as it pushed through them. "You would've asked too many questions if I told you," I admitted. "And I might not have gone."

"That's fair," he said. There was a pause—an opportunity for Luke to decide what came next. We both knew I was done with the decision-making. At least for now.

"Finn said he told you what happened senior year."

I nodded. Then, before thinking about it, I lifted my head from my hands, my face feeling flushed and warm when I did. "Finn told me. Ronan told me," I started, emphasizing the fact that I had a list. "You didn't tell me."

"I'm sorry," he said, and I felt that he really was. "I didn't know what we were doing or why we were doing it. I think I was ashamed."

"I just wish I knew back then. Maybe things could have been different."

Luke chuckled. "Maybe. Everything has its ifs, right?"

This was just the thing. Every moment had an opposite, a result that could lead to a different world or a different life if just one thing changed. If a yes was instead a no. If you went in the water instead of staying on the sand. If you ignored the way people were looking at you instead of taking it to heart. Everything had its ifs. And maybe this moment, the one in between the ones we'd lived and the ones we looked forward to, was its best possible version. We'd never know, and maybe that was what made it so special.

Luke and I sat on the steps for a few more minutes before he headed inside to get Adrienne and I woke a sleepy Ronan. When I retreated to bed myself, I vowed to give the next day the best of myself, to make sure that every moment was as good as it could get. I was in control, after all. It was about time I realized it.

Chapter Twenty-Three

Elliana

Though the creation of the boys' posters was interrupted by sunshower dancing, they turned out to be exceptional. My mother's words, not mine.

Mo and I arrived at the field early so that we could hang the posters without having to push through the imminent crowds of people that would grow closer to game time. This was a big night for the St. Jane's varsity lacrosse team, for more reasons than just it being their Senior Night. They were playing the Palm Hill Cougars, whose signature black and red jerseys were bringing me flashbacks I certainly didn't want, and a win would mean a bid to the playoffs for either team. The bleachers, with five minutes left until the ceremony, were packed. When Mo and I finally reached the rest of the crew, my head was spinning.

"Oh, thank God," Sydney sighed when she spotted us. Her two braids were dotted with glitter that matched her purple St. Jane's shirt, and I couldn't help but smile at her school spirit. "I thought we were going to have to send out a search team."

"You don't have enough faith in us," Mo laughed. She situated herself on the bleacher just beside Adrienne, leaving enough room for me to sit between her and Syd. It was that kind of thought, and the grouping together of she and I as an *us*, that had my head spinning again. Truthfully, it hadn't stopped since the night before.

Once we left the garden, Mo walked herself home and I retreated to my bedroom, but I didn't sleep. And it wasn't because I could hear Luke, Ronan, and Finn giggling downstairs. I was on cloud nine.

The mere confirmation I'd gotten that Mo felt the same way I did, or was at least on the same side, was enough to keep me awake and giddy all night. I didn't know what was going to come next, but I was beginning to imagine a life with her.

Maybe it wasn't an elaborate plan complete with trimmed hedges and a big backyard, but I started to think about visiting New York, or Mo visiting home, once fall came. I thought about the things we could do together, the conversations we could have if we never ran out of time. I was starting to dream without closing my eyes.

Even now, I had to make a real effort to pay attention to my surroundings, and this was a big night. It had always been a big night.

I was snapped back in, my focus keen, when the announcer—a girl in the senior class named Willa who was going to school for broadcasting—began the ceremony with the tapping of her mic. She had the job of announcing the senior players as they walked onto the field with their parents, describing their time on the team and their future goals in just a few words. Finn took the field first, sandwiched between his two parents.

Willa proudly announced to the crowd that Finn had been on varsity for four years, and that he broke the school's goal-scoring record earlier in the season. She said that Finn planned on attending Carnegie Mellon University to study theater and drama, and that he was in the top ten of St. Jane's graduating class. Willa also announced that Finn was being escorted to the field by his mother, Lisa and his father, Jed. But what she didn't know, what she didn't include in her description of them, was that Finn had spent every night in the past week at our house because of how horribly his parents were fighting in the middle of the night. She didn't know that this was the first game they had attended all year, or that they didn't deserve to be by his side, or that Finn wasn't sure he'd even have parents to walk him out. Even if Willa did know any of this, she wouldn't have said it. Because you didn't talk about those things on nights like this. Finn didn't talk about them ever.

I let my eyes linger on Finn, who stood with barely a smile as his parents were beaming. Ronan was next, and I was surprised to see that he wasn't gushing, either. Not even when Willa described his being on the team as "integral," and not even when she said that he was headed to Ohio State, so far undecided on his major but on scholarship to play lacrosse. His parents, Barb and Gabriel, seemed so happy, so proud. I was surprised to not find the same things on Ronan's face. Maybe he was just nervous.

Finally, there was Luke. My mother was crying before they'd even begun walking, but she masked it well with her characteristic smile. Willa announced that Luke was headed to UNC Wilmington to study business, and mentioned his later goal to attend culinary school. She described him as a "light," both on the team and in school, and said that his four years on the lacrosse team were "surely going to leave a mark on the program forever." This was all so kind, so well-spoken, that I was sure it was going to lead Luke to tears, or at least close. But even though I was far away, I could tell he wasn't hearing any of it. He was coasting, walking between my parents only because he had to. I was beginning to think I was reading into it too much when Adrienne, from the other side of Mo, leaned forward, her eyes on me.

"Did you talk to them last night?"

I shook my head, watched as the school's photographer and a couple of local media people snapped photos of all three boys and their parents standing on the sideline. All around us, the chatter had picked back up.

"The boys?"

Adrienne nodded.

"When?"

"I left right after the fire," she told me. "They were all weird in school today. Finn especially."

I turned my head back to the field. The parents were dispersing, mine headed back in our direction, while the boys joined the team's scattered huddle. Nothing seemed particularly off about them, although Finn wasn't anywhere near Ronan and Luke, who stood side-by-side. But they were in game-mode, determined. I was sure it meant nothing.

"I was— I was showing Mo the garden." I felt Mo look at me, then hesitate as she looked back to Adrienne. I wasn't sure what her expression was, but it didn't feel like a smile. "They were still in the living room when I went up to bed."

"Huh," Adrienne mumbled. She crossed her arms, looking both nervous and determined as she studied the field.

Five minutes later, when the game started and my parents finally made their way back to us, something else happened. I wasn't the first to notice, but I was preoccupied.

"...would just be one semester unless I found a different program," Mo was saying, answering the question I'd asked about her plans to study abroad. "But I could really go anywhere."

"Would you go by yourself?"

Her lip curled, and she was readying herself to answer when we heard Adrienne again.

"Where are they?"

Mo wasn't upset by the interruption, and I wasn't either. I could tell just by Adrienne's tone that this was important.

"Who?" Mo asked.

I followed Adrienne's gaze to the field. The game had just started—only fourteen seconds had fallen from the scoreboard so far—and the Cougars were slowly moving the ball up the field. Everything was normal, uniform. But Ronan and Luke weren't there.

Technically, they were there, but not on the field like Finn. He'd just gotten possession of the ball when my dad noticed, too.

"Ronan and Luke." He leaned closer to my mom and pointed to the bench. The two of them were sitting with a sophomore between them. "There."

Adrienne shook her head. "Something's not right."

"Have they ever not started before?" Henry asked. Beside him, Sydney wore a confused expression too.

She was the next to chime in. "I've never seen them on the bench at all."

"That one time when Ronan had a nosebleed," Braeden added. "He sat for, like, four minutes."

262

"Huh," my mother muttered. She and Adrienne both wore the same concerned expression, while everyone else sat confused, watching as the players moved and listening as the whistles were blown. I was somewhere in between. The combination of their sullen faces and now the game's lineup was certainly not a good one. But two minutes into the game, the three of them were on the field together again, and all seemed to be okay. Whatever it was, I was sure I'd hear about it later. There was nothing that could take me back down to Earth from the cloud I was on. Not even this.

And then there was halftime.

The scoreboard horn rang out and all of the players from the field returned to their benches before retreating to the locker rooms, their coaches in tow with a tied score to work through. Adrienne and my mother kept a keen eye on all three boys, watching their behavior now that there was a gap in playing time. Which, ever since those first two minutes ended, had been normal. Not one of the three had a turn on the bench since then, if we were keeping count.

It had been a tense first half, and an exciting one. The crowd around us, as the break allowed, began to disperse from the bleachers. Next to me, Sydney sat down, the side of her head finding Henry's shoulder as a convenient pillow. I was trying to think of a way to comment on its wholesomeness when my arm was brushed by Mo's.

"I'm going to go get some waters," she started, her eyes easily landing on mine. "Want to come?"

I nodded, melting as I followed a curly red ponytail past my peers and down the steps. I left behind an onlooking Sydney. Beside her, my parents watched us walk away. I felt it. I wondered what we looked like to them.

We were just passing the posters of the boys when, all of a sudden, I realized how much they really meant. This was their last game. With it, the last time all of the people here would watch them play. The last time seniors would attend a game as students.

"I can't believe you're all leaving," I said aloud as I thought this.

We'd made it to the concession stand line in the nick of time, only standing behind a group of junior girls who had their stomachs painted with various jersey numbers to represent players. I couldn't help but notice that one was sporting the number seven. It seemed as though Ronan had a not-so-secret admirer.

"I know," Mo said in response to me. "I feel like I just got here."

"You did," I told her. "I mean, in the grand scheme of things."

"In the grand scheme of things," she repeated, her tone indicating that she found it sweet. She turned to me then, while the group of painted stomachs ordered. "I can't imagine how it feels to have everyone else leave. You've known Finn and Ronan forever, yeah?"

"Pretty much," I told her. "Adrienne a little less than forever, but still. I don't know what I'm going to do when Luke moves out."

"It's sweet that you're so close." Her voice carried over the sound of laughter from the group in front of us, a result of a girl painted with the number twelve flirting with a student working the stand. Mo ignored it. "Everyone will be back," she assured me. "Soon enough it'll be your turn to go. Maybe I'll be able to sell you on New York by then."

If we weren't called to order, I would've likely melted into the pavement at the sound of Mo's suggestion. By then, she'd said. *Then* was years away, literally. She was thinking of the future too.

It was that exact feeling—the smile I wore, the one I saw on Mo, the jitter in my chest—that I wished I could have bottled. Because, in the next beat, everything changed.

"What can I get for you?" said Corey Robins, a senior boy with a buzz cut and long eyelashes. He was wearing a purple St. Jane's shirt, like everyone else, and had worked the stand on game nights for a few years. He'd always been nice.

Behind him, though, I could see faces that I wasn't so sure about, at least not this time. First, there was Emmet Jackson, a boy in my class who'd never spoken a word to me and whose kindness I'd never particularly felt. There was also Alison Abbott, a senior who was Finn's opposite in the musical two years before, who I didn't know. Then, there was Sonny Rosenthal. He was wearing a shirt with its sleeves cut off, and he was standing by the cooler. He was also looking right at me.

"Just three waters," Mo said with a smile. She handed over a five dollar bill. "Thanks."

I swallowed and put an extra inch between Mo and me while Corey walked toward Sonny to retrieve the waters. I watched as they exchanged a hushed word, and when Corey returned, waters in hand, all four of them were looking at me. At us.

"Enjoy the game," Corey said, still smiling politely.

When we turned away, Mo handed me a cool bottle while she held onto the other two. A crowd had formed around the stand and all the way to the bleachers. We were back in the middle of it before I knew it. I could feel heat radiating from the bodies around me.

"So I went to the boardwalk with my dad the other day, and you know that store that was vacant for a while in the spring?"

I just nodded, hoping she'd see it and keep talking so I didn't have to. As we walked, we passed the end of the now-stretched concession line. Coach Pieter and his wife were at the end of it. He lit up and waved at me as we got closer, a crowd of people between us and them. I waved back, but I felt like I saw something else in his eyes. I shook it away.

"It's a record store now. This couple from Chicago just moved here and opened it up. They were sick of the corporate scene, or whatever, so now they want to do the whole beach bum thing. Cool, right?"

I took a deep breath. I could feel people staring at us. They were stabbing into my back, and I felt itchy.

"Yeah. Cool."

In the next beat, we passed Bax. He was standing with a group of boys our age, his hair shining in even the dim lights beside the bleachers. When we made eye contact, there was no sign of googly eyes. No smile, no nothing. Maybe it was because of the way I left him on the boardwalk, or maybe it was that Henry had been keeping his distance since then, too. Maybe he thought it was all my fault. But there was that part of me, that voice screaming inside my brain, telling me that he was piecing it together. Perhaps he'd been right all along. What he'd said was personal, and I was proving it to him.

Mo, oblivious to the way I was feeling and the way all eyes were on us, took a sip of water. "We should go before I leave," she said.

Piper Frag and Amari Watson were just ahead of us now. I turned to Mo before they could meet my eyes.

"Like, on a date?"

Mo's face was soft as she studied me. We walked slowly past my lab partner, my mom's coworker, Ronan's cousin. What were they all thinking?

Elliana's will be perfect, Piper had said. My whole life was so clear to everyone else. It was common sense to think that I would live exactly the way I presented myself. What if I had to explain to everyone that I didn't want that kind of life anymore? I never really knew what I wanted before, but what if it didn't make sense to anyone else? What if *I* didn't make sense?

"Are you okay?" Mo asked. We'd stopped walking now. I hadn't noticed.

I shook my head, tucking my straight hair back behind my ears when it fell in front of my face. I could feel my jeans sitting against my legs, my bra squeezing my back. I wasn't anything like Mo. I couldn't handle the way people were looking at us. I couldn't do anything that I wasn't meant to do, and I wasn't sure that I was meant to do this. Maybe I mistook my friendship and admiration. Maybe it wasn't something else entirely. Maybe it was just that.

"I can't do this," I said breathlessly. I couldn't look away from the ground.

"Walk up the stairs?" Mo joked.

She was so relaxed, so oblivious. She didn't get it.

"This," I repeated, looking only at her now. I watched as her smile fell, the people around us carrying on as it did, as if it didn't shake the earth. Apparently, I planned to shatter it. "Look, whatever this is, it isn't."

Mo lowered the water bottles she was carrying. Her eyes got softer, glassier.

"I don't understand." Her voice was even, serious. I hated it.

I took a breath that wasn't deep enough. I didn't want anything about myself to change, and it was happening too fast. I felt wrong. I didn't want to feel anything anymore.

"I'm sorry if I gave you the wrong impression," I said quietly. "But I can't do this."

Mo shook her head. "Nell—"

"It's Elliana," I said, louder this time. A group of students was passing us to return to the bleachers. Two of them heard me, while the others pretended not to.

"I'm sorry," I said finally, my voice low, before turning away.

I'd only just made it behind the bleachers when I heard footsteps right behind me. I didn't want to turn around, but I did. I had to.

"We're not going to talk about it?" Mo asked, her voice desperate and breathless and everything I never wanted it to be.

I just looked at her, a warm tear rolling down my cheek, and shook my head. Mo nodded as she came to the conclusion herself. She was disappointed in me and I could tell. But I didn't want this. I never wanted this.

"I wasn't insinuating that it had to be a date," she said gently. "We don't have to do anything you're not comfortable with. I just thought last night—"

"Last night was a mistake."

Mo's mouth hung open partially, her cut-off sentence completely ripped away by me. I'd hurt her, and I knew it. But for some reason, I had to make it clear. What it was, I didn't know.

"I don't want to be with you," I said. "Ever."

I studied Mo's face as she comprehended what I said. She was frozen for a moment, in disbelief just as I was that I'd uttered such words. She took a deep breath, blinked rapidly a few times, and wiped her eyes. But then, unlike the brokenhearted people in those books Henry showed me or the movies I watched with Finn, she stood tall. She held care in her eyes, somehow.

"You know that person you look for in the sky?"

I couldn't feel any of myself. I was outside of my body, watching her study my face like it was the last time.

"I hope you find her," she told me. In the next beat, she was gone.

I stood still, feeling cold and colorless and dark. I couldn't breathe and I couldn't cry but I knew I was breathing and crying because I felt everything and everything felt bad. Everything hurt. The worst part was that I didn't know if I regretted it. Not while it was happening and not after. What I knew was that I let go, and there wasn't any getting it back.

I felt my pulse slow down after a moment, just as I heard a series of cleats pounding against the pavement. I turned halfway to see the lacrosse team—our lacrosse team—returning to the field, walking in two lines. I made eye contact with the last player in line, who broke from the team and made his way to me without hesitation. I wiped tears from both eyes before he reached his hands out to my shoulders.

"Are you okay?" he asked.

There were various funny looks being thrown his way from the rest of the team as they entered another huddle. Ronan and Luke had been at the front of the line, and I assumed they didn't see me. I didn't want anyone to see me.

I shook my head and avoided looking at the team. I tried to do the same to Finn, but somehow my eyes met his.

"What was that with Mo?" he asked. Then, again, "Are you okay?"

"Later," I told him. I nodded toward the team.

"Cooper, you joining us today?" Coach Allenson shouted, his red face growing redder.

Now, the looks from the team were becoming more uniform, more full of concern. Luke saw me, and I watched him step out of the circle. When I shook my head, adamantly, in his direction, he stayed put.

"Go," I said quietly to Finn.

He turned back toward me, his kind eyes softening mine. He pulled my weak body in for a hug, like always making me feel whole. Then, I watched him walk away. I heard the scoreboard horn ring out once I'd made it to the parking lot.

I was a bad sister and an even worse friend for leaving the game. But returning to the bleachers either meant facing Mo or facing my friends and family without Mo, neither of which I could handle. Not then.

I couldn't shake the pit in my stomach. I wanted to be someone else. I wanted to be a person who could find answers on her own and who didn't feel the way other people saw her. It wasn't just that I cared; it was that I existed through them— through their perception and their validation and their happiness with who I was.

There was always going to be that version of me somewhere. Maybe she was too far out of reach or maybe she was in the vibrant clouds that danced above the ocean every time I sat on the sand and watched. Maybe she wasn't really so different from the person I saw staring back at me when the water was glassy enough to give off a reflection, or maybe she was the complete opposite.

I wished I didn't have to search for her, and I wished she was just me. But if Mo's words left me with anything, it was ambition, drive. I never wanted to feel like this again. So, I hoped I'd find her, too. Maybe she'd know how to fix what I'd just broken.

Chapter Twenty-Four

Nell

"Found it, Nell!"

It was still morning, and yet the day had been long already—hair, makeup, dresses, photographers snapping pictures through every movement we made. I'd been oversaturated in wedding preparation, and though it was glamorous, I wasn't sure I wanted to be a part of another one for the rest of my life.

In just the two hours that we'd been in Adrienne's bridal suite, I'd used a day's worth of energy. For starters, I'd assured Jess that her hair looked "just fine," roughly twenty-five times (and counting), and assisted Logan in sewing a tear on Renna's dress that was a result of her (all of us) dancing to Adrienne's pre-wedding playlist. Apparently, "Look at Me I'm Sandra Dee" from *Grease* was a hit in Logan's dorm room at college, and Adrienne and Renna exemplified just how much fun they had while listening to it. I was having a blast, and I'd downed a mimosa, so I was feeling warm. All things considered, it was turning out to be a better day than I'd imagined. Especially since my mother had just entered the room holding the necklace I misplaced.

"Thank God," I sighed.

"I told you!" Logan exclaimed from behind me. "Mother knows best!"

I watched through the mirror in front of me as my mother approached, wearing a simple, light blue dress and a smile that hadn't faded since she woke up. She was holding a delicate silver chain with a simple *E* charm dangling from it. It was Adrienne's gift to me the day I graduated high school, and I wore it on special occasions.

"How's she doing?" I asked as my mom unhooked the necklace's clasp for me.

She shook her head, tears pooling the bottoms of her eyes. "She's the happiest I've ever seen her."

Adrienne had been in the room across the hall with my mother and her own for twenty minutes. The photographers recommended that she put her dress on with just the two of them so they could capture the bridesmaids' reactions to her walking in the room. While I appreciated the gesture, I was much too anxious to be waiting so long. I couldn't imagine how Luke felt.

I turned to the mirror, standing still as my mom lowered the necklace onto my collarbones and shifted my hair so she could fasten it. I caught a glimpse of myself then, and I was relieved to see a familiar face staring back at me. For the first time in a long time, she wasn't just someone I knew, but someone I loved.

She had rosy cheeks and her hair was curled but not perfectly. She was happy with the body she lived in just as much as she was with her mind and her soul. She liked to take risks and she was proud of herself for trying. There was something in her eyes—something beside the reflection of water or the vibrant ocean sky that usually flooded them when she was being introspective. There was a sparkle, not unlike the one coming from the charm on her neck. This one was different, though, because she'd put it there herself.

Looking at her now, I was proud of who she was. As much as she'd hurt and struggled and changed and grown, she still had the same heart. That was worth something, at least to me.

Once I finally ripped my eyes away from my own, I found the same type of girl—the same type of woman—standing just beside me, her hands resting on my shoulders as she studied who I was, too. She'd seen so much more than my eyes ever had, but she carried all of it with such grace. Today, all of her kids were finally under the same roof again. So the glow on her skin wasn't just secondhand happiness or pride for her son on his big day. She was happy for her too, and she had every right to be.

"You look–" She shook her head, took a deep breath as she swallowed a cry. "You look radiant, Nell."

I turned away from the mirror and faced my mom, taking in her eyes and her freckles and her spirit, all which matched mine.

"So do you," I told her before wrapping my arms around her. I didn't care about my makeup or my hair, and I was sure she didn't either. We held each other tight because we could. "I love you, Mom."

"I love you."

"*Incoming!*"

My mother and I exchanged a smile before turning to find the subject of Logan's outburst. It wasn't long before we found it.

Lena, the spunky wedding photographer with round glasses and an always-smiling face, was positioned in the corner of the room, ready for the moment that was already unfolding. I watched in slow motion as the door to the room opened. Ms. Brenda, who Adrienne uncannily resembled, stepped in first, wearing a light gray dress and a simple updo. The smile on her face was worth everything that the morning had held. I was glad to see that Lena's lens had captured it.

I lost all sight of Lena in the next moment, because my heart just about stopped.

When Adrienne entered the room, I was speechless, breathless, lacking everything a human needed to function properly. Her dress was angelic, and it fit her body and her spirit like a glove. Its off-white shade complemented her tanned skin and her rosy cheeks and her dark blue eyes, while its shape complemented everything else.

"Immaculate," Lena mumbled. I was pretty sure I heard Logan choke on something.

When I caught a glimpse of Adrienne's face, and the sheer euphoria beaming from it, I knew I was living in a moment I was going to remember forever. There was her smile and the lightness in her step and the color of her dress, but there was also the white glow coming through the windows and the pure love surrounding me that made me feel like I was living in a memory. It was out-of-body, and I only found myself back in mine when Adrienne met my eyes.

I shook my head, my hand covering my mouth. "Adrienne—"

"Do I look like a bride?" she asked, spinning when her name was all I could mutter.

"You look like *the* bride," Renna answered. "The only one. Ever."

I took three steps forward, hearing Lena's camera shutter as I did, and pulled Adrienne into a hug. She received it like a gift, holding me tight as we told each other how grateful we were without using words. I took a step back, taking all of her in as I shook my head.

"Luke is going to lose it when he sees you."

And he did.

But before he got the chance, I had the honor of watching as the nerves poured from his skin. The list of my Highlights of the Day was getting longer and longer.

We were standing in a hallway larger than any room I'd ever been in, and my mother and Ms. Brenda had just left us to find their places in front of the next set of doors. So it was just Adrienne and me, in the nicest hallway in The Royal and in our beach town alone, waiting for the person who was going to wait with her.

Adrienne's father wasn't there to walk her down the aisle, which wasn't a big deal. She never really liked the idea of anyone giving her away, anyways. She was always her own person, and her heart had always been Luke's. Nothing was going to change when she walked into the Coastal Room in just a few moments.

But there was also something about standing alone on her wedding day that wasn't very enticing, either. So she asked someone to stand with her until she made her entrance. Since Luke and I were going to be preoccupied, she found the next best thing. Her words, not mine.

"Sorry, I'm late," Mo said as soon as she turned the corner and headed for us. "Jess asked me to touch-up her makeup and wouldn't let me go."

"You're perfectly on time," Adrienne said in her soothing voice. She greeted Mo with a hug while I stood to the side and studied the two of them. Mo's hair was braided and styled into a bun that was meant to look a little messy and, like always, suited her well. She wore a floor-length, mauve dress made of velvet and, when she stepped away from Adrienne, a smile that said just how happy she was to be there.

As I watched her dress shimmer subtly in the light, I realized that Mo herself was like velvet. She was old school, but also timeless. Bold, but romantic. She carried light in a way others didn't.

"Alright," I said, interrupting my own thoughts before they got lost. I pulled Adrienne in once more, this moment being the last we shared before we were really family. "I better go before a siren goes off, or something."

Adrienne laughed. "I'll see you in there."

I shared in Adrienne's laughter, then stood by helplessly as my eyes flickered back to Mo. She was watching me, and the happy look she wore when she hugged Adrienne had now faded. But her eyes—they'd gotten brighter, somehow.

Every interaction we'd had since her return to North Carolina had been different. In Archie's, I was nervous. On the beach, I rambled. At the party, I felt like we'd gotten somewhere. But then, on the steps outside of my house just a number of hours ago, it was obvious that we hadn't. It felt like we'd gone back four years and were standing behind the bleachers, Mo full of hope that I would find the missing piece of me while in reality I was looking right at it. The only difference now was that I knew it, and I was sure she didn't.

I was thinking all of this when I slipped through the doors, certain that I wouldn't be able to shake any of it from my mind. But then I saw Ronan.

He was amidst the mess of people standing before the double doors that led into the Coastal Room, his head one of the few towering over the others. I watched as his eyes searched desperately for something, and my cold heart was warmed when I realized it was me.

"There you are," he breathed. I had to admit, he looked handsome. His hair was curly but somehow neat, and his tuxedo looked as if it were made for him. It was only a matter of time before it was stained or torn, so I knew I had to take it all in now.

"Were you doubting me?" I asked, flashing him a smile before turning to Luke.

I straightened his tux, balancing the bouquet of flowers I was holding in one hand and avoiding his eyes because I knew tears would flood mine when I looked at him. And so it went.

"How are you doing?"

My eyes moved up first, and the rest of me followed. I found Luke's expression to be genuine and whole, like every single part of him was standing in that room with us. I was impressed.

"How am I?" I asked. "You're the one about to marry the love of your life."

Marrying the love of your life. What an impossible feat. And there we were, just moments away from watching two people so young and so certain conquer it. What a day.

To punctuate this thought, Luke took a deep breath. He was nervous, I could tell. But he wasn't wishing any of the time away. He was in that room with us as much as he was going to be on the altar with Adrienne.

"You look good, Puke," I told him, hoping to calm him with a bit of humor. I turned to Braeden, a spitting image of Luke five years ago, and found him to be smiling, too. "Not as nice as B, but that was a given."

Luke laughed just as the music started, which was our cue to find our places, and Luke's cue to find my mom and start their trek down the aisle. I turned to him one more time, tears lining my eyelids and my throat, if that was possible.

"Best day ever," I told him.

He just nodded, another deep breath raising his chest like the tide. "Best day ever." He turned away then, headed for his spot, but flashed one last look at us—at me—before he went. "Don't trip him."

Luke was off, then, and Braeden turned himself to face forward as he stood beside Logan. The music—an instrumental version of Queen's "Love Of My Life"—was building softly as the crowd in the back of the room thinned.

I watched Renna and Brett start up the aisle, leaving only Logan and Braeden between us and the ceremony. Ronan's presence next to me was like a pillow. I knew if I had to head up the aisle by myself, all eyes on me, I would've crumbled. It didn't matter how much I knew myself or how comfortable I was in my skin. Eyes were eyes, and I still didn't love when so many were directed at me.

"I take it back," I said quietly to Ronan.

We were merely seconds away from our cue, but I had Ronan's full attention as he turned my way. He was bursting with nerves and excitement, just as I would've expected. But I wanted to make him smile.

I turned forward as Braeden and Logan started up the aisle. "I think you could pull off Banner," I whispered, "like Ruffalo."

Ronan audibly gasped, and I could feel his smile without seeing his face.

"If you tell anyone I said that, I'll deny it," I said then.

He threw his arm around my shoulders, testing time as I heard our cue and watched Braeden and Logan cross the halfway point of their trek.

"I know you will," Ronan laughed.

We made our way up the aisle then, past family members and old friends dressed to the nines. There were my grandparents and all of their descendants, both sides of the family sitting together as one. Sydney and Henry, whose flight from Europe landed early that morning, sat beside faces I recognized from high school and random days in the years after. There were classmates and teammates and colleagues and peers, all gathered like the sea to celebrate one love between two very special people. My eyes, of course, lingered on one particular family for the majority of my trek, and I felt that Ronan's did too. Maybe it was Freya's bouncy pigtails, or the toothy smile on her face. Either way.

I parted from Ronan once we reached the front of the room. The second we were settled just as everyone else was, the chorus started to play.

This next moment was one that I usually found to be wildly dramatized, overplayed. Whenever I watched a video or a scene in a film that focused on the groom's reaction to his bride walking through those back doors, her father on her arm, I thought it was fake. I thought they reacted just to react, because not doing so would mess with the flow of the wedding and slash everyone's expectations. Standing across from Luke when that very moment came for him, I didn't find my usual suspicions to be true.

Luke's eyes, upon seeing Adrienne, were filled with pure bliss. He was as happy and grateful as he possibly could've been. I knew it because I remembered a certain thirteen-year-old boy slinging his backpack onto the floor and sitting at the kitchen table with the same exact expression.

Luke's face and Adrienne's subsequent arrival, which resulted in tears from every person in the room, were a collective stamp on the day that would already go down in history as the best one my family had experienced. I was still thinking about the scene an hour later, when Ronan and I were walking back into the Royal for the reception after running to his car together.

I was carrying my shoes across the paved parking lot, which felt more like walking across lava since the sun had been beating down on it for hours. But it was better than the heels. Anything was better than the heels.

"You know," Ronan started when he saw me tip-toeing, "we could walk on the beach."

"We're almost there," I answered. "And it's not that bad."

"My feet are hot, and I'm wearing shoes."

I shot him a look that said I wasn't straying from the parking lot, then went out of my way to walk on a patch of sand that had snuck onto it from the beach. Ronan laughed.

"This isn't how I pictured today going," he said then.

I turned to him, my steps reverting back onto the pavement. "What do you mean?"

He shrugged. His hands were in his pockets, and his shoulders were relaxed. It was a stark contrast from his demeanor in the Coastal Room. "I've had this pit in my stomach telling me something was going to go wrong," he told me. "I think I was worried I was going to mess everything up."

"Well, the night is still young," I joked.

Ronan grinned, but I could tell he was being genuine, vulnerable. I almost regretted making a joke.

"The pit's gone," he told me. "I think you're mostly to thank for that."

"Me?"

We were just a moment away from the reception now. I could hear the wedding guests gathered on the deck of the Royal—a perfect setting, which overlooked the ocean and was big enough for two wedding receptions—and could see stragglers walking up its steps.

Ronan nodded. "Today wouldn't have been perfect without Finn," he admitted. "I knew it the day Luke proposed. I'm just glad you had the guts to act on it."

I was proud of Ronan. Feeling that way was a feat in itself. Speaking it aloud was on another level.

I nudged him with my elbow. "It wouldn't have been perfect without you, either. I hope you know that. Luke and Adrienne both adore you."

He smiled again, but this one was short lived. He'd never been great at taking compliments. I just wished he knew he was appreciated.

"Are you nervous for your speech?" I asked, in part to switch the subject and also because I was nervous for mine. I wanted to make sure we were going in with the same mindset.

Instead, Ronan stopped in his tracks. His jaw fell and his mouth was quickly covered by his hand.

No. No way.

"Ronan, are you joking?"

His eyes were wide as could be. We spoke too soon. What were we thinking, throwing around the word "perfect" like it was confetti? Now, we had a Best Man who hadn't prepared a toast. As far as I was concerned, that was his sole duty. His one job.

"I had so many other things to do," he blurted. "I completely forgot."

We were steps away from the deck now, but it might've been in our best interest to book it in the other direction.

I was breathing heavily, like I'd just finished a run. "Okay, okay," I said in one breath, the gears in my brain moving in full force. "We can– I can help you. We can skip the rest of the cocktail hour and write it together."

He shook his head. His eyes were starting to pool with tears. God, I couldn't handle this.

"We don't have time," he said.

"It'll be easy," I assured him. "It just has to come from your heart, right? Luke will love it no matter what."

"I don't know, Nell."

"You really don't have another choice," I explained, forcing him to meet my eyes. "Look, I'll go find some paper and a pen and we'll write a great toast."

Like magic, Ronan's fearful look faded. The tears in his eyes were swallowed as he reached into his coat pocket, slowly revealing an off-white sheet of paper whose ink was visible in the sunlight.

"Like this one?"

I looked away from the paper to Ronan's eyes, which were filled with amusement, then immediately began strapping my shoes back on.

"I hate you."

"You love me," he countered.

"I do not," I said, slipping on my second shoe. "And I take back my take-back. Effective immediately."

"If it helps," Ronan said as we started up the steps together, me treading carefully with clicking heels while he just bounced alongside, "I only finished it last night."

"Seriously?"

He laughed. "Well, I've had it written for a while. But I made some last-minute changes. I'm sure it won't compare to yours."

"Oh, now you're buttering me up?"

"I'm serious," Ronan said, his signature grin on his face as we reached the top of the stairs.

I shoved him, effectively pushing out a laugh. We'd arrived at the reception and though I'd seen the Banquet Hall and its adjoining deck before, I hadn't imagined it would look quite this extravagant. Everything was lit tastefully, creating a party atmosphere unlike any other. There were high-top tables and chairs scattered about the deck, leaving room for mingling and cocktail-devouring. I could see how beautifully the inside of the Banquet Hall was decorated, too, but what took my breath away was the view of the ocean. Living on the coast, I was sure I'd taken for granted the privilege of having the shore at our fingertips, and I was worried the magic of it had been lost on me. Standing on the deck now, a jittery Ronan taking it all in beside me, I felt like we were on top of the world. I couldn't wait for Luke and Adrienne to see it.

"I'm going to go make sure your mom found her table," Ronan said, turning only halfway to me. "Want to come with?"

I shook my head, spotting Logan and Renna across the way, talking to guests. "I'd prefer to save the You And Ronan Are Next comments until the end of the night."

He grinned. "You don't like those comments?"

"Go," I said. He did.

With Ronan's departure, my view was blocked momentarily by his body. Once it was clear again, my eyes found their way to the mauve dress I'd so diligently studied earlier. She was talking to a former lacrosse player—one of the

280

ones Luke had remained close to. I couldn't hear their conversation, but he seemed captivated by her. He wasn't the only one.

"Mel!" said a tiny voice from behind me, one that made the heartbreak I was starting to relive feel like a memory once again.

I spun around to find a purple ball of energy flying my way. She jumped into my arms a split second before I was ready, but I held my ground.

"My favorite girl!"

Freya stepped back from me, her eyes wide. When she smiled, I noticed something was missing.

"Did you lose a tooth?"

She nodded enthusiastically. "Two days ago. Before we got on the airplane," she said. Then, without a breath, "I've collected seven seashells."

I couldn't help but laugh. "That's so many!"

Freya nodded, giving me an opportunity to stand and meet the eyes of her parents. I still couldn't believe they'd come all this way so soon. By the looks on their faces, they couldn't either.

I greeted Sutton with a hug, taking in her outfit once we parted. She wore a brown jumpsuit and a simple gold necklace. Her hair was pulled back into a ponytail, and her round glasses were sitting atop her nose. Just like the first time I met her, I was ready to buy whatever she was pitching. The creativity was pulsating from her.

"Can we trade?" I asked her.

She shook her head, flashing her perfect teeth as she smiled. "What?"

"Lives," I said. Finn pulled me in then. We embraced for longer, and once again, I didn't want to let go. If it was up to me, I never would've.

"There's my hot girl," said, well, not Finn.

I was smiling even before I saw Sydney, and well after I eyed her hand, which was interlocked with Henry's. He wore a red tie that matched her dress, and his lips wore a permanent smile. He was next to Sydney, after all.

"You can't call me hot while you're wearing that," I said, then I turned to Henry, whose baby face was long gone. "How's Europe?"

"Amazing," he told us. "I'd be lying if I said I didn't miss this, though."

"The ocean?" Finn asked.

Henry turned, and was surprised by Finn's presence. In response, he squeezed Sydney's hand a little tighter. I hoped I wasn't the only one who saw it.

"Yeah, that too," he said.

This comment made everyone smile and settle at once, and it was the exact kind of moment I'd been waiting for. It was peaceful, kind. I felt at home, and I was with the people who belonged there, too. As I was thinking this, however, the moment itself got bigger. It must've heard me.

"...should've seen her face. Seriously," Ronan was saying. He entered the group seamlessly, as did Mo, who he was talking to. She laughed at his comment, then watched just as I did when he turned toward the group. "Hey, Sutton. You were right. It's purple."

"Purple?" Freya asked.

Sutton laughed, grabbing ahold of Freya's hand at her waist. "Your grandmother's dress," she said, her words directed at me.

"What color did you think it was?" I asked.

"Yellow."

I was almost over Ronan's antics for the day, and all I'd really dealt with was his toast prank. But I had to admit, this was funny. Across our impromptu circle, I watched Finn laugh.

"Hey, Mo," Sydney said then. The expression she wore was one of intrigue, though Mo wasn't talking, and was in no way drawing attention to herself.

"Dippy," Mo said delightfully, making me laugh, mostly on the inside. "Hey."

"Nell, we've got to line up in a minute," Ronan said, his laughter finally subsiding.

I nodded, already full of adrenaline for the wedding party's official entrance into the reception. I wasn't exactly excited to dance in front of everyone with Ronan, but I wasn't dreading it, either. I was mostly just anxious to see Luke and Adrienne—The Roses—for the first time as a married couple. I was shaking just thinking about it.

As I did, though, I saw Finn and Sydney exchange a rare look. It was unique because I couldn't decipher it, at least not until their actions laid it all out in front of me. After all this time, I was amazed at how quickly they found themselves on the same page about what might've been best for me. If this move could be considered best, that is.

"Freya," Sydney started, crouching down in front of her, "I've got some really funny stories about your dad, if you want to hear them."

Finn, like clockwork, threw his arm around Ronan's shoulder, sparking confusion in several of us around the group, including Ronan.

"One of them includes Ronan and a wakeboard," Finn said, turning to Sydney. "You know that one?"

"A wakeboard?" Freya asked, spinning around to face a smiling Sutton. "Is that like the skeeters?"

Ronan tilted his head.

"Skis," Finn explained before facing Freya. "Sort of."

Henry had joined in on the conversation, though silent, leaving me standing almost alone. Ronan, whose discomfort under Finn's arm had vanished, was tuned in now, too. The move was obvious, as Sydney and Finn moved the group away from Mo and me. We'd been cut out, left to speak only to one another. But, like Ronan mentioned, we had to line up soon, so in the split-second of silence that followed the group's departure, I started to head that way.

And then there was her voice.

"Smooth," she said, standing with her arms crossed and an impressed look on her face.

I settled back into my spot, my gaze focused on the back of Ronan's head, which tipped back in laughter a second later.

"They think they are," I said.

Mo chuckled. I wondered what went through her head then. Maybe she was thinking about how easily Sydney and Finn singled out the two of us or wondering if they knew the whole story. Our story. Or maybe she was wishing they hadn't cut us out, longing to be part of a conversation that didn't only feature me.

"I couldn't believe that was you this morning," she said instead.

My eyes jumped from Ronan to Mo immediately. "Meaning what?"

When she turned to me, I could tell she was nervous, treading carefully with me. This hadn't ever happened before, at least as far as I remembered. She always had words. I was the one who had to search for them.

"You just looked— you look—" She shook her head and took a breath. "I know Adrienne wore that dress to Ball, but it looks like it was made for you. You look happy and— and like yourself. It's almost like—"

"Like I'm her?"

She shook her head. I guess we didn't read each other's minds anymore. Time takes its toll.

"Like I'm the person you wanted me to find," I clarified.

Around us, the chatter was abundant. The music inside was playing softly, the waves were crashing into the distant shore. We were standing in the middle of a song of sorts. I could hear it all, but was still experiencing the look in Mo's eyes and the rasp in her voice. It was freeing, to be there fully.

"Nell! Ronan!" Across the deck, Renna waved us in her direction. "Game time!"

Mo was still sitting with what I'd said, but she heard Renna beckon me, too. She wore a polite smile when I faced her again, and God, it broke my heart.

If I'd known what to say next, I would've said it. It wasn't that I needed to be told how I felt. I'd known for years that seeing her again would light something inside of me. I knew I loved her when we were younger and I knew that hadn't faded, no matter how hard I tried to force it away.

"I should go," I said.

Mo nodded, her polite smile remaining. The guests around us were starting to make their way inside, their conversations surrounding us like paparazzi intruding on a celebrity's peace. I stepped forward to join the flow, my eyes grazing the crowd for my friends who were too far away to be eavesdropping. But then my heart told my feet to stop, and so they did. When I turned back around, Mo hadn't moved, but her smile had gone.

I couldn't change what happened four years ago. I couldn't take back what I'd said and I couldn't erase the amount of time between those moments and these ones. But maybe I had the power to change what happened next.

"I'll see you in there," I told her, extending my theoretical olive branch. "Maybe we can talk. Really talk, I mean."

Mo's eyes softened, her shoulders falling a bit with them. The smile she wore then wasn't forced or polite or courteous. It was real.

"I'd like that."

Chapter Twenty-Five

Elliana

It was that time of night when the grass felt cool as it brushed along your ankles, when the mosquitos finally received their invitation to the party. I knew this because these were the things I was noticing, all I could focus on as I sat at a picnic table filled with people gathered to celebrate someone who deserved it the most.

Finn's graduation party was being held on the outskirts of our town, a relative hike for anyone who lived on the coast and had to come inland for the afternoon. But the outskirts were where Finn's grandparents lived, thus the obvious location for his party, since his parents weren't apt to throw one. So no one minded the hike. Not one bit.

We'd been at the party for hours, and the graduation ceremony in the morning had lasted just as long. I sat with my parents and Braeden as we watched everyone walk across the outdoor stage to receive their long-awaited sheet of paper that indicated they'd made it through four of the most formative and confusing years of their lives. One piece of paper for everything they'd been through, all that they'd achieved, every day they'd woken up and put themselves on the line, each one different from the next.

And now, we were celebrating those exact things for Finn. Well, most of us.

Braeden, Adrienne, and I rode in the backseat of my parents' car to Finn's grandparents' house, playing yard games and eating barbecued food immediately upon our arrival. Ronan and Luke told us they'd be coming with the rest of the lacrosse team. I'd been sitting at the table for twenty minutes since the lacrosse team left. I still hadn't seen Ronan or Luke.

"We're going to head out," my father said, his hands in his pockets as he stood beside my mother. They'd been talking to Ronan's parents across the yard for a while. "Are you guys riding with us?"

I looked sideways at Adrienne, whose expression had only grown more and more defeated every minute we'd been there. She shrugged, so I took her answer for what it was, standing up from the table with as much energy as my body would allow me. So, none.

"We should go say goodbye to Finn," my mom suggested.

He was standing underneath a tent, next to a board filled with photos of him from kindergarten to now. Most of the pictures included a member of my immediate family, or Adrienne or Ronan, who might as well have been. The solo pictures of Finn were ones his grandparents took at theater performances or the vacation they took him on in ninth grade.

"Something's wrong," Adrienne whispered to me.

I met her eyes, and immediately I believed her. I hadn't been paying much attention to anything that wasn't touching my skin—the grass, the sand, the ocean breeze. The past few days had been gloomy, though the sky wasn't saying so. I was having a hard time figuring out whether it was my fault, so I wasn't thinking about it at all. But this—the look in Adrienne's eyes, the tension I could see in Finn's chest, Luke and Ronan's absence—wasn't just a sullen day in the ones leading up to the end of youth as we knew it so far. It was wrong.

"Heading out?" Finn asked. There was a smile on his face, but it wasn't his. There wasn't a spark behind it, a charm that surrounded it.

Adrienne nodded, then wrapped her arms around him, pulling him close to her. This was normal for our goodbyes, on any night really. Except this looked different, and I didn't know why. But then Finn pulled me in next. My mom was exchanging words with his grandmother, who stood close by, as I held onto him. I couldn't hear what they were saying, because I could feel the way he was clinging to me. It was distracting because it was so desperate, emotional. Maybe my feelings were off.

"I'm proud of you," I told him, since this was most appropriate given the occasion. But I laced my voice with something else. A question, maybe. But it was Finn's eyes looking back at me, filled with more concern than I was expressing toward him, that reminded me of the reason behind our last embrace. And, all of a sudden, I was back—blocking it all out, feeling only the shirt on my back and the socks hugging my ankles. Everything else was dark.

"I'll see you soon," he said to Adrienne and to me.

Adrienne shook her head, her eyes darting back and forth between his. "Why do I feel like I need to make you promise me that?"

"Adrienne—"

"Where are they, Finn?" she asked, demanding an answer with the edge in her voice. "Why aren't they here?"

His face sank. He took a deep breath. "I don't know."

"That's not true."

"It is true," he insisted, his voice hushed.

From behind me, an older woman called out Finn's name. I looked over my shoulder to find her, with rosy cheeks and graying hair, holding a blue envelope. She waved him over.

Finn looked at the two of us once more. Mostly, he was being attentive to Adrienne, trying, and failing, to put her at ease. She was still frowning, unconvinced.

But Finn just gave Braeden a fist bump, said goodbye to my parents, and then flashed the two of us a weak smile.

"I'll see you soon," he repeated. Then he walked away.

If I could feel anything, I was pretty sure I would've felt Adrienne's heart breaking beside me. It was written all over her face. As we walked to the car, I was pretty sure my mother noticed it. She'd asked if she was okay twice, which to both Adrienne replied with a smile and an affirmation. My mother didn't buy it. I wasn't sure if I did.

When we got back to the house, Adrienne spotted Luke's shoes by the door, then marched up to his bedroom where the door was cracked, determined to find answers to the questions she didn't even know. I didn't know if Ronan was around, or where Braeden was headed with his phone lighting up his nose and chin.

I was in a daze as I walked through the house, its usual summer scent—sunscreen, flowers, fresh air—in full-swing since the day school let out. It was almost like I'd reverted to the state I didn't know I was in before spring. I was happy to be inside, glad the day of activities was over.

And yet, the next morning, my feet and my heart took me to the beach just after breakfast. I was aching to watch the ocean glimmer, to hear the waves dancing their way to my toes in the sand. Among all of the changes, that was the only constant. The one thing I knew would always be there.

Of course, there was something, or someone, else that I should've known would always be there, too. She was sitting on the beach, waiting for me, I presumed. Her hair was in a messy bun and her basketball t-shirt was rolled at the sleeves. The picture of her was a picture of comfort, even when I sat beside her and her face was angry.

"Were you just going to ignore me all summer?"

"No," I said, like it was the most ridiculous suggestion ever. It was. "I've just been busy."

Sydney turned to the waves, her anger settling but her words hitting all the same. "You've been sad, not busy," she said. "I don't have to see you to know that, Elliana."

I was silent for a moment. Not because I was angry or offended or confused. Because I spent three days thinking no one would get what I was feeling. It might not have been my first mistake, but it was a big one.

"Did something happen with Mo?" she asked, her voice soft again.

I shook my head, but it faded quickly. "Something happened with me," I admitted, to Sydney and to myself. "And now it's all over."

For a moment, the two of us turned our attention back to the water. It had been a while since we sat beside one another, watching this exact scene in search of some sort of otherworldly meaning that we couldn't find behind us. Sitting there now, staring at the same sky I'd put my faith in all along, I realized something.

All of its characteristics—its warmth and vibrance and billowy clouds—belonged to the sky alone. The ocean, always underneath it, could only be understood fully by the ocean itself. What was surface-level to me would always be that way, no matter how hard I tried to go deeper. No matter how many times I stepped off of the beach and found myself dancing in its grasp.

If I'd really been in search of who I was, maybe I should've turned my gaze in the other direction. The answers weren't here, on the outside. To anyone but me, they could only be surface-level.

Sydney, if you could believe it, seemed to have the same idea. And I didn't have to tell her what happened for her to get the point. She knew me, and I was grateful for it in every moment. In this one, however, I needed it. And that was okay.

"You know what Mo told me once?" Syd asked quietly. "That the greatest gift you can give someone is showing them exactly who you are."

I took another breath. A single, warm tear fell down my cheek. I hadn't felt it coming.

"You gave her that," she told me. "For the first time. You'd never given it to anyone before."

Now, I wasn't thinking about Mo, but about everyone else in my life. My parents, my brothers, my friends. Sydney. They'd been trying for years to see all of me, for me to look at myself the way they did. I hoped it didn't hurt them to see that it only took a couple of words and glances from Mo for me to start looking a little deeper.

"I messed up," I said quietly, thinking about her again.

"So fix it."

"It's not that easy."

"Isn't it?" I turned to her then, finding the most familiar of her expressions: her game face. "Mo leaves in three days.

You're going to regret it for the rest of your life if you don't go after her. Besides, if you don't, I will."

It was enticing, really. Months ago, I wouldn't have been so apt to stand from where I was sitting and march in the direction of Mo's house. I was proud of myself for that. But still, I'd said what I said. I felt how I felt that day at the lacrosse game. There wasn't any changing that.

"I felt so wrong when I was next to her," I said to Sydney, shaking my head. "I didn't like the way people were looking at us. At me."

"You and Mo— you're like a work of art. People are going to look at you," she told me.

"But what if no one gets it?" I asked.

"Isn't that the whole point of being in love? That no one else understands it? The feeling you get when you're around her is something new and phenomenal that the universe only crafted for you." She paused, settled her shoulders. "If everyone understood it, you wouldn't feel the way you do right now. You wouldn't have a pit in your stomach at the idea of it being gone."

Sydney might've been speaking from experience, or she might've been pulling words from the air on the fly, but those words were speaking to me. They were resonating deeply and finding their way to the feeling that she was talking about. I felt them wrap their hands around it, holding it up to the light inside me.

Maybe I shouldn't have been so quick to run away. Maybe, all of those times I felt something move inside of me— that day behind the bleachers, that night in the garden, the afternoon in the ocean—I wasn't doing something wrong, but falling instead. Whether I landed with a thud on the basketball court or in the middle of someone else's heart, there was always something to be said about getting back up and trying again.

So I stood, huffing with another deep breath that my tears tried to swallow. I wiped them away, and I watched a proud smile grow on Sydney's face as I stood above her.

"I'll be here," she told me.

With that, I was gone. I walked pointedly up and through my house, fully unaware and admittedly careless of what was going on upstairs. I walked through the front door, down the steps and the driveway, and took a right once I reached the sidewalk.

The sun was hitting every inch of me as I began to think about what I was going to say. After a moment, I diverted my thinking to what Mo would've done if she were in my shoes, though she never would've been.

She'd have started with something attention-grabbing, urgent. Maybe it wouldn't have made perfect sense at first, but once it did, it would've been heartbreaking in the best way. She would have told me exactly how she felt. She wouldn't have been afraid of how I was going to react. She would have been completely and unapologetically herself in every way. That was all I had to do. The greatest gift.

I knocked on the door to Mo's beautiful green house before I realized I was standing in front of it. A few days without her in my life had been enough. Whatever happened once she opened the door, I could handle it.

Still, when I heard footsteps approaching, I tucked my hair behind my ears and tried to calm my heartbeat.

But then the door opened, and a man appeared in it. He was tall with curly, blonde-brown hair. He wore a gray t-shirt and a kind expression that I had a feeling was always there. Most importantly, he had Mo's eyes. It was probably more accurate to assume that she had his.

"Hi," he said, his tone both curious and welcoming.

"Hi," I said, attempting to make myself sound confident with even the smallest of syllables. "Is, um– is Mo home?"

I felt like a child again, knocking on the door at Sydney's house asking if she could come fly kites with Luke and me on the beach. If only that were the case.

"She left a few hours ago," he said, shaking his head with his eyebrows a bit lower.

"Oh," I answered, only slightly defeated. "Okay. Do you know when she might be back?"

Now, the confusion on his face grew a bit more sullen. He took a breath as he studied my face, his eyes seeming as if he saw something on it.

"Thanksgiving, I assume," he joked, his voice airy.

I didn't get it. Maybe my brain did, but my heart certainly didn't. "What?"

"She left for New York this morning."

He was wrong. She wouldn't have left without telling me. I knew that.

"She wasn't supposed to leave for three days," I said, my voice quieter than I intended. I certainly wasn't planning on crying in front of this man I didn't know. But as the realization continued to set in, I was getting close.

"She decided to go early," he said, his words intentionally soft. He could sense the hurt in my eyes, my voice. "Is there any chance that you're Nell?"

All I could do was nod.

"I'm Benen, Mo's Dad," he said, reaching his hand out to shake mine. "I've heard a lot about you. Mo really admires you."

This was almost as surprising as the news of her departure. Almost.

"I admire her, too," I said. I wished that summed up the way I felt about her. Standing there, hearing this, wouldn't have hurt nearly as bad.

I couldn't think straight. I could barely focus on Benen standing in front of me. I was the reason she left. I knew I was. There couldn't be another one.

"Well, I'd better go," I said, hurriedly. "It was really nice to meet you, Benen."

"You too, Nell," he said.

I started toward the driveway, and when I hadn't heard the door shut yet behind me, I turned back around. I wasn't entirely sure why, but then I opened my mouth.

"Hey, Benen? You and Mo– you dance in the rain together, and you get gas station pizza in the middle of the night. Right?

Benen grinned a bit, a flash of his white teeth showing between his lips. He was with me.

"Do you ever do those things alone? When you're not together?"

He nodded, though I could tell he had no idea where I was going with these questions. For once, I did.

"I do," he said. "Even if she's not here, she's still with me. You know?"

I nodded. "Yeah. Yeah, I do," I said, the last word dropping. "Thanks, I'll see you around."

He smiled once more. "I hope so."

I was back inside my house in record time. I could still feel the heat sitting on my skin as I was welcomed by the cool air of our living room, then kitchen, then my bedroom. In the next room over, I heard Adrienne's voice, stern, speaking words I couldn't make out. There was Luke, too, and maybe even Ronan. I didn't try to hear what they were saying, and I didn't immediately run out to the beach to tell Sydney what had, or hadn't, happened. All I could do was look at myself in the mirror that sat upon my dresser.

My cheeks were dotted with freckles that had been hidden for years. I had a spark in my eyes, history on my lips, the sun's touch on my shoulders. There were versions of myself staring back at me that I hadn't been introduced to until this year. There was the part of me who liked to dance, who yearned to hear the sound of laughter in the middle of the night. There was the part that was daring, unafraid. There was the girl capable of love who wanted it so badly that the worst thing she could've done was let it go.

Mo was the reason that I could see all of those things. She was the reason I'd stepped into myself, the reason I wanted to in the first place. Staring at my reflection now, seeing all of these things on my face, I knew that wasn't enough. I had to be the reason. I had to do it for me and no one else. Maybe, then, I wouldn't feel so bad.

I vowed to my reflection that the next time Mo came home, I wouldn't have to try so hard to be myself. There wouldn't be an image of a girl that I was looking for anymore, because that girl would be me. Maybe, then, we could really be together and stay that way. I was willing to put in the effort until then. Even if I had to wait until Thanksgiving.

Chapter Twenty-Six

Nell

The leader of the band was ecstatic as he gripped the microphone, his tattoos peeking out under the sleeves of his button-down shirt. A drumroll sounded softly from behind him.

"And now, for the first time as husband and wife, Lucas and Adrienne Rose!"

The Banquet Hall erupted in applause, cheers, whistles, cries. If it was a happy noise, it was thrown into the air, and deservedly so. I found myself tearing up at the sight of my brother and Adrienne, fingers intertwined as they made their way to the center of the dance floor. I couldn't get enough of their faces, so relieved and blissful. I was clapping so enthusiastically that my hands were beginning to sting.

In the next breath, Luke and Adrienne were dancing sweetly to Gavin Degraw's "More Than Anyone," looking at one another and softly conversing like they were the only ones in the room for just a moment. The song, which the wedding band played a stripped-down version of, set a smooth tone for the rest of the night.

After the music faded out, the food was served—a choice of prime rib, lemon chicken, or salmon, all served with a colorful side salad. Everyone dug in as the energy in the room only grew brighter, the anticipation for the looming dance party with it. And then, all of a sudden, it was time for the toasts.

Ronan required no introduction, as just the clinking of his glass settled the room in seconds. I was already glad he was going first, but especially then. I would have never been able to grab everyone's attention like he did.

He cleared his throat, straightening his bowtie as the band's leader handed him the microphone. I wondered then if he was as nervous as I was, to speak in front of so many people. Then again, the crowd before him didn't consist of his own distant family members who held an unrealistic expectation of him. Or the one person in the entire world that he needed to find the right words for, but knew he never would. Lucky him.

As awful as it was, I was sort of hoping he stumbled over a word, or something. Then the pressure would be off.

"Good evening everyone. For those of you who don't know me, I'm Ronan, Luke's Best Man today, though we all know that I stand in a pretty long line of them," he started, his charming smile beaming. Somewhere, my grandmother was swooning. "I'd like to start off by saying that Adrienne, you look absolutely incredible tonight. Luke, I'd compliment you, too, but you said I couldn't do that in public anymore. I'm not sure if this counts."

Luke and Adrienne sat at the end of our table, both of them already breaking out into laughter with the rest of the room. Ronan took a deep breath, turning his attention back to the rest of the guests, following his visual nod of approval from the married couple. The wrinkled paper he was holding remained at his side.

"I think I speak for everyone when I say that we've been looking forward to today for a long time. But what most of you don't know is that Luke has been planning this day since he was thirteen-years-old." He paused, and I saw Luke's smile grow wider. "Luke and I have been best friends since we were babies. We met in elementary school in Ms. Lucy's class. I believe it was the second day of first grade when the two of us– the three of us–"

Technically, I manifested the slip-up with my wishful thinking, but I didn't think it would present itself like this. I looked over my shoulder to Finn, who was shocked by his mention, and he hadn't even said his name yet.

"Lucas, Finn, and I, we were placed together in a group, by complete chance, to work on an art project."

Ronan went on to tell a story about the project—a paper mache turtle, which, if my memory serves me, looked more like a platypus—and detailed how much of a disaster it was, crediting the chaos to how well the three of them got along.

I wasn't exactly sure of the logic there, but considering where we were, it made sense for the time being. I guess we had Ms. Lucy to thank.

"I was drawn to Luke, even in the first grade, because of how big and how kind his heart was. I wanted to stick around to see the person he became, and I thought I had an idea of who that person would be. But then Adrienne came along." Ronan took another breath, settling himself as his eyes glistened.

"We were in the seventh grade when Adrienne transferred into our class. Lucas, Finn, and I were sitting at the back of our homeroom when Adrienne walked in wearing her yellow backpack, a white dress with sunflowers, and her hair in two braids. I am not kidding when I say that the kid almost fell out of his chair." The room erupted in laughter again, successfully willing Ronan to keep going.

"It only took him five minutes to gather up the courage to talk to her. Finn and I sat back and actually watched him fall in love, right there. It was incredible." I snuck a glimpse at Finn again, just as much of the room did. He, too, was tearing up. I had to keep it together, so I reverted my eyes to Ronan. "That was the day that Luke started planning this one. He wasn't presumptuous, and he really wasn't a big dreamer at the time. He just knew that the universe put them in that room together for a reason. They both did."

This sentiment was sweet, and astoundingly true. Sure, everything had its ifs. But I was certain that there wasn't a world, a possibility caused by a turned moment, that didn't have Luke and Adrienne in that room. And then, in this one.

"If there's one thing you need to leave here knowing about Luke, it's that he's thoughtful. In the sixth grade, a girl named Janie Melfield asked him what his type was, because that was our eleven-year-old hyperfixation of the week." Another round of laughter. "Luke said that he didn't have one. He said that once he found his person, they'd be unlike anyone he'd ever met, and they wouldn't fit into a category. That person would be his type, he said. So, to Janie Melfield and anyone else who has ever wondered…"

Ronan turned his body again and held his hand out to Adrienne, as if presenting her to the room for the first time. This was the punctuation mark to a great speech, and it was met with laughter and applause as Adrienne's cheeks reddened. Although I was exponentially more anxious for mine, I was grateful to have listened to Ronan's. Luke, who squeezed Adrienne's arm at Ronan's final sentiment, seemed to be too. The tears in his eyes told me so.

Ronan finished with another round of compliments, a shout out to my parents and Adrienne's mother, and a joyful wish for a happy marriage. After he held up his glass and we all toasted, Luke and Adrienne both stood to hug him. It was such a moment that my nerves slipped away upon watching it.

"And now," Ronan said, turning to me, "you all have the honor of hearing from the *Maid* of Honor, Nell."

Shit.

Ronan handed the microphone to my free hand, the other one holding loosely onto an almost-full glass of champagne. He looked me in the eyes as he did so, giving me luck and his love with just a glance. I felt it, and it calmed me.

"I'm not sure how I'm going to follow that," I mumbled, intending to only reach Ronan's ears. But when everyone around me laughed, I realized I'd said it into the microphone. Great start, Nell.

I cleared my throat, wasting no time, and began to recount the words I'd memorized over the past six months.

"I assume everyone here knows this already, or guessed it based on our resemblance, but for those of you who aren't aware, I am Luke's little sister, which is one of the biggest blessings of my life. I grew up as the middle child, with a brother on either side. This means that I've always felt equally loved and picked on, and I learned at a young age to hold my ground when it came to my time in the bathroom every morning."

There was a round of laughter, which I wasn't expecting. I tried not to look at all of the faces staring back at me as everyone awaited more of my voice, but it wasn't exactly helping the sinking feeling in my chest. So, to start, I just looked at my father. He wasn't crying already, like my mother was, and I could always say anything to him. This didn't exactly classify as a tough conversation, but it had started on my terms. What was the difference?

"Having two brothers made me who I am. I'll always be grateful for Luke's guidance and Braeden's support, the way both of them have always included me. But, being the only girl, that also meant something else.

"When my mom asked me what I wanted for my birthday when I was five, I said I wanted a sister. The same thing happened when I turned seven, and at Christmas when I was eight." Without intending to, I found myself looking at my mom then. There were tears rolling down her face, as they had been since Ronan stood up a few moments earlier, but she was smiling. "I'd never wanted a sister more than when I was eleven years old, which just so happens to be the year that Adrienne walked into Luke's life. His homeroom, first."

I was finding comfort in my skin as I went on. As it turned out, this story was the one I knew the most, and it wasn't as hard to describe as I thought. I lifted my eyes from my parents to see that every person in the room was with me, each wearing a delighted or intrigued expression. I felt good, and it was more than enough to keep me going.

"The first time I met Adrienne was at Luke's fourteenth birthday party. He was having a pancake-themed bash on the beach, and I was hiding upstairs in my room, like I always did. But Lucas, annoyingly persistent, managed to drag me outside, insisting that I just had to meet the girl named Adrienne that had finally made her way over to our house," I said, readying myself to drop the bomb that was the next sentence. "I wasn't excited at all. I knew how Luke felt about her, but my hopes weren't high. I'd had a beautiful and romantic example of love sitting in front of me at the kitchen table every night, and I had every doubt in my body telling me that whoever Luke liked would never measure up to that."

My next pause was intentional. I'd even written it in the first draft of my notes when preparing for the speech. I could practically see the bolded ink.

"I have never been more wrong in my life," I said, earning more laughter. I turned to my brother. "Luke, I would like to formally apologize for stealing Adrienne away from you that day. And the week after that."

Through the next series of chuckles and giggles, I saw Luke say something, to which Adrienne laughed. But I hadn't heard him, and no one else did, so I pointed the microphone in his direction.

"I think it was a month," he said.

Now, I was laughing. I waited for myself and everyone else to settle before continuing on. I was getting to the part of the speech I was nervous about. Vulnerability is never easy.

"Right. So, obviously, Adrienne and I were immediately best friends. She quickly became the person that I told all of my junior high gossip to, and the person I heard all of the high school drama from. I was always excited to receive her hand-me-downs. If this dress is familiar to anyone, for example, it's because Adrienne wore it to Prom her senior year."

I felt the reaction from everyone after mentioning the dress, and I basked in it. But my favorite was Finn's. His eyes grew wide and his jaw dropped, a telltale sign that he hadn't put the pieces together until I explained them. I bit my lip, held back a laugh.

"Adrienne became my advice-giver, my card game and karaoke partner, my source of humor when the boys were being boys, as in not funny. Once I realized all of this, and really thought about it, I knew I finally had the sister I always wanted. And, I knew just by the way she and Luke glanced at each other from across the room, that I'd never lose her."

I was finally able to glance at Adrienne then. Her eyelids were wet with tears, which she was wiping away as her smile remained cemented on her face. God, it felt good to see that. To have someone smiling because of my words. It was even better that that person, among many others in the room, was Adrienne.

Onto the home stretch.

"When I was a sophomore in high school, I asked Adrienne how she knew that Luke and she were meant to be together. How she knew it was really love and he was really the one. I thought her answer was going to be complicated, because I thought that was what love was.

"But her answer was simple. She said that every day with Luke was the best day of her life. Everything about him made her feel more like herself, and he was always showing her new things about the world. She said she knew her heart."

Luke's attention was on Adrienne the next time I looked. His eyes were glistening too, and Adrienne's tears had moved to her cheeks. I wondered if she remembered that conversation. I knew I'd never forget it.

"I think every one of us in this room would be lying if we said we didn't want the kind of love that Adrienne described. The kind of love that changes your world and changes who you are, in all of the good ways and none of the bad."

Mo's eyes were vibrant and inescapable when I met them. My words weren't meant to be an allusion towards her, but they'd come from my heart. Though I knew and owned every inch of myself, that part of me was still in her grasp. So, of course I looked at her. Of course I heard Lena snap a picture of my face when I did. And of course Mo smiled as she looked down. I didn't know what she was thinking; I didn't have that instinct anymore. But there was something new in her expression. Hope, maybe.

I looked away then, while I still had the power to do so. Then, I turned back to Adrienne and Luke, the smile on my face the realest I'd ever worn.

"For most of my life, you two have shown me what it looks like to love and to be loved. Maybe it's simple to you, but it's invaluable to me. To all of us." I raised my glass, my mother wiping a tear from her face in my peripheral. "I can't wait to keep learning from the two of you, and I wish nothing more

302

than for you to feel this way forever. For nothing to change. So here's to that."

My toast wasn't only met by the clinking of glasses and sipping of champagne, but an abundance of applause, cheers, kind words as I took the few steps remaining between me and Adrienne. I was elated because the toast was over, and although I was honored to give it, I would've been lying if I said I hadn't been dreading it. But as I met Adrienne, and she embraced me with her warmth and her smile, I knew my words really meant something. That, in itself, was worth it.

"Thank you," she said softly as she held me tight. "I love you so much."

I found her eyes as we broke apart. "I love you."

Luke pulled me in next. We didn't exchange any words, but we didn't need to. His eyes were watering when I looked into them, so I knew just how he felt.

When I sat down, my father stood up. Then, over the next hour, a myriad of wonderful things occurred. My dad and Ms. Brenda both gave heartwarming and spirit-lifting toasts, showcasing just how grateful they were for the joining of their two families. Adrienne and Luke cut into their wedding cake, which was beautifully decorated with flowers in every shade of pink. Luke and my mother shared a tear-jerking dance to Elton John's "Your Song," while my grandmother, standing beside me, pointed out Ronan's charming grin as he stood just a few feet away. I entertained her with a smile, and was relieved when the next song started playing, and a dance circle formed.

Luke was pushed in first, by no one other than Ronan and Finn. Though everyone was expecting him to pull his bride into the circle with him, Adrienne beat him to the punch, shoving Braeden into Luke's arms before the two laughed their faces off as they tried to recall a dance they made up together when they were little. I danced along the outside, and knew the one they were trying to remember by heart. Adrienne, who I instantly regretted calling my sister, could see it on my face, so she pushed me in, too.

Once the three of us made our exit, Freya was the next to jump in. She stole everyone's hearts and attention as she twirled along to a Beyoncé song. I watched as Sutton laughed uncontrollably, then encouraged her daughter to keep going once she started to get shy. But Freya, unbeknownst to us, had ulterior motives. She moved around the circle, taking her time and stealing the show while she considered who to choose as her dance partner. My heart melted when she reached her hand up to Ronan.

This was it. Ronan having the time of his life, sacrificing his toes as Finn's daughter stood on top of them throughout the next song. Adrienne and Braeden dancing together to a song they'd bonded over for years. Finn and Sutton finding themselves nearly on the outskirts, my parents getting to know every detail of their life together. Sydney and Henry looking just as in love as the first time I'd sensed they were. Luke and me, dancing side by side as we identified a movie that every consecutive song had played in within the first ten seconds of each one starting. It wasn't exactly what I'd been dreaming of all along, but only because I never could have pictured it. This was the best day. There wasn't a doubt.

And the night went on just like that. I didn't know how many songs had played by the time Taylor Swift's "Paper Rings" blasted over the speakers, the band taking their short intermission. I stole Adrienne from Luke after I heard the first few beats of the song, and felt no regret in doing it. We scream-sung the lyrics shamelessly, while countless others around us did the same.

Then, I was thirsty.

It was the first break I'd taken all night, but it really felt like days since I'd taken a seat. I found my glass of water shimmering on my table, and I took my time sipping it so as to not look too desperate.

I watched as the night continued to unfold around me, and glanced over the heads and past the shoulders of everyone to see one of the most important guests of the night.

It was sitting happily past the deck, which was littered with guests seeking fresh air and a view. I could feel its blueness still. Its sparkle intrigued me, and although it was constantly calling my name, I took comfort in knowing that it would be there when the night was over. Still blue, still sparkling, still vast.

After all this time, the ocean and me still had something in common. We desired to be loved, fiercely and endlessly. It was only now, standing in a room full of so much emotion and warmth, that I realized we both were. And by the same people, nonetheless.

It was then that I saw her. She'd been sitting at a table closer to the deck talking to a few girls from high school. The two of them stood, blocking my view of the ocean momentarily, and headed for the bathroom, leaving Mo sitting alone. I was sure she didn't mind; she never had before. But maybe now was my chance. I knew that those didn't come around very often, so I took it.

"All danced out?" Mo asked, breaking the ice before it had even formed.

I took the seat next to her at the table, hoping that she didn't take her leave immediately after my doing so. I flashed her a smile.

"For now," I said.

There were only a few tables between us and the dance floor, on which Finn and Sutton had a part of my attention, one of each of their hands intertwined with one of Freya's.

"How about that?" Mo said as she followed my eyes.

I shook my head. "Everywhere I look, I need someone to pinch me so I know what I'm seeing is real."

"And it was all your doing," Mo added.

I turned to her then. There wasn't a trace of the hurt she wore the night before or the confusion she wore days earlier.

"Not all of it," I said, turning back to the floor before I launched into a minutes-long explanation of why, of all the people here, her presence was the one that stunned me the most. It always was. "Everyone was meant to be here for Adrienne and Luke, I just did a little bit of pushing."

There was a beat, and then we both watched as Ronan and Freya re-entered our view, this time accompanied by Braeden, who was pretending to beat-box next to a rapping Freya. Ronan was doing the Robot.

"I'm surprised his suit hasn't ripped yet," Mo observed.

"Oh it has," I told her. "He danced too hard to Dave Matthews Band earlier. Pants ripped right on the crotch."

I turned to find Mo biting her lip, withholding laughter. When she read my face, we both broke out in it. After a moment, it settled. Then, Mo said something that I'm not sure she knew was on her mind, much less her lips.

"Well, I'm glad not everyone has changed."

Her statement was bold, and though it might not have been directly aimed at me, it applied all the same. I couldn't possibly mind it. We needed to talk about it, and her words might have just done the trick.

"Mo—"

"I'm sorry," she said, looking down and fiddling with the flower ring on her thumb. "I didn't mean it as a bad thing."

I just nodded, giving her the floor. She took it.

"I've tried really hard to be angry at you," she said, knocking the breath from my lungs. "I can never decide if I am or not. But I didn't think it would matter because I wasn't sure I'd ever see you again."

"And now?" I dared to ask.

"And now," she said slowly, "I see your face and I can't possibly be angry. I can't feel anything bad when I look at you."

This was good. This was the best thing she could've said. This filled my heart and my lungs and my soul and—

"And I hate it."

The wind was knocked out of me again. I was beginning to feel like a punching bag, and we hadn't even gotten anywhere. I was beginning to think we never would.

"You—" I shook my head. "You hate it?"

She meant what she said, but she shook her head slightly at the sound of my question. "At the party on Thursday, there was that video of Luke and Adrienne from Ball. I don't know if you noticed us in the background of it."

"I did."

She nodded, pausing as she returned to fiddling with her ring. "I was naive," she told me. "I shouldn't have assumed you felt the way I did that whole time."

"I did feel that way."

I still felt that way.

"Then why'd you walk away?" She lifted her eyes back up after asking the question, as if my face would reveal the answer before my words. If it did, I wasn't sure what it was saying.

"I don't know," I said, wishing more than anything that I had an answer to give her. I wished I could've told her why I said those things that I didn't mean, or why I felt so adamantly that the best thing for me was really the worst.

Mo nodded, like she was expecting my answer to be that way. "I asked myself that a lot, and the only answer I could think of was me," she said. I wasn't sure how much more I could take. "And then I tried to get over it. I dated a girl at school. A whole year."

I stood corrected. I knew exactly how much more I could take, and that was it.

"She was really cool, actually. An art student. She spoke four languages, lived in three different countries before moving to the city. We were good together, everyone said."

Maybe there was a point to all of this. There had to have been things Mo wanted to say for the past four years, and perhaps that was what I was hearing. Maybe there was still a chance. I just had to muscle through it.

I swallowed hard. I could feel my heart beating in my ears. I had to ask. "Why did it end?"

She shook her head, and I saw her eyes as they fell upon mine. "She wasn't you. As much as I thought she could be, she just wasn't," she said. Then, before I could say anything, "And she hated the rain."

This, to me, felt like an olive branch. Maybe Mo didn't need me to give my piece, but I did. And I was in the business of putting myself first lately.

"I was with a boy and a girl at school. Not at the same time, obviously," I told her. Technically, outside of Sydney and Genevieve, Mo was the first person to hear this. Not because I was ashamed or wanted to hide the fact. It had just never come up anywhere else.

Mo, though she was trying not to show it, was utterly surprised. The way her head cocked backwards slightly and her eyes blinked twice rapidly told me so.

"I never thought they could be you, but I did think that maybe I didn't need you," I told her.

My eyes lingered from Mo to my hands to the dance floor, where the party was still in full-force. Except for Finn. He was out there, still participating in the dancing and the love-fest that was the night, but every so often, he'd glance my way. This one, I caught, and I could tell just by his eyes that he was asking if I was okay. So I flashed him a smile, because I was okay. Or, getting there.

"And maybe- maybe I don't," I started, hoping to God that my words didn't sound too concrete, too sure. "But I know for a fact that no one has ever made me feel the way you did. And I'm not sure anyone ever will."

I was proud of myself for saying what I meant, even if I didn't know where the conversation had us standing. Thankfully, I could always count on Mo to get us there. I should've known.

"You said you were different. Or– or that version of yourself. What did you mean?"

I shrugged, though I knew exactly what I meant. "I just know who I am now. I'm still the same person, just without all the—"

"Straight hair?" she interrupted. There was that smile.

I laughed. "Yeah. Without the straight hair," I said. "And the hesitancy, and the rules. The naivety, I hope. Plus, my posture's gotten worse."

"I did see you slouching earlier," she laughed. "I liked it."

I felt so unbelievably good to hear her laughing because of me. To see a smile on my account.

"Of course you did," I said. I shook my head, taking a deep breath. "I am who I am still, just more so, I guess. That's never going to change, I just—"

"Good," she interrupted, forcing me to meet her eyes. "I never wanted you to change. I just wanted you to see yourself."

I nodded. "I do."

I sat back in my seat, allowing the music to make its way back to my ears and the air to find my skin again. I was relieved, and I hoped I had a reason to be.

"I've been wanting to say that for a while," I admitted.

"I've been wanting to hear it." Mo smiled. She was sitting back, too. It was like the two of us had been running a marathon for years, unaware that we were side-by-side, experiencing the same hills and long stretches together. Now, we'd reached the finish line, and it was time to relax.

But, inside, I was desperate to know what happened next. We couldn't just leave it at that. What we'd both said was so pressing, wasn't it? I needed to feel the way she made me feel, and she couldn't be with someone who wasn't me.

I couldn't just be her friend. If it was what she wanted, then I could've. But I wasn't going to spend the next four years wondering what would've happened if I didn't push her away the first time. If this resolve wasn't just a band-aid.

"Is there any chance—" I started, my gaze taking its aim back on the dance floor before turning to Mo. She looked at me with her vibrant eyes, daring me to ask what I wanted to. "Do you want to dance with me?"

I extended my hand, just above the table with a half-eaten piece of cake on a dessert plate, and watched Mo's eyes as she considered the offer. We both knew it meant more than the two of us joining the rest of the party. My question was built on the regret I had, the second chance I knew was so fleeting at that moment.

My heart skipped a beat when I felt her hand on mine. Two beats, even.

We joined the dance floor seamlessly, finding all of our people grouped into the center of it. My mother and Ms. Brenda were singing to each other, my father and Henry doing the same. Sydney was beside Jess who was beside Adrienne and Finn. I saw Sutton laugh at something Ronan said and Freya was standing on Braeden's toes, his hands interlocked with hers so she didn't fall over.

The song was "Signed, Sealed, Delivered," by Stevie Wonder, and the band was singing it with such gumption that I could feel the beat in my veins. Though it was fast-paced, I didn't let go of Mo's hand, and she didn't let go of mine. We sang the words together, and I couldn't take my eyes off of her. I'd never been happier, not by a long shot.

When the song faded out, I made a mental note to thank Genevieve for never letting me skip a 2 a.m. dance party in our dorm room. The hours she spent teaching me how to move without seeming stiff had paid off. At least I hoped so.

The next song that the band played was by a rock group that Adrienne loved. I couldn't quite put my finger on their name, because I felt a strong pair of eyes on me. I turned around as the beat picked up to find my grandmother standing just off of the dance floor, her eyes digging into me and her expression one of utter disapproval. It was then that I realized she wasn't looking at my eyes, however, but my hand.

I shook it away, because I didn't care. Of course I didn't. Mo was happy to be by my side, and it was all I'd ever wanted.

The next look came from Jess. She'd always had a smug look on her face, so I told myself not to think anything of the way she was looking at me. When she turned away, I saw Logan and Renna, both so welcoming and kind-hearted. I had to be paranoid about the way they were staring, about the way their eyes were saying I didn't belong next to someone so bright. I had to be.

The night was about Lucas and Adrienne, not me. Everyone noticing my hand in Mo's was missing the point. But that didn't stop my heart from racing.

My grandmother hadn't moved. Aunt Marley was beside her now, her face blank yet disapproving. Uncle Drake and Aunt Lucy were across the dance floor. She whispered something in his ear and he laughed. Jonah Kravitz, a former lacrosse player, raised his eyebrows at something Brett said. Uncle Paul shook his head.

The tattooed lead singer of the band had just belted out a note when I started to lose my breath. I looked at Mo. She was happy, dancing away just like me. She was so much more vibrant than I was. She had so much more to give, with our hands interlocked.

I tried to hold the picture of her in my mind as I closed my eyes and attempted to slow my breathing. I looked at my feet, the ceiling, the ocean, anything else but the eyes of people around me. I couldn't believe it was happening again.

I couldn't believe what I was about to do.

In one swift motion, I dropped Mo's hand and slowed my dancing to a full stop. I felt her mood change. I felt everyone's mood change. I felt everything.

Mo lowered her head so our eyes could meet. She was concerned, and not for herself.

"I can't," I said quietly.

Everyone around us was still dancing, but I knew this was causing a scene. I wished I could've stopped it.

"Nell," Mo said softly. She wanted me to look at her. I couldn't. My mind was telling me to pull her aside, to start slower. My heart was telling me to stay, to convince her that I really was the person I said I was. So, for the life of me, I couldn't figure out why I didn't.

"I'm sorry," I said.

"Nell." Mo's voice was louder this time, a hint that this was the last chance I had.

By the time I made it to the deck, my face was full of tears and my chest hurt so bad that I needed to sit down. I planted myself onto a wooden bench facing the ocean, my head immediately falling into my hands. I didn't want to think about what had happened but it was all I could do. I hated myself. I hated everything about me. I pushed away everything that was good for me, and I didn't only do it once.

My whole body jerked upwards when I felt a hand on my back. It was a gentle touch, but I hadn't expected it. I turned my head to see a concerned Ronan, his face illuminated by the decorative lights above us. He didn't say anything before he sat down and pulled me into a hug.

"Nell—"

"Did everyone notice?" I said into his chest. Between the muffled voice and the way it broke, I was surprised he understood me.

"No. No, not at all," he assured me. I felt him shake his head as I pulled myself away from him slowly, if only to get more air. He sat for a moment before saying what I could read on his face. "What exactly was that, though?"

"I ran away," I explained.

He nodded, slowly. "Right, but— from what? Did something happen? Did someone say something to you?"

I shook my head. "Was Mo upset?"

"I don't know, I came right out here," he told me. "Why would Mo be upset?"

"Because I convinced her that I could do it," I said quietly. There were only a few other people on the deck, and I didn't care if they heard, but I was still ashamed of the words I was saying. "And I just proved that I most definitely can't."

"Do what?"

I looked at Ronan then. I knew he didn't get it, and I guess I didn't have much in me to slowly spell it out for him.

"Be with her," I told him. "I want to be with her."

"Be with—" He stopped himself, and I watched the thought make it all the way from his ears to his eyes to his brain. "You're—"

"Gay," I said, finishing his sentence in case he didn't actually get it. I was impatient. "Or– or not straight. I don't know."

Ronan's eyebrows eventually lowered to a normal height. He wasn't at all offended or hurt or showing any signs of disapproval. It's not that he would have been warranted in doing so, but I would've expected more than the pure acceptance immediately bursting from his eyes. I knew how he felt about me, so the care I knew he was about to show meant more than anything. Except now, he knew how badly I'd messed up.

"Thank you for telling me that," he said, his voice soft. "I didn't mean to force it out of you."

"You didn't." I shook my head. "I just– I couldn't stand the way people were looking at me, and I don't know why."

Ronan took a breath, and I gave him the time to do so. Of all of the things that he was expecting to have to deal with tonight, I was pretty sure this was a curveball. Hopefully the pit wasn't back.

"I don't know how any of that feels, Nell, but I can assure you that anyone who matters isn't going to think any differently of you because of who you love. I know I don't."

This wasn't exactly what I needed to hear, but it did mean something more than he knew. The part that hurt the most was that I knew that what he said was true, and I knew it before Mo took my hand.

"Mel, are you sad?"

I turned to find Freya, purple dress and all, standing next to Ronan with her eyebrows lowered. I let a laugh out of my nose, one I didn't know I could release. Freya had that effect, I guess.

"Yeah, I'm a little sad."

She nodded as if she understood my statement to its fullest extent.

"Sorry, Nell," Finn said breathlessly as he, too, approached. "I couldn't catch her."

Finn and I exchanged a look while Freya comfied herself on Ronan's lap.

"Freya?"

He shook his head. "Mo. She left."

When I didn't answer, because I knew right then that I really had ruined not only my night, but everyone else's, Finn broke the silence again. Checking in, like always.

"Are you—"

"Please tell me Luke and Adrienne are still inside," I begged.

Finn nodded, and immediately I was relieved. "I told them you and Ronan ran out here to take a picture. Sydney asked, too."

Ronan grinned. "What do they think you're doing?"

Finn shrugged. "I don't know. Taking the picture?"

"There you are," Sutton said, emerging from the darkness and appearing beside Finn. She stretched her arms out to Freya, who stretched back. In the next beat, she was in her arms, but her attention was still on me. "I'm going to take her up, Finn," Sutton said. "The sugar crash is coming."

"Okay," Finn said. He planted a kiss on Freya's cheek when Sutton tipped her his way. She smiled.

"Goodnight, daddy."

"Goodnight, Fish," he said. Ronan, his arm still around me, smiled.

"Nell?" Freya said then. "Daddy says that sometimes it's good to be sad. It means the happy will be bigger when it comes."

It might not have been poetic or philosophical or literary. But the gist of it was. All of the happiness in the world wouldn't be so extraordinary if there were no darkness to contrast it. Maybe this was the end of it for Mo and me. But I was lucky to even have a taste of something so great. This darkness was proof of it.

"Thanks, Freya," I said to her with a smile, wiping another tear from my cheek. "You're very wise. Just like your dad."

Before Finn could blush, Freya spoke up again. She was nodding, triumphant as she'd earned the two of them a compliment. But Sutton was right. I could see the sugar crash looming in her eyes.

"He also says something about noodles," she told us. "I don't get it."

Ronan gasped, the mere possibility of Finn having a stance on the pasta debate being enough to liven him back up. This was all that had ever really mattered, wasn't it?

"I'll explain when you're older," I said.

With that, Sutton flashed us all a smile. "We'll see you guys tomorrow."

"Goodnight," Finn and I said in unison. Ronan's jaw was still floored.

But, considering the circumstances, he canned the pasta conversation. I had a feeling, come morning, the debate would be back in full force.

Finn sat himself beside me on the bench, so I was sandwiched between him and Ronan. It was such a strange phenomenon, having one thing feel so realigned just moments after I'd torn another thing apart. I was beside the two people whose presence in my life I likely wouldn't have survived without. Even more, they were close to one another again, and that proximity was enough to get me through the night.

"I love that kid," Ronan said, breaking my silence but filling one of the holes in my heart.

"She worships you," Finn told him. Then, he nudged my shoulder with his. "And you."

There was so much radiating from Freya both times I had the privilege of meeting her that I felt I needed to take note. She was so little—in age and every other variation of the term— but held such hope and curiosity and sheer passion for the world she was living in. I wondered if the two of us could possibly have anything in common.

And then, without realizing it, Finn hinted at just how much we did, at the same time reminding me where I came from. Where I belonged.

315

It was Ronan who started it, though. Like always.

"She went on all night about those damn seashells," Ronan laughed. "Made me swear on my life that I'd help her find more tomorrow."

Finn grinned, his forearm grazing mine with the subtle movement of his body. "She loves the ocean."

Chapter Twenty-Seven

Elliana

"This is just about the worst thing that could possibly happen."

I laughed. "You're acting like we're never going to see each other again."

She frowned. "Well, look at your brother."

Sydney had a point, but I didn't like it. My brother and his friends had been in college for two years now, most of them bouncing back and forth between their dorm rooms and the coast. Every time they came home, I felt like they'd missed so much, even if it had only been a few months or weeks. For one, though, it had been so much more than that.

Just like everyone my age, I'd always heard that you tend to lose contact with many of the people you grow up with once you graduate high school. I always thought I'd see those kinds of relationships flailing, however. I figured I'd have a chance to hold onto them if I wanted to. But it had been two years since they moved away—both years full of milestones of my own, that my family and friends made themselves available to witness—and I hadn't heard from Finn once.

Luke advised me early on to stay out of whatever happened between them, and he'd never wanted me to stay away before, so I had a feeling it was serious. But, as time went on, I felt myself having more and more to tell Finn. I was growing, changing, experiencing things I'd never been inclined to experience before, and I often felt a tug to share everything with him. To have my voice float to him in the middle of the night, and to listen as his floated back. His absence was a void, and it was only a matter of time before I had to fill it.

For now, though, I had bigger fish to fry, the current one being Sydney's uncharacteristic panic about our departure from one another. I wasn't quite sure when I became the voice of reason.

"I'm not my brother," I told her.

She raised her eyebrows. "But you haven't talked to Finn either."

I let out a sigh. I was done with the conversation, and she knew it. "Well, you're not Finn," I said. I placed my hands on her warm, tanned shoulders. "This isn't going to change anything."

"You're not going to find a new best friend at college that you tell everything to? That you video call when you're crying in front of a movie or when you need an honest outfit opinion on? Think about it, Elliana, you're going to find someone for that."

"Well, if I meet them at college, I probably won't have to video call them."

"Nell."

"Sydney," I groaned. "You're my best friend, okay? I'm going to go to Vermont and have an awful time and meet absolutely no people while you go to Georgia to build your basketball empire and steal the hearts of all the boys who can never have you anyways."

"Basketball isn't going to be the same without you," she said. "I wish you could be out there with me."

I smiled. For once, I wished I could've kept playing, too. But my time on the court was over, and I was at peace with it. "I'll be watching every game. Just like always."

Sydney threw her arms around me then, and I threw mine back. I heard the characteristic sound of her mother pulling into our driveway, her sister's favorite pop song playing through the cracked windows. But we took our time.

The last two years for Sydney and me had been nothing short of memorable. We vowed before junior year to cherish every minute we had left in our beloved hometown together, and I was pretty sure we couldn't have kept the promise more firmly. She was still my rock, still my go-to for any and everything. It didn't matter that we'd branched out, or that we started going to Archie's with bigger groups of friends and surfing with the kids Henry introduced us to along the coast. It didn't matter that I did group projects with people that weren't Sydney and enjoyed their company, or that our late-night fires were open to anyone in our class, not just the two of us. She was still who I looked for in any room, no matter how many people were in it.

For the first time in my life, I felt my age, and I was no longer worried that I wasn't being enough of a kid. I liked the way the sun felt on my skin so much that I embraced it daily, with proper UV-protection, of course (I was living in the moment, not being stupid). I looked forward to our school's dances, and found that the hours of preparation that led up to them were often as eventful as the nights themselves. I listened to so much music in the car with Sydney and on my solo morning runs that I had a music taste that was uniquely mine, which had never happened before. I had a rotating list of favorite movies, many of which I used to think were too cliché for my attention. I liked to fish with my dad and shop for flowers with my mom. I learned how to surf and then I taught Braeden. Maybe I was even cool.

The most important addition to my life since that dreadful day two summers before—a day whose repercussions still haunted my subconscious—was that I was happy, despite what I might have been missing. I knew I wasn't perfect, but I didn't want to be anymore. More than that, there was the always-present relief I saw on Sydney's face when we were together. She wasn't worried about me anymore, and neither of us were afraid. That is, until we decided to attend schools on opposite ends of the East Coast.

"Alright," she said as she wiped a tear from her eye. "I'm going to go but I'm not going to say goodbye."

"You just did." I smirked and let the tear coming from my eye roll right down my cheek.

Sydney just looked at me, as if she was both taking me in as I was for the last time and cursing me for having changed into someone who could keep up with her in conversation. But then she pulled me in again.

"I hate Vermont," she said.

I laughed. "I'll call you in ten minutes. I promise."

Truthfully, I'd never been a big fan of the North either, but only because it was so far away from everything I knew. But now, I wanted to discover the parts of me that didn't grow up at home, the parts that bloomed when I wasn't beside the coastline in my backyard. I was desperate to find comfort in something new and out of place. I knew I'd feel alive then, just like the first time.

An hour after Sydney closed the door of her mom's Jeep, it was my turn to go. There was a heaviness in my chest as I sat in the living room with Braeden and Luke, for the last time as a permanent resident in the house. There was all of the childhood nostalgia swirling around me like it had been for weeks and months, but there was also the proximity to my brothers that I wished I could've brought with me. But it was time to move on, and they weren't going anywhere. That, I was sure of.

"Elliana, you left your hair straightener in the bathroom," my mom said as she hurried halfway down the stairs, stopping when she met my eyes. "Did you mean to pack it?"

I shook my head, feeling the weight of Luke's eyes on me. "No."

She flashed me a smile then continued down the stairs, rustling through her purse in the kitchen for her car keys. That was our cue, I guess.

Braeden hugged me first. I took in his warmth, feeling a bit like I was about to leave a newborn at home for a few months. When I came back, he'd be a different person. Even now, every time I looked at him, he'd grown another inch. He just offered a smile as we stepped aside; he wasn't much for showing his emotions, but we were working on it.

Then, there was Luke.

I was glad I didn't have to put into words how much his being there—not just that day, but every one since I was born—meant to me, because I would've failed to do it. He held me tight, and when we parted, I felt cold.

"Adrienne and I will be there in a few weeks," he told me. "Don't have too much fun before then."

"I won't," I said. But, for once, we both knew I was lying. And man, I liked lying. It was freeing.

Luke laughed, reading my face like his favorite novel, then shook his head. My mom entered the room then, rustling Braeden's hair with her free hand.

"Alright. Ready, honey?"

I swallowed the urge to look around the house and study the ocean one last time before I headed off. I was ready, and I had to go before I changed my mind.

Our car ride to the airport was mostly silent, save for the music I was playing. I'd already suffered through a long goodbye with my father that morning. We went for a run together before he headed off to a conference in Georgia. It was funny; the look I always saw in my mother's eyes was gleaming in his for those few hours. They'd been in love for so long that even their eyes were bonded.

So, I wasn't at all surprised when I saw it in my mother's, too. She kept glancing over at me, at stop lights and during our small conversations that popped up here and there. I'd always hated seeing my mother down, and this time, it really was because of me. I hoped, deep down, it was a good kind of sad. But I just couldn't be sure.

We arrived at the airport with plenty of time. I slipped my backpack onto my shoulders as soon as I stepped out of the car. My mom retrieved my carry-on bag from the trunk—the rest of my belongings were already in Vermont, courtesy of our full-family road trip for orientation a few weeks earlier. And then, it was time for the moment I knew we were both dreading.

"Do you have everything you need?" she asked.

She was trying not to look at me, but I couldn't look away from her. I knew that Luke, Braeden, and I were her world. I knew how hard it was to see a second one go, to be one bird away from an empty nest. So, even though we were awaiting a flight that would officially take me into my next chapter, I was the proud one. I was proud of her for being present, a battle we'd both fought so differently.

To answer her question, I wrapped my arms around her. I did have everything I needed. In that moment, it was only her.

"Call me when you're settled, okay?" she said in a voice that was battling tears.

"I will," I assured her. "I love you."

"I love you too," she said. "Now, go. Change that world of yours."

I left her and North Carolina with one last smile, and then I did as she said. Or, I planned to, at least.

After I made my way through two airports, and sat on a four-hour flight with a bouncy leg, I made it to campus. I was a *college student*. A real one. Whatever that meant, it was exciting.

I found my way to my dorm room easily, mostly because the first time I found it, Adrienne was with me. She made sure to point out all of the signs I could follow to reassure myself I was going the right way. I liked that I thought about her when I saw them now. The place already felt a little bit like home.

When I opened the heavy door, though, the noises of move-in playing like a movie soundtrack from the hallway surrounding me, I noticed a change. Or, lots of changes. My bedspread and unpacked bags weren't the only things in the room.

The wall on my right was empty, so far. I didn't want to decorate too much until I settled in, so the only thing that revealed anything about me was my blue bedspread and the few colorful pillows my mother had gifted me that sat on top of it. With one look at the left wall, however, I felt I already knew a bit about my new roommate.

First, there were pictures. I didn't have the time and my eyes hadn't adjusted enough to look at all of them, but I saw lots of people. Friends, family, maybe even foes. There were strings of flowers, a mirror, a map with colorful pins on it, most of them sitting idle on the West Coast and a few stuck into countries in

Europe. My eyes fell onto France, where there was a red pin grabbing my attention.

I looked away for a few reasons, but mainly because of the next and biggest part of my roommate's chosen wall display. It was a flag, and it hung a bit crooked toward the foot of her bed. There was a horizontal purple stripe sandwiched by a pink one on top and blue on the bottom. I immediately felt comfort in my stomach as I studied it. And then I heard footsteps.

"Is it too much?"

I whipped my head around, my low messy bun bouncing on my neck as I did.

The girl who met my eyes was about my height. She had wavy black hair and wide, round glasses with silver frames. A yellow tank top hung from her shoulders and there was a small gap between her front teeth when she smiled.

"No," I laughed. "I love it."

"I'm Genevieve," she said, her smile still beaming. She glanced down at her feet before I could, revealing silently that she was only wearing one shoe. "I– uh I lost the other one."

I laughed again, then bent down and reached behind my duffel bag, where I'd spotted a red Converse when I came in. I handed it to her.

"I think I found it."

"You have no idea how long I've been looking for that," she breathed. She met my eyes again. "You must be Elliana."

I nodded. I already liked her. I liked the way the room started buzzing when she walked in and how colorful she was— not just her outfit and her side of the room but her aura. I was already breaking my promise to Sydney, but we both knew it didn't matter.

"I am." I smiled. "But you can call me Nell."

Chapter Twenty-Eight

Nell

Her name was Sabrina, and it started as a double date with Genevieve and a boy named Manny.

I liked the way she laughed and I loved the way she spoke about her family. Her friends called her Brina, which meant that I called her Sab, because I was more than that. We were together for six months, the majority of my sophomore year and her freshman, though her gap year before college made us the same age—our birthdays were actually only three days apart. Being alone together became my new favorite oxymoron when I was with Sabrina. But I couldn't love her.

Maybe I could, and maybe I did. But I couldn't love her as much as I knew I was capable of loving a person. Every morning I woke up knowing that turned into an entire day where I felt like I wasn't being honest with her or with myself. I'd learned to have compassion for the person I was becoming, so when I ended it, I told Sabrina everything. She wanted the best for me, so she hoped I would find my way back to that kind of love one day. I'd resolved to believe I was going to spend the rest of my life alone or settling.

And now, I was back there, in that place.

Technically, I was walking down the stairs. My hair was heavy, soaking wet from the long, necessary shower I sat in for thirty minutes after my morning run, which, if I was honest, was really a walk. I had a headache the size of the ocean, and it wasn't the same kind that my mother had. While the source of hers was a series of emptied champagne glasses, mine was the tears that soaked my pillow beginning the moment I arrived home. I would've thought that the second heartbreak I caused myself would've been easier, lighter to hold. But this was a hurricane compared to the rain storm I caused four years ago.

I was thinking about Sabrina as I approached the bottom of the stairs. I'd held her hand in public. I sat right beside her in the dining hall with our joint group of friends surrounding us. I sat at parties with my peers while my attention was solely fixated on her, not a thought of how they were perceiving us or how we looked. The only eyes I felt on me were hers. I never felt a bad thing.

So I couldn't figure out, for the life of me, why it was any different with Mo. Maybe my instinct was to run away whenever I felt something intense because it used to be so foreign to me. Maybe I really did feel all of those eyes on me both of those times, and my anxiety was merely caused by the attention and not the idea of my being with a girl. I knew that what Ronan said the night before was true, that anyone who mattered wouldn't bat an eyelash at the idea.

Or maybe I was wrong. Maybe that feeling in my heart that told me Mo was the only person I could ever love fully was dishonest. If that was the case, then I didn't know where I stood. Then, I didn't even know who I was anymore. Lucky for me, I'd blown my chance to figure it out anyways.

"Everyone was wondering where you were this morning," my mother said from the kitchen.

I'd just reached the ground floor. Outside, I could see everyone on the beach, enjoying a sunny day that was supposed to be filled with thunderstorms. I could see Ronan and Finn in shin-high water with Sutton and Freya, Braeden pointing his camera toward them. Adrienne and Luke were there too, insistent that they couldn't miss a day on the beach with everyone together again, even if they had only been married for a number of hours. It was a good thing they didn't leave for their honeymoon until the next day.

"I went for a walk."

"For two hours?"

I shrugged, reaching in the freezer for the bin of frozen strawberries as I attempted to hide my mood. "It was a long walk."

She nodded, turning her attention toward the window above the sink as she rinsed a glass. Through it, I watched Freya jump between Ronan and Adrienne's arms in the water. I was thinking about how whole our house felt again, how good it was to have everyone there. And then my mother read my mind.

"That's nice, isn't it?"

I nodded, looking away only to pour apple juice into the blender cup.

"You know who's not out there?"

"Sydney's spending the morning with Henry then coming over," I told her. "He leaves for Europe again tomorrow."

My mother chuckled. "I didn't mean Sydney."

"Who did you mean?"

"Your friend Mo."

I bit my lip. "She leaves for New York again today."

It physically hurt me to say it. There was a burning in my chest that made its way to my throat, like I was already preparing to spend months getting over that one little sentence. But then my mom didn't answer, and I could feel her looking at me.

She knew. All she did was breathe, shift her body slightly. But God, she knew.

"I, um– I noticed that she left a bit early last night," she said carefully. "Around the same time you went out to get some air."

My hands were gripping the sides of the blender. I released them, because I looked insane, but my jaw remained clenched. I turned toward my mother slowly, trying to get a quick and subtle read of exactly how much she knew. And how, if that was possible with a glance.

"Did someone tell you?"

Maybe it was Ronan, I thought. That wouldn't have been so bad. I wondered if he told Luke, too. I had a feeling Adrienne was suspecting already. Really, it would've been easier this way. But then my mother shook her head.

"No."

Before I felt the tears reaching my cheek and then my chin, my mother was letting out a sympathetic sigh. Her face quickly turned from curious to soft to empathetic. I had a conscious battle between wiping my tears away and letting them continue their streak down my face, and the latter won just as my mother pulled me close to her, her arms secure around my body.

"Oh, Nell," she said. "It's okay, don't cry."

"She's not just my friend," I mumbled into her shoulder.

I felt her nod. "I know, honey."

"You know?"

"I suspected," she said, her voice light.

I wiped the tears away once I was standing on my own again. My mother was smiling, looking into my eyes with such softness in hers it nearly blew me away.

"First of all, I love you. So much," she said.

I took a deep breath, feeling thankful even in a split second for the kind of family I was blessed with. Not everyone was met with these kinds of words when they revealed who they were, who they loved. I knew I was lucky.

"I love you too," I said quietly.

My mother paused, considering her next move. I didn't need consolation, and I wasn't sure I really wanted to talk about the whole Mo thing just yet. So I was happy when I didn't have to. Not exactly.

"Do you know how badly I wanted a big family?" When I nodded, she said, "So many kids, so many mouths to feed that your dad and I would have a hard time keeping track."

I nodded again.

"And then we only had you three—the biggest blessings in our lives, and you know how much I mean that. But it was hard to hear that we wouldn't be able to meet any more of you, that ten quickly became three, no exceptions."

I already knew all of this, but hearing it again made me sad. For my parents, for my brothers, even for me. I would've loved to meet more of us, too.

"Well, what I didn't know was that three was a much bigger blessing than ten."

I looked at her then. I was starting to feel better, if you could believe it.

I shook my head. "Why?"

She smiled. "Because I get to *see* everything," she told me. "I got to watch you and your brothers playing on the rug or on the beach together when you were little. I got to watch every game you played in, attend every school play. We could all ride in the car together on road trips. I could sit back while you and Sydney watched sunsets together when the sky was too beautiful to photograph because everyone else was taken care of."

She shook her head as a heavy breath made its way to my chest. It made perfect sense, but I didn't know exactly what it had to do with what we were talking about.

"I've been very lucky because I was given the opportunity to know you better. To be your friend as well as your mother," she told me. "I could tell just by how red your cheeks were if you had a good basketball practice or a bad one. I know when you've checked out of a conversation by the way you look in another direction for just *half* a second." She smiled, this one simpler, almost involuntary. "I can tell by the sparkle in your eyes when you think of someone as more than a friend. A different sparkle when you're in love."

There it was. For so long, I rolled my eyes and squirmed at the look my mother gave me whenever I did something remotely grown-up. Looking at her now, I could finally see what she saw. She wasn't wishing we would stop growing up or regretting what she couldn't have. The look she gave us was pride, gratitude that she was there for it all.

Nothing could take away the pain that losing Paisley caused, and there wasn't a doubt in my mind that getting to know and love her would've been a blessing to all of us. But there was something to be said about finding a light in a dark place. This was ours, and that was okay.

Instead of thanking her for her sentiment or for allowing me into her heart the way she did, I just leaned forward and pulled her close again. I wasn't sure if she needed it, but I did.

"Are you going to go after her?" she asked, breaking the comfortable silence.

I paused as we separated. "I don't think there's really a point."

Just outside the window, we could now see the whole crew jogging up to the house with towels and footballs and sunscreen in hand. I looked just above them and saw that the sky had turned a dark shade of gray, and it was beginning to rain.

My mother nodded. "There's always a point."

They'd made it to the back deck now, and were just about to barrel inside when she turned to me once more.

"We've been rooting for you two, by the way."

I shook my head. "We?"

"Your father and I. Luke, too." She raised her eyebrows. "Just because you weren't as forward as Luke doesn't mean we weren't speculating behind closed doors."

She elbowed me, knocking my dropped jaw back upright.

"Loosen up. It was fun."

I couldn't help it. By the time everyone made it in the house—barely wet but still noticeably tussled by the wind—I was laughing. For most of my life I'd been trying to find out who I was and what I wanted the hard way. Maybe I should have just started by asking my mom.

The first pair to make it into my line of vision was Ronan and Freya, though I could see everyone else gathered behind them. Ronan held his hand in hers, and she looked right up at him after spotting me in the kitchen.

"Alright, Freya, tell her!"

Freya flashed her toothy smile. "Ronan is just as strong as the Folk!"

Finn laughed audibly, patting Ronan on the back as he commended his effort.

"The *Hulk*," Ronan whispered.

Freya looked up at him. "What?"

Adrienne caught my gaze next while everyone else began to disperse. Beside her, Luke was watching something on Braeden's camera and laughing.

"We're going to find a musical to watch. Join us?" Adrienne said.

I grinned, then nodded in Adrienne's direction. Sure, I'd still messed up, and I still wanted a do-over for the night before. But at least this time, all of the people I needed to preoccupy me while I nursed my heartache were here. And, as evident by the way my mother bent down and started talking to Freya, her eyes lighting up as she spoke, we'd even added two to the family this time. Things could have been worse.

I planned to return to my smoothie-making, but then Finn made his way into the kitchen as everyone else headed for the living room. Within seconds, his arm was around me and my head was on his shoulder. We were the same two people looking out at the same waves, the same sky that was now nearing a dark peak, so I was half-expecting to feel like I did all those years ago. But that was a world away now.

"Is that from your sophomore year?" Finn asked.

I stood corrected; we were not both looking out at the waves. Finn was looking at a picture frame on the kitchen counter. In the photo on the left, which I assumed he was referring to, I stood sandwiched between a smiling Luke and Braeden, a basketball in my hands and the St. Jane's gym almost-blurred in the background.

I nodded. "The semi-final game," I told him. "Braeden found that ball in the corner of the gym and made me hold it.'"

I felt Finn smile. "Well, you deserved the game ball that day if I remember correctly," he said. And he did. He nodded to the picture next to it. "What about that one?"

The adjoining frame held another photo taken after a basketball game. In this one, I was wearing the same St. Jane's uniform, but with pride written blatantly across my face, and was holding a purple basketball with a bold white stripe. I'd grown a bit in height and in muscle volume, my hair was in a messy ponytail and missing all of its straightness. I stood between Braeden and Luke, who'd both matured in their respective ways, too. We were all smiling so brightly I could feel it through the frame.

"My senior night," I said, remembering that night like it was just days ago. I could still hear the crowd in the gym. It was louder than any one I'd played for.

"And why are you holding that ball?"

This question was a joke, I assumed, since I'd given the justification for the first picture. So Finn was surprised when I actually had a reason.

"I broke the single-season scoring record."

Finn's jaw dropped. Literally. I heard it fall. "You did– what? *You did?*"

I couldn't help but laugh. "I did."

"You beat Sydney?" he asked, this time biting his tongue as he tried to hide his surprise. "I mean– I'm sorry. I don't mean to sound so shocked, I just–"

"No, I know. Trust me." Then, as if he'd asked how I did it, I said, "I just started shooting the ball, and it happened to go in."

This wasn't exactly the whole truth, but I wasn't lying. I did start shooting the ball more, and it did go in. But I also had to credit my soaring basketball success to the confidence I'd gained over those years too. I was putting work in at the gym, both in and outside of practice, but I was also putting the work in at home. I spent time learning how to love my body and my personality and my life in general. I found it perplexing how much easier basketball became. Once I convinced myself I belonged, there was no stopping me.

"I'm sorry I missed it," Finn said then.

I shook my head, offered him a smile that said it was okay. "You're here now."

Finn nodded. Both of us turned then and watched the scene that was unfolding in the living room. The couch was nearly full, with Braeden and Freya on one end and Sutton on the other. Adrienne was sitting in the love seat. I assumed she was saving the other half for me since Ronan and Luke were beside one another on the floor.

"You know," Finn started quietly. "It wasn't all their fault."

"What wasn't?"

"Me not coming back," he explained. "I made a choice to go or stay. I didn't really put up a fight and I should've." He paused, his eyes shifting slightly. "I almost did the same thing with Sutton."

This was new. "You did?"

He nodded. "I barely knew her, and she was raising a baby. I thought I was way out of my league, you know?"

I didn't exactly understand, because I'd never been in Finn's situation and because I didn't think anything was out of his league, quite frankly. But I did empathize.

"What made you stay, then?"

He shrugged. "Well, I knew nothing could change the way I felt about her. I knew I'd always wonder what would've happened if I did stay. That was the main reason," he explained. "And running away never really got me anywhere before."

I turned to Finn then. The way he was looking at Sutton was remarkable, to say the least.

"I'm proud of you for that," I told him.

He smiled, turning to me then with a look that was almost the same yet wildly different.

"Sometimes you've got to fight against yourself for yourself," he said. "It's not always as hard a choice as you think."

I was thinking about his words, desperately so, when my attention was pulled again to the window. Outside, the rain was pounding down on the deck and the sand and everything else underneath the dark clouds. But then, right at that moment, a golden haze started to creep over the ocean, highlighting the raindrops as they continued to fall freely to the ground. It was unmistakable, what was happening.

She said it wouldn't matter where she was, or what she was doing. She would dance in every one. I wondered if it mattered now.

I'd never really been a firm believer in anything. The closest I'd ever had to a personal credence was that the ocean and me had something in common. Now, I was sure of it. That haze, the glow that was stretching its arms out over the earth as the sky continued to open up—we both needed it. And it wasn't just by chance. We were meant to find it, to exist in harmony with it. One way or another.

Finn watched my eyes. I had a feeling he was recalling the story I told him long ago about sunshowers. About what happened during them.

"You're going to go after her, aren't you?"

I could feel the pressure of the ground with every step I took. It was rocking my knees, catching in my breath. I'd taken the beach route, for a reason I knew but couldn't explain, and the rain was pouring in sheets all around me. Still, the sun was lighting the way.

I wanted so badly for so long to know who I was. To find the person I was capable of being. Now, in this moment, I knew that I was the kind of person who did this.

I was human. I made mistakes, and I felt their wake so deeply that it was nearly catastrophic. I was capable of falling in love and falling flat on my face. I was strong and I was sensitive. I was brave and I was scared. Realizing that I was more than just one thing, more than just one type of girl, was what pushed me further along the beach. It was what got me there.

After all, I was Nell, and I loved her. But I was doing this for Elliana. She deserved a second chance. I was the only one who had the power to give her that.

The parts of my hair that had dried since my shower were now soaked-through again, just like my clothes. My skin was dripping and I felt alive. Then, I saw her, standing on the back deck of her green house, and I felt more than that.

My heart sank and jumped and broke and swelled at the sight of her curly hair and bright eyes. She wore a pair of ripped jeans and a faded Led Zeppelin shirt. She was soaking wet, and she was standing still. But she was there and so was I.

"You're not dancing," I pointed out when I was close enough that she would hear me.

Her eyes remained forward, on the ocean. I wondered if she saw me coming, or if she just knew.

"I'm doing my best."

When I got closer, I started to feel that weight on my chest. The one that usually told me to turn around, to find somewhere quieter, safer. So I kept going.

"Mo—"

"No." She shook her head.

"Mo, listen to me. Please."

I was beside her now. When she finally turned to me, I couldn't breathe. She was still shaking her head slowly, tears welling in her eyes.

"You didn't have to, you know," she said. "You didn't have to act like you were different, like you wanted to try again. You could've just left it alone."

"I didn't want to leave it alone," I said, wanting so badly for her to hear me. "And neither did you—"

"Don't do that," she demanded. "Don't pull my feelings into it."

"I'm sorry," I said breathlessly. "I'm sorry."

I was at a loss then, but not because I didn't want to make things better. Because I didn't know how. This wasn't a wedding toast. I wasn't prepared.

Evidently, Mo was.

"I was embarrassed," she said, looking down and biting her lip. Every tear that fell from her eyes became one with the rain. "But that wasn't even the worst part."

She turned to me then, her green eyes igniting the air around us. I'd never seen a person so full of sorrow with such strong shoulders. I'd never stop envying the way she held herself.

334

"You turned me into someone who didn't understand," she told me, her words like a knife. "You did it twice."

"That was never my intention. You have to believe me," I said, realizing very quickly that I had no way to prove it. I turned back to the ocean then, too, watching as the sun's light started to fade. It wasn't quite gone yet.

The only noise to be heard then was the rain, and it made me think. Maybe I was the one who needed to understand.

"Why did you go back early?"

She shook her head. "What?"

"Four years ago. Why did you go back to New York early?"

"Because I didn't want this," she told me immediately. "I didn't want to be convinced that things could change."

"It wasn't things that needed to change. It was me," I said. "I'm not going to put words in your mouth but I know what we were back then. It was a mistake to walk away."

She didn't have a response to this, and maybe it's because it wasn't anything new. We both knew I'd messed up.

"I know you have no reason to believe me, but I found her. I found her before I ran away the first time."

She just looked at me.

"That girl that I thought would change my life," I explained. "I found her the day you walked up to Sydney and me on that beach, wearing a Bon Iver shirt and holding your shoes in your hand."

"Nell—" she started, not wanting to hear another speal about how I could do what I'd proved time and time again that I couldn't. I understood. And maybe there was a chance that it would happen again. But there was one thing we'd never given ourselves, and that was time. It was what I was fighting for now.

"No, please," I said, my voice breaking. "I know that I did the worst thing I could have done. I know I broke your trust. I'm sorry it happened again and I wish I could take it back, but—"

Just before my rambling could turn incomprehensible, the sky reminded me why I'd started across the beach in the first place. The sun disappeared back behind the clouds, the curtains closing on the beautiful sunshower. Now, like before it had come out, we were in the dark.

I turned to Mo again. She was still in front of me, her hair flattening and her clothes turning dark as they stuck to her skin. At the same time, she was walking out of her house in the early hours of the daylight, a smile on her face as she impressed me with her radiance once again.

"You're the sun," I told her. There was a smile making its way to my face. I pushed it away.

She shook her head, and I did too.

"You told me in high school that— that the thing you love about the sun is that it takes the darkness and makes it brighter. The mundane becomes vibrant. The ocean becomes blue. Our eyes light up."

And right at that moment, hers did. She remembered.

"That's you," I told her, and I was confident that it was true. I believed it more than I'd ever believed anything.

"I don't get what you're—"

"My life was black and white," I started. "Right and wrong. There was so much monotony, and everything had to be perfectly straight in order for me to be comfortable living. And then you came along, and everything was bursting in color."

I could feel my smile now, but was still searching for one on Mo's face. It would come. I knew it would.

I shook my head again. "You are sunshine to me," I said. "The person that I've been looking for all along is the person that I am with you."

Her eyes didn't wander from me as she tried to understand. I watched her face soften as she did. And then she looked down, biting her lip again.

"I can't let myself feel unwanted again, Nell. I won't."

I wasn't going to give up. I couldn't. But she wasn't budging, and it hurt.

"I know," I said quietly. "I'm sorry—"

"I don't want you to think that I don't understand how you feel," she said, her voice bolder. "I've been there. I've been scared. I would've waited for you. Both times."

I began to nod, scraping the bottom of my heart for the words to thank her or keep her going somehow. But then she turned on her heel, slid open the glass door to her house, and stepped inside. She nodded her head toward the house before disappearing inside of it, so I followed her, completely unsure of what to expect.

The house—an open-concept floor that was mostly empty with the exception of some of the furniture that her dad must've been leaving behind—was beautiful. In it, Mo stopped at a stool that sat beside the kitchen island, and pulled open the zipper of the black backpack that sat on top of it. She began to rustle through its contents, and stopped abruptly when she found a small, blue-covered notebook with papers sticking out of it. She took a deep breath before flipping through its pages.

The flipping stopped when she found a page full of folded papers. She took them out and handed them to me.

"What is this?" I asked as they sat unidentified in my hands.

She said nothing, only looked down at the papers, willing me to unfold them. So I did.

I was still confused upon opening the first one, my brain incapable of comprehending something that wasn't spelled out for me. But then, in the top right corner of the sheet, I saw the name of an airline. It was a plane ticket.

My eyes jumped from the ticket to Mo. Her eyes were soft. She wasn't angry.

I studied the ticket again. It was a flight from New York to North Carolina three months into my junior year. She was going to come home.

"Look at the next one."

Mo's eyes were on the papers, not me, when I unfolded the next one. It was another ticket. This time to Vermont, last winter.

"What?" I blurted, my voice a whisper.

I opened the third and final paper. A ticket to North Carolina the weekend I graduated high school.

There were tears in my eyes, a rasp building in my throat. "I don't understand."

"You were mine, too," she said, her voice fading. "My sunshine."

Were. Past tense.

"I didn't get on those flights because I was afraid. I didn't want to be wrong about us. About you. I didn't want to feel like that again," she told me. "But I thought about it more than just those three times."

"And now?" I asked, desperately awaiting an answer.

"Now—" She looked down, blinking away a tear. "I feel that way again."

I was exhausted, and I wasn't sure I had much fight left in me. I was prepared to leave with nothing again.

"Mo—"

"Nell, I know why you run away," she said softly. "I don't think it's because you're afraid of loving someone who's different."

This was it. This was what I needed to hear and say and believe for the past four years.

"It's because I'm afraid of loving you," I said.

Mo nodded. She was sad, but only because her fear of being the reason I walked out had come to fruition. It was true, and it was hanging in the air between us. But maybe it was a good thing.

"I just know what losing you will feel like," I told her.

"I know."

"And I have a hard time believing that I'm enough for someone like you."

"You—" She shook her head, finally meeting my eyes again. "The only person you have to be enough for is yourself."

This was typical of Mo—to end a conversation with something motivational that I'd go on thinking about for days, wondering how long I could stretch out its effects. But this wasn't the end of the conversation. It couldn't be. Could it?

I watched Mo's eyes as they sat fixated on the floor, and I had a sinking feeling in my chest. She held the cards now. I didn't have anything left to say that I hadn't said already.

"There's still a chance you'll feel that way again. The bad feeling. There's a chance it comes back," she said as she broke the silence, like this was what she'd been thinking all along.

"I'm not going to walk away," I assured her, begging for her eyes to meet mine. "I can't."

"I know."

She knew. But her eyes were still on the floor, her thoughts still forming, so I stayed silent. The rain outside was pouring down harder than before. But I couldn't see it, and I couldn't hear it. Because in the next beat, she looked at me.

"Can we agree on something?"

I swallowed hard, then nodded so slightly I wasn't sure she saw it.

"Nothing matters when we're together," she said. "So if you ever feel like you can't do it, or if it ever feels scary again, tell me. Just tell me. Okay?"

I couldn't nod and I couldn't breathe and I couldn't speak. There was no way this was happening. There was no chance I'd found my way back to her, and she'd let me in.

But then I looked into those eyes, at the freckles on her face and the way her lips were curling at the ends. Those things alone were enough to make me believe anything.

"I never mind a risk," she said, her smile now evident though not overwhelming. "You know that."

I couldn't tell what my face looked like, but I had a feeling. "So—"

"So," Mo started, taking the papers from me and replacing them with her hand, "if you're going to run away, take me with you."

I was smiling so hard that it almost hurt. "You're right," I told her. "Nothing matters."

"Absolutely nothing," she agreed.

This back-and-forth was Mo O'Brien summed up into just a few words, and these ones were perfectly timed. Of course our solution to my years-long stretch of thinking about everything all the time was to agree that nothing mattered. I was still scared, but only because of how precious I knew this feeling was. I couldn't have been angry with myself for taking so long to realize it. I was here now, and that was everything.

This was the kind of moment you're supposed to live for. There are the ones that break you, the instances of failure and regret that you feel like you'll never recover from. There are the in-between moments and the nail-biting bouts of tension before the result of a decision goes one way or another. There are the happy times with something missing and the dark times with silver linings. And then there are ones like this, where everything falls into place like rain into the ocean.

This was the moment I'd remember forever as the beginning and the middle and the end all at once. It was messy and perfect and so long overdue that I knew it had been waiting for us. This was also the moment that Mo kissed me again, and the moment that we decided we wouldn't be breaking our tradition. Sunshowers were made for dancing.

Epilogue

"Pizza! *Pizza!*"

Despite Ronan's helpful instruction, Mo continued to hurl downhill toward me. Her curls were sticking out from under her helmet and her legs wobbled in her gray snow pants, but somehow she was still graceful. And lucky for me, we hadn't made it past the Bunny Hill, so I was able to catch her without being taken out.

Ronan, out of breath, approached the two of us just as Mo laid back on the snow, her goggles slipping off of her helmet as she did.

"That wasn't pizza," Ronan pointed out.

"Don't," I warned him.

Mo rolled her eyes as Ronan plopped down on the ground beside her. "I don't know what pizza is."

Suddenly, a pink orb flashed before our eyes. Before we knew it, it was approaching the bottom of the hill.

"Now!" Sutton yelled from beside me.

Like a well-oiled, five-year-old machine, the ball of pink snow gear pointed the tips of her skis toward one another, the two of them forming a triangle as she slowed to a stop. Finn smiled wide as he caught Freya who, unlike Mo, remained vertical.

"That," Ronan started, pausing for dramatic effect, "is pizza."

I laughed, taking note of Mo's rosy cheeks before I turned and spotted Freya again. "Good job!"

Finn flashed us a thumbs-up, then leaned down to better hear whatever Freya was trying to muster through her fleece neck warmer.

"She's getting hungry," Sutton pointed out.

Ronan nodded. "Me too. And cold. Should we get out of here?"

"Yes, please," Mo mumbled from beside me.

I turned to her, amused. "What happened to living life to its fullest? No challenge too big?"

She lowered her eyebrows. "I've been rolling down a mountain for four hours with sticks strapped to my feet."

I grinned, offering my hand instead of another remark. When I pulled Mo to her feet, she returned my grin and pinched my cheek with her free hand.

Within the next hour, every ski and snowboard boot was packed into the car, and we were headed home. And by home, I mean the mountainside condo we'd rented for the weekend.

I'd been wanting to have everyone in Vermont since the summer ended, but it would've been a squeeze to fit eight adults and a very small child into the small, off-campus dorm room Genevieve and I had been renting. So, just as March began to roll around in our calendars, we splurged. It hadn't even been a full day, and so far it had been paying off.

When we arrived at the house, Finn instructed everyone to get out of the car before he tried to squeeze it into the uphill, skinny garage. I made my way inside—I didn't want to bear witness to the inevitable scratches on the rental—and was blissfully surprised by who I saw at the kitchen counter.

"You made it!"

I practically sprinted to Adrienne, throwing my arms around her before I did the same to Luke. They'd been working tirelessly for weeks to finish the kitchen in their house, and this weekend were caught up in the chaos of it. They were supposed to arrive the night before.

"Just in time, apparently," Luke said, smiling.

Genevieve, who was sitting at the kitchen table with her laptop open in front of her and her favorite sweater hanging from her shoulders, nodded toward me.

"How were the boots?"

"Unreal," I told her. "I need to invest in a pair."

Genevieve smiled, mostly because she'd won an argument we didn't ever really have. I was insistent on believing that the hand-me-down ski boots her sister had given me freshman year were "perfectly fine" and "could last me five more seasons." But really, they tortured my feet. Genevieve's boots were like clouds.

"Cookie!" Freya said upon entering the door. She headed straight for Luke, galloping into his arms. The rest of the crew piled in slowly behind her, Ronan acting as the caboose.

Luke, basking in the glory of being chosen by the five-year-old, muttered the nickname he'd learned from Finn.

"Fish!"

Genevieve laughed. "Do any of you go by your real names?"

"It's about fifty-fifty," Adrienne explained.

"Nell sometimes calls me Bruce," Ronan said, tugging at the bottom of my messy braid as he passed by me to get to the kitchen.

"That's very far from the truth," I said.

Despite our banter, Ronan and I, since the summer, had been better friends than ever before. I had a feeling that the air had changed between us once the pressure to be more than friends vanished. So, although we were always picking on each other, I was grateful to have him in this way, and I knew he wasn't going anywhere. Just like the rest of the people beside me.

It felt good to have everyone in town—with the exception of Braeden who was spending a week in California with his official girlfriend Rowan and her family—and I already didn't want the weekend to end.

"So, uh, Sutton has been going on and on about the hot tub," Finn said then, raising his eyebrows with his hands in his hoodie pocket.

Sutton tilted her head. "Also very far from the truth."

"I'm in," Ronan said, turning to Mo and me.

I nodded, and so did she. It seemed we were always on the same page lately. "I just have to find my suit," Mo said.

"That's what I forgot!" Adrienne exclaimed, her hand lightly slapping her own forehead.

Everyone turned, feeling instant empathy for a rookie mistake, while Luke chuckled.

"It's in your bag."

"No, it's not," Adrienne said.

He nodded. "I put it in there last night."

"Man, it's like you've been married for eight years, not eight months," Ronan commented.

For once, there was no disagreeing with him. And so we all parted on a good note as we inched up staircases and down hallways to our rooms. Mo and I were the first to make it outside, the air between the sliding glass door and the hot tub biting at our skin. That was the thing about being so far from the ocean—the air wasn't always so kind. At least the company was still good.

I was climbing into the steaming water, holding onto Mo's hand so I didn't slip, when I felt her smile on me.

When I met her eyes, she shook her head.

"I still can't believe you got that," she said.

I glanced down at my ribcage. The words were sitting proudly under the thin strap of my bikini. I looked back at Mo as I sank down further into the water, letting its warmth envelope me as I sat down.

"You meant everything to me then," I told her. "So did your words."

A soft laugh escaped her chest. "Those particular words were a little harsh, though."

It was almost the same conversation we had the first time she saw the tattoo. That time, it was darker, and we were laying on a towel under the stars as another summer night slipped out of our grasp. It was the light of the moon that revealed the words that time, and I couldn't help but laugh at how surprised she was that I'd done something so permanent. And this time, I didn't mind repeating myself. In fact, I would've told her this every day. I often did.

I shook my head. "It was the nicest thing anyone's ever done for me," I told her. "I knew I'd never regret it."

She nodded, running her finger along it once and sending a spark through my body.

"And you still don't?"

She lifted her eyes to mine, and I couldn't have looked away if I tried. I didn't understand how I'd gotten so lucky.

"No," I said, my voice soft. "I don't regret a single thing."

I'd never been so comfortable, in every sense of the term. At that moment, sure. But I'd also never felt so good in my skin and my conscience as I did. I didn't know what the future looked like, but my forever was turning out to be very promising. Truthfully, all of ours were.

Finn and Sutton were moving to North Carolina. They wanted to give Freya a life beside the ocean, and they wanted to be closer to Luke and Adrienne, who often told me late at night about their plans to start a family of their own. Ronan was moving to New York. He figured that a city like that one was more his pace than his rural apartment complex in Ohio. He also wanted to be closer to Mo and hopefully, eventually, me.

There was so much more to come for all of us. I knew there would be as many downs as there would be ups, because that was how life was. But what kept me smiling as I woke up every morning, other than the love I was so lucky to finally have as mine, was knowing that we'd face every good and bad thing together. We all had each other, all the time. Finally.

When the screen door to the condo slid open, snapping me out of my trance, I was holding Mo's hand in mine, toying with the flower ring on her thumb.

The first two to join us were Ronan and Genevieve. Ronan slid the door shut behind him, holding a couple of towels with his other arm. He set them on the clear table while Genevieve stepped into the hot tub across from me. I stuck my tongue out at her, and she returned the gesture.

"Alright, Genevieve," Ronan said, his goofy grin making its presence known in Vermont, and not for the first time. "I have a very important question to ask you."

"Oh, dear God," Mo sighed, sharing my sentiment.

Genevieve laughed, then glanced curiously at Ronan as she began spinning her curly hair into a low bun. "Hit me."

With just one look at Ronan, I knew what was coming.

"Alright," he said. "What would you call an individual piece of spaghetti?"

ACKNOWLEDGEMENTS

This story and I have spent so much time together that I'd dare to call it one of my friends. I'm elated that I can finally share this book in a way I am proud of, but I must admit that I didn't do this all by myself. The writing, yes. But this book was built on experience, and was pushed forward by more support than I could've ever dreamed of having.

I must begin by thanking my parents and step-parent for giving me two warm, welcoming, and safe homes. I grew up in houses with always-open doors and walls that comforted me when I was learning who I was going to be. The Rose House was given life by you, and I will always be grateful for that.

I was lucky to have remarkable friendships in high school that I still carry with me today, and that largely inspired the lifelong bonds between many of these characters. To my friends—Lauryn, Emma, and Rachael—the friendships we share are among the most important things in my life. I wouldn't have been able to write this story without them.

While I am proud of the Elliana and Nell inside of me, I am also lucky to have been the Braeden of my story, as well as the Luke. I must thank my older sister, Emily, for showing me that sisters can be synonymous with friends and maids of honor. I'm proud of who you are and thankful for how much you let me in. To my little sisters, Nora and Juliet, thanks for teaching me just how much love I can hold in this little heart of mine. I hope you're proud of this one day (when you can read, that is).

To my Grandma Bets, and my late Grandma Sharon, my knowledge of and love for family begins with you. Grandma Bets, you are the only grandmother I know that recommends Young Adult Fiction to her friends. You will always be my first reader.

A very special thanks to Dr. Sodano, who is directly responsible for my love of storytelling. This debut, and everything else I've written, is driven by a passion that began the day I walked into Video Storytelling. I hope Nell's switch into the Communication major serves her just as well as mine did.

The biggest of thank-yous to Meleah, who is always reminding me that I am, in fact, a writer, and who makes sure that even the smallest of wins are acknowledged and celebrated. I'm as grateful for our shared passion for telling stories as I am for our collective and unapologetic love for Taylor Swift. Also, I apologize in advance for how many copies of this book are going to be stacked on our coffee table.

Thank you times a million to Katy Teets, for so enthusiastically helping me format the book's cover when all hope was momentarily lost. You are a serif queen and I hope you know it.

To my friends and family members that read an early version of this book: Rachael, Allie, Sam, Christian, Alex, Karly, Josh, Aunt Bets, Emily, Paris, Olivia, Caleb, Hannah, and Shelley Skibitski—my trusty editor, whose support for my writing began all the way back at *Ready, Set*. Thank you for reaching the end with me again. I hope you stick around for the next one.

Finally, I must thank Kate Graziano. For promoting this book to everyone you meet. For loving and caring for these characters like they're your friends and family. For reading every word I write, even the ones that get deleted. This version of *Tossed by the Waves* would not exist without you. I am as serious about this as Ronan is about pasta (and bagels, apparently). Thank you.

Read on for an excerpt from *Pearl Cove,*

Erin Reilly's upcoming novel.

CHAPTER ONE

PRESSLEY

Sending love and hugs! xoxo, Luna

"Are you ready, Pressley?"

Though it was posed as a question, it was more of a cue. The funeral director stood above me, his salt and pepper hair glistening in the yellow lights of the lobby. His face was soft and his eyes were kind. But then, I guess they had to be.

I slipped my phone back into my purse, stood up, and flattened the back of my dress. Everyone was waiting for me in front of the doors. Almost everyone, I guess. My parents were there, as they had been all morning and most of the night before. Grandpa was waiting in the back, watching as everyone else began to fall into line. He was having a hard time keeping his eyes open, but not because he was sleepy. Because he didn't want to see any of it.

I made my way past aunts and uncles and cousins and friends until I stopped beside Laurel. Her eyes remained forward, as did her belly, whose bump wasn't going anywhere. Not for the past six months, and certainly not today. Though I wouldn't admit it, she looked good in Mom's old maternity dress. She looked good in everything.

"Nervous?" she asked quietly.

Everyone around us was trying to distract themselves. They were conversing softly, fixing their dresses and suits and ties, looking around at the church like they hadn't been there a million times before. Laurel and I could've done it, too. We could've acted as though we weren't about to participate in the inevitable, in order to spare ourselves or something. But Laurel never liked to play pretend. Truthfully, I didn't either.

I shrugged my shoulders. I didn't know whether or not I was nervous. I knew I was sad, and I knew I was disappointed. But, nervous? I wasn't sure I'd ever been.

Laurel's eyes turned glassy, and she sniffled as quietly as possible. She turned to me then. "You'll do great."

Rare was the day that Laurel offered me words of encouragement, or any compliment for that matter. We weren't like that. So, now, I was nervous.

I took a deep breath and stared forward, listening again as everyone else played pretend. Moments later, the doors opened, revealing a church packed to its brim, not an inch of standing room left in the back or the sides. Then, the music began, and so did the processional.

The beginning of the mass went by in a blur. My ears prickled at the sound of every cry, every deep, staggered breath. I wondered if the priest was supposed to sound so happy when he spoke. He was saying nice things, some funny things, even, but joy sounded so foreign in those moments. I wasn't sure where to put it.

The readings were done by two of my aunts, both of whom I hadn't seen in a few years. They looked older than I remembered them. Time does that, I guess. But maybe grief does, too. More moments passed, ones I didn't recognize and ones I already couldn't remember. And then, all of a sudden, it was my turn.

Everyone sitting in my row stood up when I did, in an attempt to make my trek up to the altar easier. The truth was, nothing could make it easier. Not the look of encouragement I got from my dad, the sad yet potent smile my mom offered me, or the way that my grandpa placed his hand on my shoulder when I passed him. Although, that one did the most.

The altar, only a few steps up from ground level, felt like a mountain. If it was, the people staring back at me were pine trees. There were so many that I couldn't count, nor did I want to. However, like pine trees, there weren't too many of them. There couldn't be. Not today.

"Good morning," I started, making an effort not to look anyone in the eyes.

The beginning of the eulogy was like a form; it was a continuation of the pattern that anyone who had ever been to a funeral had encountered. I introduced myself and told everyone why I was up there, though I wasn't really sure of that myself. I used the phrase *born to*, which I didn't like. I talked about the beginning of her life and the challenges she faced to be a good person. I went on about her successes and her failures, because I knew she wouldn't have wanted me to say one without the other. I tried my best to summarize how she became who she was. It wasn't easy, though. She was so many things.

Then, I talked about how they met. I talked about Grandpa, and the way that his eyes would flicker momentarily towards the door every time Grandma wasn't in the room. I talked about their love story, the one I knew like the back of my hand. I talked about the void that would be left in Grandpa's heart now, among everyone else's in the room. I talked about how I felt it, too.

"My grandma was an exceptional sister, mother, grandmother, wife, and friend. She was a successful professor, had the best eye for Christmas Decorations, and was blessed with a mind that worked like nobody else's, though she often hid that part of herself."

My voice cracked then and, when it did, the silence in the room was loud. It was hesitant. I ignored it and took a deep breath.

"Mostly, she was wise. She used to tell me that it didn't matter what my hair looked like, or if I had the same kinds of clothes as everyone else. She said that those wouldn't be the things that people would think about at my funeral. 'People will think about how you made them feel,' she'd say."

I thought about this now, the way she would look me in the eyes whenever she told me something like this. I thought about how she'd jump into the next thing, a conversation about birds or fettuccine alfredo or the new song she'd heard

3

on the radio and just couldn't get enough of. But I always remained on what she said at first. Her words had a way of doing that.

"Standing here, now, with all of you, I can say for certain that she's right. I know that none of us are thinking about the way her hair used to fall out of her braid and stick to her face when it was hot, or how she never threw out an item of clothing in her entire life, no matter how ripped it had gotten."

At this, the mood lifted, ever so slightly, and a number of laughs bounced off of the walls of the church. This joy felt like it had a place, and it was heartening.

"Maybe we are," I said with a smile. "But that's what she would want. For us to be thinking about the messy and the chaos right along with the joy and love that she surrounded all of us with. We may have seen her for the last time-"

I paused, my eyes shifting to my grandpa. He was sad, maybe the saddest I'd ever seen him, but he was proud. He wiped a tear from his eyes and offered me a nod.

"But her memory is going to live forever, just like her spirit." I turned to the casket. *The casket.* I shook my head and the frozen feeling that began to rise in my throat. "We'll miss you, Grandma Essie. We already do."

After the recessional, where I kept my eyes on the floor and felt Laurel doing the same, we headed to the cemetery. It was cold—freezing, even—as the December air loomed in the distance. No one made any noise when the casket was lowered into the ground. I felt something fall from my cheekbones once I couldn't see it anymore. Relief, maybe, that the day was finally over. Or at least this part of it.

I didn't find warmth until we made it back to Grandma and Grandpa's house. I guess it would've just been Grandpa's house, or Grandpa's and my house. Maybe I'd just call it home. I never had a problem doing that before.

"You did good, Press," my dad said when he found me in the foyer, hanging my hat up on the hook under my coat.

He pulled me into a side-hug, and I felt him take a deep breath when he did.

I offered him a smile. "You did, too."

He nodded, the tears that had been sitting idle in his eyelids all week sparkling in the warm light from above us. He noticed that I noticed, quickly wiped them away and sniffled. Again.

"Lots of food in the kitchen. Better get some before everyone arrives," he said. "There's butternut squash ravioli and breaded green beans."

I smiled again, something that felt so strange after so many days without it. "Grandma's favorites?"

He nodded. "Even the desserts."

My jaw nearly dropped. "Éclairs and pusties?"

He raised his eyebrows. That was enough of an answer.

I shook my head, a breath escaping my nose. "If she's already looking down on us, she'll be pissed we're not sharing."

At this, my dad laughed, and it felt good. We didn't always see eye-to-eye, that was true. But we understood each other. I liked hearing him laugh.

A few hours later, the house felt just about as full as the church was in the morning. Even though the ceilings were high and the rooms were spacey, it was always warm on the first floor. I usually loved that about the house. Walking through the front doors felt like walking into a hug, probably because I was always greeted with one. But it was also because of the ambience.

Every light in the house was a warm-toned one, as were the decorations. Wood lined the walls and a fireplace—a big one—sat at the head of the living room. The couches didn't match, and neither did the rug, but if they did they wouldn't have fit inside. Nothing about the interior of the house was plain or uniform or, dare I say, normal. Grandma and Grandpa weren't like that, and I knew nothing would change now.

5

Though it was always warm in the house, the amount of people inside made it feel hot. I weaved in and out of family and friends for several minutes, trying to find a space where the air felt cool instead of sticky. I wasn't successful, nor was I in avoiding conversations. Many of them had good intentions, or just didn't want to let me pass by without acknowledging me.

"I'm so sorry about your grandma, Pressley."

"You did so good, honey. Your grandma would be so proud."

"Your grandmother would have loved seeing you up there."

"God, I can't believe how much you look like her."

I smiled and melted into those conversations, finding it hard to pass on them when I'd spoken all morning about the joy that my grandma was always spreading. It was the more intrusive comments that I pretended not to hear.

"How are you holding up?"

"You two were so close, I can't imagine how you must feel."

"How long did it take you to write the eulogy?"

"Pressley, come. You have to meet my son."

"Is it going to be weird living here without her?"

The day had been long, and it was barely the afternoon. When I finally made it to the back dining room, where the desserts had been picked over and only a few people were milling about, I felt almost refreshed. The air didn't feel cool on my skin, but it wasn't hot, either. It seemed I wasn't alone in my journey to find open space.

Laurel looked at me sideways when I sat beside her. She pushed her paper plate subtly in front of me.

"Hungry?"

I shook my head and took the deepest breath I could. Still not enough.

For a moment, there was silence. Not in the house, of course. The conversations between everyone I knew and many that I didn't were running in circles around my head. The silence was between Laurel and me. It was comfortable because it was usually there. We weren't always on the same playing field. The difference between Laurel and my dad, though, was that we didn't always understand one another. In fact, we rarely did.

"Where's Luna?" she asked, breaking the silence that I was beginning to enjoy.

I took a breath. Luna's text was still sitting unanswered on my phone, whose location I couldn't have even guessed.

"She's coming after indoor track practice."

Laurel nodded, but showed no emotion one way or another. I knew exactly what that meant.

"The practice was mandatory."

Laurel looked at me now, her pale face flat. "I didn't ask."

"But you were thinking it," I countered.

Laurel sighed. For a few seconds, it looked as though she was done with the conversation. But then she turned to me, her eyes trying their hardest to scream empathy but instead offering a bit of annoyance.

"You gave the eulogy at your grandmother's funeral." Before I could defend Luna, which I knew would've been pointless, Laurel stood up, albeit slowly, with her hand on her belly. "Is Cole still in the kitchen with Dad?"

I nodded.

With that, Laurel was gone, and so was my desire to argue.

Moments passed, though I wasn't sure how many, before I was completely anchored in my chair. I wasn't going anywhere, not even if the house caught on fire. My feet hurt as much as my heart, and for once in my life, my eyelids were heavy.

Then came Aunt Poppy.

"Pressley Grace, you'd better not be sleeping in the middle of your grandmother's funeral celebration."

Aunt Poppy was Grandma Essie's sister. She'd been around my whole life, and she knew me better than most of my friends did. Just like Grandma, her heart was young and her mind never wandered. She and I spent many summer mornings on Anchor Bridge trying to see who could throw the furthest rock. She always won.

I opened my eyes. "What, that's not allowed?"

Poppy smiled, taking the seat that probably still had some warmth left from Laurel's presence in it. "I'd be lying if I said I wasn't jealous when I saw you with your eyes closed."

"I'm sure there's an open bedroom upstairs," I told her. "I can stand watch."

At this, Poppy laughed. She shook her head then, taking a look around at the dressed up and grieving people that stood in small groups in front of us.

"What a day, huh?" she said.

I nodded, taking a moment to survey the room myself. "There were so many people."

"I know."

I tilted my head. Poppy and I were nothing if not honest. "She would've hated it."

Poppy grinned, tilted her head, then let the grin fade. "She wouldn't have believed it."

She was right. Grandma had an impact on every person that she'd ever spoken to, as was evident today. But she didn't know it. There were very few people that she kept in her circle. Though I was family, I was lucky enough to be one of the closest.

Poppy sighed. Unlike Laurel and me, she hated silence.

"So where's that Luna? Did she head home already?"

I shook my head, then glanced at the grandfather clock sitting in the corner of the room. It was nearly five. She should've been done with track by now.

"She should be here soon," I told her. "Track practice."

"Ah," Poppy said. "Good. I haven't seen her since Halloween."

8

I looked at Poppy, just to be sure that she was sure. She was, which made me a little sad. But I understood. Luna had a lot going on.

"She'll be around a lot more now," I said, forcing a smile on my own lips as well as Poppy's.

Poppy patted my leg the way she always did when we talked. "Your grandpa is happy you'll be here. Even if he's not showing it yet."

She looked at me with empathy and a lot of love in her eyes, all of it which I returned.

"He's showing it."

She was right, partially. Grandpa had been mostly sad lately, but I couldn't blame him. I wouldn't even think of blaming him. Grandma was his entire life, way more than he was hers. He began losing her a few months before she was gone, and I could see the pain in his eyes when that started. Sure, it was all over now. But he had to learn how to live again. I was more than willing to cut him some slack.

My parents, however, weren't willing to cut him much slack. They were expecting him to be sad, just as they were, but they didn't think he'd change. They didn't think he'd get quieter and more pensive. They didn't think he'd forget to put up the Halloween decorations or neglect the leaf raking for so long that the neighbors would call my dad. They certainly didn't think he'd forget his own birthday. That was three days before Grandma died, and the same day that my parents decided he wouldn't be living alone when she did.

"So, are you ready for Castle?"

I peeled my eyes away from the ticking second arm on the clock and brought them all the way back to Poppy.

"Castle?"

"You know, every twenty-five years-"

I shook my head. "Yeah, I remember. But I thought that was only for kids who go to Pearl Cove."

"Kids who *live* in Pearl Cove." Poppy raised her eyebrows. "I think your bedroom upstairs is proof enough that you're one of those now."

I lowered my eyebrows, a rush of adrenaline lifting my eyelids to their normal height and restoring whatever energy I had left from the day.

I opened my mouth again. I wanted to ask Poppy everything now. I had no idea I would be able to participate in Castle and, even then, I wasn't sure I wanted to. But I was interrupted anyway.

"Press?" My dad yelled. "Door!"

"Must be Luna." I turned away from my dad's voice and back to Poppy, an apology across my face.

Poppy winked. "We'll talk."

Printed in Great Britain
by Amazon

14888135R00212